THE HEARTBREAKER PRINCE

BY

KIM LAWRENCE

Published in Great Britain 2014
by Mills & Boon, an imprint of Harlequin (UK) Limited,
Eton House, 18-24 Paradise Road, Richmond, Surrey, TW9 1SR

© 2014 Kim Lawrence

ISBN: 978 0 263 24647 6

Harlequin (UK) Limited's policy is to use papers that are natural,
renewable and recyclable products and made from wood grown in
sustainable forests. The logging and manufacturing processes conform
to the legal environmental regulations of the country of origin.

Printed and bound in Spain
by Blackprint CPI, Barcelona

Though lacking much authentic Welsh blood—she comes from English/Irish stock—**Kim Lawrence** was born and brought up in North Wales. She returned there when she married, and her sons were both born on Anglesey, an island off the coast. Though not isolated, Anglesey is a little off the beaten track, but lively Dublin, which Kim loves, is only a short ferry ride away.

Today they live on the farm her husband was brought up on. Welsh is the first language of many people in this area and Kim's husband and sons are all bilingual—she is having a lot of fun, not to mention a few headaches, trying to learn the language!

With small children, the unsocial hours of nursing didn't look attractive so, encouraged by a husband who thinks she can do anything she sets her mind to, Kim tried her hand at writing. Always a keen Mills & Boon® reader, it seemed natural for her to write a romance novel—now she can't imagine doing anything else.

She is a keen gardener and cook and enjoys running—often on the beach as, living on an island, the sea is never very far away. She is usually accompanied by her Jack Russell, Sprout—don't ask...it's long story!

Recent titles by the same author:

A SECRET UNTIL NOW
CAPTIVATED BY HER INNOCENCE
MAID FOR MONTERO (At His Service)
THE PETRELLI HEIR

For Barbara, thanks for all your support.

CHAPTER ONE

HANNAH WAS NOT sleeping when the key turned in the lock. Apart from a few snatched moments she had not slept for forty-eight hours straight but she was lying down, her eyes closed against the fluorescent light above her head, when the sound made her sit bolt upright and swing her legs over the side of the narrow metal bed.

She made a few frantic attempts to smooth her tousled hair back from her face and clasped her shaking hands on her lap. She was able to mould her expression into a mask of composure, but recognised that it was no longer a matter of *whether* she lost it and cracked wide open, but *when*. For now at least she cared about maintaining an illusion of dignity.

She blinked against the threat of tears that stung like hot gravel pricking the backs of her eyes. Gouging her teeth into her plump lower lip, she found the pain helped her focus as she lifted her chin and pulled her shoulders back, drawing her narrow back ramrod straight. For the moment at least she was determined she wouldn't give the bastards the satisfaction of seeing her cry.

This was what happened when you tried to prove...

prove…what? And to whom? The tabloids? Your father? Yourself…?

She took a deep breath. Focus on the facts, Hannah. The fact is you messed up big time! You should have accepted what everyone else thinks: you are not meant for serious thoughts or fieldwork. Stick to your safe desk job, and your perfect nails… She curled her fingers to reveal a row of nails bitten below the quick and swallowed a bubble of hysteria.

'Stiff upper lip, Hannah.'

She had always thought that was an absurd phrase.

About as absurd as thinking working a desk job for a charity qualified you for working in the field in any capacity!

'I won't let you down.'

Only she had.

She lowered her eyelids like a shield and tensed in every nerve fibre of her body just before the door swung in. Focusing on the wall, she uttered the words that had become almost a mantra.

'I'm not hungry, but I require a toothbrush and toothpaste. When can I see the British consul?'

She wasn't expecting a straight answer. She hadn't had one to this, or any of the other questions she had asked, since she had been arrested on the wrong side of the border. Geography never had been her strong point. No answers, but there had been questions, many questions, the same questions over and over again. Questions and unbelieving silences.

Humanitarian aid did not translate into Quagani military speak. She told them she was not a spy and she had never belonged to a political party, and when they tried to refute her claim with a picture of her waving a banner at a protest to stop the closure of a local village infant school, she laughed—perhaps ill-advisedly.

When they weren't calling her a spy they were accusing her of being a drug runner. The evidence they used to illustrate this was boxes of precious vaccines that were now useless because they had clearly not been kept refrigerated.

For the first day she had clung to her belief that she had nothing to worry about if she told the truth. But now she couldn't believe she had ever been so naïve.

Thirty-six hours had passed, the news hadn't even made the headlines, and the diplomatic cogs had not even thought about turning when the King of Surana picked up his phone and dialled his counterpart in a neighbouring country, Sheikh Malek Sa'idi.

Two very different men stood awaiting the outcome of that conversation, and both had a vested interest.

The older was in his early sixties, of moderate height with a straggly beard and shaggy salt-and-pepper hair that curled on his collar and stuck up in tufts around his face. With his tweed jacket and comically mismatched socks, he had the look of a distracted professor.

But his horn-rimmed glasses hid eyes that were sharp and hard, and his unkempt hair covered a brain that, combined with risk-taking inclinations and a liberal measure of ruthlessness, had enabled him to make and lose two fortunes by the time he was fifty.

Right now he stood once more on the brink of either major success or financial ruin, but his mind was not focused on his financial situation. There was one thing in the world that meant more to Charles Latimer and that was his only child. In this room, behind closed doors, his poker face had gone, leaving only a pale and terrified parent.

The other man wore his raven-black hair close cropped, and his olive-toned skin looked gold in the light that flooded the room through massive windows that looked out over a courtyard. He was several inches over six feet tall, with long legs and broad shoulders that had made him a natural for the rowing teams at school and university. Rowing was not a career in his uncle's eyes, so his first Olympics had been his last. He had gold to show for it, even if the medal lay forgotten in a drawer somewhere. He liked to push himself, he liked winning, but he did not value prizes.

Charles Latimer's restless, hand-wringing pacing contrasted with this younger man's immobility—although he was motionless apart from the spasmodic clenching of a muscle in the hollow of one lean cheek, there was an edgy, explosive quality about him.

This man was of a different generation from the anguished parent—it was actually his thirtieth birthday that day. This was not the way he had planned to celebrate, though nothing in his manner hinted at this frustration. He accepted that his feelings were secondary to duty, and duty was bred into his every bone and sinew.

He got up suddenly, his actions betraying a tension that his expression concealed. Tall and innately elegant, he walked to the full-length window, his feet silent on the centuries-old intricate ceramic tiles. Fighting a feeling of claustrophobia, he flung open the window, allowing the sound of the falling water in the courtyard below to muffle his uncle's voice. The air was humid, heavy with the scent of jasmine, but there was no sign of the dust storm that had blown up after he had landed.

It was a good twenty degrees hotter than it would have been in Antibes. Through half-closed eyes he saw Charlotte Denning, her lithe, tanned body arranged on a sun lounger by the infinity pool, a bottle of champagne on ice, ready to fulfil her promise of a special birthday treat.

Recently divorced and enjoying her freedom, she was making up for a year spent married to a man who did not share her sexual appetites.

In short she was pretty much his ideal woman.

She would be angry at his no-show and later, when she found out the reason, she would be even angrier— not that marriage would put him out of bounds. Knowing Charlotte, he thought it might even add an extra illicit thrill.

There would be no thrills for him. Marriage would put the Charlottes of this world off-limits. He had his memories to keep him warm. The ironic curve of his lips that accompanied the thought flattened into a hard line of resolve. He would marry because it was his duty. For a lucky few duty and desire were one and the same… Once he had considered himself one of the lucky ones.

He took a deep breath of fragrant air, and closed the window, refusing to allow the insidious tendrils of resentment and self-pity to take hold. If he ever thought he'd got a bad deal he simply reminded himself that he was alive. Unlike his little niece, Leila, the baby who might have become his, had things been different. She died when the plane that was carrying her and her parents crashed into the side of a mountain, killing all on board, starting an avalanche of speculation and changing his future for ever.

He *had* a future, one he had inherited from Leila's father. Since becoming the heir and not the spare he had not thought about marriage except as something that would happen and sooner rather than later. With limited time he had set about enjoying what there was of it and in his determined pursuit of this ambition he had gained a reputation. At some point someone had called him the Heartbreaker Prince, and the title had stuck.

And now a freak set of circumstances had conspired to provide him with a ready-made bride who had a reputation to match his own. There would be no twelve-month marriage for him; it was a life sentence to Heartless Hannah. Those tabloids did so love their alliteration.

'It is done.'

Kamel turned back and nodded calmly. 'I'll set things in motion.'

As the King put the phone back down on its cradle Charles Latimer shocked himself and the others present by bursting into tears.

It took Kamel slightly less than an hour to put arrangements in place and then he returned to give the two older men a run-through of the way he saw it happening. As a courtesy he got the plan signed off by his uncle, who nodded and turned to his old college friend and business partner.

'So we should have her with you by tonight, Charlie.'

Kamel could have pointed out that more factually she would be with *him*, but he refrained. It was all about priorities: get the girl out, then deal with the consequences.

Kamel felt obliged to point out the possibility he

had not been able to factor in. Not that this was a deal-breaker—in life sometimes you just had to wing it and he was confident of his ability to do so in most situations. 'Of course, if she's hysterical or—'

'Don't worry, Hannah is tough and smart. She catches on quick. She'll walk out of there under her own steam.'

And now he was within moments of discovering if the parental confidence had been justified.

He doubted it.

Kamel thought it much more likely the man had not allowed himself to believe anything else. Clearly he had indulged the girl all her life. The chances of a spoilt English society brat lasting half a day in a prison cell before she fell apart were slender at best.

So having been fully prepared for the worst, he should have been relieved to find the object of his rescue mission wasn't the anticipated hysterical wreck. For some reason the sight of this slim, stunningly beautiful woman—sitting there on the narrow iron cot with its bare mattress, hands folded in her lap, head tilted at a confident angle, wearing a creased, shapeless prison gown with the confidence and poise of someone wearing a designer outfit—did not fill him with relief, and definitely not admiration, but a blast of anger.

Unbelievable! On her behalf people were moving heaven and earth and she was sitting there acting as though the bloody butler had entered the room! A butler she hadn't even deigned to notice. Was she simply too stupid to understand the danger of her position or was she so used to Daddy rescuing her from unpleasant situations that she thought she was invulnerable?

Then she turned her head, the dark lashes lifting

from the curve of her smooth cheek, and Kamel realised that under the cool blonde Hitchcock heroine attitude she was scared witless. He took a step closer and could almost smell the tension that was visible in the taut muscles around her delicate jaw, and the fine mist of sweat on her pale skin.

He frowned. He'd save his sympathy for those who deserved it. Scared or not, Hannah Latimer did not come into that category. This was a mess of her own making.

It was easy to see how men went after her, though, despite the fact she was obviously poison. He even experienced a slug of attraction himself—but then luckily she opened her mouth. Her voice was as cut glass as her profile, her attitude a mixture of disdain and superiority, which could not have won her any friends around here.

'I must demand to see the—' She stopped, her violet-blue eyes flying wide as she released an involuntary gasp. The man standing there was not holding a tray with a plate of inedible slop on it.

There had been several interrogators but always the same two guards, neither of whom spoke. One was short and squat, and the other was tall and had a problem with body odour—after he had gone the room was filled with a sour smell for ages.

This man was tall too, very tall. She found herself tilting her head to frame all of him; beyond height there was no similarity whatsoever to her round-shouldered, sour-smelling jailors. He wasn't wearing the drab utilitarian khaki of the guards or the showy uniform with gold epaulettes of the man who sat in on all the interrogations.

This man was clean-shaven and he was wearing

snowy white ceremonial desert robes. The fabric carried a scent of fresh air and clean male into the enclosed space. Rather bizarrely he carried a swathe of blue silk over one arm. Her round-eyed, fearful stare shifted from the incongruous item to his face.

If it hadn't been for the slight scar that stood out white on his golden skin, and the slight off-centre kink in his nose, he might have been classed as pretty. Instead he was simply beautiful… She stared at his wide, sensual mouth and looked away a moment before he said in a voice that had no discernible accent and even less warmth, 'I need you to put this on, Miss Latimer.'

The soft, sinister demand made her guts clench in fear. Before she clamped her trembling lips together a whisper slipped through. 'No!'

This man represented the nightmare she had kept at bay and up to this point her treatment had been civilised, if not gentle. She had deliberately not dwelt on her vulnerability; she hadn't seen another woman since her arrest, and she was at the mercy of men who sometimes looked at her… The close-set eyes of the man who sat in on the interviews flashed into her head and a quiver of disgust slid through her body.

People in her situation simply vanished.

Staring at the blue fabric and the hand that held it as if it were a striking snake, she surged to her feet—too fast. The room began to swirl as she struggled to focus on the silk square, bright against the clinical white of the walls and tiled floor…blue, white, blue, white…

'Breathe.' Her legs folded as he pressed her down onto the bed and pushed her head towards her knees.

The habit of a lifetime kicked in and she took refuge behind an air of cool disdain.

'I don't need a change of clothing. I'm fine with this.'
She clutched the fabric of the baggy shift that reached
mid-calf with both hands and aimed her gaze at the
middle of his chest.

Two large hands came to rest on her shoulders, stopping the rhythmic swaying motion she had been unaware of, but not the spasms of fear that were rippling
through her body.

Kamel was controlling his anger and resentment: he
didn't want to be here; he didn't want to be doing this,
and he didn't want to feel any empathy for the person
who was totally responsible for the situation, a spoilt
English brat who had a well-documented history of bolt-
ing at the final hurdle.

Had she felt any sort of remorse for the wave of emotional destruction she'd left in her wake? Had her own
emotions ever been involved? he wondered.

Still, she hadn't got off scot-free. Some enterprising
journalist had linked the car smash of her first victim
with the aborted wedding.

Driven over the Edge, the headline had screamed,
and the media had crucified Heartless Hannah. Perhaps
if she had shown even a scrap of emotion they might
have softened when it turned out that the guy had been
over the drink-drive limit when he drove his car off a
bridge, but she had looked down her aristocratic little
nose and ignored the flashing cameras.

In London at the time, he had followed the story
partly because he knew her father and partly because,
like the man who had written off his car, Kamel knew
what it felt like to lose the love you planned to spend
your life with. Not that Amira had dumped him—if
he hadn't released her she would have married him

rather than cause him pain. She had been everything this woman was not.

And yet it was hard not to look into that grubby flower-like face, perfect in every detail, and feel a flicker of something that came perilously close to pity. He sternly squashed it.

She deserved everything that was going to happen to her. If there was any victim in this it was him. Luckily he had no romantic illusions about marriage, or at least his. It was never going to be a love match—he'd loved and lost and disbelieved the popular idea that this was better than not to have loved at all. Still, it was a mistake he would not make in the future. Only an imbecile would want to lay himself open to that sort of pain again. A marriage of practicality suited him.

Though Kamel had imagined his bride would be someone whom he could respect.

Why couldn't the brainless little bimbo have found meaning in her life by buying some shoes? Even facing financial collapse, Kamel was sure Daddy dear would have bought her the whole shop. Instead she decided to become an angel of mercy. While he could see the selfish delusion that had led her to do this, he couldn't understand why any legitimate medical charity would have taken her on, even on a voluntary basis.

'I asked you to put this on, not take anything off.' Kamel let out a hissing sound of irritation as she sat there looking up at him like some sort of sacrificial virgin...though there was nothing even vaguely virginal about Miss Hannah Latimer, and that quality was about the only one he didn't have a problem with in his future bride!

Digging deep into reserves she didn't know she had, Hannah got to her feet.

'If you touch me I will report you and when I get out of here—' Don't you mean *if,* Hannah? '—I'm going to be sick.'

'No, you are not,' Kamel said. 'If you want to get out of here do as I say so put the damned thing on.'

Breathing hard, staring at him with wide eyes, she backed away, holding her hands out in a warning gesture. 'If you touch me in an inappropriate way...' You'll what, Hannah? Scream? And then who will come running?

'I promise you, angel, that sex is the last thing on my mind and if it was...' His heavy-lidded eyes moved in a contemptuous sweep from her feet to her face before he added, 'I'm not asking you to strip.' He enunciated each scathing word slowly, the words very clear despite the fact he had not raised his voice above a low menacing purr since he'd come in. 'I'm asking you to cover up.'

Hannah barely heard him. The nightmare images she had so far kept at bay were crowding in.

Kamel had had a varied life, but having a woman look at him as though he were all her nightmares come true was a first. Conquering a natural impulse to shake her rather than comfort her, he struggled to inject some soothing quality into his voice as he leaned in closer. 'Your father says to tell you that...' He stopped and closed his eyes. What was the name of the damned dog? His eyes opened again as it came to him. 'Olive had five puppies.'

It had been a last thought: I need a detail, something that a stranger wouldn't know. Something that will tell her I'm one of the good guys.

Hannah froze, her wild eyes returning to his face at the specific reference to the rescue dog she had adopted.

'Yes, I'm the cavalry—' he watched as she took a shuddering sigh and closed her eyes '—so just do as you're told and cover up.' His glance moved to the honey-blonde tresses that were tangled and limp. 'And be grateful you're having a bad-hair day.'

Hannah didn't register his words past cavalry; her thoughts were whirling. 'My father sent you?'

She gave a watery smile. Her father had come through! She exhaled and sent up a silent thank you to her absent parent.

She took the fabric and looked at it. What did he expect her to do with it? 'Who are you?'

Possibilities buzzed like a restless bee through her head. An actor? Some sort of mercenary? A corrupt official? Someone willing to do anything for money or the adrenalin buzz?

'Your ticket out of here.'

Hannah tilted her head in acknowledgement. The important thing was he had successfully blagged or bribed his way in here and represented a shot at freedom.

Her jaw firmed. Suddenly she felt the optimism she had not allowed herself to feel during her incarceration. It had been an hour to hour—hard to believe there had only been forty-eight, but then, in a room illuminated twenty-four-seven by the harsh fluorescent light, it was hard to judge time.

'Is Dad...?'

He responded to the quiver of hope in her voice with a stern, 'Forget your father and focus. Do not allow yourself to become distracted.'

The tone enabled her to retain her grip on her unravelling control. He had the shoulders but he clearly had no intention of offering them up for tears, which was fine by her. If a girl didn't learn after two failed engagements that the only person she could rely on was herself, she deserved everything she got!

'Yes…of course.'

Her fingers shook as she took the shimmering blue fabric. It fell in a tangled skein on the floor, the fabric unravelling… Just like me, she thought.

She took a deep breath and released it, slowly able to lift her chin and meet his gaze with something approaching composure as she asked, 'What do you want me to do?'

Kamel felt an unwilling stab of admiration.

'I want you to keep your mouth closed, your head covered, and follow my lead.'

He bent forward and took the fold of fabric from her fingers. The fabric billowed out of his hands and she was suddenly swathed in the stuff, covering her head and most of the ugly shift.

He stood back to see the effect, then nodded and threw the remaining fabric over her shoulder. His hand stayed there, heavy, the contact more reassuring than his stern stare.

'Can you do that?'

'Yes,' she said, hoping it was true.

'Right. You are going to leave here and you are going to do so with your head held high. Just channel all your…just be yourself.'

She blinked up into his dark eyes, noticing the little silver flecks, and struggled to swallow a giggle—she knew that once she gave in to hysteria that was it.

'And they are just going to let us out?' His confidence

bordered the insane but maybe that was a good thing for someone in charge of a jail break.

'Yes.'

'I don't know why they let you just walk in here but—'

'They let me just walk in here because to refuse me access would have caused offence and they have a lot of ground to make up.' They could arrest, interrogate and imprison a foreign national on charges that carried the death penalty, but not the bride-to-be of the heir to the Suranian throne.

Maybe if she had chosen another moment to stray across the border his uncle's influence alone would have been enough to gain her freedom, but with impeccable timing Hannah Latimer had wandered into an armed border patrol at a time when the ruling family of Quagani was politically vulnerable. Accused by rival factions of being unable to protect the country's interests against foreign exploitation, the royals had responded by instigating a draconian zero-tolerance policy: no second chances, no leniency, no special cases...*almost*.

His uncle had not ordered, he had not played the duty card—instead he had spoken of a debt he owed Charles Latimer and asked with uncharacteristic humility if Kamel would be willing to marry Hannah Latimer.

'She is not ideal,' the King admitted, 'and not the person I would have wanted for you, but I'm sure with guidance... She was a lovely child, as I recall. Very like her mother, poor Emily.' He sighed.

'She grew up.'

'It is your decision, Kamel.'

This was the first thing ever asked of him by his uncle—who was not just his King but also the man who had stepped in after his father's death and treated him as his own son. Kamel's response had never been in doubt.

Hannah heard the irony in her rescuer's voice but didn't have a clue what it meant. 'I don't understand a word you're saying.' Though he said it in a voice that had a tactile shiver-down-your-spine quality.

'You will.' Despite the smile that went with the words, she sensed an underlying threat that was echoed in the bleakness of his stare.

'Look, no one is about to ask you anything, but if they do, don't say anything. Burst into tears or something.'

That would not require much effort. The walking might, though—her knees felt like cotton wool.

'Just pretend you're running away from some sucker at the altar.'

Her shocked violet eyes widened to their fullest extent. The reputation she pretended not to care about had followed her to a jail halfway around the world. Ironically she had come here in the hope of rebuilding her reputation, or at least escaping the cameras.

'I believe you've had some practice,' he murmured before seamlessly raising his voice from the soft, for-her-ears-only undertone, to an authoritative command to the prison guards.

The words were unintelligible to her but the effect was magic. The guards she recognised stood either side of the open door, their heads bowed. Along the corridor there were uniformed figures standing to attention.

The man beside her spoke and the guards bowed lower. Hannah stared, astonished—it wasn't just their reaction; it was the man himself. He seemed to have as-

sumed a totally new persona, and it fitted him as well
as the flowing robes. He was clearly immersing himself
in his role; even his body language had changed. The
arrogance was still there but it was combined with an
air of haughty authority as he strode along, shortening
his step so that she could keep pace.

What the hell was happening?

She had expected to be smuggled out of some back
entrance, not to receive the red-carpet treatment.

Like a sleepwalker, Hannah allowed her tall escort to
guide her down the corridor. Nobody looked directly at
her or her companion as they walked past. The silence
was so intense she could feel it.

Outside, the heat hit her—it was like walking into
a shimmering wall, but the sun was infinitely preferable to the ten-foot-square, white-walled cell. It was the
thought of being discovered and ending up back there
and not the temperature that brought Hannah out in a
cold sweat.

A leashed guard dog began to bark, straining at the
lead as they walked on. Could dogs really smell fear?
As his handler fought to control the animal the man
beside her turned, clicked his fingers and looked at the
dog, who immediately dropped down on his belly and
whimpered.

Neat trick, Hannah thought, momentarily losing her
balance as a jet flew low overhead. She had heard the
sound before many times over the last days but it was
a lot quieter in her cell.

'I'm fine,' she mumbled as the hand on her elbow
slid to her waist. In that moment of contact she registered the fact that his body had no give—it was all hard

muscle. For a moment she enjoyed an illusion of safety before she was released.

Hannah, who had been totally disorientated when she had arrived in darkness, realised for the first time that she had been incarcerated on a military base.

Almost as if some of his strength had seeped into her, she felt more confident, enabling her to adopt a fatalistic attitude when they were approached by a mean-looking man with shoulders the size of a hangar, dressed similarly to the man she struggled to keep pace with.

Hannah wanted to run, every survival instinct she had was screaming at her to do so, but the hand that reached down and took her own had other ideas. Her escort had stopped when he saw the other man and waited. Under her blue silk and grubby shift Hannah sucked in a shaky breath and began to sweat—but the hand that held her own was cool and dry.

'This is Rafiq.'

So clearly friend, not foe. She managed a shaky half-smile when the big man acknowledged her presence with a respectful tip of his covered head. He responded with calm, one-word replies to the questions her escort threw at him, even earning a tight smile that might have been approval.

Hannah, who hadn't been able to follow a word, was unable to restrain herself. 'Is everything all right?'

'You mean are you about to escape justice?'

'I'm innocent!'

Her protest drew a sardonic smile from her rescuer. She had the impression he wasn't her greatest fan, but she didn't mind so long as he got her out of here.

'We are all guilty of something, angel. As the man

said, there's no such thing as a free meal, but, yes, your taxi awaits.'

Hannah spun to face the direction in which he had nodded and saw a jet with a crest on the side that seemed vaguely familiar.

CHAPTER TWO

AT THE SIGHT of the private jet Hannah felt her heart race. Her anticipation of imminent escape and the possibility that her father was inside waiting were mingled with the equally powerful conviction that any minute someone would catch on. To be caught when freedom was literally within sight, touch and smell would be so much harder than if she had never hoped.

'Keep it together.'

She turned her head sharply, the action causing the silk to fall away from her cheek. She could not believe he could look so relaxed. Did the man have ice in his veins? No—she remained conscious of the warmth of his guiding hand on her elbow.

Hannah twitched the silk back into place and in doing so caught sight of someone who was approaching across the tarmac. Her eyes widened to large pools of blue terror in a face that had become dramatically pale.

'Do not run.'

Fear clutched her belly. 'He…'

Kamel watched as she licked her dry lips. Her eyes were darting from side to side like a cornered animal seeking an avenue of escape, but they kept moving back to the army colonel who carried a cane and an air of self-importance as he approached them, flanked by a small armed guard.

It didn't take a second for Kamel to experience a flash of vengeful rage that reminded him strongly of a time in his youth when, after escaping the security that he hated, he had encountered three much older boys in a narrow side street. He had not known at first what was lying on the ground there, but he had seen one boy aim a kick at it, and they had all laughed. It was the laughter he had reacted to with sheer, blinding, red-mist rage.

He had arrived back at the palace later, looking worse than the poor stray dog the trio had been systematically kicking the hell out of. He had freed the dog in the end, not by physical means but by offering them the ring he wore.

His father, the antithesis of a tyrannical parent, had been more bemused than angry when he'd discovered the ring was gone.

'You gave a priceless heirloom for this flea-ridden thing?' He had then progressed to remind Kamel how important breeding was.

It was an important lesson, not in breeding but in negotiation. In a tight situation, it was often a clear head rather than physical force that turned the tide. He controlled his instinctive rage now. Summing up the man in a glance, he knew he had come across the kind before many times: a bully who took pleasure from intimidating those he controlled.

'Did he interrogate you?'

Hannah shivered, not from the ice in Kamel's voice, but the memory.

'He watched.' And tapped a cane on the floor, she thought, shivering again as she remembered the sound.

The man's silence had seemed more threatening to her than the men who asked the questions. That and the look in his eyes.

Kamel's jaw was taut, and his voice flat. 'Lift your head up. He can't do a thing to you.'

'Highness, I am here to offer our sincere apologies for any misunderstanding. I hope it has not given Miss Latimer a dislike of our beautiful country.'

And now it was his turn.

His turn to smile and lie through his teeth. It was a talent that he had worked on to the point where his diplomacy looked effortless even though it frequently veiled less civilised instincts.

He uncurled his clenched fingers, unmaking the fists they had instinctively balled into, but he was spared having to produce the words that stuck in his throat by sudden activity around the waiting jet.

As something came screaming down towards them, one man raised a pistol. Kamel, who had the advantage of faster reflexes, reached casually out and chopped the man's arm, causing him to drop the gun to the ground. It went off, sending a bullet into a distant brick wall.

'Relax, it's just…'

He stopped as the hawk that had been flying above their heads dropped down, claws extended, straight onto the head of the uniformed colonel. His hat went flying and he covered his head protectively as the hooded hawk swooped again—this time escaping with what looked like a dead animal in his talons.

The colonel stood there, his hands on his bald head.

Releasing a hissing signal from between his teeth,

Kamel extended his arm. The hawk responded to the sound and landed on his wrist.

'You are quite safe now, Colonel.' Kamel took the toupee from the bird and, holding it on one finger, extended it to the man who had curled into a foetal crouch, his head between his hands.

Red-faced, the older man rose to his feet, his dignity less intact than his face, which had only suffered a couple of superficial scratches, oozing blood onto the ground.

He took the hairpiece and crammed it on his head, drawing a smothered laugh from one of his escorts. When he spun around the men stared ahead stonily.

'That thing should be destroyed. It nearly blinded me.'

Kamel touched the jewel attached to that bird's hood. 'My apologies, Colonel. No matter how many jewels you put on a bird of prey, she remains at heart a creature of impulse. But then that is the attraction of wild things, don't you think?'

The other man opened his mouth and a grunt emerged through his clenched teeth as he bowed.

Kamel smiled. He handed back the pistol to the man who had tried to shoot it, having first emptied the barrel with a mild reproach of, 'Unwise.' He then turned to Rafiq and issued a soft-voiced command in French that Hannah struggled to make sense of.

The big man bowed his head, murmured, 'Highness,' and took Hannah's elbow.

Hannah, who had remained glued to the spot while the drama had played out around her, did not respond to the pressure.

Kamel, his dark eyes flashing warning, touched her cheek.

Like someone waking from a deep sleep, she started and lifted her blue eyes to his face. 'Go with Rafiq. I will be with you presently, my little dove.' Without waiting to see if she responded, he turned to the bleeding and humiliated colonel. 'Please forgive Emerald. She is very protective and responds when she senses danger. She is…unpredictable. But as you see—' he ran a finger down the bird's neck '—quite docile.'

Kamel could feel the effort it cost the man to smile. 'You have an unusual pet, Prince Kamel.'

Kamel produced a smile that was equally insincere. 'She is not a pet, Colonel.'

He could feel the man's eyes in his back as he walked away. Still, a poisonous stare was less painful than the bullet he would no doubt have preferred to deliver.

'No.' Hannah shook her head and refused to take the seat that she was guided to. 'Where is he?' she asked the monolith of a man who didn't react to her question. 'My father! Where is he?'

As the door closed behind him the hawk flew off Kamel's hand and onto her perch, the tinkle of bells making Hannah turn her head. 'Where is my father? I want my—'

He cut across her, his tone as bleak as winter, but not as cold and derisive as his eyes. 'You should know I have no taste for hysteria.'

'And you should know I don't give a damn.'

Kamel, who had anticipated her reaction to be of the standard 'poor little me' variety, was actually pleasantly surprised by her anger. If nothing else the girl was resilient. Just as well—as it was a quality she was going to need.

'I suppose it was too much to hope that you have learnt anything from your experience.' He arched a sardonic ebony brow. 'Like humility.'

Now wasn't that the ultimate in irony? She was being lectured on humility by a man who had just produced a master class in arrogance.

She hadn't expected to be told she'd done brilliantly or receive a pat on the back…but a lecture?

'You got me out of there, so thanks. But I'm damned if I'm going to be lectured by the hired help!' It came out all wrong. But what did it matter if he thought she was a snob? She needed to know what the hell was happening and he wouldn't even give her a straight answer.

At last she was now living down to his expectations. He peeled off his head gear, revealing a head of close-cropped raven-black hair. The austere style emphasised the classical strength of his strongly sculpted features. 'I suggest that we postpone this discussion until we are actually in the air.'

It wasn't a suggestion so much as an order, and his back was already to her. She had just spent two days in a cell experiencing a total lack of control—this man was going to give her answers!

'Don't walk away from me like that!'

Dragging a hand back and forth over his hair, causing it to stand up in spikes, he paused and turned his head towards her without immediately responding. Instead in a low aside he spoke to his massive stone-faced sidekick, who bowed his head respectfully before he whisked away—moving surprisingly quickly for such a large man.

His attentions switched back to Hannah. 'It's called prioritising, my little dove.'

Hannah felt her stomach muscles tighten at the reminder that the last hurdle was still to be negotiated. At least most of the quivering was associated with fear. Some of it…well, it wasn't as if she were struck dumb with lust, but a little dry-mouthed maybe? Previously her fear levels had given her some protection from the aura of raw sexuality this man exuded, but she felt it even more strongly when he hooked a finger under her chin and looked down into her face for a moment before letting his hand drop away.

The contact and the deep dark stare had been uncomfortable, but now it was gone she wasn't sure what she felt. She gave her head a tiny shake to clear the low-level buzz—or was that the jet engines? She was clearly suffering the effects of an adrenalin dip; the chemical circulating in her blood had got her this far, but now she was shaking.

'Sit down, belt up and switch off your phone,' he drawled, wondering if he hadn't been a bit too tough on her. But she acted tough, and looked… His eyes slid over the soft contours of her fine-boned face. She was possibly one of the few women on the planet who could look beautiful after two days in a ten-foot-square prison cell.

She sat down with a bump because it was preferable to falling. Had she thanked him yet?

'Thank you.' Hannah had been brought up to be polite, after all, and he had just rescued her.

She closed her eyes and missed the look of shock on his face. As the jet took off she released a long, slow sigh and didn't open her eyes again, even when she felt the light brush of hands on her shoulder and midriff as a belt was snapped shut.

Was it possible that she had jumped from the proverbial frying pan straight into…what? And with whom? It was only the knowledge that he carried the personal message from her father that had stopped her tipping over into panic as her imagination threatened to go wild on her.

'If you would like anything, just ask Rafiq. I have some work to do.'

She opened her eyes in time to see her rescuer shrug off his imposing desert robes to reveal a pale coffee-coloured tee shirt and black jeans. The resulting relaxed image should have been less imposing, but actually wasn't—even though he appeared to have shrugged off the icy-eyed hauteur that had reduced the aggressive colonel to red-faced docility.

He might be dressed casually, his attitude might be relaxed when he glanced her way, but this didn't change the fact that he exuded a level of sexuality that was unlike anything she had ever encountered.

He took a couple of steps, then turned back, his dark, dispassionate stare moving across her face. So many questions—Hannah asked the one that she felt took priority. 'Who are you?'

His mouth lifted at one corner but the dark silver-flecked eyes stayed coolly dispassionate as he responded, 'Your future husband.'

Then he was gone.

CHAPTER THREE

'Is THERE ANYTHING I can get for you?'

The words roused Hannah from her semi catatonic state. She surged to her feet and flung the man mountain before her a look of profound scorn before pushing past him into the adjoining cabin, which contained a seating area and a bed on which her tall, rude rescuer was stretched out, one booted foot crossed over the other, his forearm pressed across his eyes.

'I thought you were working.'

'This is a power nap. I want to look good in the wedding photos.'

Breathing hard, she stood there, hands on her hips, glaring at his concealed face—noticing as she did the small bloody indentations on the sides of his wrist, presumably from where the hawk had landed on his bare skin.

'Can you be serious for one moment, please?'

He lifted a dark brow and with a long-suffering sigh dropped his arm. Then, in one sinuous motion, he pulled himself up into a sitting position and lowered his feet to the ground.

He planted his hands on his thighs and leaned forward. 'I'm all yours. Shoot.'

Hannah heard *shoot* and shuddered, recalling the scene on the tarmac where but for his lightning reflexes there might have been more than one bullet discharged—a disaster narrowly averted.

'You should put some antiseptic on those.'

His dark brows twitched into a puzzled line.

She pointed to his arm. 'The bird.' She angled a wary glance at the big bird. 'You're bleeding.'

He turned his wrist and shrugged in an irritatingly tough fashion. 'I'll live.'

'I, on the other hand, am feeling a little insecure about being on a plane with a total stranger going...' she gave an expressive shrug '...God knows where. So do you mind filling in a few blanks?'

He nodded. She didn't sound insecure. She sounded and looked confident and sexy and in control. What would it take to make her lose it? It could be he was about to find out.

'My father sent you?'

He tipped his head in acknowledgement and she gave a gusty sigh of relief. 'He sends his love.'

'I'm sure Dad appreciates your sense of humour, but I'm a bit...'

'Uptight? Humourless?'

Her blue eyes narrowed to slits. She had very little energy left, and being angry with him was using it all up. She took a deep breath and thought, Rise above it, Hannah. People had said a lot worse about her and she'd maintained her dignity.

It was a power thing. If *they* saw it got to her *they* had the power and she lost it. It didn't matter who *they* were—school bullies, journalists—the same rule applied. If you showed weakness they reacted like pack animals scenting blood.

'I'd prefer to know what's happening, so if you could just fill me in…? Tell me where the plane is headed and then I'll let you sleep in peace.'

'Surana.'

The mention of the oil-rich desert state fired a memory. That was where she'd seen the crest on the plane before, and it fitted: her father had called in some favours. She knew he counted the King of Surana as a personal friend; the two men had met forty years earlier at the public school they had attended as boys. The friendship had survived the years—apparently the King had once dandled her on his knee but Hannah had no recollection of the event.

'So Dad will be there to meet us?'

'No, he'll be waiting at the chapel.'

Hannah fought for composure. Was this man on something? 'Hilarious.' She tried to laugh but laughing in the face of the ruthless resolve stamped on his hard-boned face was difficult. She hefted a weary sigh and reminded herself she was free. It was all up from here, once she got a straight answer from this man. 'This is not a joke that has the legs to run and run.'

His broad shoulders lifted in a shrug that suggested he didn't care. 'Look, I wish it were a joke. I have no more wish to marry you than you have me, but before you start bleating for Daddy ask yourself what you would have preferred if I'd offered you the option back there: marrying me, or spending twenty years in a boiling-hot jail where luxury is considered a tap shared by several hundred. Or even worse—'

'How does it get worse?'

'How about the death penalty?'

'That was never a possibility.' Her scorn faltered and her stomach clenched with terror. Had she really been that close? 'Was it?'

He arched a sardonic brow.

'So if I'd signed the confession...?' Her voice trailed away as she spoke until 'confession' emerged from her white lips as a husky whisper.

'You didn't.' Kamel fought the irrational feeling of guilt. He was only spelling out the ugly facts; he was not responsible. Still, it gave him no pleasure to see the shadow of terror in her wide eyes. 'So don't think about it.'

The advice brought her chin up with a snap. 'I wouldn't be thinking about it at all if you hadn't told me.'

'Maybe it's about time you faced unpleasant facts and accepted that there are some things we cannot run away from.'

Not several thousand feet off the ground, but once they landed Hannah intended to run very fast indeed from this man. 'I'm grateful to be free, obviously, but I didn't do anything wrong.'

'You entered a sovereign state illegally, carrying drugs.'

Hannah's clenched teeth ached. His righteous attitude was really getting under her skin.

'I got lost and I was carrying medicine. Vaccines and antibiotics.'

'Morphine?'

Feeling defensive, Hannah rubbed her damp palms against her thighs. With his steely eyes and relentless delivery he was a much more effective interrogator than her captors had been. 'Yes.'

'And a camera.'

'No!'

'Isn't there a camera on your phone?'

He would have thought better of her if she had the guts to hold up her hands and take responsibility for her own actions, but that obviously wasn't her style.

'Weren't you told to stay with the vehicle if it broke down?'

How did he know? 'It was an emergency.' And that was the only reason she had been entrusted the responsibility. There simply had been no one else available.

'And you were the one on the ground and you made a tough call…fine. But now you have to take the consequences for that decision.'

Struggling to keep pace with the relentless pace of his reasoning, she shook her head. 'So I have to marry you because you rescued me? Sure, *obvious*. I should have realised.'

The bored façade and the last shades of cynical amusement in his manner fell away as he vaulted to his feet.

He towered over her, eyes blazing with contempt. She could feel the anger spilling out of him and presumably so could the bird sitting on its perch—it began to squawk and Hannah lifted her hands to her head to protect herself.

The act of soothing the spooked creature seemed to help Kamel regain some semblance of control. 'She won't hurt you.'

Hannah dropped her hands, cast a quick sideways glance at the fascinating wild creature, and then returned her attention to the man. 'I wasn't worried about the *bird*.'

His jaw tightened in response to the pointed comment, and he stared at the mouth that delivered it...her wide, full, sexy lower lip. Hers was a mouth actually made for kissing.

'I wouldn't marry you even if you *were* sane!'

She might have a point. Wasn't it insane to be checking out her impossibly long legs? Wasn't it even more insane to actually like the fact she didn't back away from him, that her pride made her give as good as she got?

'And came gift-wrapped!' Hannah caught herself wondering how many women would have liked to unwrap him, and felt a lick of fear before she told herself that she was not one of them.

'You want facts? Fine. When we land in Surana in —' He turned his wrist and glanced at the watch that glinted against his dark skin.

'Thirty minutes. There will be a red carpet and reception committee for Your Royal Highness,' she finished his sentence for him, and, keeping her eyes on his face, she performed a graceful bow.

He took her sarcasm at face value.

'There will be no official reception under the circumstances. Things will be low-key. We will go straight to the palace where my uncle, the King—'

Her eyes flew wide. '*King?* You're asking me to believe you're really a prince?'

He stared at her hard. 'Who did you think I was?'

'Someone my father paid to get me out of jail. I thought you were pretending to—'

'I can't decide if you're just plain stupid or incredibly naïve.' He shook his head from side to side in an attitude of weary incredulity. 'You thought all I had to do was walk in, claim to be of royal blood and all the doors would open to release you?' What alternative universe did this woman live in?

Her eyes narrowed with dislike as he threw back his head and laughed.

'What was I meant to think?'

'That you were extremely lucky you have a father who cares so much about you, a father who is waiting with my uncle and Sheikh Sa'idi of Quagani. The only reason you are not now facing the consequences of your actions is because the Sheikh has been told that you are my fiancée.'

'And he believed that?'

'I think the wedding invite swung it.'

'Well, I'm out, so job done. You can tell him the wedding's off.'

'I can see that that is the way things work in your world.' A world with no honour.

'What is that meant to mean?'

The plane hit a pocket and he braced himself as it sank and rose while she staggered and grabbed the back of a chair. 'That you step away from commitment when it suits you.'

Hannah was waiting for her stomach to find its level but this not so veiled reference to her engagements brought an angry flush to her cheeks. 'I'm fine, thanks for asking,' she murmured, rubbing the area where her wrist had banged against the chair.

He continued as though she had not spoken. 'But that is not the way it works here. My uncle feels indebted to your father and he has given his word.'

'I didn't give my word.'

'*Your word!*' he echoed with acid scorn.

She felt the burn of tears in her eyes and furiously blinked to clear them. 'I won't be lectured by you!'

'Your word means...' he clicked his fingers '...nothing. It is otherwise with my uncle. He is a man of integrity, honour. I suppose I'm speaking a foreign language to you?'

'So your uncle would be embarrassed. I'm sorry about that—'

'But not sorry enough to accept the consequences of your actions?'

Consequences...consequences... Hannah fought the urge to cover her ears. 'This is stupid. What terrible thing is going to happen if we don't get married?' Hannah hoped the question didn't give him the false impression that she would even consider this.

'I'm glad you asked that.'

He opened the laptop that lay on a table and spun it around, stabbing it with his finger. 'We are a small country but oil rich, and we have enjoyed relative political stability. Since the discovery last year of these new reserves, we are set to be even more rich.'

She pursed her lips at his lecturing tone and stuck out her chin. 'I do read an occasional newspaper.'

'Don't boast about your IQ, angel, because,' he drawled, 'stupidity is the only possible excuse for your little escapade.'

An angry hissing sound escaped her clenched teeth. 'I know the country is a shining light of political stability and religious tolerance. What I didn't know was that the ruling family had a history of insanity—but that's what happens when you marry cousins.'

'Well, you will be a new injection of blood, won't you, angel? This will happen, you know. The sooner you accept it, the easier it will be.'

Hannah bit her lip. Even her interrogators had never looked at her with such open contempt and, though she refused to admit it even to herself, it hurt. As had the headlines and the inches of gossip all vilifying her.

'Shall I tell you why?'

He waited a moment, then tipped his head, acknowledging her silence.

'We have a problem. We are landlocked and the oil needs to get to the sea.' He flicked his finger across the screen and traced a line. 'Which means we rely on the cooperation of others. The new pipeline is at present being constructed in Quagani, and it crosses three separate countries. Did you know your father is building the pipeline?'

Hannah didn't but she would have died before admitting it. 'I'm surprised they haven't already married you off to some Quagani princess to seal the deal.'

'They were going to, but she met my cousin.' Kamel had fallen in love with Amira slowly. It had been a gradual process and he'd thought it had been the same for her. Had he not seen it with his own eyes, Kamel would have laughed at the idea of love at first sight. He had tried very hard not to see it. 'When she found him... preferable, her family were fine with it because he was the heir and I was, as they say, the spare.'

'Then where is the problem? If your families are linked they're not going to fall out.'

'He died...she died...their baby died.' The only thing that linked the rulers now was shared grief and a need to blame someone.

Like a sandcastle hit by a wave, Hannah's snooty attitude dissolved. Despite some throat-clearing her voice was husky as she said softly, 'I'm so sorry. But my father wouldn't force me to marry for any amount of money.'

He looked at the woman who sat there with spoilt brat written all over her pretty face.

'Has it occurred to you that your father, being human, might jump at the chance to get you off his hands? And if he did I don't think there are many who would blame him.'

'My father doesn't think of me as a piece of property.'

He might, however, think of her as a lead weight around his neck.

'Do you care for your father as much as he does you?'

'What does that mean?'

'It means if Quagani closes the new pipeline it won't just be the school programme in our country that suffers. Your father has a stake in the new refinery too.'

It was the mention of a school programme that brought a worried furrow to her brow. In her job she knew what a difference education could make. 'My father has a stake in many things.'

'My uncle let your father in on this deal as a favour. He knew of his situation.'

She tensed and then relaxed.

'What situation? Are you trying to tell me my father has lost all of his money again?'

Over the years her father's reckless, impulsive approach to business had led to dramatic fluctuations in fortune, but that was in the past. After the heart attack he had actually listened to the doctors' warnings about the danger of stress. He had *promised* her faithfully that the risky deals were a thing of the past.

'Not all of it.'

Hannah met his dark, implacable stare and felt the walls of the cabin close in. Even as she was shaking her head in denial she knew deep down that he was telling her the truth.

Kamel watched, arms folded across his chest, as the comment sank in. The prospect of being the daughter of a poor man seemed to affect her more than anything he had said so far. The idea of slumming it or being forced to make her own way in the world without the cushion of Daddy's money had driven what little colour she had out of her face.

'He has made a number of unfortunate ventures, and if the pipeline deal fails your father faces bankruptcy.'

Hannah's heart started to thud faster and her heart was healthy. *Stress*...what could be more stressful than bankruptcy? Unless it was the humiliation of telling a cathedral full of people that your daughter's wedding was off.

She had accepted her share of responsibility for the heart attack that very few people knew about. At the time her father had sworn Hannah to secrecy, saying the markets would react badly to the news. Hannah didn't give a damn about the markets, but she cared a lot about her father. He was not as young as he liked to think. With his medical history, having to rebuild his company from scratch—what would that do to a man with a cardiac problem?

Struggling desperately to hide her concern behind a composed mask, she turned her clear, critical stare on her prospective husband and discovered as she stared at his lean, bronzed, beautiful face that she hadn't, as she had thought, relinquished all her childish romantic fantasies, even after her two engagements had ended so disastrously.

'So you have made a case for me doing this,' she admitted, trying to sound calm. 'But why *would you*? Why would you marry someone you can't stand the sight of? Are you really willing to marry a total stranger just because your uncle tells you to?'

'I could talk about duty and service,' he flung back, 'but I would be wasting my breath. They are concepts that you have no grasp of. And my motivation is not the issue here. I had a choice and I made it. Now it is your turn.'

She sank onto a day bed, her head bent forward and her hands clenched in her lap. After a few moments she lifted her head. She'd made her decision, but she wasn't ready to admit it.

'What will happen? If we get married…after…?' She lifted a hank of heavy hair from her eyes and caught sight of her reflection in the shiny surface of a metallic lamp on the wall beside her. There had been no mirrors in her cell and her appearance had not occupied her thoughts so it took her a few seconds before she realised the wild hair attached to a haggard face was her own. With a grimace she looked away.

'You would have a title, so not only could you act like a little princess, you could actually be one, which has some limited value when it comes to getting a dinner table or theatre ticket.'

'Princess…?' Could this get any more surreal?

The ingenuous, wide-eyed act irritated Kamel. 'Oh,

don't get too excited. In our family,' he drawled, 'a title is almost obligatory. It means little.'

As his had, but all that had changed the day that his cousin's plane had gone down and he had become the Crown prince.

That was two years ago now, and there remained those conspiracy theorists who still insisted there had been a cover-up—that the royal heir and his family had been the victims of a terrorist bomb, rather than a mechanical malfunction.

There was a more sinister school of thought that had gone farther, so at a time when Kamel had been struggling with the intense grief and anger he felt for the senseless deaths—his cousin was a man he had admired and loved—Kamel had also had to deal with the fact that some believed he had orchestrated the tragedy that wiped out the heirs standing between him and the crown.

He had inherited a position he'd never wanted, and a future that, when he allowed himself to think about it, filled him with dread. He'd also inherited a reputation for bumping off anyone who got in his way.

And now he had a lovely bride—what more could a man want?

'My official residence is inside the palace. I have an apartment in Paris, and also a place outside London, and a villa in Antibes.' Would the lovely Charlotte still be there waiting? No, not likely. Charlotte was not the waiting kind. 'I imagine, should we wish it, we could go a whole year without bumping into one another.'

'So I could carry on with my life—nothing would change?'

'You like the life you have so much?'

His voice held zero inflection but she could feel his contempt. She struggled to read the expression in his eyes, but the dark silver-flecked depths were like the mirrored surface of a lake, deep and inscrutable yet strangely hypnotic.

She pushed away a mental image of sinking into a lake, feeling the cool water embrace her, close over her head. She lowered her gaze, running her tongue across her lips to moisten them.

When she lifted her head she'd fixed a cool smile in place…though it was hard to channel cool when you knew you looked like a victim of a natural disaster. But her disaster was of her own making.

Her delicate jaw clenched at the insight that had only made her imprisonment worse. The knowledge that she was the author of her own disaster movie, that she had ignored the advice to wait until a driver was available, and then she had chosen not to stay with the vehicle as had been drilled into them.

'I like my freedom.' It had not escaped his notice that she had sidestepped his question.

'At last we have something in common.'

'So you…we…?' This was the world's craziest conversation. 'Is there any chance of a drink?' With a heavy sigh she let her head fall back, her eyes closed.

Exhausted but not relaxed, he decided. His glance moved from her lashes—fanning out across the marble-pale curve of her smooth cheeks and hiding the dark shadows beneath her eyes—to her slim, shapely hands with the bitten untidy nails. Presumably her manicure had been a victim of her incarceration.

She had some way to go before she could collapse. Would she make it? It appeared to him that she was running on a combination of adrenalin and sheer bloody-minded obstinacy. His expression clinical, he scrutinised the visible, blue-veined pulse hammering away in the hollow at the base of her throat. There was something vulnerable about it… His mouth twisted as he reminded himself that the last two dumb guys she'd left high and dry at the altar had probably thought the same thing.

'I'm not sure alcohol would be a good idea.'

Her blue eyes flew open. 'I was thinking more along the lines of tea.'

'I can do that.' He spoke to Rafiq, who had a habit of silently materialising, before turning his attention back to Hannah. 'Well, at least our marriage will put an end to your heartbreaking activities.'

'I didn't break anyone's—' She stopped, biting back the retort. She'd promised Craig—who had loved her but, it turned out, not in 'that' way—that she'd take responsibility.

'You're more like a sister to me,' Craig had told her. 'Well, actually, not like a sister because you know Sal and she's a total…no, more like a best friend.'

'Sal is my best friend,' Hannah had replied. And Sal had been, before she'd slept with treacherous Rob.

'That's why I'm asking you not to tell her I called it off. When we got engaged she got really weird, and told me she'd never ever forgive me if I hurt you. But I haven't hurt you, have I…? We were both on the rebound—me after Natalie and you after Rob.' He had patted her shoulder. 'I think you still love him.'

Somehow Hannah had loved the man who had slept his way through her friends while they were together.

She had only known about Sal when she had given him back his ring after he stopped denying it.

She hated Rob now but he had taught her about trust. Mainly that it wasn't possible. Craig, who she had known all her life, was different. He was totally predictable; he would never hurt her. But she had forgotten one thing—Craig was a man.

'You know me so well, Craig.'

'So, are you all right with this?'

'I'm fine.'

'So what happens now?'

People who had never met you felt qualified to spend time and a lot of effort ripping you to shreds. 'I don't know,' she lied.

Her lips twitched as she recalled her ex-fiancé's response. Craig never had been known for his tact.

'Well, what happened last time?'

Hannah had shrugged guiltily. The last time her dad had done everything. Even though pride had stopped her revealing that her fiancé had slept with all her friends— pride and the fact that her father would have blamed himself, as Charles Latimer had introduced her to Rob and had encouraged the relationship.

The second time he'd run out of understanding. He'd been furious and dumped the whole nightmare mess in her lap. Her glance flickered to the tall, imposing figure of her future husband and she struggled to see a way through the nightmare he represented.

CHAPTER FOUR

THIS TIME HANNAH was aware of the man mountain before he appeared—just as they hit another air pocket, he entered apologising for the tea he had slopped over the tray he was carrying.

'I will get a fresh tray.'

'It'll be fine,' Kamel responded impatiently. 'We need not stand on ceremony with Miss Latimer. She is one of the family now. Considering the nature of my trip I kept staffing down to a minimum.' He murmured something in what she assumed was Arabic to the other man, who left the compartment. 'Rafiq can turn his hand to most things but his culinary skills are limited.' He lifted the domed lid on the plate to reveal a pile of thickly cut sandwiches. 'I hope you like chicken.'

'I'm not hungry,' she said dully.

'I don't recall asking you if you were hungry, Hannah,' he returned in a bored drawl as he piled an extra sandwich onto a plate and pushed it her way.

She slung him an angry look. 'How am I meant to think about food when I'm being asked to sacrifice my freedom?' That had been her comfort after the battering her self-esteem had taken after being basically told she was not physically attractive by two men who had

claimed to love her. At the very least she still had her
freedom.

He smiled, with contempt glittering in his deep-set
eyes.

'You will eat because you have a long day ahead
of you.'

The thought of the long day ahead and what it involved drew a weak whimper from Hannah's throat.
Ashamed of the weakness, she shook her head. 'This
can't have been Dad's idea.'

She looked and sounded so distraught, so young and
bewildered that Kamel struggled not to react to the
wave of protective tenderness that rose up in him, de-
fying logic and good sense.

'It was something of a committee decision and if
there is an innocent victim in this it is me.'

This analysis made her jaw drop. Innocent and victim were two terms she could not imagine anyone using
about this man.

'However, if I am prepared to put a brave face on it
I don't see what your problem is.'

'My problem is I don't love you. I don't even know
you.'

I am Kamel Al Safar, and now you have all the time
in the world to get to know me.'

Her eyes narrowed. He had a smart answer for everything. 'I can hardly wait.'

'I think you're being unnecessarily dramatic. It's not
as if we'd be the first two people to marry for reasons
other than *love*.'

'So you're all right with someone telling you who
to marry.' Sure that his ego would not be able to take

such a suggestion, she was disappointed when he gave a negligent shrug.

'If I weren't, you'd still be languishing in a jail cell.'

She opened her mouth, heard the tap, tap of the uniformed officer's stick on the floor and closed it again. 'Don't think I'm not grateful.'

He arched a brow. 'Is that so? Strange, I'm not feeling the love,' he drawled.

Her face went blank. 'There isn't any love.'

'True, but then basing a marriage on something as transitory as *love*—' again he said the word as though it left a bad taste in his mouth '—makes about as much sense as building a house on sand.'

Was this a man trying to put a positive spin on it or was he genuinely that cynical?

'Have you ever been in love?' It was a weird thing to ask a total stranger, but then this was a very weird situation.

And just as weird was the expression she glimpsed on the tall prince's face. But even as she registered the bleakness in his eyes his heavy lids half closed. When he turned to look directly at her there was only cynicism shining in the dark depths.

'I defer to you as an expert on that subject. Two engagements is impressive. Do you get engaged to every man you sleep with?'

'I'm twenty-three,' she tossed back.

He tipped his dark head. 'My apologies,' he intoned with smiling contempt. 'That was a stupid question.'

Hannah didn't give a damn if he thought she had casual sex with every man she met. What made her want to slap the look of smug superiority off his face were the double standards his attitude betrayed.

How dared a man who had probably had more notches in his bedpost than she'd had pedicures look down his nose at her?

'And this is all about money and power. You have it and you're prepared to do anything to keep it. You carry on calling it duty if it makes you feel any better about yourself, but I call it greed!'

Kamel struggled to contain the flash of rage he felt at the insult. 'Only a woman who has always had access to her rich daddy's wallet and has never had to work for anything in her life could be so scornful about money. Or maybe you're just stupid.'

Stupid! The word throbbed like an infected wound in her brain. 'I do work.' If only to prove to all those people who called her stupid that people with dyslexia could do as well as anyone else if they had the help they needed.

'I think you might find your role is no longer available.'

'You couldn't say or think anything about me that hasn't been said,' she told him in a voice that shook with all the emotion she normally cloaked behind a cold mask. 'Thought or written. But enough about me. What's your contribution to society? I forget,' she drawled, adopting a dumb expression. 'What qualifications do you need to be a future King? Oh, that's right, an accident of birth.' She stopped and released a long fractured sigh. 'That's not what I wanted to say.'

He stared at her through narrowed eyes, resisting the possibility that a woman with feelings, that a woman who could be hurt, lurked behind the icy disdain.

'Well, what did you want to say?'

Relief rippled through her. This was not the response she had anticipated to her outburst.

'Would this marriage be a…paper one?'

'*Will*…get the tense right,' he chided. 'There will be official duties, occasions when we would be expected to be seen together.' He studied her face. 'But that isn't what you're talking about, is it?'

She gnawed on her lower lip and shook her head.

'It will be expected that we produce an heir.'

Shaken by the image that popped into her head, she looked away but not before her mind had stripped him naked. The image refused to budge, as did the uncomfortable feeling low in her belly.

'You might find it educational.'

The drawled comment made her expression freeze over; it hid her panic. 'The offer of lessons in sex is not a big selling point!' My God, he was really in for a disappointment.

His laugh cut over her words. 'I wasn't referring to your carnal education, though if you want to teach me a thing or two I have no problem.'

The riposte he had anticipated didn't come. Instead, astonishingly, she blushed. Kamel was not often disconcerted, but he was by her response.

Hannah, who had conquered many things but not her infuriating habit of blushing, hated feeling gauche and immature. From somewhere she dredged up some cool. 'So what were you referring to?'

'I'm assuming that your average lover is besotted. I'm not.'

'What, besotted or average?' Stupid question, she thought as her eyes slid down his long, lean, powerful frame—average was not a word anyone would use when referring to this man. 'I can't just jump into bed with you. I don't know you!'

'We have time.' He produced a thin-lipped smile. 'A lot of it. But relax, I don't expect our union to be consummated any time soon, if you can cope with that?'

'With what?'

'No sex.'

Her lashes came down in a concealing curtain. 'I'll manage.'

'Because your little adventures will be over. There can be no questioning the legitimacy of the heir to the throne,' he warned.

'And does the same rule apply to you?' Without waiting for him to reply she gave a snort of disgust. 'Don't answer that. But perhaps you could answer me this…'

He turned and she dropped the hand she self-consciously had extended to him. 'Do you know…' he seemed to know everything else with a few exceptions '…did they get the vaccinations to the village in time?'

The anxiety in her blue eyes was too genuine to be feigned. Perhaps the woman did have a conscience, but not one that stopped her doing exactly what she wanted, Kamel reminded himself.

'It is a pity you didn't think about the village when you decided to cross a border without papers or—'

'My Jeep broke down. I got lost.' Hating the whining note of self-justification, she bit her lip. 'Do you know? Could you find out?' The report that had reached the storage facility where she had been organising local distribution had said the infection was spreading rapidly; the death toll would be horrific if it wasn't contained.

'I have no idea.'

She watched as he moved away, not just in the physical sense to the other end of the cabin, but in every way. He tuned her out totally, appearing to be immersed in whatever was on the laptop he scrolled through.

Studying the back of his neck, she had to crane her own to see more than the top of his dark head. Hannah envied him and wished she could forget he existed. Was this a foretaste of the rest of her life? Occupying the same space when forced to, but not interacting? She had given up on romance but the thought of such a clinical union lay like an icy fist in her stomach.

He didn't even glance at her when the plane landed; he just left his seat, leaving her sitting there. It was the massive bodyguard who indicated she should follow Kamel down the aisle to the exit with one of his trademark tilts of the head.

She was between the two men as they disembarked. Hannah blinked in the bright sun—the blinds had been down in the cabin and for some reason she had expected it to be dark. She had lost all sense of time. She glanced down at her wrist and felt a pang when she remembered they had taken her watch. It was one of the few things she had that had been her mother's. When she was arrested they'd taken everything she had, including her sunglasses, and she would have given a lot for dark lenses to hide behind.

Her eyes flew wide with alarm.

'I don't have my passport!'

At the bottom of the steps he paused and looked up at her, his cold eyes moving across her face in a zero-tolerance sweep. 'You will not need your passport.'

'One of the perks of being royal?' Like the daunting armed presence and salutes, she thought, watching the suited figure who was bowing deferentially in response to what Kamel was saying.

Glad to be off his radar, she ran her tongue across her dry lips, frightened by how close to total panic she had come in that moment she'd thought that without a passport she would be denied entry. The thought of the cell she had escaped made her knees shake as she negotiated the rest of the steps and stood on terra firma.

There were three massive limos with darkened glass parked a few feet away on the concrete, waiting to whisk them away. One each? Unable to smile at her own joke in the presence of such an overt armed presence, she took a hurried step towards Kamel, who was striding across to the farthest car, only to be restrained by a heavy hand on her shoulder.

She angled a questioning look up and the massive bodyguard shook his head slowly from side to side.

She pulled herself back from another panic precipice and called after Kamel. 'You're leaving?'

She was literally sweating with her effort to project calm but she could still hear the sharp anxiety in her voice.

He turned his head and paused, his dark eyes sweeping her face. 'You'll be looked after.'

Hannah lifted her chin, ignoring the tight knot of loneliness in her chest. She hated the feeling; she hated him. She would not cry—she would not let that damned man make her cry.

Kamel ruthlessly quashed a pang of empathy, but remained conscious of her standing there looking like some sort of sacrificial virgin as he got into the car. He resented the way her accusing blue eyes followed him, making him feel like an exploitative monster. It was illogical—he'd saved her. He hadn't expected to be hailed as a hero but he hadn't counted on becoming the villain of the piece. It was a tough situation, but life required sacrifice and compromise—a fact that she refused to recognise.

He pressed a button and the dark tinted window slid up. She could no longer see him but he could see her.

'What's happening to me?' She managed to wrench the question from her aching throat as she watched the sleek car draw away.

She had not directed the question at anyone in particular so she started when Rafiq, the man of few words, responded.

'My instructions are to take you to Dr Raini's home.'

He tipped his head in the direction of the open car door, clearly expecting her to get in. It hadn't even crossed his mind that she wouldn't.

Hannah felt a tiny bubble of rebellion. She'd had her independence taken away from her during the past few days, and she would not allow it to happen again. She would not become some decorative, docile wife producing stage-managed performances to enhance her husband's standing, only to become invisible when she was not needed.

Then show a bit of backbone, Hannah.

She lifted her chin and didn't move towards the open car door. 'I don't need a doctor.'

The big man, who looked thrown by her response, took his time before responding. 'No, you misunderstand. She is not that sort of doctor. She is a professor of philosophy at the university. She will help you dress for the ceremony, and will act as your maid of honour.'

He stood by the door but Hannah stayed where she was.

'What about my father?'

'I believe your father is to meet you at the royal chapel.'

The mention of a chapel drew her delicate brows into a bemused frown. She recalled the rest of the article in the Sunday supplement where she had garnered most of her knowledge about Surana—as well as being a peaceful melting pot of religions, the country was known for its royal family being Christian, which made them a rarity in the region.

After the car left the airport it turned onto a wide, palm-fringed boulevard where the sun glinted off the glass on the tall modern buildings that lined it. From there they entered what was clearly an older part of the city, where the roads were narrow and the design less geometric.

The screen between the front and back seat came down.

'We are nearly there, miss.'

Hannah nodded her thanks to Rafiq and realised they had entered what appeared to be a prosperous suburb. Almost immediately she had registered the air of affluence, and their car turned sharply through an open pair of high ornate gates and into a small cobbled courtyard hidden from the street by a high wall.

The driver spoke into his earpiece as the gates closed behind them and a suited figure appeared. The big bodyguard spoke to the man and then, with the manner of someone who habitually expected to find danger lurking behind every bush, he scanned the area before opening the door for her.

Hannah's feet hit the cobbles when the wide wooden door of the three-storey whitewashed house was flung open.

'Welcome. I'm Raini, Kamel's cousin.'

The professor turned out to be an attractive woman in her mid-thirties. Tall and slim, she wore her dark hair in a short twenties bob, and her smile was warm as she held out her hands to Hannah.

'I'd ask what sort of journey you had but I can see—'

The kindness and genuine warmth cut through all Hannah's defences and the tears started oozing out of her eyes. Embarrassed, she took the tissue that was pushed into her hand and blew her nose. 'I'm so sorry, I don't normally, it's just…I know I look like a nightmare.'

The woman gave her a hug and ushered her into the house, throwing a comment over her shoulder to the bodyguard as she closed the door very firmly behind them.

Hannah half expected the door to be knocked down; her respect for the woman went up when it wasn't.

'No need to apologise. If I'd been through what you have I'd be a basket case.'

'I am.' Hannah blinked. Inside the house was nothing like the exterior suggested: the décor was minimalist and the ground floor appeared to be totally open-plan.

'Of course you are.' She laid a comforting hand on Hannah's arm. 'This way,' she added, and opened a door that led into a long corridor. Several of the doors lining it were open, and it appeared to be a bedroom wing.

The older woman caught Hannah's bewildered expression. 'I know, it's bigger than it looks.' She smiled sympathetically. 'I'd love to give you the guided tour and I know you must be dead on your feet but we're on the clock, I'm afraid. Just in here.' She pushed open a door and waited for Hannah to enter ahead of her.

It was a big square room with tiled floors. One wall had French doors and another a row of fitted wardrobes. The large low platform bed was the only piece of furniture in the room.

'I know, bleak. I love clutter, not to mention a bit of glitz, but Steve is a minimalist with borderline OCD.' The thought of Steve, presumably her husband, brought a fond smile to her face.

The look reminded Hannah of what she wouldn't have, what she had refused to acknowledge she still wanted. She looked away, conscious of a pain in her chest, and sank down onto the bed. It was a long way down but she barely noticed the soft impact as she landed on the deep duvet. She lifted her hands to her face and shook her head.

'None of this should be happening.'

Watching her, the other woman gave a sympathetic grimace. 'I know this isn't how you envisioned your wedding day,' she said gently, 'but really it's not the wedding that counts. Everything that could go wrong did at mine. It's the person you're going to spend the rest of your life with that matters. How did you and Kamel meet?'

Hannah lifted her head. 'Sorry?'

The other woman misinterpreted her blank look. 'Don't worry, it's a story for another day, I'm just so glad he's found someone. All that playboy stuff, it was so *not* like him, but he isn't as bad as those awful tabloids painted him, you know.'

'I never read the tabloids,' Hannah responded honestly.

The other woman patted her hand and Hannah, who was more confused by these tantalising snippets of information than she had been before, realised two things: that his cousin thought the marriage was for real, and that she would be married to a man who, even his very fond cousin had to admit, had a horrific reputation.

'I prayed he'd recover from Amira one day, but when you lose someone that way…' She gave an expressive shrug. 'I ask myself sometimes, could I have been as noble if I knew that Steve had fallen for someone?'

For a moment a frustrated Hannah thought the flow of confidences had ended, but then Raini's voice dropped to a confidential whisper.

'Amira told me that Kamel said she'd make a beautiful queen, and that all he wanted was for her to be happy. He and Hakim were like brothers—talk about triangles.'

Hannah gave a non-committal grunt, struggling to put the people and places mentioned in context, and then she remembered what he had said: '*She found him… preferable.*' This love that Hannah was meant to be replacing was the woman who had married Kamel's cousin, only to lose her life in the plane crash that had moved Kamel up the line of succession. He had acted as though he didn't care but if his cousin had it right…? She shook her head, struggling to see the man who had showed her zero empathy caring for anyone. It was almost as strange an idea as him being rejected. Whether he wore a crown or not, Kamel was not the sort of man women ran away from.

'She would have, too.'

Hannah wrenched her wandering thoughts back to the present and shook her head, mumbling, 'Sorry?'

'She would have made a beautiful queen. But she never got the chance…' Raini breathed a deep sigh. 'So sad.' Then, visibly pulling herself together, she produced a warm smile. 'But this is not a day for tears. *You will* make a beautiful queen, and you're marrying a man in a million.'

Hannah knew she was meant to respond. 'I would still be in the jail cell if it hadn't been for him.'

The other woman looked mistily emotional as she nodded. 'He's the man you need in an emergency. When Steve was kidnapped…' She gave her head a tiny shake and pulled open the wardrobe door. 'Like I said, Kamel is a guy in a million but patience is not one of his virtues, and my instructions are to have you on the road in thirty minutes.

'Take your pick of the dresses, Hannah.' She indicated a row of white gowns. 'They delivered a few.'

Hannah blinked at the understatement, and Raini continued to deliver the information at the same shotgun speed.

'Your father wasn't sure of your size so I got them to send them all in three sizes, but…' Her bright eyes moved in an assessing sweep up and down Hannah. 'You're an eight?'

Hannah nodded.

'Shower that way.' Her efficient mother hen nodded at a door. 'You'll find toiletries and make-up by the mirror—anything you want just yell. I'll just go and get changed into something much less comfortable.'

The shower was bliss. All the gowns were beautiful but she selected the simplest: a column with the hem and high neck heavily encrusted with beads and crystals. It fitted like a silken glove. Smooth and butter-soft, in dramatic contrast to the emotional rawness of her emotions. She took a deep breath and pulled the shattered threads of her protective composure tight about her shoulders, refusing to acknowledge the fear in her belly.

When Raini returned, looking elegant in a tailored silk trouser suit, Hannah was struggling with her hair. Freshly washed, it was evading her efforts to secure it in an elegant chignon.

'You look beautiful,' the older woman said, standing back to view her. 'I thought you might like this.'

Hannah's eyes travelled from the mist of emotional tears in the other woman's eyes to the lace veil she held out and her armour of cool detachment crumbled.

'It's beautiful,' she said, hating the fact she couldn't tell this woman who was so genuine the truth—that this marriage was all an awful sham.

'It was my grandmother's. I wore it when I was married. I thought you might like it.'

Hannah backed away, feeling even more wretched that she was playing the loving bride for this woman. 'I couldn't—it looks so delicate.'

'I insist. Besides, it will go perfectly with this.' She presented what Hannah had assumed was a clutch bag, but turned out to be a large rectangular wooden box.

'What beautiful work.' Hannah ran a finger along the intricate engraving work that covered the rosewood lid.

'Not nearly as beautiful as this.' With a magician's

flourish Raini flicked the lid open. Her eyes were not on the contents, but on Hannah's face. She gave a smile as Hannah's jaw dropped.

'No, you're really kind, but I *really* couldn't wear that. It's far too precious. This is lovely,' she said, draping the lace veil over her head, 'but really, no.' She stepped back, waving her hands in a fluttering gesture of refusal.

'It's not mine...I wish.' Raini laughed, removing the tiara from its silken bed. The diamonds in the delicately wrought gold circlet glittered as she held it up. 'Kamel had it couriered over. He wants you to wear it. Let me...' Her face a mask of serious concentration, she placed the tiara carefully on top of the lace. *'Dieu,'* she breathed reverently. 'You look like something out of a book of fairy tales. You really are a princess.'

Hannah lifted her hands to remove it. 'I haven't put my hair up yet.'

'If I were you I'd leave it loose. It's very beautiful.'

Hannah shrugged. Her hairstyle was the least of her worries.

CHAPTER FIVE

HANNAH'S FIRST GLIMPSE of her future home drew a pained gasp from her lips.

'I know.' Raini was all amused sympathy. 'I'd like to tell you it's not as awe-inspiring as it looks, but actually,' she admitted, directing her critical stare at the multitude of minarets, 'it is. Even Hollywood couldn't build a set like this. The family, as you'll learn, has never been into less is more. When I lived here—'

'You lived here?' How did anyone ever relax in a setting this ostentatiously grand?

Raini gave a warm chuckle. 'Oh, my parents occupied a small attic,' she joked. 'Until Dad got posted. He's a diplomat,' she explained. 'By the time I was eighteen I'd lived in a dozen cities.' They drove under a gilded archway into a courtyard the size of a football pitch, filled with fountains. 'But nothing ever came close to this.'

Hannah believed her.

Rafiq escorted them into the building through a small antechamber that had seemed large until they stepped through the next door and entered a massive hall. The wall sconces in there were all lit, creating swirling patterns on the mosaic floor.

The awful sense of impending doom that lay like a cold stone in Hannah's chest became heavier as they followed the tall, gowned figure down a maze of marble-floored empty corridors. By the time she saw a familiar figure, she was struggling to breathe past the oppressive weight.

'Dad!'

'Hello, Hannah! You look very beautiful, child.'

Hannah struggled to hide her shock at her father's appearance. She had never seen him look so pale and haggard. Not even when he'd lain in a hospital bed attached to bleeping machines had he looked this frail. He seemed to have aged ten years since she last saw him.

Any lingering mental image of her walking into his arms and asking him to make everything right vanished as the tears began to slide down his cheeks. She had never seen her ebullient parent cry except on the anniversary of her mother's death—her birthday. On that day he always vanished to be alone with his grief, and the sight of tears now was as painful to her as a knife thrust.

Intentionally or not, it always felt as if she was the cause of his tears. If she hadn't been born the woman he loved would not have died and now this was her fault. About that much Kamel was right.

She had been doing a job that she was ill qualified to do and she'd messed up. But the consequences had not been just hers. Other people had suffered. She lifted her chin. Well, that was going to stop. She'd made the mistake and she'd take the nasty-tasting medicine, though in this instance it came in the shape of the dark and impossibly handsome and arrogant Prince of Surana.

'I thought I'd lost you,' her father cried. 'They have

the death penalty in Quagani, Hannah. It was the only way we could get you out. They wanted to make an example of you, and without the King's personal intervention they would have. Kamel is a good man.'

It seemed to be a universally held opinion. Hannah didn't believe it. Nonetheless, it was clear that he had not just freed her, he had saved her life.

'I know, Dad. I'm fine about this,' she lied.

'Really?'

She nodded. 'It's about time I finally made it down the aisle, don't you think?'

'He'll take care of you.' He squeezed her hand. 'You'll take care of each other. You know your mother was the love of my life…'

Hannah felt a heart-squeezing clutch of sadness. 'Yes, Dad.'

'She didn't love me when we got married. She was pregnant, and I persuaded her… What I'm trying to say is that it's possible to grow to love someone. She did.'

Incredibly moved by his confidences, she nodded, her throat aching with unshed tears. There was no point telling him the cases were totally dissimilar. Her father had loved the woman he had married, whereas Hannah was marrying a man who despised her.

A man who had saved her life.

Any moment she would wake up.

But it wasn't a dream. However surreal it felt, she really was standing there with her hand on her father's arm, about to walk down the aisle to be married to a stranger.

'Ready?' her father asked.

She struggled to relearn the forgotten skill of smiling for his benefit and nodded. Ahead of her the elegant

Raini spoke to someone outside Hannah's line of vision and the big doors swung open.

Hannah had anticipated more of the same magnificence she had encountered so far, but she had the impression of a space that was relatively small, almost intimate…peaceful. The tranquillity was a dramatic contrast to the emotional storm that raged just below her calm surface.

If you discounted the priest and choir there were only four people present: two robed rulers in the pews, and the two men who stood waiting, one tall and fair, the other…the other tall and very dark. She closed her eyes and willed herself to relax, to breathe, to do this… She opened them again and smiled at her father. He felt bad enough about this without her falling apart.

'Nervous?'

Kamel glanced at his best man. 'No.' Resigned would be a more accurate description of his mindset. There had only ever been one woman he had imagined walking down the aisle towards him and he had watched her make that walk to someone else. He would never forget the expression on her face—she had been incandescent with joy. Yet now when he did think of it he found another face superimposing itself over Amira's. A face framed by blonde hair.

'I suppose you could call this a version of a shotgun wedding,' the other man mused, glancing at the two royal personages who occupied the empty front pews. 'She's not…?'

He tried to imagine those blue eyes soft as she held a child. 'No, she is not.'

'There's going to be a hell of a lot of pressure for you

to change that. I hope she knows what she's letting herself in for.'

'Did you?' Kamel countered, genuinely curious.

'No, but then I didn't marry the heir apparent…which
is maybe just as well. Raini and I have decided not to go
for another round of IVF. It's been eight years now and
there has to be a cut-off point. There is a limit to how
many times she can put herself through this.'

Kamel clasped the other man's shoulder. 'Sorry.'

The word had never sounded less adequate. Kamel
never lost sight of the fact that life was unfair, but if he
had this would have reminded him. The world was filled
with children who were unloved and unwanted and here
were two people who had all the love in the world to
give a child and it wasn't going to happen for them.

One of life's cruelties.

'Thanks.' Steven looked towards a security guy who
nodded and spoke into his earpiece. 'Looks like she's
arrived on time. You're a lucky man.'

Kamel glanced at Steven and followed the direction
of his gaze. The breath caught in his throat. Bedraggled,
she had been a beautiful woman, but this tall, slender
creature was a dream vision in white—hair falling like
a golden cloud down her back, the diamonds glittering on her lacy veil fading beside the brilliance of her
wide blue eyes.

'That remains to be seen.'

Kamel's murmured comment drew a quizzical look
from his best man but no response that could be heard
above the strains of 'Ave Maria' sung by the choir as
the bride on her father's arm, preceded by her matron
of honour, began her progression.

A weird sense of calm settled on Hannah as she stood

facing her bridegroom. It did not cross her mind until afterwards that the whole thing resembled an out-of-body experience: she was floating somewhere above the heads of the people gathered to witness this parody, watching herself give her responses in a voice that didn't even hold a tremor.

The tremor came at the end when they were pronounced man and wife and Kamel looked directly at her for the first time. His dark eyes held hers as he brushed a fold of gossamer lace from her cheek and stared down at her with a soul-stripping intensity.

In her emotionally heightened state she had no idea who leaned in to whom; Hannah just knew she experienced the weirdest sensation, as though she were being pulled by an invisible thread towards him.

Her eyes were wide open as he covered her lips with his, then as the warm pressure deepened her eyelids lowered and her lips parted without any coercion and she kissed him back.

It was Kamel who broke the contact. Without it, her head was no longer filled with the taste, the texture and the smell of him, and reality came flooding back with a vengeance. She'd just kissed her husband and she'd enjoyed it—more than a little. That was wrong, so *very* wrong on every level. It was as if he had flicked a switch she didn't know she had. She shivered, unable to control the fresh wave of heat that washed over her skin.

He took her hand and raised it to his lips, watching the rapt glow of sensual invitation in her velvet eyes be replaced by something close to panic. He was not shocked but he was surprised by the strength of the physical response she had shown.

'Smile. You're the radiant bride, *ma belle*,' he warned.

Hannah smiled until her jaw ached. She smiled all the way through the formality of signatures, and all she could think about was that kiss. The memory felt like a hot prickle under her skin. For the first time in her life she understood the power of sex and how a person could forget who they were under the influence of that particular drug.

She was kissed on both cheeks by the leaders of two countries, and then rather more robustly by her father, who held her hand tightly.

'You know that I am always there for you, Hannah.'

'I know, Dad. I'm fine.' She blinked away emotional tears but couldn't dislodge the massive lump in her throat.

'I will take care of her, Charles.'

His sincerity made her teeth ache. You couldn't trust a man who could lie so well, not that Hannah had any intention of trusting him. Aware that her father was watching, she let it lie when Kamel took her hand in his, not snatching it away until they were out of sight.

His only reaction was a sardonic smirk.

It took ten minutes after the farewells for them to walk back to his private apartments. His bride didn't say a word the whole time.

It was hard not to contrast the brittle ice queen beside him with the woman whose soft warm lips he had tasted. That small taste, the heat that had flared between them, shocking with its intensity and urgency, had left him curious, and eager to repeat the experience.

He was lusting after his bride. Well, life was full of surprises and not all of them were bad. The situation suited a man who had a very pragmatic approach to sex.

her sleep-deprived brain shut down—she just clung on for the ride.

Kamel was a man who was rarely surprised—but Hannah had surprised him twice already. First when she kissed him, and second when lust slammed through his body.

Had he ever wanted a woman this badly?

Then he identified the flavour of her kiss. As he pulled away she clung like a limpet, a very soft, warm, inviting limpet, but he gritted his teeth. He knew that if he let it go on a moment longer he wouldn't be able to stop. And when he made love to his wife he wanted her not just willing but awake and sober!

He studied her flushed face, the bright, almost febrile glitter in her eyes. He had seen the same look in the eyes of a friend who, after pulling three consecutive all-nighters before an exam, had fallen asleep halfway through the actual exam. Hannah was seriously sleep deprived, and more than a bit tipsy.

As a rule he thought it was nice if the person you were making love to stayed conscious. He gave a self-mocking smile. Being noble was really overrated—no wonder it had fallen out of fashion.

'You've been drinking.'

She blinked at the accusation, then insisted loudly, 'I'm not drunk!'

The pout she gave him almost broke his resolve. 'We won't argue the point,' he said wearily. 'I think we should sleep on this. Goodnight, Hannah.'

And he walked away and left her standing there feeling like…like…like a woman who'd just made a pass at her own husband and got knocked back. So not only did she now feel cheap, she felt unattractive.

Rejected by two fiancés, and now a husband, but she couldn't summon the energy to care as, with a sigh, she fell backwards fully clothed onto the bed, closed her eyes and was immediately asleep.

CHAPTER SIX

Too proud to ask for help, Hannah was lost. She finally located Kamel in the fourth room she tried—one that opened off a square, windowless hallway that might have been dark but for the daylight that filtered through the blue glass of the dome high above.

Like the ones before it, this room was massive and imposing, and also came complete with a built-in echo, and her heels were particularly noisy on the inlaid floor. But Kamel didn't look up. The hawk on its perch followed her with its dark eyes while her master continued to stare at the screen of his mobile phone with a frown of concentration that drew his dark brows into a straight line above his aquiline nose.

Choosing not to acknowledge the strange achy feeling in the pit of her stomach, she walked up to the desk and cleared her throat.

When his dark head didn't lift she felt her temper fizz and embraced the feeling. If he wanted to be awkward, fine. She could do awkward. She felt damned awkward after last night.

'Is this your doing?' Realising that her posture, with her arms folded tightly across her stomach, might be construed as protective, she dropped them to her sides.

Kamel stopped scrolling through his emails, looked up from his phone and smiled. 'Good morning, dear wife.'

Kamel did not feel it was a particularly good morning and it had been a very bad night. He felt tired, and more frustrated than any man should be after his wedding night. A cold shower, a long run and he had regained a little perspective this morning. But then she walked in the room and just the scent of her perfume... He wanted her here and now. *The difference between want and need* was important to Kamel. He had not allowed himself to *need* a woman since Amira.

He *needed* sex, not Hannah. And the sex would be good—his icy bride turned out to have more fire in her than any woman he had ever met. But afterwards he would feel as he always did—the escape from the tight knot of brutal loneliness in his chest was only ever temporary.

Hannah's lips tightened at the mockery but she did not react to it; instead she simply arched a feathery brow. *'Well?'*

'I feel as though I am walking into this conversation midway through. Coffee?' He lifted the pot on the desk beside him and topped up his half-filled cup and allowed his gaze to drift over her face. 'Hangover?'

'No,' she lied. The delicious aroma drifted her way, making her mouth water. She felt shivery as she struggled to tear her eyes off his long brown fingers. 'I don't want coffee.'

'So can I help you with something?'

She emitted a soft hissing sound of annoyance. Without looking back, she pointed to the open doorway where a suited figure stood, complete with enigmatic expression and concealed weapon. 'Did you arrange for him to follow me?'

Kamel stood up from the desk and walked past her towards the open door. Nodding to the man standing outside, he closed it with a soft thud and turned back to Hannah, though his attention appeared to be on the lie of his narrow silk tie that lay in a flash of subdued colour against his white shirt. The jacket that matched the dove-grey trousers was draped across the back of the chair.

'For heaven's sake, you look ridiculously perfect.'

Her delivery lacked the scornful punch she had intended, possibly because the comment was no exaggeration. The pale grey trousers that matched the jacket were clearly bespoke and could have been cut to disguise a multitude of sins if he'd had any, but there was no escaping the fact that physically at least he was flawless.

He raised his brows and she felt her cheeks colour. 'I despise men who spend more time looking in the mirror than I do.'

'Rather a sexist thing to say,' he remarked, his tone mildly amused and his eyes uncomfortably observant. 'But each to his own. I'm sorry I don't measure up to your unwashed grunge ideal.'

Having dug herself a hole, she let the subject drop. He could never fail to live up to any woman's ideal, on a purely eye-candy level, of course. 'I do not require a bodyguard.'

'No, obviously not.'

Her pleased smile at a battle so easily won had barely formed when his next words made it vanish.

'You will require a team of them.'

'That's ludicrous!' she contended furiously.

The amusement in his manner vanished as he countered, 'It's necessary, so I suggest you stop acting like a diva and accept it.'

'I refuse.'

His glance slid from her flashing eyes to her heaving bosom, lingering there long enough to bring her hand to her throat. 'Refuse all you like, it won't alter anything. I appreciate this is an adjustment and I'll make allowances.'

That was big of him. 'Allowances! This is a palace! How do I adjust to that?'

'I have been to Brent Hall and it is hardly a council flat,' he retorted, thinking of the portrait that hung above the fireplace in the drawing room. Had Hannah Latimer ever possessed the dreamy innocence that shone in the eyes of her portrait, or had the artist been keen to flatter the man who was paying him?

She opened her mouth to retort and then his comment sank in. 'You've been to my home?'

He tipped his head. 'I stood in for my uncle on one social occasion, actually two. I predict you will adjust to your change in status. After all, you have played the pampered princess all your life. The only difference now is you have an actual title, and, of course, me.'

'I'm trying to forget.'

'Not the best idea.'

Despite the monotone delivery, she heard the warning and she didn't like it, or him.

Kamel gave a tolerant nod and picked up a pen from the desk. 'It is a fact of life. You will not leave this building without a security presence.'

'I wasn't outside the building. He was waiting outside my bedroom. What harm was I likely to come to there?'

'Oh, so your concern is for your privacy.'

'Well, yes. Obviously.' The idea of living like a bird in a golden cage did not hold any appeal. She'd given up her freedom but there had to be boundaries. Where were your boundaries last night, Hannah?

'We will be private enough, I promise you.'

The seductive promise in his voice sent a beat of white-hot excitement whipping through her body. As it ebbed she was consumed by hot-cheeked embarrassment.

'You blush very easily.'

She slung him a belligerent glare. 'I'm not used to the heat.' The desert heat she might grow accustomed to, but being around a man who could make her feel... feel...she gave a tiny gusty sigh as she sought for a word to describe how he made her feel, and it came— *hungry*! That was something she would never get used to. She just hoped it would pass quickly like a twenty-four-hour bug.

'So this is an example of how my life will not change?' she charged shrilly. 'I left one cell with a guard outside for another.'

'But the facilities and décor are much better,' he came back smoothly.

The languid smile that tugged the corner of his mouth upwards did not improve her mood. Neither did looking at his mouth. It was a struggle not to lift a hand to her own tingling lips. So far he hadn't mentioned the kiss. Had he forgotten?

She wished she had, but her memory loss only lasted until she had stood under a shower and then the whole mortifying scene came rushing back.

'This isn't a joke.'

The shriller she got, the calmer he became. 'Neither is it a subject for screaming and shouting and stamping your little foot.'

He glanced down at the part of her under discussion. She had very nice ankles but she had even nicer calves. He found his eyes drawn to the silky smooth contours and higher... The skirt of the dress she wore, a silky blue thing, sleeveless and cinched in at the waist with a narrow plaited tan belt, ended just above the knee. The entire image was cool, perfectly groomed...regal.

He refused to allow the image of his hands sliding under the fabric up and over the smooth curves—but the suggestion had been enough to send a streak of heat through his body where it coalesced into a heavy ache in his groin. He could have woken up this morning in her arms. Even while he had called himself a fool during the long wakeful night, he had known it was the right decision.

'I did not stamp my foot,' Hannah retorted and immediately wanted to do just that.

'But you have a tendency to turn everything into a drama, angel.'

Her brows hit her smooth hairline exposed by the severe hairstyle she had adopted that morning. The woman who had looked back at her from the mirror after she had speared the last hair grip into the smooth coil did not even look like a distant relative of the woman with the flushed face, feverishly bright eyes and swollen lips she had glimpsed in the mirror last night before she had fallen onto the bed fully dressed.

'If *this* isn't a drama, what is?'

'I appreciate this is not easy, but we are *both* living with the consequences of your actions.'

She threw up her hands and didn't even register the discomfort as one of the pearl studs she wore went flying across the room. She sighed heavily and asked, 'How many times a day are you going to remind me it's all my fault?'

'It depends on how many times you irritate me.' Kamel left his desk and walked to the spot where the pearl had landed beside the window.

'My breathing irritates you,' she said.

He elevated a dark brow. 'Not if you do it quietly.' He half closed his eyes, imagining hearing her breath quicken as he moved in and out of her body.

Hannah was not breathing quietly now. The closer he got, the louder her breathing became, then she stopped altogether. 'You are...' The trapped air left her lungs in one soft, sibilant sigh as he stopped just in front of her, close enough for her to feel the heat from his body.

'Have you ever heard of personal space?' she asked, tilting back her head to meet his challenging dark stare as she fought an increasingly strong impulse to step back. Her cool vanished into shrill panic as he leaned in towards her. 'What are you doing?'

More to the point, what was she doing?

She had tried so hard *not* to look at his mouth, *not* to think of that kiss, it became inevitable that she was now staring and not in a casual way at his mouth and the only thing she could think about was that kiss—the firm texture of his lips, the heat of his mouth, the moist...

'You lost this.'

It took a few seconds to bring into focus the stud he held between his thumb and forefinger. When she realised what he was holding her hand went jerkily to her ear...the wrong one.

'No, this one.' He touched her ear lobe, catching it for a moment between his thumb and forefinger before letting it drop away. 'Pretty.' Her head jerked to one side, causing a fresh stab of pain to slide like a knife through her skull. How long before the headache tablets she had swallowed kicked in?

The strength of her physical response to the light contact sent a stab of alarm through Hannah. She swayed slightly and shifted her position, taking a step back. It no longer seemed so important to stand her ground. Live to fight another day—wasn't that what they said about those who ran away?

'Thank you,' she breathed, holding out her hand as she focused on his left shoulder.

He ignored the hand and leaned in closer. *Help,* she thought, her smile little more now than a scared fixed grimace painted on. Her nostrils quivered in reaction to the warm scent of his body, his nearness. She could feel the heat of his body through his clothes and hers... imagine how hot his skin would feel without...

And she did imagine; her core temperature immediately jumped by several painful degrees as she stood there in an agony of shame and arousal while he placed a thumb under her chin to angle her face up to him.

She'd decided that the only plus point in being married to a man she loathed was that she would never again suffer the pain and humiliation of rejection. She wouldn't care. A lovely theory, but hard to cling to when every cell in her body craved his touch. She had never felt this way before.

She bit her lip, fearing that if she set free the ironic laugh locked in her throat there would be a chain reaction—she would lose it and she couldn't do that. Pretty much all she had left was her pride.

Listen to yourself, Hannah, mocked the voice in her head. Your pride is all you have left? Go down that road of self-pity and you'd pretty much end up being the spoilt shallow bitch your husband thinks you are.

Husband.

I'm married.

Third time lucky. Or as it happened, *unlucky*. She knew there were many women who would have envied her *unlucky* fate just as there had been girls at school who had envied her.

The influential clique who had decided to make the new girl's life a misery even before they'd discovered she was stupid. She'd thought so too until she'd been diagnosed as dyslexic at fourteen.

For a long time Hannah had wondered why—what had she done or said?—and then she'd had the opportunity to ask when she'd found herself sitting in a train compartment with one of her former tormentors, all grown up now.

Hannah had immediately got up to leave but had paused by the door when the other woman had spoken.

'I'm sorry.'

And Hannah had asked the question that she had always wanted to ask.

'Why?'

The answer had been the same one her father had given her when she had sobbed, 'What have I done? What's wrong with me?'

'It's got nothing to do with you, Hannah. They do it because they can. I could move you to another school, sweetheart, but what happens if the same thing happens there? You can't carry on running away. The way to cope with bullies is not to react. Don't let them see they get to you.'

The strategy had worked perhaps too well because, not only had her cool mask put off the bullies, but potential friends too, except for Sal.

What would Sal say? She closed off that line of thought, but not before she experienced a wave of deep sadness. She didn't share secrets with Sal any more; she had lost her best friend the day she had found her in bed with her fiancé. It was to have been her wedding day.

And now here she was, a married woman. Kamel's touch was deft, almost clinical, but there was nothing clinical about the shimmies of sensation that zigzagged through her body as his fingers brushed her ear lobe.

Hannah breathed again when he straightened up, keeping her expression as neutral as his.

'Thank you,' she murmured distantly. 'Could you tell me where the kitchen is?'

He looked surprised by the question. 'I haven't the faintest idea.'

'You don't know where your own kitchen is?'

Kamel, who still looked bemused, ignored her question. 'Why were you going to the kitchen?' he persisted. 'If you want a tour of the place the housekeeper will...'

'I didn't want a tour. I wanted breakfast.' She had eaten nothing the previous evening. Unfortunately she had not shown similar restraint when it came to the champagne.

'Why didn't you ring for something?'

'Do you really not know where your kitchen is?'

He arched a sardonic brow. 'And am I meant to believe you do? That you are a regular visitor to the kitchens at Brent Hall?' It was not an area he had seen on the occasion he had been a guest at Charles Latimer's country estate, a vast Elizabethan manor with a full complement of staff. The daughter of the house had not been home at the time but her presence had been very much felt.

There was barely a polished surface in the place that did not have a framed photo of her and her accomplishments through the years—playing the violin, riding a horse, looking athletic with a tennis racket, looking academic in a gown and mortar board.

And looking beautiful in the portrait in the drawing room over the fireplace.

'He really caught her,' the proud father had said when he'd found Kamel looking at it.

His sarcastic drawl set her teeth on edge. 'I left home at eighteen.'

And by then Hannah had been a very good cook, thanks to her father's chef at Brent Hall. Sarah Curtis had an impressive professional pedigree, she had worked in top kitchens around Europe and she had a daughter who had no interest in food or cooking. When she'd realised that Hannah did, she'd encouraged that interest.

For Hannah the kitchen was a happy place, the place her father came and sat in the evenings, where he shed his jacket and his formality. She had not realised then why…now she did.

'Yes, I can imagine the hardship of picking out an outfit and booking a table every night must have been difficult. What taxing subject did you study?'

'Classics,' she snapped.

'So you spent a happy three years learning something incredibly useful.'

'Four actually. I needed extra time because I'm dyslexic.'

'You have dyslexia?'

'Which doesn't mean I'm stupid.'

It was a taunt she had obviously heard before, and taunts left scars. Kamel experienced a swift surge of anger as he thought of the people responsible for creating this defensive reflex. In his opinion it was them, not Hannah, who could be accused of stupidity...ignorance...cruelty.

Kamel was looking at her oddly. The silence stretched. Was he worried their child might inherit her condition? He might be right, but at least she'd know what signs to look for—he or she wouldn't have to wait until they were a teenager before they had a diagnosis.

'You have dyslexia and you got a degree in Classics?' Now that was something that required serious determination.

'Not a first, but I can make a cup of tea and toast a slice of bread, and at least I don't judge people I don't know...' She stopped and thought, Why am I playing it down? 'I got an upper second and actually I'm a good cook—*very* good.' She'd be even better if she had accepted the internship at the restaurant that Sarah had wangled for her: awful hours, menial repetitive tasks and the chance to work under a three-star Michelin chef.

For once she hadn't been able to coax her father around to her way of thinking—he had exploded when he'd learnt of the plan. It hadn't just been to please him that instead she had accepted the prestigious university place she had been offered; it had been because she had realised that the contentious issue of her career had become a major issue between her father and his cook.

His mistress.

The smile that hitched one corner of Kamel's mouth upwards did not touch his eyes; they remained thoughtful, almost wary. 'I have married a clever woman and a domestic goddess. Lucky me.'

Her jaw tightened at what she perceived as sarcasm.

'Lucky me,' he repeated, seeing her in the wedding dress, her face clustered with damp curls, her lips looking pink and bruised, her passion-glazed eyes heavy and deep blue, not cold, but hot. He rubbed his thumb absently against his palm, mimicking the action when he had stroked her cheek, feeling the invisible fuzz of invisible downy hair on the soft surface.

The contrast with the cold, classy woman before him could not have been more dramatic; they were both beautiful but the woman last night had been sexy, sinfully hot, available—but married. He didn't sleep with drunk women; the choice was normally an end-of-story shrug, not hours of seething frustration while he wrestled his passion into submission, cursing his black and white sense of honour.

The same honour that had made him push Amira into Hakim's arms.

He was either a saint or an idiot!

Hannah gave a mental shrug and turned a slender shoulder, telling herself that it didn't matter what he thought of her...she still wanted to hit him.

Or kiss him.

Dusting an invisible speck off her silk dress, she gave a faint smile and thought about slapping that expression of smug superiority off his hateful face.

'Relax, we leave at twelve-thirty.'

Relax, no. But this was the best news she had had in several nightmare days.

'Where are you off to?' She didn't care but it seemed polite to ask.

'*We.*'

Her expression froze. 'We? What are you talking about? There is no we!'

'Please do not treat me to another bout of your histrionics. Behind closed doors there is no we.' Lips twisted into a sardonic smile, he sat on the edge of the desk. 'But in public we are a loving couple and you will show me respect.'

'When you stop lying to me. You said we would not have to live together.'

'You didn't really believe that. I said what you wanted to hear. It seemed the kindest thing at the time.'

She let out a snort of sheer disbelief—was this man for real? 'Perhaps I should thank you for kindly lying through your teeth.'

He glanced at the watch on his wrist, exposing the fine dark hairs on his arm as he flicked his cuff. 'Quite clearly we have things to discuss,' he conceded.

Hannah, who was breathing hard, flashed a bitter smile. 'Discuss' implied reasonable and flexible. It implied listening. *You think?*'

He refused to recognise the irony in her voice. 'Yes, I do think.'

'You are giving me a time slot?' She was married to a man she was expected to make an appointment to talk to? Now that really brought home how awful this entire situation was. She had walked into it with her eyes wide open and her brain in denial. The fact was that

deep down she had never stopped being a person who
believed in happy ever after, who believed that everything happened for a reason.

A spasm of irritation crossed his lean, hard features.

She shook her head and gave a laugh of sheer disbelief. 'Or should that be granting me an audience?' she
wondered, letting her head tip forward as she performed
a mocking curtsey.

The childish reaction made his jaw clench.

'You're used to people dropping everything when
you require attention. But I've got a newsflash…' He let
the sentence hang, but the languid contempt in his voice
made it easy to fill in the blanks as he glanced down at
the stack of papers spread out on the inlaid table.

It wasn't that she wanted to be important to him, but
a little empathy—she'd have settled for civility—would
have made him human. Instead he intended to map out
just how insignificant she was in the scheme of things
from the outset. Did he really think she didn't know she
was on the bottom rung of his priorities?

Hannah could feel the defensive ice forming on her
features. 'Sorry,' she said coldly. 'I'm still living in a
world where people have marriages based on mutual
respect, not mutual contempt! It was unrealistic of me,
and it won't happen again,' she promised. 'I won't dis-
turb you any longer. Have your people talk to my people and…' The ice chips left her voice as it quivered…
My people. I have no people. The total isolation of her
position hit home for the first time.

She squeezed her eyes shut.

'I need an hour.'

She opened her eyes and found he was looking right
at her. Her stomach immediately went into a dive.

'I could postpone this but I assumed you would prefer to arrive early at Brent.'

Her eyes flew wide. 'Brent!' She gave a shaky smile. 'You're taking me home?'

'This is your home.'

Swallowing the hurt and annoyed with herself for leaping to conclusions, she lifted her chin and stared at him coldly. 'This will never be my home.'

'That, *ma belle*, is up to you. But your father wanted to hold a wedding party for us, and for your friends. I think it would only be polite for us to be there. I will have some breakfast sent up to your room.'

Jaw clenched at the dismissal, Hannah left the room with her head held high.

CHAPTER SEVEN

HER FATHER WAS there to greet them at the private airstrip where they landed, and Hannah was relieved he looked better than the previous day, almost his old self. She was sandwiched between the two men in the back seat of the limo and by the time they arrived at Brent Hall the effort of maintaining a reassuring pretence for her father's sake had taken its toll, her persistent nagging headache showing signs of becoming a full-blown migraine.

'I think I might go to my room, unless you want me to help.' There was evidence of the preparations for tonight everywhere.

'No, you have a rest. Good idea. Tonight is all under control. I got a new firm in and they seem excellent— they're doing the lot. I have a few ideas I want to run past your husband.' He glanced towards Kamel and joked, 'Not much point having a financial genius in the family if you don't make use of him, is there? I'm sure he'll even write your thank-you letters.'

Hannah laughed and her father winked conspiratorially at her. 'A family joke.'

And one that was at his daughter's expense, thought Kamel, who had seen the flinch before the smile. How many times, he wondered, had she been on the receiving end of such jokes? For a man who cared deeply for his daughter, Charles Latimer seemed remarkably blind to her sensitivity.

'I am aware of Hannah's dyslexia. Is that the family joke?'

'She told you?' Hannah's father looked startled.

'She did. But even if she hadn't I would have noticed how uncomfortable the family *joke* made her.'

Hannah's father looked horrified by the suggestion. 'It's just that some of her mistakes have been so…' His stammering explanation ground to a halt in the face of his new son-in-law's fixed, unsmiling stare. 'Hannah has a great sense of humour.'

'I don't.'

Instead of heading for her room, Hannah made her way down to the kitchens. But finding the place had been taken over by outside caterers, she made her way to Sarah's private flat.

The cook was delighted to see her. So was Olive, the dog sitting in her basket, surrounded by her puppies, who licked Hannah's hand and wagged her stumpy little tail.

Without being asked, Sarah produced some painkillers along with the coffee and cakes. 'Now, tell me all about it.'

Hannah did—or at least the approved version. She stayed half an hour before she got up to leave.

'Where are you going?' Sarah called after her.

'To my room. I need to get ready.' She pulled a face.

'Not that way, Hannah.' Sarah laughed. 'You can't sleep in your old bedroom. You're a married woman now.'

'Oh, God, I forgot!' Hannah groaned.

If the cook thought this was an odd thing to say she didn't let on. Instead she enthused about the complete refurbishment of the guest suite that Hannah was to stay in. 'Mind you, if you're used to palaces...'

'I'm not used to palaces. I'll never be used to palaces. I hate them and I hate him!' Then it all came tumbling out—the whole story.

'I knew something was wrong,' Sarah said as she piled sugar in a cup of tea and made Hannah drink it. 'I don't know what to say, Hannah. I really don't.'

'There's nothing to say. I'm sorry I dumped on you like this.'

'Heavens, girl, that's what I'm here for. You know I've always thought of you as my second daughter.'

'I wish I was,' Hannah replied fiercely, envying Eve her mother. 'Dad thinks I'm all right with it. You won't tell him, will you? I worry so much that the stress will…' She didn't have to explain her worries to Sarah, who knew about the heart attack. She'd been with Hannah when she'd got the call and had travelled with her to the hospital.

Having extracted a firm promise that Sarah would not reveal how unhappy she was, Hannah made her way to the guest room and discovered that Sarah had not exaggerated about the makeover.

She explored the luxurious bedroom. An opulent silk curtained four-poster bed occupied one end of the room. She quickly looked away, but not before several illicit images slipped through her mental block. Her stomach was still flipping lazily as she focused on the opposite end of the room where a bathtub deep enough to swim in sat on a raised dais.

Behind it there were two doors. One opened, she discovered, into a massive wet room—she pressed one of the buttons on a glass control panel that would have looked at home in a space station and the room was filled with the sounds of the ocean. Unable to locate a button that turned it off, she closed the door and pushed open the other door. The lights inside automatically lit up, revealing a space that was the size of her entire flat, lined with hanging space, mirrors and shelves.

It was not a full wardrobe, but neither was it empty. The selection of clothes and shoes that were hung and neatly folded were her own. Shoes, bags, underclothes—there was something for every occasion, including an obvious choice for this evening where all eyes would be on her. She pushed away the thought of the evening ahead and lifted a silk shirt to her face. Feeling the sharp prick of tears behind her eyelids, she blinked them back.

After the last few days Hannah had imagined that nothing could shock her ever again. But when she opened the large velvet box on the dressing table and looked at the contents displayed on the silk lining, she knew that she had been wrong!

Kamel glanced at the closed door, then at his watch. He was expecting her to be late and he was expecting her to be hostile; she was neither. At seven on the dot the door opened and his wife stepped into the room.

Kamel struggled to contain his gasp. He had seen her at her worst and that had been beautiful. At her best she was simply breathtaking. The satin gown she wore with such queenly confidence left one shoulder bare, Grecian style. The bodice cut snugly across her breasts, continued in a body-hugging column to the knee where it flared out, sweeping the ground. Her skin against the black glowed with a pearly opalescence.

The silence stretched and Hannah fought the absurd urge to curtsey. What was she meant to do—ask for marks out of ten?

Anxiety gnawed her stomach lining and tension tied the muscles in her shoulders but her expression was serene as she took a step towards him and fought the ridiculous urge to ask for his approval. 'Am I late?'

'You are not wearing the diamonds,' he said, noticing the absence of the jewels he had had removed from the vault that morning.

'I'm a "less is more" kind of girl.' She could not explain even to herself her reluctance to wear the jewels.

He arched a sardonic brow. 'And I'm an "if you have it flaunt it" sort of guy.'

'All right, I'll put them on,' she agreed without good grace before sweeping from the room. 'Satisfied now?' she asked when she returned a short while later wearing the jewellery. On the plus side, nobody would be looking at her now—they'd be staring at the king's ransom she wore.

Hannah watched the lift doors opening and felt her stomach go into a steep dive. She did not question the instinct that warned her not to be in an enclosed space with this man. She picked up her skirt in one hand. 'I'm fine with the stairs.'

'I'm not.'

Not anticipating the hand against the small of her back that propelled her forward, she tensed before retreating into a corner and standing there trying not to meet her own eyes in the mirrors that covered four walls of the lift.

She exited the lift a step ahead of him, almost falling out in the process.

'Relax.'

The advice drew a disbelieving laugh from the resentful recipient, who turned her head sharply and was reminded of the chandelier earrings she wore as they brushed her skin. '*Seriously?*'

The man had spent most of their flight giving her a last-minute crash course in how princesses were meant to behave. The consequences of her failing had not been spelt out, but had left her with the impression the political stability of a nation—or possibly even a continent—could be jeopardised by her saying the wrong word to the wrong person or using the wrong fork.

So no pressure, then!

'If I'd been listening to a word you said I'd be a gibbering wreck, but happily I've started as I mean to go on. I tuned you out.' She smiled at his expression, catching the flicker of shock in his eyes, and chalked a mental point in the air. Then, producing a brilliant smile, she laid a hand on his arm as they reached the double doors of the ballroom.

'I do know how to work a room, you know.'

Despite the assurance, she was actually glad to enter the room beside a figure who oozed authority. She'd been acting as a hostess for her father for years, but it was a shock to find few faces she recognised in the room.

Despite her initial misgivings, a glass of champagne later she was circulating, accepting congratulations, smiling and doing a pretty good job of lying through her clenched teeth. Until she saw a familiar figure. She went to wave, and then the man he was speaking to turned his head.

She knew, of course, that her father and Rob Preston still saw one another on a personal and professional level, but her ex-fiancé had never been invited to any event when she was present previously.

Hannah moved across the room to where her father stood chatting.

'Excuse me, can I borrow my father for one minute?'

'What's wrong, Hannah?'

'Rob is here!'

'He is one of my oldest friends. You're married now, and I think it's time we drew a line under what happened, if Rob is willing to forgive and forget.'

'I should too.' She took a deep breath. This was what happened when you put your pride before the truth. 'You're right, Dad. Fine,' she said, thinking that it was so not fine.

As the party progressed a few people began to drift outside into the courtyard, and Hannah joined them, having spent the evening avoiding Rob, who to her relief had shown no inclination to speak to her.

With the tree branches filled with white lights and the sound of laughter and music from inside drifting out through the open doors, it was a magical scene. Most people had sensibly avoided the damp grass and remained on the paved area around the pool, laughing and talking, all except a middle-aged couple who reappeared from amongst the trees. The woman's hair was mussed and her shoes were in her hand.

Hannah looked down at her own feet—they ached in the high heels that matched her gown. She wriggled her cramped toes, forcing blood back into the cramped extremities and wincing at the painful burn. What page on the princess handbook said you weren't allowed to take off your shoes and walk on the grass? It would be there along with anything else spontaneous and fun. The wistful ache in her throat grew heavier as she watched the man…maybe her husband…slide a shoe back onto the pretty woman's foot while she balanced precariously on the other. The woman tottered and her partner caught her. There was a lot of soft laughter and a brief kiss before they went back indoors.

Hannah was taking a last deep breath of fresh air and painting on a smile just as a figure emerged, his eyes scanning as if he was searching for something or someone. Her bodyguard stood out like a sore thumb, albeit one in black tie.

Hannah found herself moving backwards into the shadow of a tree. She realised she was holding her breath and closing her eyes like a child who wanted to disappear. She looked down at her hands clenched into tight fists and slowly unfurled them. The sight of the deep grooves her nails had cut into the flesh of her palm drew a fleeting frown of acknowledgement but didn't lessen her defiance.

The buzz lasted a few moments, but as the exhilaration of her small rebellion faded away she stared at her shoes sinking into the damp ground. Was this going to be her life in future? Ignoring 'don't walk on the grass' signs just to feel alive?

As rebellions went it was pathetic.

She was pathetic.

She took a deep breath and, taking her shoes off and holding them in one hand, she used the other to lift her skirt free of the damp grass as she straightened her slender shoulder. 'Man up, Hannah,' she muttered to herself as she moved towards the lights that filtered through the bank of trees.

'Hello, Hannah. I knew you wanted me to follow you.'

Hannah let out a soft yelp of shock and dropped both her shoes and skirt. The fabric trailed on the wet ground as she turned around.

The comment came from a man with a massive ego, a man who thought everything was about him.

The acknowledgement shocked Hannah more than the fact Rob had followed her. Even after she had discovered his infidelities there had been a small, irrational corner of her brain that had made excuses for him.

There were no excuses, not for him and not for her either for being so damned gullible—for not seeing past the perfect manners, the practised smile and the thoughtful gifts. She'd seen little flashes of the real Rob and she'd chosen to ignore them and the growing unease she had felt. If she hadn't walked into Sal's room and found them…

She closed her eyes to blot out the mental image, and lifted her chin. She had been dreading this moment but now that it was here…how bad could it be? She'd spent two days in a prison cell. She could definitely cope with an awkward situation.

'Hello, Rob.' He'd been drinking heavily. She could smell it even before he stepped into the patch of moonlight and she was able to see his high colour and glazed eyes. Seeing Rob when she had thought he was the love of her life had always made her stomach quiver, but now it quivered with distaste.

'No, I didn't want you to follow me. I *really* didn't.'

He looked taken aback by her reaction. Clearly I'm not following the script he wrote, she thought. Drunk or not drunk, he was still a very handsome man, the premature silvered wings of hair giving him a distinguished look, along with the horn-rimmed glasses that she had been amazed to discover were plain glass, though they gave a superficial impression of intellect and sensitivity.

But then Rob always had been more about style than substance. Deep down Hannah had always known that, she had just chosen not to think about it. But for the first time now she was struck by a softness about him. Not just the thickness around the middle that regular sessions with a personal trainer could never quite eliminate, but in his features… Had he always looked that way or was it just the contrast? She had spent the last two days in the company of a man who made granite look soft.

An image of Kamel floated into her mind: his strong-boned aristocratic features, his mobile, sensual mouth.

'Just like old times. Remember the time we brought a bottle of champagne out here and—?'

Hannah stiffened and matched his hot stare with one of cold contempt. 'That wasn't me.'

He stopped, his eyes falling as his lips compressed in a petulant line. 'Oh! She never meant anything—'

Did he even remember who *she* was? The anger and bitterness was still there, and most of all the knowledge that she had been a total fool. But now she could see the black humour in it…in him.

He was a joke.

'And now you mean nothing to me.'

As he sensed her shift of attitude, sensed he had lost his power, his expression darkened. 'That's not true and we both know it.'

'Look, Rob, Dad wanted you to be here and that's fine. But you and I are never going to be friends. Let's settle for civil…?' She gave a sigh and felt relief. This was the moment she had been dreading—coming face to face with the man she had considered the love of her life only to discover he meant nothing.

Her relieved sigh became a sharp intake of alarm as Rob lumbered drunkenly towards her, forcing Hannah to retreat until her back hit the tree trunk. She winced as the bark grazed her back through the thin fabric of her gown.

'You were meant to be with me. We are soul mates… What went wrong, Hannah?'

A contemptuous laugh came from Hannah's lips. She was too angry at being manhandled to be afraid. 'Maybe all my friends—the ones you bedded after we were engaged?' She made the sarcastic suggestion without particular rancour. Rob was pathetic.

'I told you, they meant nothing. They were just cheap…' His lips curled. 'Not like you—you're pure and perfect. I was willing to wait for you. It would have been different after we were married. I would have given you everything.' He clasped a hand to his heart.

The dramatic gesture caused Hannah's discomfort to tip over into amusement. He looked so ridiculous.

His eyes narrowed at her laugh, then slid to the jewels that gleamed against the skin of her throat. 'But I wasn't enough for you, was I?'

She swallowed; the laugh had been a bad idea. 'I think I'd better go.'

'A love match, is it? Or should that be an oil deal?' He saw her look of shock and smiled. 'People talk, and I know a lot of people.'

On the receiving end of his fixed lascivious stare, she felt sick. 'Well, I'm not pure or perfect but I am extremely pis—'

Rob, in full florid flow, cut across her. 'A work of art,' he raved. 'Sheer perfection, my perfect queen, not his—he doesn't appreciate you like I would have. I'd have looked after you...the other women, they meant nothing to me,' he slurred. 'You must know that—you are the only woman I have ever loved.'

How did I ever think he was the man of my dreams? she wondered, feeling queasy as he planted a hand on the tree trunk beside her head and leaned in closer.

Struggling not to breathe in the fumes, she countered acidly, 'Well, you know, you can't miss what you've never had.'

Having followed the spiky imprints of her heels across the wet grass, Kamel took only a few minutes to locate the couple in the tree. He didn't pause. Unable to see them, he heard their voices as with a face like thunder he charged straight through a shrub.

This wasn't a moment to stop and consider, not a moment for subtlety. He'd bent over backwards to be reasonable but she wasn't a woman who responded to reasonable. Was she pushing boundaries, checking just how far she could push him? Or maybe she simply lacked any normal sense of propriety? This wasn't about jealousy. It was one thing to have a pragmatic approach to marriage, but she had not just crossed the line, she had obliterated it!

The couple came into his line of vision about the

same moment that he mentally processed the inter-
change he had just heard. It was astonishing enough to
stop him in his tracks.

'Well, he's welcome to you!'

Hannah struggled and failed to swallow a caustic retort to this petulant response. 'Well, the idea that I was
your soul mate didn't last long, did it?'

'Bitch!' Rob snarled. 'You think you've landed on
your feet now, but we all know what happens to people
when they get in your husband's way…'

Hannah was shaken by the malice and ugly jealousy
in his face. *Jealousy…!* She shook her head in disbelief.
Perhaps he'd been acting the injured party so long he
actually believed it.

The full realisation of just how lucky she had been
hit home. She could have been married to him.

Her stomach gave a fresh shudder of disgust as she
pulled in a breath, trying to surreptitiously ease away
from him. As nice as it would have been to drop the
icy dignity that had got her through that awful day, this
wasn't the time and definitely not the place, she thought,
to have the last word.

This could get ugly.

'They have a habit of disappearing.' He mimed a
slashing action across his throat. 'So watch yourself.'

The sinister comment drew a startled laugh from
her. It was clearly not the reaction Rob had wanted,
as his face darkened and he grabbed for her. Things
happened with dizzying speed so that later when she
thought about it Hannah couldn't recall the exact sequence of events.

Kamel surged forward but Hannah was quicker. Unable to escape, she ducked and her attacker's head hit the tree trunk with a dull thud.

Her attempt to slip under his arm was less successful, and by the time Kamel reached her the man, with blood streaming from a superficial head wound, had caught her arm and swung her back.

'Bitch!'

Hannah hit out blindly with her free hand and then quite suddenly she was free. Off balance, she fell and landed on her bottom on the wet grass. When she looked up Rob was standing with one hand twisted behind his back with Kamel whispering what she doubted were sweet nothings into the older man's ear, if the white-lipped fury stamped on his face was any indication.

Rob, who had blood seeping from a gash on his head, seemed to shrink before her eyes and started muttering excuses in full self-preservation mode.

'If I ever see you in the same postcode as my wife… if you so much as *look* in her direction…' Kamel leaned in closer, his nostrils flaring in distaste at the smell of booze and fear that enveloped the man like a cloud, and told him what would happen to him, sparing little detail.

Hannah struggled to her feet imagining the headlines. 'Don't hurt him!'

The plea caused Kamel's attention to swivel from the man he held to Hannah.

'Please?'

A muscle along his jaw clenched as he stared at her. Then, with a nod that caused two invisible figures to emerge from the trees, he stood aside and the trio walked away.

'Sure you don't want to go and hold his hand?'

'I wasn't protecting him. I was protecting you.' Why

are you explaining yourself to him? she wondered. It's not as if he's going to believe you and it's not like you care what he thinks.

A look of scowling incredulity spread across his face. '*Me?* You are protecting *me*?' He had no idea why her caring about someone who was clearly an abusive loser bothered him so much, but it did.

Her eyes moved slowly up the long, lean length of his muscle-packed body. It was hard to imagine anyone who looked less like he needed looking after.

'The press could dub you something worse than The Heartbreaker Prince.' She paused and saw him absorb her comment. His anger still permeated the air around them but it simmered now where it had boiled before. 'Rob likes to play the victim. I can just see the head-lines now...'

'I wasn't going to hit him, but if I had he wouldn't have been running to any scandal sheet,' he retorted, managing to sound every bit as sinister as Rob had im-plied he was. While Hannah believed Rob's comments were motivated by malice, there was no escaping the fact that she knew very little about the man she had married and what he was capable of.

Unwilling to release his image of her as a cold-hearted, unapproachable ice bitch, he asked, 'What the hell were you thinking of meeting him out here?'

What the hell had she been thinking about getting involved with him to begin with? The man had been mentally filed in his head as a victim. Stupid, but a vic-tim, and now he turned out to be a... His fists clenched as he found himself wishing he had not shown restraint.

Temper fizzed through her body, sparking wrathful

blue flames in her eyes. 'Are you implying that I arranged this? Rob followed me!'

'And I followed him.' It was an impulse that he had not checked even though it was a situation that had not required his personal intervention. In fact his abrupt departure had probably caused more speculation than Hannah's.

'Why? I thought you delegated all that sort of thing.'

'There are some things that a husband cannot delegate.' She might not be wife material but she was definitely mistress material. She might be the sort of woman he would normally cross the road to avoid, but there was no denying that physically she was perfect.

'So you thought it was your duty to rescue me.' She had about as much luck injecting amusement into her voice as she had escaping his dark, relentless stare. It was becoming harder to rationalise her response to his strong personal magnetism, or control the pulse-racing mixture of dread and excitement whenever he was close by.

'Little did I know you had it all under control.'

Her clenched teeth ached at the sarcasm. 'My hero riding to the rescue yet again.'

'I thought I was rescuing your...'

'Victim?'

He dragged his smouldering glance free of her cushiony soft lips and found himself staring at her heaving bosom. 'The man is...' He said a word that she didn't understand but it was not hard to get the drift. 'What is your ex doing at our wedding party?'

The accusation made her blink. 'The word party suggests celebration. Tonight has felt more like a punishment. And yes, we all know this is my fault, though

I have to tell you that line is getting a bit boring. I'm willing to take my medicine and make nice and pretend you're almost as marvellous as you think you are, but if this marriage is going to last, and I'm talking beyond the next few seconds, it won't be on a speak-when-you're-spoken-to, walk-two-steps-behind-me way. I am *not* willing to be a doormat!'

She released a shuddering sigh and warmed to her theme. 'So from now on I expect to be treated with some damned respect, and not just in public!' Oh, God! Overwhelmed with a mixture of horror and exhilaration, she could not recall losing control of herself quite so completely in her life. Hannah brought her lashes down in a protective veil as she gulped in several shallow breaths while her heart rate continued to race.

The ice queen is dead! Long live the princess of passion! His mental headline tugged the corners of his mouth upwards, but the curve flattened out as he felt his body stir lustfully. It wasn't the physical response that bothered him; it was the strength of it and the fact it kept intruding.

Mentally and physically, discipline and order were important to Kamel. He had never made a conscious decision to compartmentalise the disparate aspects of his life, but he took the ability for granted and it enabled him to combine the role he had unexpectedly inherited and any sort of personal life.

It had not crossed his mind that being married would lead to any overlap. Tonight came under the heading of duty, with a capital D. Such occasions were more than useful, they were essential, and he *definitely* shouldn't be thinking about how she'd look naked, and how soft and inviting her mouth was. Had she just said what he thought she had? He clenched his teeth and struggled to regroup his thoughts. Focus, Kamel—but not on her mouth.

'Would I be right in thinking that was an...' he spoke slowly, winged brows drawn into a straight line, and shaking his head slightly as though the concept he was about to voice was just so off the planet as to be unreal '...*ultimatum?*'

Hannah didn't pause to analyse the weirdness in his voice. If he wanted to call it that it was fine by her! Like an angry curtain, the protective veil of her lashes lifted, but her militant response was delayed as their glances connected and the subsequent sensual jolt caused her brain to stall.

'I if...I...?'

The nerve endings in her brain might have stopped sending messages, but during that long, nerve-shredding pause those elsewhere had stepped up to fill the vacuum. She could almost feel the blood racing through her veins—it felt dark and hot like the ache low in her pelvis. She snatched a breath, let it out in a quivering sigh, and lifted her chin.

'Yes, it is, and,' she added, wagging her finger as she took a squelchy step towards him, 'if you want to know about the damned guest list why ask me? Ask Dad. I probably know half a dozen people here by first name. You're the one in the loop. I'm here to smile and take one for the team.'

'*Take one for the team?*'

'What else would you call it?' His outrage struck her as the height of hypocrisy. 'Apologies to your ego, but don't expect me to pretend I like the situation when we're alone!'

'No. You'll just pretend you haven't thought about what it will be like.'

'What *what* would be like?'

His slow predatory smile sent a pulse of sexual heat through her body.

'Oh, that.' She faked amusement to cover her embarrassment. 'Now? Here?' She laughed a high-pitched laugh. 'Has anyone ever mentioned your awful timing?'

'Actually, no.'

She swallowed hard, thinking, That I can believe. 'Silly me! Of course, even if you were lousy in bed they'd still tell you how marvellous you were because you're—' She broke off and finished lamely, 'You're… a prince.'

'You're a princess.'

'What?'

'You're a princess.'

As in dignified, serene, gracious, aloof…qualities that when she'd been plain old Hannah Latimer she'd had in abundance. Now she was the real deal—a real princess—she'd turned into some sort of fishwife!

It isn't me, it's him, she thought, levelling a look of breathless resentment up at his impossibly handsome face. He was the one who was making her act this way, the one who was making her feel…out of control. Because of him she was saying the first thing that popped into her head. She'd lost every vestige of mental censorship; she was saying things she didn't know she felt…

'Oh, God!' Without warning, the adrenalin wave that she'd been riding suddenly broke and she started shaking.

Watching her wrap her arms around herself, an action that didn't disguise the fact she was shaking like a leaf, Kamel felt a sharp stab of guilt. 'You've had a bad experience.' A fact he was a little late acknowledging.

She slung him a look. Anybody hearing him would think he gave a damn. 'I'm fine. Look, it was handy you turned up when you did.' He was the last person in the world she would have wanted to see her in that position, but that didn't alter the fact she had needed saving. 'And if the opportunity ever arises and some ex-girlfriend of yours comes to scratch your eyes out I'll return the favour.' By the time the last syllable had left her lips Hannah was utterly drained; her ironic smile was not weak, it was non-existent.

'So you will rescue me?' He was torn between amusement, astonishment and an uncharacteristic impulse that he firmly quashed. Comforting embraces were so *not* his style.

She felt the colour rush to her cheeks. 'You think that's funny because I'm a woman.' Hopping on one foot while she bent to try and retrieve the shoe that had been sucked into a patch of mud, she turned her head and threw him a look of frowning dislike. 'You going to stand there and watch?'

He held up his phone, his eyes trained on her bottom, the firm, curvy outline very clear against the silk of her gown. 'That really is a good look for you!'

'You dare!' she growled.

Still grinning—the grin made him look normal and nice and far too good-looking—he shrugged and slid the phone back into his pocket before he bent and grabbed the protruded strap of her shoe. It came free with a massive slurping sound.

'Well, Cinderella, you can go to the ball but I don't think that you're going to be doing much dancing in this,' he said, shaking free the larger dollops of mud that clung to the heel. His brows suddenly lifted.

'What?'

'I never realised,' he said, his glance transferring from the wrecked shoe to her foot and back again, 'that you actually have really big feet.'

Hannah's jaw dropped.

'As for women being weaker...Have you ever *seen* a tigress protecting her young?' It was not the image of a tigress that formed in his mind, though. It was Hannah with a baby in her arms at her breast.

'I suppose you have.' There was an air of resignation in her response. He'd done all the things she hadn't... An image that she had seen in a magazine during her last hairdresser's appointment superimposed itself over his face: the gorgeous scantily clad model strutting her stuff at a red-carpet event while her escort looked on indulgently.

'I have no doubt that a woman can be fierce in defence of what she considers hers.'

'You're not mine,' she blurted, embarrassed by the suggestion and slightly queasy. In her head the damned supermodel was now doing things to the man she had married that Hannah knew she never could...which was a good thing, she reminded herself.

'And I'm not fierce. I'm...I just like to pay my debts.'

'And you shall.'

Promise, threat...Hannah was beyond differentiating between the two even in her own head. 'By having sex with you?'

Anger drew the skin tight across his hard-boned features. 'I have no intention of negotiating sex with my own wife,' he asserted proudly.

'You think I'm going to have sex with a man I don't like or respect?' She barely spoke above a whisper but her low voice sounded loud in the charged silence.

'You don't have to respect or like someone to want to rip off their clothes.'

'My God, you do love yourself.'

'This isn't love, but it is a strong mutual attraction.'

Heart thudding, she dodged his stare and snatched the shoe from him, grimacing as she slid her foot back in. 'Thank you.' She managed two steps before the heel snapped and threw her off balance. The jolt as she struggled to stay upright caused her chignon to come free, effectively blinding her. She took several more lopsided strides forward before she stopped and swore.

Throwing him a look that dared him to comment, she took off both shoes and threw them in a bush. Hitching her skirt a little higher, she continued barefoot, feeling his eyes in her back.

'Go on, say it!' she challenged him.

'Say what?'

'Say whatever sarcastic little gem you're just aching to say. Go ahead,' she said, opening her arms wide in invitation. 'I can take it.'

Their eyes connected and her challenging smile vanished. She dropped her arms so fast she almost lost her balance. She would have lowered her gaze had his dark, glittered stare not held her captive. The silence settled like a heavy velvet blanket around them. She had to fight for breath and fight the weird compulsion that made her want to...

'You want to take me, *ma belle*?' His eyes cancelled out the joke in his voice.

She could feel the heat inside her swell and she thought, Yes, I do. 'You can't say things like that to me.'

'What do you expect? You are a very confrontational woman.'

'I'm cold.'

'So the rumour goes, but we both know different. What were you doing with a man who wants to put you on a pedestal and worship you from afar?'

'Many girls dream of that.'

'Not you, though. You want to be touched and you looked like you'd seen a ghost when you saw him.' Kamel had made it his business to find out who the man was who was responsible for her shaken look.

Hannah heaved in a deep breath. She *longed* to be touched. She shivered; he saw it and frowned. 'You're cold.'

'Oh, and I was just getting used to the idea of being hot,' she quipped back.

He threw her a look. 'I will explain to the guests that you are feeling unwell. Rafiq will see you to your room.'

On cue the big man appeared. Hannah was getting used to it—she didn't jump, but she did accept with gratitude the wrap he placed across her shoulders.

CHAPTER EIGHT

HANNAH ACTUALLY PERSUADED Rafiq to leave her in the hallway and made her way upstairs alone. It was an area of the house that no guests had entered and it was very quiet. She found herself walking past the door to the guest suite, drawn by a need to experience the comfort of familiar things. She took the extra flight of narrow winding oak stairs hidden behind a door that led up to the next floor.

The attic rooms had been the servants' quarters years before. Later on they became the nursery and more recently a semi self-contained unit, complete with mini kitchen. She opened the door of her old bedroom and stepped inside. The paintwork was bright and fresh but it was the same colour scheme she had chosen when she was twelve. The bed was piled high with stuffed toys, and the doll's house she had had for her tenth birthday stood on the table by the window. It was like being caught in a time warp.

She picked up a stuffed toy from the pile on the bed and flicked the latch on the doll's house. The door swung open, automatically illuminating the neat rooms inside.

She stood there, a frown pleating her brow, and

waited. She didn't even recognise she was waiting until nothing happened. There was no warm glow, no lessening of tension. She didn't feel safe or secure.

In the past, she realised, this room had represented a sanctuary. She had closed the door and shut out the world. But even though the familiar things that had given her a sense of security were still the same—she had changed.

She closed the door of the doll's house with a decisive click. It was time to look forward, not back.

In the guest suite she showered and pulled a matching robe on over her silk pyjamas. Her hair hung loose and damp down her back. Leaving the steamy bathroom, she walked across to the interconnecting door and, after a pause, turned the key. Locked doors were no solution. Hugging a teddy bear had not helped, and hiding from the situation was not going to make it go away. Would talking help? Hannah didn't know, but she was willing to give it a try.

So long as he didn't construe the open door as an invitation to do more than talk.

She cinched the belt of her robe tight and walked across to the bed, trying not to think about the flare of sexual heat in her stomach as she heard his voice in her mind—*You don't have to respect or like someone to want to rip off their clothes.*

'Oh, God!'

She didn't know if the dismayed moan was in her head or she'd actually cried out, but when she opened her eyes there was no room for debate—he was no creation of her subconscious. A very real Kamel stood framed in the doorway, one shoulder wedged against the jamb, as he pulled his tie free from his neck.

'I'm glad that's over.'

He sounded almost human. He *was* human, she realised, noticing the lines of fatigue etched into his face—a fatigue that was emphasised by the shadow of dark stubble across his jaw. So he could get tired. It was a tiny chink in his armour, but she still struggled to see him suffering the same doubts and fears as the rest of the human race, and it went without saying that fatigue didn't stop him looking stupendously attractive. No, *beautiful*, she corrected, her eyes running over the angles and planes of his darkly lean face, a face that she found endlessly fascinating. She compressed her lips and closed a door on the thought. She knew it would be foolish to lower her defences around him.

He pulled the tie through his long fingers and let it dangle there, arching a sardonic brow as his dark eyes swept her face. 'So, no locked doors?'

'That was childish.'

The admission surprised him but he hid it. It was harder to hide his reaction to the way she looked. The only trace of make-up was the pink varnish on her toenails. With her hair hanging damply down her back and her face bare she looked incredibly young, incredibly vulnerable and incredibly beautiful.

There was a wary caution in the blue eyes that met his, but not the hostility that he had come to expect.

'I thought you'd be asleep by now.' The purple smudges under her eyes no longer smoothed away by a skilful application of make-up made it clear she still desperately needed sleep. Kamel reminded himself that her nightmare had been going on forty-eight hours longer than his. He felt a flash of grudging admiration for her—whatever else the woman he had married was, she was not weak.

Hannah absently rubbed the toes of one foot against the arch of the other until she saw him staring and she tucked them under her. She pushed her hair behind her ears as she admitted, 'I felt bad letting you make excuses for me. Was it awkward?' She had probably broken about a hundred unwritten rules of protocol.

'Awkward?' He arched a brow. 'You mean did anyone see you leave with—?'

'I didn't leave with him. He f—'

He held up his hands in a gesture of surrender. 'I know.'

'Me not being there. What did you say?'

'I did not go into detail. I simply told my uncle that you had retired early.' He had actually told Charles Latimer a little more. He had made it clear to his father-in-law that if he wanted his daughter to spend any time under his roof he would guarantee that Rob Preston would not be there.

'Did they believe you?'

He took a step into the room and dropped his tie onto a chair. 'Why should we care?'

The *we* was not symbolic of some new togetherness so the small glow of pleasure it gave her was totally out of proportion.

'So how long were you standing there watching?' She had gone through the scene enough times to realise that Kamel could have heard some, if not all, of the exchange with Rob.

Grave-eyed, she looked up from her contemplation of her hands and heard him say, 'Long enough.'

She ground her teeth in exasperation at this deliberately cryptic response.

'So he cheated on you?'

Oh, yes, he would have heard that bit.

'It happens.'

There was no pity in his voice; Hannah let out a tiny sigh of relief.

'Dumping him on the actual wedding day was a pretty good revenge.' Kamel understood the attraction of retribution, though, being a man to whom patience did not come easily, he struggled with the concept of a dish served cold.

'I didn't plan it.' She looked startled by the idea. 'That's when I found out.'

He looked at her incredulously. 'On the actual day?'

She nodded, experiencing the familiar sick feeling in the pit of her stomach as the memory surfaced. It had been an hour before the photographers, hairdressers and make-up artists were due to arrive. She had knocked on Sal's door under the pretext of collecting the something blue her best friend had promised her, though what she had actually wanted was reassurance—someone to tell her she was suffering from last-minute nerves and it was all normal.

'I walked in on him with Sal, my chief bridesmaid. They were... It wasn't until later that I discovered he'd worked his way through most of my circle.'

She didn't look at him to see his reaction. She told herself she was past caring whether she came across as self-pitying and pathetic, but it wasn't true. She simply didn't have the strength left to maintain the illusion.

The last few days one hit after another combined with exhaustion had destroyed her normal coping mechanisms... What pride she had left had been used up in her encounter with Rob.

'So he slept with everyone but you.'

Her eyes flew to his face. 'So you heard that too.'

He nodded. He had heard, but not quite understood. It was not a new strategy, and she was the sort of woman who was capable of inspiring obsession in susceptible men, though why a man who was willing to marry to get a woman in his bed would then choose to sleep around was more difficult to understand. Especially when the woman in question would make all others look like pale imitations.

'So the only way he could have you was marriage.' Twenty-four hours ago the discovery would not have left him with a sense of disappointment. Twenty-four hours ago he'd had no expectations that could be disappointed—he had only expected the worst of her.

His cynical interpretation caused her cobalt-blue eyes to fly wide open in shocked horror. 'No, I wanted to.' She gave a tiny grimace and added more honestly, 'I would have.' The fact was she simply wasn't a very sexual creature, which did beg the question as to why she couldn't look at Kamel or even hear his voice without feeling her insides melt. 'But he...'

Kamel watched her fumble for words, looking a million miles from the controlled woman reputed to have a block of ice for a heart, and felt something tighten in his chest.

'Apparently he wanted to worship me, not—'

'Take you to bed,' Kamel supplied, thinking the man was even more of a loser than he'd thought.

'I don't actually think he thought of me as a woman. More an addition to his art collection. He likes beautiful things…not that I'm saying I'm—'

'Don't spoil all this honesty by going coy. We both know you're beautiful. So why is it everyone thinks he's the injured party?'

'I'd prefer to be thought a bitch than an idiot.' The explanation was not one she had previously articulated. She was startled to hear the words. It was something she had not admitted to anyone before.

'And your father still invited the man here?' If a man had treated his daughter that way he would have— Kamel dragged a chair out from the dressing table, swung it around and straddled it.

'Oh, it was easier to let him think I'd had second thoughts. They've been friends for a long time and Dad had already had an awful time telling everyone the wedding was cancelled. A lot of people turned up and it was terrible for him—'

'And you were having such a great day…'

Hannah's protective instincts surfaced at the implied criticism of her father.

'You were right. It was my fault. This is my fault, totally my fault.'

He shook his head, bemused by her vehemence, and protested, 'You didn't ask the guy to jump you!'

'No, not Rob. Getting arrested, getting you mixed up in it, terrifying Dad half to death. If he has another heart attack, it would be down to me.'

It was news to Kamel that he had had one. The man certainly hadn't been scared enough to change his lifestyle. 'I think a doctor might disagree. Your father does not hold back when it comes to saturated fat.'

'You're trying to make me feel better.'

He studied her face. 'It's clearly not working.'

'Why are you being nice? It's my fault we had to get married. I should have waited for help. I shouldn't have left the Land Rover. I shouldn't have been there at all.' She shook her head, her face settling into a mask of bitter self-recrimination as she loosed a fractured sob. 'All the things you said.'

'The village did get the vaccines, and the help they needed.'

Lost in a morass of self-loathing, she didn't seem to hear him. 'I couldn't even help myself, let alone anyone else. I was only there to prove a point. I've spent my life playing it safe.' She planted her hand flat on her heaving chest and lifted her tear-filled eyes to his.

'I always played by the rules. I even wanted a safe man... I didn't even have the guts to do what I really wanted.' She shook her head slowly from side to side and sniffed. 'I went to university and did a course I had absolutely no interest in rather than stand up to my dad. I got engaged to a man who seemed safe and solid, and when he turned out to be a total bastard did I learn? No, I got engaged to a man I knew would never hurt me because...I always go for the safe option.'

He let out a long, low whistle. '*Dieu*, I wanted you to take responsibility for your own actions—not the financial crisis, world hunger and bad days in the week that have a Y in them.'

Startled, Hannah lifted her head. Her eyes connected with his and a small laugh was shaken from her chest. 'I just want...' She stopped, her husky voice suspended by tears, her control still unravelling so fast she could not keep pace.

With a muttered imprecation he dropped down to his knees beside the bed and pushed the hair back from her damp face.

'What do you want?'

Her wide brimming blue eyes lifted. 'I just want to be…to feel…not like this.' She gnawed at her lower lip and brought her lashes down in a protective veil. 'Sorry, I don't know why I'm saying this stuff to you.'

Responding to the painful tug in his chest, Kamel stood up and gently pushed her down. Sliding his hand behind her knees, he swung her legs onto the bed, pulling a pillow under her head before joining her.

'Go to sleep,' he said, lowering his long length onto the bed beside her.

'I can't sleep. I have dreams that I'm back in that cell and he is…' She struggled to sit up. A light touch on her breastbone stopped her rising and after a moment she stopped fighting. 'I can't sleep.'

He touched a finger to her lips. 'Move over.' Pausing to slide an arm under her shoulders, he pulled her head back onto his shoulder.

'Why are you being nice to me?' she whispered into his neck—and then a moment later she was asleep.

Kamel, who preferred his own bed, realised this was the first time in his life that he had slept with a woman, in the literal sense. Only he wasn't sleeping and he seriously doubted he would. A state of semi-arousal combined with seething frustration was not in his experience conducive to sleep, especially when there was zero chance of doing anything to relieve that frustration.

On the plus side at least the scenery was rather special. Asleep she looked like a wanton angel. There were probably a lot of men out there who would be willing to give up a night's sleep to look at that face. He was aware of an ache of desire somewhere deep inside him so strong it hurt. Ignoring it didn't make it go away, and not looking at her was not an option because his eyes, like the north arrow on a compass, kept going back to the same place.

So in the end he didn't question it; he just accepted it.

Hannah fought her way out of a dream, struggling to shake off the lingering sense of dread.

'Wake up. You're safe.'

Still half asleep, she opened her eyes, saw his face and sighed. 'I love your mouth,' she said before pressing her own lips to the sensual curve.

'Hannah.' He pulled away.

She blinked, the confusion slowly filtering from her.

'Sorry, I thought you were a dream.' She had kissed him and he hadn't kissed her back. He hadn't done anything. Once was bad, but twice was humiliating.

'I thought you were a bitch.' And that had made the politically expedient marriage not right, but not this wrong. 'I was wrong.'

'Not a bitch.' Great, I feel so much better.

Suddenly she felt very angry. She struggled to sit up. 'So what is wrong with me?' she asked, looking down at him for once. 'I mean, there has to be, doesn't there? I've been engaged twice, and no sex.' Hannah could hear the words coming out of her mouth. She knew she shouldn't be saying them but she couldn't stop. 'Now I'm married, and you don't even want to kiss me!'

With a dry sob she flung herself down and rolled over, her back to him.

It was the sight of her heaving shoulders that snapped

the last threads of Kamel's self-imposed restraint. 'Don't cry,' he begged.

'I'm not crying,' she retorted, sniffing. 'I've just realised something. I don't know why I was so bothered about marrying you.'

'I'm flattered.'

Hannah rolled over until she was able to stare straight at him. She had barely registered his dry comment, as her thoughts—dark ones—were turned inward.

'I can't even do sex so what would the point have been of waiting for someone who can give me...*more*?'

Kamel had never felt any driving desire to be a with a woman who considered him her soul mate. On the other hand, being basically told that you were an *all right* consolation prize for someone with low expectations was a bit below the belt even for someone with his ego.

Well at least the pressure is off, he thought. She's not expecting much of you!

His sudden laugh made her look up.

'So you are willing to settle for me?'

A small puzzled indent appeared between her feathery brows as she struggled to read his expression. 'Doesn't seem like I have a lot of choice in the matter, does it?' She glanced at the ring on her finger.

'So you are willing to...how did you put it—take one for the team?'

'I thought you'd have been glad to know that you don't have to pretend, that I don't expect—'

'Much?'

This drew an exasperated hiss from Hannah.

'Well, the mystery of why you're a virgin is solved,' he drawled. 'You talked them to sleep.'

With an angry snort Hannah reached behind her for

one of the pillows that had been spread across the bed while she slept.

'I don't think so, angel.'

Somewhere between picking it up and lobbing it at him she found the pillow was removed from her fingers and a moment later she was lying with her wrists held either side of her head, with his body suspended above her.

She could hear a sound above the thunderous clamour of her frantic heartbeat—it was her panting. She couldn't draw enough air into her lungs to stop her head spinning. His mouth was a whisper away from hers; she could feel the warmth of his breath on her lips.

The dark intent shining in his heavy-lidded eyes made the heat prickle under her skin.

'Just—' he ran his tongue lightly across the surface of her lips '—how—' he kissed one corner of her mouth '—much—' he kissed the other corner, smiling as she gave a deep languid sigh and lifted her head towards him '—are you willing—' he kissed her full on her trembling lips before trailing a series of burning kisses down the smooth column of her neck '—to take for the team?'

'I...don't...God...stop...please don't stop!' she moaned, terrified at the thought he might.

Her beating heart stumbled as his beautiful mouth came crashing down to claim her lips. The relief she felt as she opened her mouth to him in silent invitation was quickly consumed by the response of her body to the thrust of his tongue: low in her belly each carnal incursion caused a tight clenching; between her legs the dampness ran hot.

While he kissed her with something approaching

desperation his hands were busy in her hair, on her face, sliding under her nightdress to caress the warm skin of her smooth thighs then reaching to curve over one taut, tingling breast. As he found the loop of the top button and slipped it off his patience snapped and he tugged hard, causing the remainder to tear from the fabric as he pushed the two sides apart to reveal her breasts to his hungry stare.

She arched up into him as he took first one turgid rosy peak and then the other into his mouth, leaving her gasping and moaning; her entire body reached fever pitch in seconds. He pressed a kiss to her belly and the frustration building inside got higher and higher as his finger slid lower and lower, inscribing a tingling line between her aching breasts and then down her quivering belly.

Nakedness turned out not to be inhibiting—it was liberating. She lifted her arms and tugged him down to her. The slow, drugging kisses continued as she arched, pushing her breasts up against his hard chest, frantic for skin-to-skin contact. Her hands ran down the strong, smooth lines of his back, revealing his strength, his sleek hardness.

The liquid heat in her belly had a new urgency as he began to fumble with the buckle on his belt. A moment later she heard the sound of his zipper.

Afflicted by a belated bout of virginal modesty, she closed her eyes, opening them only when he took her hands in his and curled them around the hot, silky, rock-hard erection.

She couldn't prevent the little gasp that was wrenched from somewhere in her chest.

At least make an effort to look like you know what you're doing, Hannah.

The voice in her head was critical but he was not.

A deep feral moan was wrenched from his throat as her fingers began to experimentally tighten then release the pressure around the throbbing column. His eyes drifted shut and he began to breathe hard. Then without warning he took her hand and tipped her back onto the pillows.

She let out a series of fractured gasps that terminated in a higher-pitched wailing moan as he touched the dampness between her thighs.

'This is good?' he slurred thickly as he continued to stroke and torment, making her ache everywhere.

She nodded vigorously and pushed against the heel of his hand. 'Oh, yes...very good.'

He raised himself up, took her hand and, holding her gaze, laid it against his chest. Not looking away from her eyes for an instant, he fought his way out of his shirt and flung it away.

'You're beautiful,' she breathed, unable to take her greedy stare off his tautly muscled, gleaming torso.

Kamel swallowed. He wanted her badly. At that moment he could not think of anything he had wanted more.

'I've wanted to be inside you since the moment I saw you.' He pushed against her, letting her share the relentless ache in his groin.

'I want that too.' Delighting in the discovery of an inherent sensuality, she parted her thighs.

Responding to the silent invitation with a fierce groan, he came over her and settled between her legs. She had expected to tense at that final point of no return, but she relaxed. It was easy, not so painful as she'd imagined—and then as her body tightened around him she felt her blood tingle and squeezed her eyelids tight, just focusing on all the things that were happening inside and Kamel filling her so wonderfully, Kamel moving, pushing her somewhere...

Then just as the itch got too intense to bear, she found out where she was going and let go. She heard Kamel cry out, felt the flood of his release and wrapped her legs around him, afraid that she'd be washed away, lost.

She wasn't. She finished up where she'd started, under Kamel.

Some time later she did recover the power of speech but she couldn't do full sentences.

'Wow!' she said, staring at the ceiling. Beside her, his chest heaving, Kamel was doing the same.

He turned his head. 'For a first effort, I have to say you show promise.'

This time he did not prevent her lobbing the pillow at his head, but in the subsequent tussle it ended on the floor and they ended up in a tangle of limbs.

CHAPTER NINE

WHEN HANNAH WOKE it was light and she was alone.

She felt the bed beside her—it was still warm. She gave a wistful sigh. She hadn't expected him to be there but it would have been…no, *nice* was not part of their relationship. Though yesterday she would have said the same about sex. It was crazy, in a good way, that the area of this marriage she'd thought would be hardest—that she had been dreading—turned out to be the easiest and the most pleasurable.

She gave a voluptuous sigh and smiled. It had been easy, natural, and totally incredible.

She sat up suddenly, her eyes flying wide in dawning alarm. She was assuming that it would be happening again soon and often. But what if last night wasn't going to be something that happened regularly? While she hadn't known what she was missing, celibacy had been easy—but now she did know. She gave an anxious sigh.

It would be…terrible. One night and Kamel was her drug of choice; she was a total addict.

She showered and dressed in record time, wondering if she should just come out and ask him. She was on her way to see Sarah when she literally bumped into him.

He was dressed in running shorts and a tee shirt and looked so gorgeous that she was struck dumb.

'I've been running.'

She nodded, and thought that there really was such a thing as being paralysed with lust. If she'd stayed in bed, would he have walked in? Her eyelids drooped as she imagined him peeling off his top and—

'And you are…?' he prompted.

Hannah started guiltily, the colour rushing to her cheeks. 'I'm going to see Sarah, and Olive and the puppies.'

'Sarah?'

'The cook…but she's more than that. I'll be ready for the flight.'

'I'm sure you will. See you then.'

He actually saw her much sooner. He had showered and was beginning to wade through his emails when he heard her bedroom door slam, quite loudly. A slamming door was not in itself indicative of a problem. He cut off the pointless line of speculation and focused on work. Luckily his ability to ignore distractions was almost as legendary as his reputation for zero patience for those undisciplined individuals who brought their personal lives into the workplace.

Five minutes later he closed his laptop, realising that in the interests of efficiency it would save time if he just went and checked she was all right.

He didn't ask. It was obvious she wasn't.

'What's wrong?'

Hannah stopped pacing and turned around. 'Nothing.'

He arched a brow.

'I can't tell you.' She pressed a fist to her mouth.

He walked over, removed her fist and said calmly, 'What can't you tell me?'

'I walked in on Sarah with Dad, They were...' her eyes slid towards the bed '...you know.'

Kamel blinked. 'You walked in on your father having sex with the cook?'

She covered her ears with her hands. 'Don't say it out loud!'

Kamel fought back a smile. 'It always comes as a shock to a child when they learn their parents have sex.'

'I know my father has sex. I just don't want to see it!'

This time he couldn't fight the smile. 'It's going to be tough for him—'

'No, they didn't see me. That really would be awful. No, the door was half open and...' She stopped, closed her eyes and shook her head, shuddered. 'I backed out and ran.'

'I imagine you did.' His lips quivered.

'This isn't funny,' she protested.

Unable to stop himself, Kamel began to laugh.

A laugh bubbled in her throat. 'I want to delete the image from my mind. I really do.' The laugh escaped.

Five minutes later Hannah was all laughed out, and Kamel was sprawled on the bed, one arm under his head, telling her that when he had walked in he had thought there had been some major disaster.

'Your face! Honestly it was...' He sat up and sighed. 'I should get back to it. I've got a stack of—'

'I'm sorry I stopped you working.'

He gave a sudden grin. 'No, you're not.' He patted the bed beside him and leaned back against the pillows.

Hannah came across the room, hesitating only a moment before she manoeuvred herself to sit straddling him.

'I like your thinking,' he purred, his eyes flaring hot as she pulled the top over her head. 'I like other things even more.'

'Are you all right?'

Hannah shrugged and put down the book she had been holding. Her interest in the novel was feigned but her confusion was not. 'With flying, you mean...?'

A spasm of irritation crossed his face. 'Your father and the cook? It happens—the attraction between people from different backgrounds.'

Her brow smoothed and she laughed. 'You think I didn't know? Or that I have some sort of problem with it?'

His brows lifted. 'You are telling me you don't?'

In defiance of his open scepticism, she shook her head from side to side. 'Beyond the fact that discovering that your parent has a sex life, which is a bit...uncomfortable...no, I like Sarah.'

'And the fact she is the cook?'

'I know you think I'm a snob. She's probably the best thing that has ever happened to my dad. I just wish he... I wish they'd come out into the open about it. I wish...' She caught the expression on Kamel's face and, taking it for boredom, brought her ramble to a juddering stop.

It would be a massive mistake to assume that, because Kamel had seemed to have an endless fascination with her body, his interest extended beyond the bedroom. She knew that any woman would only ever be a substitute for the woman he had lost, Amira. Kamel must have thought nothing could be worse than seeing the woman he loved happy with another man—until he'd found out that there was something much worse.

'You wish?'

I wish I could look at you and not ache. 'Forget it.'

It was sex—fantastic, incredible sex—but she had to stop thinking about it.

'I don't want to bore you.'

He unclipped his seat belt and stretched his long legs out in front of him. 'Don't worry. If you bore me I'll let you know,' he promised.

'I think that Sarah deserves more than to be a secret...' She gave a self-conscious shrug.

'Maybe this Sarah is happy with just sex.'

She looked away. Was there a message, a warning even, in there for her?

'Maybe she is,' Hannah agreed without conviction. She turned her head to angle a curious look at his face. 'You expected me to be devastated to find my father in bed with the cook, didn't you? Sarah has been my father's mistress for the past five years that I know of. Probably longer.

'The truth is I've no idea how Sarah is content to be treated like some sort of...' She stopped, wondering whether that wasn't exactly what she was doing. 'We both worry about her.'

'We?'

'Sarah's daughter, Eve, and I. She's a year younger than me.' She noticed the airstrip below and pressed her face to the window to get a better view. 'Is it far to the villa?'

'Not by helicopter.'

'Helicopter?'

He nodded. 'It beats being stuck in a traffic jam.'

That, she thought, was a matter of opinion.

As the helicopter landed Hannah closed her eyes—but even with them squeezed tightly shut she retained the stomach-clenching image of them falling directly into the ocean.

The pilot landed the helicopter smoothly but Hannah appeared oblivious, her eyes tightly shut, hands clenched into white-knuckled fists. Her lips continued to move, presumably in a silent prayer. Watching her silent but abject terror, he had felt like an inconsiderate monster for subjecting her to what had clearly been an ordeal. He wanted to be irritated with her but she looked so fragile, her big eyes reminding him of a scared child. But she wasn't a child. She was all woman—*his* woman. The reminder should have made him feel resentful— after all, he was paying the price for her stupidity—but instead the thought came with an accompanying shaft of possessive pride.

'You can breathe now.'

Hannah opened her eyes and collided instantly with Kamel's dark, intense stare. The feeling of falling into the abyss didn't go away; if anything it intensified as, with a thudding heart, she fumbled with her seat belt.

'What time is it?' she heard herself ask.

'You have somewhere you need to be, *ma belle*?' His eyes drifted to the wide, full, plump curve of her lips and he felt the barely damped fires of passion roar into life.

She was the most responsive woman he had ever had in his bed. He still couldn't get his head around the fact that the cool, distant virgin had turned out to be a warm, giving woman who held nothing back. In the middle of figuring how long he could wait until he got her into bed again he found himself wondering about the sequence of events that had led her to hide her passionate nature behind a cool mask.

He had never felt the need to look beyond the surface of a beautiful woman, and he had no intention of looking too far now.

'Relax.'

This struck Hannah as ironic advice from someone who, as far as she could tell, never totally switched off, someone who was never *totally* off duty. Duty always came first with Kamel. If it didn't, they wouldn't be married.

While Kamel was speaking to the pilot she took the opportunity to look through the glass without fear of gibbering. The helipad was not, as it had seemed, positioned perilously on the cliff's edge, but several hundred feet away, and screened from the villa by an avenue of trees. Hannah could just make out through the branches the terracotta roof, but the rest of the villa was totally concealed by the lush greenery.

Above the whirr of the blades she could hear the men's voices. She was struggling to catch what they were saying when it happened. Previously it had only occurred when she was in a small space—the lift between floors, or in the pantry in the kitchen—but now there were no walls to close in on her, just glass. Even so, the urge to escape and the struggle to breathe were equally strong.

Her knees were shaking but Hannah was so anxious to get back on terra firma that she didn't wait. She didn't wait for Kamel, who was still deep in conversation with the pilot; she just had to get out of there.

Hannah watched as her luggage was piled onto a golf cart by two men—one of whom she had almost flattened when she missed the bottom step in her anxiety to escape the helicopter. Both men nodded respectfully to Kamel and vanished through an arch cut in the neatly trimmed green foliage.

Hannah could feel Kamel's disapproval—she'd sensed it before but it had upped several notches.

'You should have said that you have a problem with helicopters.' Seeing the surprise in the blue eyes that flew to his face, he smiled. 'Yes, it was obvious.' He took one of her hands in his and turned the palm upwards, exposing the grooves her nails had cut into her palms. 'Any tenser and I think you'd have snapped. Why on earth didn't you say anything?'

'Why didn't you ask?' she countered, wishing he would release her hand, while feeling an equally strong reluctance to break the contact. His thumb was moving in circles across her palm, and each light, impersonal caress sent wave after wave of disproportionate pleasure through her body. But then there was no sense of proportion in her response to Kamel when she thought about how completely and how quickly she had given up control, and it terrified her.

She tensed as his eyes flicked from her palm to her face. 'You have a point,' he conceded. 'Should I call them back?' He gestured in the direction of the now invisible carts. 'I thought you might like to stretch your legs, but if you prefer—?'

'No, a walk would be good.' A night of mind-blowing sex might be better, though. The reciprocal warm glow in his eyes made her wonder if underneath all the politeness an alternative dialogue wasn't just going on in his own head too. But who knew what went on in the mind of a man like Kamel?

She couldn't begin to intellectualise her response to him. How could she be standing here, thinking about him ripping her clothes off?

Shocked and more than a little excited by the thought, she lowered her gaze. 'You don't have to act as though this is a real honeymoon,' she murmured. It was duty for him. And for her it was…all so new she had no name for what she was feeling. But the ferocity of it scared her. 'I know it's window dressing.' It had never crossed her mind that she could want a man's touch this badly, to the extent it was hard to think past it.

'I like touching you.'

For a shocked instant she thought she had voiced her secret longing. 'Oh!'

'The sex wasn't window dressing.'

Experiencing a wave of lust so immense she felt as though she were drowning, she closed her fingers tight around his hand. She swallowed, suddenly unable to meet his eyes, her heart thudding fast in her chest. She felt bizarrely shy. The emotion paralysed her vocal cords and brought a rosy flush to her cheeks.

'We are expected to make a baby, so why not enjoy it?'

The glow faded. Afterwards, with his duty done, would he seek his pleasure elsewhere? His life was all duty—he would probably be glad to escape it.

'It's not far to the villa,' he said as they reached the top of the incline they had been climbing.

Hannah gasped. 'It's beautiful, Kamel.'

'Yes,' he agreed. 'So, you think you might be able to stick it here for a few days?'

How few? she wondered. And what happened after that? But then she closed down that line of thought. Better to enjoy the here and now and not think too far ahead.

'I might cope.' She looked at the sugar-pink painted villa that seemed to cling to the edge of the cliff.

'I even know where the kitchen is here.'

She lifted her brows and tried to look serious but a laugh bubbled through. 'I'm more interested in the pool today.' She mimed a fanning gesture with her hand.

'That sounds good.' He withdrew the vibrating phone from his pocket and looked at the screen. 'Sorry, I might have to take a rain check on that.' You did not hang up on a king, even—or maybe especially—if that king was your uncle. 'I really have to take this. Go have an explore.'

Hannah nodded, lowering her eyes to hide the irrational stab of hurt. It was crazy to mind that she was not at the top of his priorities.

CHAPTER TEN

WHEN SHE SLID open the wardrobes that lined one wall of the dressing room and found they weren't empty, Hannah thought she was seeing an example of Kamel's famed forward thinking.

The beginnings of a frown began to form on her brow as she lifted the top item on the stack of underclothes. Size-wise—not to mention style-wise—it was really not her! A few moments later as she flicked through the row of expensive garments the frown was fully formed and it had become obvious that even Kamel did not think of everything! She felt her self-righteous anger reach new heights as she picked up the faint but distinctive scent that clung to the garments. He thought it was fine to have his wife share wardrobe space with his mistress... maybe the economy appealed to him!

She felt physically sick, but, in the grip of a masochistic urge she could not fight, Hannah stretched out a shaking hand to the neatly folded stacks of underclothes on the shelf. They were not items that could be classed utilitarian or, by any stretch of the imagination, tasteful.

Hannah pushed the lot onto the floor and, with a vengeful cry, grabbed the most tacky, glittering thing she could see. It turned out to be a gold beaded dress with a designer label, and a split so low on the back the wearer couldn't possibly have worn any underclothes.

Had she been this angry when she discovered Rob's multiple infidelities? Hannah was incapable by this point of questioning the degree of her reaction. She was incandescent with rage. Not only did she not want a second-hand G-string, she didn't want a second-hand man!

How stupid had she been to even begin to let down her guard with him, to trust him? Experience had taught her you couldn't trust a man.

Eyes flashing, back stiff, she stalked down the glass-roofed corridor that connected the more modern bedroom wing to the main house and into the open-plan living room where she had left Kamel. The room was empty but the echoing sound of her heels on the terracotta tiles drew a call from outside.

'Come have a swim!'

Responding to the invitation with narrow-eyed determination, she exited the patio doors just as Kamel levered himself from the infinity pool.

Rising in one seamless motion, he stood with the towel he had retrieved from the pool's edge in one hand, but he made no attempt to dry himself. The water continued to stream down his lean brown body, making his skin glisten like polished copper in the sun.

She caught her breath. Not even a full-blown rage could protect her from her visceral reaction to the sight of six feet four inches of dripping-wet Kamel. She was helpless to control her quivering response to the image of earthy power in his broad shoulders, deeply muscled chest, and strong thighs. She swallowed, knowing she was staring but helpless to stop herself. The moisture clinging to his skin emphasised each individual slab of

muscle in his flat washboard torso, and he didn't carry
an ounce of surplus flesh to blur the perfect muscle
definition.

Kamel was all hard, primal male; he represented a
physical male ideal combined with an earthy sexuality
that had made him a deadly combination—the perfect
lover. As she stared at him Hannah could feel her anger
slipping away, feel the heat build inside her. She sucked
in a short shocked breath, her eyes widening in disgust
with herself as she recognised what was happening.

He looped the towel around his neck and she turned
her head slightly to avoid the rippling contraction that
moved across his flat torso as he lifted his arm to drag
a hand across his wet hair.

She would *not* turn into one of those women who
put up with all sorts of crap from a man just because
he was…well…good in bed. And Kamel was, in her defence. There were probably not enough superlatives to
describe just *how* good he was! She smothered the internal sigh and thought that he'd certainly had enough
practice at it. It was not by accident they had dubbed
him The *Heartbreaker* Prince!

One corner of his sensual mouth lifted in a lazy half-
smile, but there was nothing lazy about the gleam in
his eyes. She pressed a hand to her stomach—not that
it helped to calm the fluttering.

'I think you're a little overdressed, angel,' he rasped
throatily.

The same could not be said of him. The black shorts
he wore low on his hips left little to the imagination—
and hers was rioting as she raised the level of her stare.

'There are some swimsuits in the pool house.'

She closed her mouth with a firm and audible snap.

Clutching the dress in one hand and her anger in the other, she slung him a contemptuous look that would have frozen a normal man stone dead in his tracks. The man she had married gave a here-we-go-again look and dragged some of the excess moisture from his hair with one hand, sending a shower of silver water droplets over her heated skin.

'I just bet there are, but I'm not too keen on wearing other women's cast-offs—or, for that matter, sleeping with them!'

He responded to her hostility with a long, slow, considering look. *'Right.'*

He didn't add *I see* because he didn't. When she had left him a few minutes earlier the sexual promise in her blue eyes... Well, if she hadn't left when she had, he had been within an undiplomatic hair's breadth of doing the unthinkable—slamming the phone down on his uncle with the explanation, *I need to make love to my wife.*

Acknowledging the strength of that need had been what had driven him to the pool. He hadn't spared his body—the relentless pace through the water should have left him incapable of breath, let alone lust, but the ache was still there, and now she was looking at him as though he had just been found guilty of waging a hate campaign against kittens!

He ground his teeth at the sheer, unremitting frustration of it all. He tilted his head, a dark scowl forming on his wide forehead as he fished for a word that summed up his life before Hannah had come into it. *Centred.*

At another time he might have appreciated the black irony of the situation, but at that moment, with frustrated desire clenched like a knot, the humour passed him by. He had married her, resenting both the sense of duty that made him step up and the woman herself. And now, days later, he wanted her so badly he could barely string a coherent thought together. He was utterly consumed by it.

Not his type…well, that self-delusion had lasted about five seconds! Hannah was every man's type and once you saw the woman behind the cool mask… He shook his head, his fine-tuned steel trap of a mind finding it impossible to rationalise the fascination she exerted for him, the all-consuming need he felt to possess her and to lose himself in her.

It was just sex, he told himself, recognising an uncharacteristic tendency to over-analyse in his train of thought. Why try and read anything else into it? He'd married a woman he couldn't keep his hands off. But there was always a flip side, no heaven without hell. Not only did she have the ability to stretch the boundaries of sexual pleasure, she also had the ability to drive him crazy with her mood swings.

He forced his eyes from her face to the garment in her hand. Her mood seemed out of proportion with a wardrobe malfunction. He struggled to school his features into something that conveyed an interest he did not feel—he was more interested in peeling off her clothes than discussing fashion.

'You want to show me a new dress?'

Her brows hit her hairline. He actually thought she wanted to parade around and ask his approval!

'I suppose you've never seen this before?' Her voice shook almost as much as her hand did as she held out the backless, frontless, totally tasteless garment.

Recognition clicked in his brain. 'I have.' He had

little interest in women's clothes but this one had been hard to forget—as was the evening that had gone with it.

He hadn't been the intended victim or beneficiary of the provocative number. Neither, it turned out, had Charlotte begged him to escort her to the glittering premiere for the pleasure of his company. He and the dress had been part of her revenge on her ex-husband. Bizarrely, although Charlotte had been glad to be out of her marriage, she had resented the fact her ex had moved on too—especially as the woman he had moved on to was a younger version of herself.

'You're angry.' His eyes slid down her body, over the slim curves and long, long legs. She was, he decided, totally magnificent. 'I know because your eyes turn from summer sky to stormy sea when you're mad.'

'It can work once, even twice, but I have to tell you, Kamel, that the staring-deep-into-my-eyes thing has a shelf life,' she lied. 'So don't try and change the subject.'

'What was the subject?' he asked, continuing to stare deep into her eyes, causing major and probably permanent damage to her frazzled nervous system.

'Your girlfriend's choice of clothes. Oh, incidentally, I'm *totally* fine with sharing my wardrobe space with your harem, though I have to tell you that they are not my size!'

'I know,' he said, his fingertips twitching as he transferred his stare to Hannah's heaving breasts. They fitted almost perfectly into his palms, soft, firm and… He took a deep swallow and lifted his gaze. 'Charlotte has had help in that area. They were, I believe, an engagement present from her ex.'

Her chin went up as she enquired in a deceptively soft voice, 'Are you suggesting I need help in that area?'

The icy question drew a low smoky laugh from him. 'You are *perfect* in that area.' The humour faded from his face, leaving a restless hunger. She was perfect. His perfect lover.

The hunger in his stare as much as his flattering words brought hot colour flying to her cheeks. But this heat was mild compared to the surge of sexual warmth that settled deep in her pelvis and spread. Her mask of disdain was rice-paper thin as she gave a sniff and tossed her head.

'I have no interest,' she informed him icily. 'Not in what your idea of perfect is, or the surgical procedures your girlfriend has had, or who paid for them.' Her haughty delivery vanished as the strength of her feelings became impossible to disguise. 'I just have an interest in being treated with a modicum, a bare *modicum* of respect while we are sharing a—' on the brink of saying bed, she stopped herself; the chain of thought already set in motion was less easy to stall '—roof!' she improvised, seeing his muscled body sleek with sweat, his face taut in a mask of need.

'I'm sorry you were upset. I gave instructions for the room to be cleared.'

'*Cleared!*' she parroted, her face twisted in an ironic grimace of disgust. 'I would have thought *fumigated* would have been more appropriate when we're talking about the sort of woman who would wear this!' She directed a look of lip-curling distaste at the garment, which was a perfect example of the adage money couldn't buy class.

'Don't you think you're overreacting to what is, after

all, a simple housekeeping error? I'll speak to someone and it won't happen again.'

'You mean the next time your girlfriend leaves her clothes you'll have them tidied away *before* I arrive? My God,' she flung with sarcastic appreciation. 'I'm one hell of a lucky woman to have married such a considerate man.'

'I will not be seeing Charlotte again.' Though the lady had made it quite clear that she did not see marriage as an obstacle to continuing their relationship.

'I do not want to know her name.' Or hear how good she is in bed, Hannah thought, experiencing a wave of jealousy that felt like a knife between her ribs. She paled and lifted her hands to her ears, squeezing her eyes shut.

Unfortunately neither action blotted out the knowledge that there would be women in slutty outfits sharing his bed in the future. They just wouldn't be called Charlotte.

She drew in a deep shuddering breath, her temper reaching boiling point in the time it took her to drag air into her lungs. 'So you think I'm *overreacting*?' she quivered incredulously. 'I'm curious—are you *trying* to be an insensitive, hateful slob?'

I'm curious—are you trying to look like a tart?

Kamel laughed as he recalled his response to Charlotte in the dress his bride held in a death grip. But then he saw Hannah's face. 'I'm not laughing at you.'

'Oh, you're laughing with me. I feel *so* much better.'

His jaw clenched as he fought to contain his increasing irritation. Sexual frustration had already eaten deep chunks out of his self-control without his dealing with her emotional antics. He took a deep breath and decided he would rise above it and be reasonable, even if she wasn't!

'I wasn't thinking about you. I was thinking about Charlotte.'

If Kamel ever found himself faced with an angry and unreasonable woman he generally removed himself from that scene. By choice he avoided women likely to indulge in scenes, but you couldn't always tell and it paid to have a plan B.

He should have walked. She was asking him to explain his actions, and no woman had ever done that.

Looking into her eyes was like staring straight into a storm. Though storms were preferable to thinking too much about the flash of desperate hurt he had seen in those shimmering depths. Crazily, of all the emotions he was struggling to contain the one that rose to the surface—the compelling urge to wipe that hurt away. It made no sense. It had been her decision to enact a Greek tragedy when given the same circumstances most women would have chosen to tactfully ignore it.

'Look. I'm sorry that the room was not cleared. I'll have t—'

'You're crazy if you think I am going to sleep in that bedroom with you!'

His jaw tightened. 'You know something? I'm starting to feel quite nostalgic for Hannah the ice queen.' He jammed his thumbs into the waistband of his shorts and glared at her. 'Just what is your problem, anyway? I had a sex life before we were married.' He lifted one shoulder in a half-shrug. 'Having sex does not make me some sort of weird pervert. Most people would think that it makes me a lot more normal than a woman who is so uptight and controlling that she saves herself for marriage.'

'So now I'm not normal? Well, let me ease your mind on one thing. I sure as hell wasn't waiting for you!'

'And yet, you can't get enough of me in bed.'

'It's the novelty value.'

He clenched his teeth and glared at the gold gown in her hands. 'Give me that damned thing.'

She looked into his dark eyes and felt the answering passions surface. Heart thudding like a trip hammer, she ignored the hand extended to her and shook her head.

'You're being very childish. I have had other women. This can hardly be a surprise to you.'

Of course it wasn't—so why the hell was she acting like this?

'I don't give a damn about your girlfriends!' she contended, snapping her fingers to show how little she cared. 'You can have a damned harem for all I care!'

'I'm glad you explained that. So *this*—' his hand sketched a toe-to-head line in the air '—is someone who doesn't care a jot? If you hadn't explained I might,' he drawled, 'have thought it was jealousy.'

Her reaction to the suggestion was dramatic. The colour that had flooded her face receded, leaving her eyes a deep well of colour.

'This isn't jealousy,' she denied, trying desperately to think of an alternative and failing. 'This is wanting to be treated with respect.'

'Am I asking you to hide in the damned shadows?' The woman, he decided, took irrationality to new uncharted levels. 'This has gone on long enough. Hand it over.'

He caught the hem of the dress and Hannah responded with teeth-gritting determination, pulling it into her chest with such force she heard the sound of fabric tearing. She was clinging on so hard that when he pulled the dress she came with it.

To absorb the impact of her soft body into his, Kamel took an automatic step back and felt his foot hit the edge of the pool just as Hannah lifted her gaze.

She saw the intent gleaming in his dark eyes and shook her head. 'You wouldn't!'

His smile was answer enough.

She hit the water yelling a warning and spluttered as the water filled her nose and throat. His arm was wrapped around her waist as they both surfaced. When the water cleared from her eyes she saw he was laughing. She opened her mouth and Kamel pressed a hard kiss to it before he let go, kicking away from her.

She lifted a hand to her mouth. Thinking only of the kiss and not the fact there were several feet of water beneath her feet, she stopped treading water to stay afloat.

He waited for her to surface, breathless and angry and still, amazingly, clutching the damned dress.

'I'm drowning.'

'No, you're not.' Flipping onto his back, he kicked lazily away from her, still maintaining eye contact.

He was utterly heartless. She hit at the water surface angrily, sending a spray of silver droplets his way. None reached him, and she struck out towards him. Hannah was a reasonable swimmer but her efforts were severely hampered by her sodden clothes, and after a couple of feet she was puffing and panting.

'Stand up.'

Easy for him to say—he was ten feet tall! Cautiously she put a foot down. Her toe found the bottom, and, bouncing along for another few feet, she finally risked attempting to follow his advice.

The water reached her shoulder but it only reached Kamel's waist. He looked like a glistening statue—if cool stone had been capable of oozing the sort of restless vitality he projected. Kamel was not stone or cold. 'You did that deliberately!' she charged, focusing on her fury and not on his body—at least that was the aim.

When the sexiest man on the planet was standing there dripping wet and gorgeous it was hard to ignore.

He shrugged, fixing her with a gleaming amused gaze. 'What can I say? The temptation...' His voice trailed away as his glance dropped. The immersion had left her shirt plastered to her body; the lacy outline of her bra was clearly visible, as were the thrusting projections of her nipples. Heat pooled in his groin and the laughter faded from his heavy-lidded eyes as in his mind he saw himself drawing the ruched rosy peak into his mouth and heard her hoarse cry. He took a step towards her.

'Get away from me!' Refusing to recognise the heart-pounding excitement that made her feel light-headed, she banged the water with the heel of her hand in warning.

His response was a predatory smile. Holding out a hand to ward him off, she took a staggering step backwards and immediately sank beneath the surface. Floating on her back, kicking to stay afloat safely out of reach, she glared at him with eyes several shades deeper than the glittering water.

'That was so childish!' she accused, finding her feet again and stepping into marginally shallower water. 'I could have drowned—you'd have liked that.'

He arched a satiric brow. '*Me*, childish?'

Hannah blinked back at him, an expression of shock filtering into her eyes as their glances connected and locked. Her jaw dropped and her eyes widened as she thought, He's right. Who was the person who had charged in all guns blazing? She turned her glance downwards over her drenched clothes, and felt the clutch of cold, horrified embarrassment in her stomach. This wasn't her. She lifted her eyes, saw the way he was looking at her, and the cold in her belly turned hot and liquid.

'You're right. It is me!' she yelled. The discovery was liberating.

Kamel didn't have a clue what she was talking about and he didn't ask, because she was churning the water, windmilling her hands, sending as much spray over herself as him—and he reciprocated.

Hannah threw herself into the exertion and was not even aware of the point when she began to cry. Blinded by the spray, she didn't realise until her arms and shoulders got too tired to retaliate that Kamel had stopped splashing and he was standing right there, toe to toe with her.

The sun and the water droplets on her lashes gave a shimmering effect to his dark outline.

Everything seemed to slow, even her heartbeat. Her throat closed over, then she stopped breathing completely. She closed her eyes and felt his finger on her cheek. Leaking control from every pore, she opened her eyes. The sexual tension humming in the air had a stronger physical presence than the Mediterranean sun burning down on them.

'Are you crying?'

She shook her head, and wondered how he could tell.

'Come here!' he growled.

Afterwards, Hannah had no clue whether she stepped into him or whether he pulled her into his arms. All she knew was that it felt gloriously right to be there. His dark, hot eyes made her feel light-headed but she couldn't look away as he brushed the strands of wet hair away from her face. She couldn't take her eyes off him.

Kamel watched through eyes narrowed against the sun as the sparkling defiance faded from her blue eyes. He saw the hot glaze of desire drift in, and heard the husky little catch as she drew in a shuddering sigh and reached for his hand—not to pull it away, but to hold it there.

Kamel felt a rise of unfamiliar emotion as he looked down at her, and his fingers tightened around the slim ones that were entwined within his. He felt her shiver and frowned.

'You're cold.'

She shook her head. Turning her face into his palm, she felt anything but cold—she was burning from the inside out. She let out a gasp as Kamel dragged her into his body; the hard imprint of his erection against the softness of her belly drew another gasp, this one fractured. Her hands slid around the nape of his neck into his dark hair.

'Can I be of—?'

Kamel swore and cut across Rafiq's enquiry. 'No, we are fine. That will be all.'

The man bowed and melted away.

'You have a beautiful mouth,' she said, staring dreamily at the sculpted outline.

Kamel's face was a rigid mask of driven need as he

brought his beautiful mouth crashing hungrily down
on her soft, parted lips. Hannah's mind blanked as she
went limp in his arms, giving herself over completely
to the hungry, sensual onslaught of his deep, draining
kisses. It felt as though he would drink her dry and she
didn't mind one bit. She wanted it.

They were both breathing like sprinters crossing the
line when he lifted his head. 'I can't get enough of you,'
he confessed huskily.

'You make it sound like a bad thing,' she whispered.

He stroked her face, pulling her in even closer, feeling her breathing become more ragged as he let her feel
how much he wanted her. 'Does that feel bad?' he asked.

'Oh, God, Kamel!' It was agony to be this close and
yet not close enough, not nearly close enough. 'I feel…
you're…' Her moan was lost inside his mouth.

It wasn't until they reached the edge of the pool and
she saw her shirt floating on the water that Hannah realised that she was naked from the waist up.

How did that happen? She didn't spend long wondering. Consumed by an elemental hunger that allowed no
room for thought, just feeling—layer and layer of hot
feeling!—she plastered her aching, swollen breasts up
hard against his chest and wound her legs tight around
his waist, almost lifting herself clear of the water as
she probed Kamel's mouth with her tongue, drawing a
deep groan from his throat.

'Just hold on…let me…' He unwound her hands
from around his neck, breaking the tenacious grip as
he pushed her away from him.

'No…!' She opened her eyes and collided head-on
with the heat in his.

Evading the hands that grabbed for him, Kamel

spanned her waist with his hands and lifted her out of the water onto the edge of the pool. A moment later he was beside her, pulling her to her feet.

He lifted her into his arms and began to stride off— not in the direction of the villa, but the grassy area where a tree-lined stream ran through the sloping mani-cured lawn towards the deep forested area that bordered three sides of the property.

'We can't here…someone will see,' she protested half-heartedly.

'This is a paparazzi-free zone, I promise.'

'I wasn't thinking of intruders. People work here.'

She admired his confidence, and because he was kissing her like a starving man she allowed herself to be convinced by it. The simple truth was that she couldn't have stopped even if she had wanted to. And she didn't.

The grass he laid her on was soft against the bare skin of her back; the sun shining through the leafy can-opy above left a dappled pattern on her skin. She lay breathing hard, one arm curved above her head, and anticipation made her stomach muscles quiver as he knelt beside her.

He bent forward, his body curving over hers, every muscle in his body pulled taut as he allowed the image to imprint on his retinas. It was one he knew would stay with him. The hectic flush of arousal on her cheeks, the wanton invitation that curled her soft full lips up-wards—she was sinful temptation personified and it would take a stronger man than he was to resist.

Kamel had no intention of resisting; he just wanted to claim what was his, driven by primitive instincts as old as man.

He could feel her eyes on him as he slid the saturated

skirt down her hips. His actions were made clumsy by the urgency that burned in his blood and the thin threads of lace on the tiny pants snapped as he tried to free her of the bondage.

Stripped of everything, her body was smooth and pale—so perfect that he couldn't breathe. He touched her breasts, running his thumbs across the tight peaks before he cupped them in his big hands.

Hannah closed her eyes, focusing everything on the sensation as he ran his hands over the smooth curve of her stomach, feeling the light calluses on his palms.

She raised her arms, reaching out towards him.

Eyes blazing with a need that made him shake, he knelt astride her, then, holding her eyes, he parted her thighs. Her skin was cool to the touch but inside she was hot. He closed his eyes and thrust in deeply, not holding back as he felt her hotness, her wetness close around him.

He ran a hand down her smooth thigh. 'Hold me now.'

Her long legs wrapped around him, locking around his waist to hold him as they pushed together towards a release that left them both breathless.

As Hannah gasped her way to cogent thought one surfaced, rising above the others, swirling in her pleasure-soaked brain. For that, she would do *anything*.

Even share him?

Everything in her said that was wrong. Self-disgust curled in the pit of her stomach.

But what was the alternative? Could there be room for compromise?

'I understand that there will be women.' The truth

hurt, but she had to be grown up about this. 'I suppose I should not have reacted. If you—'

'Do not say it.' The cool command cut across her hesitant voice. 'I do not need your blessing to sleep with other women.'

She sucked in a taut breath. 'I know you don't need my permission,' she admitted unhappily.

He lifted his head from her breast, struggling against outrage even though a short time ago he would have welcomed her adult attitude. 'Only you could say something like that at a time like this. I am not thinking about other women every second of the day. I am thinking of you. And right now I am thinking of doing this again in bed. Would you prefer to talk or make a baby?'

'But I thought you wanted—'

'How could I know what I want when you insist on telling me? Come with me and I will tell you what I want.'

'That's a plan,' she agreed faintly.

CHAPTER ELEVEN

IT WAS ON the second night of their honeymoon that the telephone rang in the middle of the night. Kamel shifted her off his dead arm and reached for the phone with the other.

'I have to go.'

'What's wrong?'

Kamel put the phone back on the hook. Under his tan he was ashen.

'Your uncle?'

He shook his head. 'No, not that, thank God.'

She was relieved for his sake. She knew how fond Kamel was of his uncle and had also worked out from a few things he had said that he was in no hurry to take the throne. In fact, she had the impression that Kamel inexplicably thought he was not good enough to fill his cousin's shoes.

The few times Kamel had mentioned his cousin, the qualities he said he had possessed—the ones that made him the perfect heir apparent—were qualities that Kamel had too, in abundance!

'There has been an earthquake.'

Hannah gasped.

'Rafiq will stay here with you.'

'Good luck and take care,' she said, struggling to keep her emotions low-key but wishing he had asked her to come with him.

'It's on occasions like this that my uncle must feel the loss of Hakim. It was so senseless. It will never make any sense. He had the ability to—'

Hannah could no longer hold her tongue. 'I'm sure your cousin was a great guy and it's desperately sad he is gone, but I'm damned sure he wasn't perfect. If he had been, he wouldn't have stolen the woman you loved! You're as good as he was any day of the week! Your uncle is lucky to have someone so dedicated.'

There was a long silence, finally broken by his slow drawl.

'So the gossips have been talking? I suppose that was to be expected. Well, one thing they didn't tell you is the difference between me and Hakim is that he *wanted* to be the king. I hate the idea. And he had Amira beside him for support and that made all the difference for him.' Kamel found that lately he was able to think about their incredible devotion to one another without feeling bitter or jealous. It was one burden he no longer carried.

She gasped as though he had struck her and glanced down expecting to see a blade protruding from between her ribs. 'And you have me.'

'Don't worry,' he said, totally misinterpreting her re-action and her flat tone. 'I'm not expecting you to hold my hand.' He paused and cleared his throat. 'Amira was brought up to this life, and she knew the pressures.'

Unable to see the desperate pain and longing she knew would be in his face, Hannah looked away, hear-ing Raini's words in her head. *A beautiful queen.*

'I may not understand being royal,' she admitted quietly, 'but I do understand that, even though you hate it...' she lifted her gaze to his face and gave a quick smile '...you still put everything into it. That makes you someone who will make a great king one day.' Under the rather intense scrutiny of his dark eyes, she coloured. 'A king should have a level of arrogance that would be unacceptable in any other job.'

This drew a laugh from Kamel, who dropped a kiss on her mouth. Their lips clung...for how many seconds she didn't know, but it was long enough for Hannah to know she had fallen in love. And the man she loved would only ever see her as a pale imitation of the love of his life.

A little over a month after the earthquake, which had not actually caused any loss of life but had flattened a power plant, Hannah was breakfasting alone. She was in no hurry, as the ribbon-cutting ceremony for the opening of a new school had been unexpectedly postponed. When she'd asked why, her secretary had been strangely evasive, but then she was probably reading things into the situation that weren't there.

Like today—just because no one had remembered her birthday didn't mean that she had no friends, that nobody would miss her if she weren't there.

Struggling to divert the self-pitying direction of her thoughts, she picked up her fork and toyed with the smoked salmon and fluffy scrambled egg on her plate. It looked delicious, it smelt delicious, but she was not hungry. Her lack of hunger had nothing whatever to do with the fact it was her birthday and nobody had remembered. Actually, there had been other days this week when she had not been able to face breakfast.

She put down her fork and reminded herself that she was not a child. Birthdays no longer had the same importance, though even last year her father, who always made a fuss of her, despite the memories the day brought back for him—or perhaps because of them—had invited her friends for a pamper spa day. Hannah had known but she had pretended to be surprised.

Practically speaking you could hardly have a spa day with friends who were hundreds of miles away—and her father, it seemed, had forgotten. Out of sight, out of mind? She had rung him two nights on the run and he hadn't picked up or responded to her text messages. Presumably he had decided she was Kamel's problem now. And Kamel had left their bed at some unearthly hour. She had barely been able to open her eyes when he had kissed her and said, 'See you later.'

'How later?' she had muttered, wondering how he managed to expend so much energy during the night and still look fresh and dynamic in the morning. Would she have traded a fresh morning face for the nights of shared passion? Hannah hadn't even asked herself the question. It was a no-brainer.

The prospect of lying in Kamel's arms at night was what made the long and sometimes exhausting days bearable. It had been a steep learning curve and a shock to find herself with a personal secretary and a diary of official engagements. And part of the problem was of her own making. Initially, despite being advised to be cautious by her advisor, Hannah had agreed to lend her name to any worthy cause that approached her. Now she was snowed under by obligations to promote the numerous good causes she had lent her name to, and had been forced to be a little more discriminating.

Not only had she learnt her own life was not to be one of leisure, she had stopped thinking of Kamel's life as one of glitter and self-indulgence. He worked harder than anyone she had ever known, and as for glamour— some of what he was called upon to do was mind-numbingly boring and the flip side of that was the delicate tightrope of diplomacy he trod when he negotiated with men of power and influence.

He never complained, and she never told him how much she admired him. He had never mentioned Amira again but she was still there, the silent invisible presence. They could close the door on the rest of the world at the end of the day, but not his dead love. She was a constant. A perfect ideal that Hannah knew she could never live up to. She also worried about what would happen when those forbidden words slipped out in a moment of passion—so she really struggled to stay in control when they made love. Maybe Kamel guessed what she was doing because sometimes he looked at her oddly.

How would he react? she wondered, picking up her coffee cup. She had taken a sip from the cup before she saw what was concealed behind it: a gold-embossed envelope with her name inscribed in a bold familiar print across it.

She slopped coffee on the pristine white cloth in her haste to tear it open. It did not take long to read the message on the card inside.

Your birthday present is in the kitchen.

He knew it was her birthday and he'd bought her something! Like the child she no longer was, she leapt to her feet with a whoop of delight.

The private jet stood idling. Bad weather had delayed Kamel's flight. These things happened, and there was always a choice. A man could stress about a situation that was outside his control, fret and fume, and metaphorically or possibly literally bang his head against a brick wall.

Or he could not.

Kamel saved his energy for situations he could influence, but today he had struggled to retain this philosophical outlook. By the time his car drove through the palace gates it was almost midnight and he was in a state of teeth-clenching impatience.

He had bought women presents before, typically expensive baubles, and he took their appreciation for granted. The bauble he had bought Hannah had been in a different class. News of the record-breaking price it had fetched at auction had made the news headlines.

It had been a fortnight ago, the same night that Kamel, who normally worked in his office after dinner, had found himself wondering what Hannah did while he worked. He spent each and every night with her, he saw her in the morning and her personal secretary told him what her schedule was for the day. Sometimes they ate together in the evening but after that...? It had not previously occurred to him to wonder what she did with herself in the evenings.

So he asked.

'The princess takes a walk and usually spends some time in the small salon. She enjoys watching television.'

'Television?'

Rafiq nodded. 'I believe she follows a cookery programme. Sometimes she reads…' Without any change
of expression, he had somehow managed to sound reproachful as he added, 'I think she might be lonely.'

'That will be all.' Only a long relationship and a respect for the older man stopped him saying more, but
Kamel was incensed that his employee should think
it came within his remit to tell him he was neglecting
his wife!

If she was lonely, all she had to do was tell him. The
trouble was that she had no sense, and could not accept advice. She had taken on an excessive workload,
despite his giving her secretary explicit instructions to
keep her duties light. She had ignored him, she had…
His anger left him without warning, leaving him exposed to the inescapable fact that he had been guilty
of neglect. Outside the bedroom he actively avoided
her. But then logically if they were to be parents there
would, for the child's sake, need to be some sort of mutual understanding outside the bedroom.

Lonely. A long way from home and anyone she knew,
living in a totally foreign environment by a set of rules
that were alien to her. And Kamel had needed someone to tell him that?

She hadn't complained and he had been happy and
even relieved to take her seeming contentment at face
value. Determined to make up for his neglect, he had
gone to see for himself, but any expectation of discovering a forlorn figure had vanished when he'd walked
into the small salon and found Hannah sitting cross-
legged on a sofa giggling helplessly at the screen. She
seemed surprised to see him but not interested enough

to give him all her attention. Most of that remained on the television. Of course, it was a relief to discover she didn't need him to entertain her.

'A comedy?' He sat on the sofa arm and looked around. The room was one that he rarely entered but he recognised there had been some changes. Not just the television and bright cushions, but where a large oil painting had stood there was now a row of moody monochrome framed photographs of rugged mountain landscapes.

On the desk there was a piece of driftwood and some shells beside an untidy stack of well-thumbed paperback novels.

Hannah caught him looking. 'The painting made me depressed and the other stuff is in a cupboard somewhere.'

'What a relief. I thought you might have pawned it.'

She looked at him as though she couldn't decide if he was joking or not. 'Do not let me interrupt your comedy.'

'It's a cookery competition. His sponge sank.'

'And that is good?'

She slung him a pitying look and shook her head. 'If he doesn't pull it out of the bag with his choux buns he's out.'

Kamel had stayed, not because he found the competitive side of baking entertaining, but because he found Hannah's enjoyment contagious. She was riveting viewing. It fascinated him to watch her face while she willed on her favourite, the sound of her throaty chuckle was entrancing, and her scolding of a contestant who, as she put it, *bottled it*, made him laugh.

When the programme finished he was sitting beside

her, sharing the sofa, and it was too late to go back to work. So he accepted her suggestion of a second glass of wine and watched a documentary with her. It was then he discovered that Hannah, renowned for her icy control, cried easily and laughed even more easily. Her aloof mask concealed someone who was warm, spontaneous and frighteningly emotional.

She had been pretending to be someone she wasn't for so long that he wondered if she remembered why she had developed the mask. But then his research into the subject had said that dyslexics developed coping mechanisms.

After that first evening it had become a habit for him to break from work a little earlier and join her. On the night he had taken receipt of her birthday gift he had cut his evening work completely and when he'd entered the salon had been feeling quite pleased with himself as he'd contemplated her reaction when she opened her gift the following week.

'No cookery programme?'

'No,' she'd snuffled, looking up at him through suspiciously red eyes. 'It's too early. This is an appeal for the famine.'

The appeal had been followed by a news programme where the headline was not the famine but an item on the diamond purchased at auction by an anonymous buyer and the record-breaking price it had achieved.

When she'd expressed her condemnation of a society where the values were so skewed that people put a higher price on a shiny jewel than they did on children's lives, he'd agreed wholeheartedly with her view before going away to pass the ring he'd bought for her on to the next highest bidder, and to make a sizeable donation to the famine appeal. He'd then spent the rest of the evening wrestling with the problem of what the hell to buy for the woman who could have everything and didn't want it!

For a man who had never put any thought into a gift beyond signing a cheque it had not been easy, but he considered his solution inspired.

Would Hannah?

At some point he would have to ask himself why pleasing her mattered so much to him, but that remained a question for tomorrow. Today things were going rather well. This marriage could have been a total disaster but it wasn't.

The sound of music as he walked into the apartment drew him to the salon. A soft, sexy ballad was playing. The room was empty but the doors of the balcony were open and the dining table there was laid for two, with red roses and candles. The roses were drooping, the candles in the silver candelabra had burnt down, spilling wax on the table, and the champagne in the ice bucket was empty, as were the plates.

He was making sense of the scene when Rafiq appeared.

'Where?'

'I believe they are in the kitchen.'

'They?'

'The chef is still here.'

Rafiq opened the kitchen door, but neither his wife nor the celebrity chef he had flown in to give her a day's one-to-one teaching session heard him. Could that have had something to do with the open bottle of wine and two glasses on the table?

Or the fact they were having a great time? The guy with his fake smile and spray tan was relating an incident with enough name-dropping to make the most committed social climber wince.

Hannah wasn't wincing, though, she was eating it up, with her amazed gasps and impressed ahhs.

Well, she wasn't lonely, and she certainly wasn't missing him.

Scowling, he tugged at his tie and walked inside. He was paying the man to give his wife cooking lessons. He could manage the other things himself.

'Happy birthday.'

At the sound of the voice she had been waiting to hear all evening, Hannah's head turned. She started to her feet just in time, restraining the impulse to fling herself at him.

To his mind, her reaction had all the hallmarks of guilt.

'Have you had a good day?' His eyes slid to the chef, who had risen slowly to his feet.

'Yes, thank you.'

Her response and her demure, hand-clasped attitude reminded him of a child summoned to the headmaster's study, and he felt his temper rise.

'I made us a meal but you—'

'You missed a great meal, really great. This girl is a talent.'

'The girl is my wife.' Kamel had spent the day being pleasant to idiots but enough was enough.

'Hannah is a great pupil. Really talented.'

'Yes, you mentioned that. Well, thank you for stepping into the breach, but I would like to say happy birthday to my wife—alone. Shall I have someone show you to your room or can you—?'

'I'll be fine. Goodnight, all.'

The door closed and Hannah gave a sigh of relief. 'Thank goodness for that.'

Her reaction sent his antagonism down several levels.

'You did not enjoy your birthday present?'

'It was the best birthday present I have ever had! It was fine before he started drinking and then…' She shook her head. 'He kept telling the same story over and over and I couldn't get rid of him. Thank goodness you came when you did. I was ready to hide in the pantry, but at least it stopped me brooding. Dad didn't call. I hope he's all right. Some years he is worse than others,' she admitted, worriedly.

Kamel shook his head. *'Worse?'*

'Sorry, I was talking as if you knew.'

Kamel struggled to contain his frustration. He had to drag every bit of information out of her. 'I would like to know.'

'My mother died when I was born. Well, actually she died a few weeks earlier. She was brain dead but they kept her alive until I was strong enough to be delivered. Dad stayed by her side night and day all that time and when I was born they switched off the life support. It's hardly any wonder it was months before he could even look at me. If it hadn't been for me she'd be alive.'

The fist around his heart tightened as she raised her swimming blue eyes to him.

'Your father doesn't blame you for your mother's death.' No father could do that to an innocent child. It was more likely, knowing Hannah, that she blamed herself. How had he ever thought this woman was self-ish and shallow?

'Well, if he did I guess he's been trying to make up for it ever since by spoiling me rotten. I wish he'd ring.'

'Your father will be fine.'

Hannah nodded and stood there noticing the lines of fatigue etched into his face. Presumably he'd had a bad day—the same bad day that was responsible for the air of menace he had been radiating when he'd walked in. He'd made her think of a big panther, all leashed violence and tension.

'Come here.'

The rough invitation and the glow in his eyes made her tummy flip. 'Why?'

'I want to make up for missing your birthday.' He wanted to make up for every moment of pain in her life.

'What did you have in min—?' She let out a shriek as he scooped her up into his arms. 'What are you doing?'

He kicked open the door and grinned. 'I am taking you upstairs to give you the rest of your birthday present. It might,' he added, his eyes darkening as they swept her face, 'take some time.'

CHAPTER TWELVE

HANNAH KICKED OFF her shoes as she walked into the bedroom. Kamel stood, his shoulders propped against the door jamb, and watched as she sat at the dressing table and struggled with the clasp of the sapphire necklace she wore.

He had never imagined that the nape of a woman's neck could be erotic, but he had to accept that some of life's normal rules did not apply where his wife was concerned. When she had walked into the room at his side tonight, making him think of a graceful swan in her slim-fitting white gown, she had been literally shaking with fear but nobody would have guessed as she smiled and charmed everyone present at the formal state dinner.

The fierce pride he had felt as he had watched her across the table, graceful and lovely, had only been matched in the emotional stakes by the rush of protectiveness he had experienced when, during the press-the-flesh session following the formal banquet, when those who were being rewarded for good works got a chance to meet the royals, Hannah's interest in the diverse range of people who lined up to shake her hand had seemed real—as had the fear in her eyes when she had seen the Quagani colonel. The moment had passed and she had recovered her poise, but Kamel had kept an eye on the man. Diplomatic incident or not, he was poised to throw the guy out personally if he so much as looked at Hannah the wrong way.

In the event he had seemed to behave himself. Even so, Kamel intended to make damned sure that in the future their favourite cuddly colonel had his card marked when it came to entry into this country.

'Let me.'

She looked at him in the mirror, unable to disguise the shiver of pleasure as his fingers brushed her neck.

'Thank you,' she said, looking at him through her lashes with eyes that shone brighter than the gems he was removing.

He paused. She seemed about to say something but then, as if she had changed her mind, she tipped her head in acknowledgement as he dropped the necklace into her hand.

'You did well tonight.'

The comment smoothed the small groove in Hannah's brow and she released the sigh she'd felt she had been holding in all night. 'So I passed?'

He didn't return her smile. 'Is that how you saw tonight? As a test?' The idea troubled him. 'You're not being graded, Hannah. No one is judging you.'

Hannah shrugged. She had been here long enough to learn a little of the politics of the place, and she knew that she was resented in certain quarters. More than a few people were just waiting for her to mess up. She would never be Amira, but she was determined to prove them all wrong.

'Especially not me.'

Whatever trust issues he had with Hannah had long gone. He often watched her—which was not exactly a hardship—and found himself wondering how he had ever even for a second thought she was a cold, spoilt bitch!

He was not a man who looked deep inside himself, maybe because he knew that he wouldn't have liked what he'd have seen.

He'd once told Hannah to lose the attitude, but now he saw that it was advice he ought to have been directing at himself. He'd seen marriage as a life sentence the moment when the doors slammed shut. He had not faced his resentment of the role that had been thrust on him. Hannah had made him do that.

He'd never for one second thought that marriage might be better than the life he'd had to let go. He'd put so much effort into seeing himself as someone who had missed out on the chance of happiness when he had lost Amira that when it had fallen at his feet he'd not recognised it.

And yet there was a cloud. Hannah welcomed him into her bed but he sensed a new restraint in her. She was holding back. On more than one occasion he had nearly demanded to know what the hell was the matter—but he'd stopped himself. What if she told him and he didn't like the answer?

His quiet admission that he hadn't been judging her made her throat ache with unshed tears.

'I was dreading it,' she admitted.

'I know.'

'It was strange sitting next to the man who once held my fate in his hands.' Protocol dictated that she was seated next to the daunting Sheikh Malek. 'He could have signed my death warrant.'

'No!'

The explosive interjection made her pause and touch his hand. His fingers unclenched under the light pressure. 'Tonight he was telling me about his rose collection. He invited me to a tour of his rose gardens.'

Kamel let out a silent whistle as he brought his hands up to rest on her shoulders. 'You're honoured. I haven't made that invite yet. It's the hottest ticket in town, I promise you.'

He bent his head and Hannah closed her eyes, but the anticipated kiss did not arrive on her waiting lips. With a disgruntled little frown between her feathery brows, she opened her eyes and saw him digging into the pocket of his jacket.

'I almost forgot. This is yours, I believe.'

Her frown deepened as she shook her head and looked at the small fat brown envelope he held. 'It's not mine.'

He turned it over. 'Well, it's got your name on the front.'

Sliding her finger under the sealed flap, she split it open and angled a questioning look up at him, suspecting this was Kamel's way of delivering a surprise. 'There's no celebrity chef hiding inside, is there?'

Kamel responded to the teasing with a lopsided grin. 'The man's ego wouldn't fit into this room, let alone an envelope.'

Hannah turned the parcel around, feeling an odd reluctance suddenly to open it. 'Where did it come from?'

'Someone saw you drop it, handed it to someone who passed it on to me. I assumed it fell out of your bag.'

Her lips quirked into an amused smile. 'My bag will just about hold a lipstick.'

Her explanation drew a puzzled look. 'Then why carry it?'

'Only a man would ask that question.'

'What is it?' he asked as she tipped the contents of the envelope onto the dressing table.

'I've no idea,' she admitted, staring as several photos clipped together fell out, then, after another shake, a card. 'It says here that…' She read the logo on top of the card and her brows lifted. 'Private investigator!'

Kamel picked up the photos. He did not look beyond the one on the top. A muscle in his lean cheek clenched.

'What's wrong?' she asked, struggling to read his shuttered expression.

'See for yourself.' He slid the clip off the bundle and fanned them out, playing-card style, on the surface in front of her.

Hannah accepted the invitation, and the nausea she had been feeling intermittently all evening resurfaced with a vengeance. There were two people in each grainy print and, even though they had clearly been taken using a telephoto lens and there was some graininess, there was no mistaking one at least of the faces…or the body.

Kamel's mouth twisted in distaste.

'I thought we had all of these.'

Of course, once images made their way onto the Internet they were there for ever, but the person who had taken these had been refreshingly pragmatic. The only thing he'd been interested in was money, not causing embarrassment.

'You knew about these?' She held a clenched fist to her pale lips.

'These were taken long before we were married. You do know that, don't you?' He could have pointed out that the dress she was wearing—when she was wearing one—was the gold number that had been the trigger for their poolside tussle. But he shouldn't have to.

He had not needed to ask Hannah if she had employed a private investigator; he knew she hadn't. He recognised this for what it was—a rather obvious and malicious attempt at mischief-making, one that could only work in a marriage where there was a lack of trust that could be exploited.

'Do you believe me, Hannah? Do you trust me?'

Saying she did amounted to an admission that she loved him. Was she ready to make it?

The realisation that she was came hand in hand with the even stronger realisation that if she didn't move fast she was going to throw up all over his shiny shoes.

She threw him an agonised look, then dashed to the bathroom with her hand pressed to her lips, and slammed the door in his face.

When she finished being violently sick, Hannah got weakly to her feet and washed her face. A look in the mirror told her she looked like death warmed up. She went back into the bedroom.

She squared her shoulders and opened the door. It was time she manned up and came clean. She would tell him that, not only did she trust his word, she trusted him with her life and that of their unborn baby.

She curved a protective hand over her flat belly and whispered, 'Here goes.'

It was empty.

The anticlimax was intense, but it only lasted a moment. She looked back on their conversation before she had made her dash for the bathroom, and she saw the situation from his perspective. He had asked her if she trusted him and she had bolted.

She put herself in his shoes—what was he thinking?

The answer was not long coming. He thought she didn't trust him. The knowledge buzzed in her head and she knew it wouldn't go away until she told him how she felt.

He had to know she wasn't that person. Fuelled by an urgency that infected every cell of her body, that defied logic, she ignored the heels she had kicked off and shoved her feet into a pair of trainers.

The bodyguard standing outside the door moved to one side as she exploded through the door.

'Where is he?'

The steely face betrayed a concern as he looked down at her.

'Shall I get someone for you—?'

'No, just tell me where he went!' she screeched, fighting the impulse to beat her hands on his chest.

After a pause that seemed to Hannah to go on for ever, he nodded to the door that led to the stone spiral steps that in turn led to the side entrance to their apartment.

Hannah's grateful smile shone, causing the big man to blush but she didn't notice. Slinging a 'Thank you!' over her shoulder, she flew down the stairs at record-breaking speed, slowing only when she remembered the baby.

Outside her burst of optimism vanished as she scanned the surrounding area lit by spotlights. Her anxious gaze failed to pick up any sign of movement amongst the rows of fragrant lemon trees that grew in the manicured expanse of green, a green maintained by high-tech underground irrigation.

She was about to concede defeat when she saw a figure who had been previously concealed by a hollow in the undulating ground outlined on the horizon.

'Kamel!'

Maybe he didn't hear her, or maybe he chose to ignore her. Her jaw firmed; she'd *make* him listen, she told herself grimly, or die in the attempt!

In her head she could hear him calling her a drama queen. Tears welled in her eyes and she tried to call his name but nothing came out of her mouth. Swallowing tears and the frustration that lay like a weight in her chest, she willed herself on.

He had vanished from view before she had made it halfway across the grass, but when she reached the top of the rise she had a lucky break: she saw his tall figure enter the massive garage block.

With cruel timing as she came around the building a sports car emerged through the open doors, kicking up a cloud of dust that made her cough as it vanished.

Well, that was it.

Feeling utterly deflated, she stopped to catch her breath, pressing her hand to a stitch in her side. She experienced a moment's panic before telling herself not to be stupid. Pregnant women played sport, rode horses, did things a lot more physically demanding than jog a few hundred yards. Her only problem was she was unfit.

Actually it wasn't her only problem. Why had she hesitated? If she had told him how she felt he wouldn't have needed to be told she trusted him. He'd have known. But, no, she'd been busy covering her back, protecting herself from the man who, whether he had intended to or not, had shown her what love was about.

It had been weeks since she'd admitted it to herself and she'd been too scared to let him see she loved him. She was disgusted by her own cowardice. Maybe it was only sex for him, but she had to know. She *needed* to know. She needed to tell him she was alive and Amira was dead. She had to be brave for their baby.

Hands braced on her thighs, she leant forward to get her breath. It was time to be honest. If she didn't it would be her own insecurity that stretched the gulf that had opened up between them tonight.

She was so caught up with her own internal dialogue that as she straightened up and brushed the hair back from her face she almost missed the figure that emerged from the garage block, the figure carrying the cane. The figure of the colonel...

For a moment literally paralysed with fear, Hannah felt herself dragged back to that room of her nightmares—the bright white light, the stains on the wall that she didn't like to think about and the sinister tap, tap of that cane.

But he wasn't tapping his stick. He wasn't doing anything to attract attention to himself. As he moved towards the staff quarters he looked furtively left and right, then over his shoulder. For a moment he seemed to be looking straight at her and, standing there in the pale ball gown, she felt as though there were a neon arrow above her head. Then he turned and walked away quickly.

It was only after he had vanished that she began to breathe again.

She was ashamed that she'd felt so afraid. He couldn't

hurt her any more. He never had; he'd only been playing mind games. He was harmless really. But harmless or not, remembering the expression she had caught a glimpse of earlier that evening when his cold little eyes had followed Kamel across the room made her shudder.

'Hannah, you're way too old to believe in the bogey man.' Firmly ejecting the hateful little creep from her head, Hannah was turning to retrace her steps when she lost her footing. By some miracle she managed not to fall, but she did jar her ankle. Flexing her toes and extending her foot to see the damage, she noticed a dark patch on the ground. There was a trail of similar spots leading all the way back to the garage. Unable to shake the feeling that something was not quite right, she found herself following the breadcrumb trail of spots. It led back into the large hangar of a building that housed Kamel's collection of cars.

She had seen them before and had made a few appropriate noises of approval, though in all honesty her interest in high-end vintage cars was limited. So long as the car she drove got her from A to B she was happy.

The lights were off in the building, but as she walked inside the internal sensor switched them on, revealing the rows of gleaming cars inside. Only one was absent—the vintage sports car that Kamel had driven off in. Where it had stood in the empty space the trail came to an end.

While Hannah's interest in cars was limited, a condition of her being given driving lessons for her seventeenth birthday had been she attend some basic car-maintenance classes. Some things had stuck with her, like the unpleasant smell of brake fluid.

She dipped her finger in the pool, lifted it to her nose

and gave a whimper, the colour fading from her face. The images clicked through her head. The hate in that man's eyes, his furtive manner as he'd left the building. Why hadn't she challenged him? Would the little coward dare…?

She didn't follow the line of speculation to its conclusion; she didn't think of the security guard who might have kept a discreet distance but was undoubtedly within calling distance, or even the internal phone on the wall behind her. She just ran.

The palace compound was more like a village or small town than a single residence, and, though it was possible to take a direct route to the heavy entrance gates, there was also a more circuitous route. She had complained recently that Kamel treated it as if it were his own private racing track. He had laughed when she'd closed her eyes and squealed at the last hairpin bend, convinced they were heading straight into a wall.

Without brakes… She shook her head to clear the image and pushed on. On foot it was possible to take a much shorter, direct route. She ought to be able to cut him off before— She refused to think that she was not going to make it in time.

The information did not make it to her lungs. They already felt as though they were going to explode and when she was forced to stop to catch her breath it also gave her body time for the pain in her ankle to register. That was when she remembered the phone in the garage block. She could have rung through to the entrance gate—someone would be there now, ready to warn Kamel. She was trying to decide between the options of going back to the phone or trying to intercept him when she saw a really ancient bike propped up against a wall.

Sending up a silent thanks to whoever had left it there, she climbed aboard and began to pedal through the trees.

Kamel had gunned his way out of the garage.

It all happened so fast the sequence of events was a blur: the car appearing, throwing herself into the road, arms waving, then the crunch of metal as the front of the Aston Martin embedded itself into a tree.

I've killed him!

She felt empty, her body was numb—and then the door of the car was being wrenched open. It actually fell off its hinges as Kamel—large, very alive and in what appeared to be a towering rage—vaulted from the vehicle. The feeling rushed back and she began to laugh and cry at the same time.

'You little fool! What the hell were you doing? I could have killed you!' Looking white and shaken and a million miles from his indestructibly assured self, Kamel took her roughly by the shoulders and wrenched her around to face him. He registered the tears sliding down her face and hissed out a soft curse. How could you yell at someone who looked like that? 'You just took ten years off my life.' If he had no Hannah he would have no life; the blinding insight stretched his self-control to the limit.

'I had to stop you—the car, the brakes…'

His ferocious frown deepened. 'How the hell did you know about the brakes?'

She wiped the tears from her cheeks with the back of one hand and sniffed. 'You knew?'

'I stopped a few yards after I left the garage.' To ask himself what the hell he was doing. Throwing some sort of tantrum because she didn't immediately express unconditional trust? He'd moved the goalposts of this relationship on an almost daily basis. Hell, at the start, he hadn't even wanted a relationship. If he had to work for her trust, he would. 'Or tried to.' He had used the gears to slow down to a crawl, planning to pull over at an appropriate place, which was the only reason he had not hit Hannah.

He closed his eyes and swallowed, reliving the nightmare moment when she had rushed into the road.

'So you knew about what he tried to do?'

'Who tried to do what?'

'The colonel. He cut your brakes and I think he might be the one who sent the photos.'

Understanding softened his dark eyes as he placed a thumb under her chin, tilting her tear-stained face up to him. 'Really sweetheart, that man can't hurt you and I promise you will never have to see him again.'

She pulled away from him. 'No!' she gritted emphatically through clenched teeth. 'Don't look at me like that, and don't even think about humouring me. I am *not* imagining things and it was *you* he was trying to hurt. You humiliated him. I saw the way he looked at you tonight, and then when I followed you he was in the garage and he didn't want to be seen. So when I saw the brake fluid I knew...' She pressed a hand to her chest and gulped back a sob and whispered, 'I had to stop you.'

'You were following me?'

'I just told you—someone tried to kill you.'

'I'll look into it. He will be brought to justice if he

is guilty.' There was no hint of doubt in Kamel's voice.
'You followed me?'

She nodded.

'Why?' He hooked a finger under her chin and forced
her to look at him, Hannah met his interrogative dark
stare steadily, not trying to look away, feeling weirdly
calm now the moment was here.

'Because you asked me a question and you left before I could answer.'

'You ran away.'

'It was that or throw up all over your shoes.'

He stiffened. 'You're ill?'

'Not ill.' For the first time she struggled to hold his
gaze. 'You asked me if I trust you and the answer is yes,
I do. Totally and absolutely. I know you always have
my back—that's one of the things I love about you. Of
course, there are an awful lot of things about you that
drive me crazy but they don't matter because I love
you...' She gave a quivering smile. It hadn't been as
hard as she had anticipated, speaking the words that had
been locked within her heart. 'The whole package. You.'

This was the moment when in her dreams he confessed his love for her. But this wasn't a dream; it was
real. And he stood there, every muscle in his stark white
face frozen, tension pulling the skin tight across the
bones of his face.

Hannah walked into the wall of pain and kept going,
her expression fixed in a reasonable mask. No matter
how hard she wanted it, it just wasn't going to happen.

'It's all right. I know that love was not part of the
deal. I know that Amira...you will always love her, but
it doesn't have to be a deal breaker, does it?'

She felt the tension leave his body. 'Say it again. I want to hear it.'

The glow in his eyes was speaking not to her brain, which was counselling caution, but directly to her heart. It stopped and then soared, and she smiled.

'I love you, Kamel.' She left a gap and this time he filled it.

'Je t'aime, ma chérie. Je t'aime. I have been too stubborn, too scared to admit it to myself.'

'Amira…?'

'I loved Amira, and her memory will always be dear to me. But what I felt for her was a thing that… If I thought you loved another man I would not let you go to him. I would lock you up in a tower. I am jealous of everyone you smile at. That damned chef creep…'

'Jealous? You… You're not just saying that because of the baby?' She saw his expression and gave a comical groan. 'I didn't mention that part yet, did I?'

'Baby…there is a baby? Our baby?'

She nodded.

He pressed a hand to her stomach. 'You do know how much you have changed my life?'

'I thought that was exactly what you didn't want.'

He shrugged. 'I was a fool. And you were charming and infuriating and brave and so beautiful. You swept into my life like a cleansing breeze, a healing breeze.'

He opened his arms and, eyes shining, she stepped into them, sighing as she felt them close behind her. 'I love you so much, Kamel. It's been an *agony* not saying it. It got so that I couldn't even relax properly when we made love—I was so scared of blurting it out.'

'So it was not that you had tired of me?'

She laughed at the thought. 'That is never going to happen.'

He put a thumb under her chin, tilting her glowing face up to him. 'You can say it as often as you wish now. In fact, I insist you say it.'

She was giggling happily as he swept her into his arms, and still when the security guard accompanied by a grim-faced Rafiq found them.

'Kamel, stop him. He's calling a doctor. Tell him I'm not ill,' she urged as her husband strode on, refusing her requests to be put down.

'You have had a stressful day and you are pregnant and I think it might be a good idea if a doctor gives you a check-over.'

'And I suppose it doesn't matter what I say?'

'No.'

She touched the hard plane of his lean cheek.

'You're impossible!' she said lovingly.

'And you are mine,' he said simply.

* * * * *

'You wanted honesty—well, here's honesty...' Karim said.

Suddenly Clemmie didn't want him to say anything. That frankness she had wanted now seemed so dangerous, so threatening. Yet she had pushed him to say it and she couldn't find the words to stop him. It was too late.

'I do want you.'

Karim's black eyes burned down into her wide amber ones, searing right into her thoughts.

'Never doubt it. I want you so much that it's tearing me to pieces not to have you. But what does that do for us?'

'It... You know it was an arranged marriage. One I had no part in...no agreement given. I was just a child. My father sold me!'

'The agreement is still binding. You are here to become Nabil's Queen.'

'But not yet...' she said.

Kate Walker was born in Nottinghamshire, but as she grew up in Yorkshire she has always felt that her roots are there. She met her husband at university, and originally worked as a children's librarian, but after the birth of her son she returned to her old childhood love of writing. When she's not working she divides her time between her family, their three cats, and her interests of embroidery, antiques, film and theatre—and, of course, reading.

You can visit Kate at www.kate-walker.com

Recent titles by the same author:

A THRONE FOR THE TAKING *(Royal and Ruthless)*
THE DEVIL AND MISS JONES
THE RETURN OF THE STRANGER
  (The Powerful and the Pure)
THE PROUD WIFE

Did you know these are also available as eBooks?
Visit www.millsandboon.co.uk

A QUESTION
OF HONOUR

BY
KATE WALKER

MILLS &
BOON

A QUESTION
OF HONOUR

This book needs several dedications:

To my editor, Pippa,
whose support and understanding has been invaluable.

To Marie,
whose 'shiver down the spine' comment
told me I needed to finish it.

And to my who knows how many 'greats'
back ancestor Chevalier Charles Wogan,
whose real-life story was the inspiration
behind my fictional version.

CHAPTER ONE

'You know why I'm here.'

The man's voice was as deep and dark as his eyes, his hair…his heart, for all Clemmie knew. He filled the doorway he stood in, big and broad and dangerously strong. Worryingly so.

She didn't know what put that sense of danger into his appearance. There was nothing in the way he stood, the long body relaxed, his hands pushed deep into the pockets of the well-worn jeans that clung to narrow hips and powerful legs, that spoke of threat or any sort of menace. And his face, although rough-hewn and rugged, did not have the type of features that made her think of black shadowy novels about serial killers or vampires rising from the dead.

Not that serial killers conformed to the myth that evil had to be ugly as well. And this man was definitely not ugly. He was all hunk, if the truth was told. Those deep brown eyes were combined with unbelievably luxuriant black lashes, slashing high cheekbones, surprisingly bronze-toned skin. He was a man for whom the word 'sexy' had been created. A man whose powerfully male impact went straight to everything that was female inside her and resonated there, making her shiver. But once the image of a vampire—dark, devastating and dangerous—had settled into her brain there was no way she could shake it loose.

It was something about the eyes. Something about that cold, direct, unflinching stare. Dead-eyed and unyielding. She couldn't understand it. And because she couldn't find a reason for it, it made her shiver all the more though she forced herself not to show it and instead pasted a smile that she hoped was polite but not overly encouraging on to her face.

'I beg your pardon?'

If he caught the note of rejection and dismissal she tried to inject into the words then not a sign of it registered in that enigmatic face. He certainly didn't look discouraged or even concerned but flashed her another of those cold-eyed glances and repeated, with obvious emphasis, 'You know why I'm here.'

'I think not.'

She *was* expecting someone. Had been dreading his arrival for days—weeks. Ever since the time had approached when she would celebrate her twenty-third birthday. If 'celebrated' was the right word for marking the day that would mean the end of her old life, and the start of the new. The start of the life she had known was coming but had tried to put out of her mind. Without success. The thought of what her future was to be hung over her like a dark storm cloud, blighting each day that crept nearer to the moment her destiny changed.

But she had prayed he wouldn't come so soon. That she would have at least a few more days—just a month would be perfect—before the fate that her father had planned for her when she had been too young to understand, let alone object, closed in around her and locked her into a very different existence.

The person she had been expecting—dreading—was very different from this darkly devastating male. He was much older for a start. And would never have appeared so casually dressed, so carelessly indifferent to the demands of protocol and security.

Which was just as well because the sudden and unexpected ring at the doorbell had caught her unawares. She hadn't even brushed her hair properly after washing it and letting it dry naturally, so that it hung in wild disorder around her face. Her mascara was smudged, and although she'd decided that the lipstick she'd been trying on was really too bright and garish, she hadn't had time to take any of it off, or in any way lessen the impact of the vivid colour.

'I have no idea who you are or what you're doing here. If you're selling something, I'm not interested. If you're canvassing, I'll not be voting for your party.'

'I'm not selling anything.'

No, she'd expected that. His clothes, while too obviously casual for a salesman, had a quality and style that contradicted that thought.

'Then in that case...'

She'd had enough of this. If he wasn't going to explain just why he was here then she had no intention of wasting her time standing here in the hallway. She had been busy enough before the autocratic and impatient knock had summoned her to the door and if she hung around any longer she was going to be late for Harry's party and he would never forgive her.

'I'd appreciate it if you would just leave...'

She made a move to close the door as she spoke, wanting this over and done with. Hunk or not, he had invaded her world just at the worst possible moment.

She had so little time to spare. Correction—she had no time to spare. No time at all for herself, no time between her and the future, the fate that had once seemed so far away. She had to finish packing, organise the legal transfer of the cottage and everything else she was leaving behind. And that was always supposing that she could persuade the man she really was waiting for to give her just two days more grace.

Just forty-eight more hours. It would mean so little to him, except as a delay in the mission he'd been sent on, but it would mean the world to her—and to Harry. A tiny bubble of tension lurched up into her throat and burst there painfully as she thought about the promise she had made to Harry just the previous evening.

'I'll be there, sweetheart, I promise. I won't let anything stand in my way.'

And she wouldn't, she had vowed. She had just enough time to visit Harry, be with him through this special time, and then make it back home. Back to face the fate she now knew her dreams of escaping would never ever come true. Back to face the prospect of a future that had been signed away from her with the dictates of a peace treaty, the plans of other people so much more powerful than she could ever be. The only thing that made it bearable was the knowledge that Harry would never be trapped as she had been. Her father knew nothing about him, and she would do anything rather than let him find out.

But that had been before she had received the unwelcome news that the visitor she so dreaded seeing would be here much sooner than she had anticipated. Forty-eight hours earlier. The vital forty-eight hours she needed.

And now here was this man—this undeniably gorgeous but totally unwelcome man—invading what little was left of her privacy, and holding her up when she needed to be on her way.

'Leave right now,' she added, the uneasy feelings in her mind giving more emphasis to her words, a hard-voiced stress that she would never have shown under any other circumstances. As she spoke she moved to shut the door, knowing a nervous need to slam it into its frame, right in his face. That feeling was mixed with a creeping, disturbing conviction that if she didn't get rid of him now, once and for all, he was going to ruin her plans completely.

'I think not.'

She only just heard his low-toned words under her own sharp gasp of shock as the door hit against some unexpected blockage at its base. She suddenly became disturbingly aware of the way that he had moved forward, sudden and silent as a striking predator, firmly inserting one booted foot between the wood and its frame. A long, strong fingered hand flashed out to slam into it too, just above her head, holding it back with an ease that denied the brutal force he was employing against her own pathetic attempt at resistance. The shock of the impact ricocheted disturbingly up her arm.

'I think not,' he repeated, low and dangerous. 'I'm not going anywhere.'

'Then you'd better think again!' she tossed at him in open defiance, her head going back, bronze eyes flashing golden sparks of rejection.

He'd expected problems, Karim Al Khalifa acknowledged to himself. The way that this woman had taken herself off from the court, the sort of life she had set up for herself, ignoring all demands of protocol and safety, in a different country, all indicated that this was not going to be the straightforward task his father had led him to believe. Clementina Savanevski—or Clemmie Savens, which was the name she was masquerading under in this rural English hideaway—knew where her duty lay, or she should do. But the fact that she had run away from that duty, and had been living a carefree life on her own had always indicated that she held her family's promise very lightly. Far too lightly.

And now that he was face to face with her, he felt he understood why.

She had clearly cast off the restraint and the dignity she should be expected to have as a potential Queen of Rhastaan. She had on only a loose, faded tee shirt and shabby denim jeans, the latter so battered that they were actually threadbare in places where they clung to her tall, slender figure. The long dark hair hung wild around her face, tumbling down on to her shoulders and back in a disarray that was as shocking as it was sensual. Her face was marked with dark smudges around her deep amber eyes, a garish crimson lipstick staining her mouth.

And what a mouth.

Unexpectedly, shockingly, his senses seemed to catch on the thought, his heart lurching sharply, making his breath tangle inside his chest so that for a second he felt he would never exhale again. His own mouth burned as if it had made contact with the red-painted fullness of hers, his tongue moving involuntarily to sweep over his lower lip in instinctive response.

'I'll call the police!'

She moved back to her place by the door so that she was blocking his way if he wanted to come towards her.

The movement drew his attention to her feet on the wooden floor. Long, elegant, golden-skinned, they were tipped with an astonishingly bright pink polish on her nails. And the movement had brought a waft of some tantalising perfume stirring on the air. Flowers, but with an unexpected undertone of sexy spice.

'No need for that.' His voice was rough around the edges as he had to push it from an unexpectedly dry throat. 'I'm not going to hurt you.'

'And you expect me to believe that, do you?' she challenged, flinging another furious and flashing glare into his face.

Knowing she had caught his attention, she let her gaze drop downwards in a deliberate move to draw his attention to where his foot still came between the door and its white-painted frame, blocking the way.

'Does that look like *normal* behaviour?' she questioned roughly, nodding towards the carefully imposed barrier. Her tone was almost as raw as his but for very different reasons, he suspected. She was furious, practically spitting her anger at him. And suddenly he had the image in his head of a young, thin stray cat he had seen in a car park only that morning. A sleek black beauty who had started in violent apprehension when he had approached it and, turning, had hissed its defiance in his face.

He was handling this all wrong, Karim acknowledged uncomfortably. Somewhere in the moments between the time he had arrived here and she had answered the door, all his carefully planned tactics had gone right up in smoke and he had taken completely the wrong approach. He hadn't expected her to be so hostile, so defiant. Raw and unsettled as he was already with thoughts of the situation he had left behind at home, worry about his father's health, the way he had been forced so unexpectedly into taking this action today, he had let his usual rigid control slip shamefully.

That and the fact that he'd been without a woman for so long, he acknowledged unwillingly. Too long. There had been no one in his bed or even near it since Soraya had stormed out, accusing him of never being there for her. Never being there, full stop. Well, of course he hadn't. When had he had the time, or the freedom of thought, to be there for anyone other than his father, or the country that he now found himself so brutally and unexpectedly heir to? The problems that had flared up so suddenly had taken every second of his time, forcing him to take on his father's duties as well as his own. He wouldn't be here otherwise. Not willingly.

And, face it, he had never expected her to be so physically gorgeous. So incredibly sexy. He had seen photographs of her, of course, but not a single one of those pictures had the sensual impact of the molten bronze eyes, golden skin, tousled black hair and the intoxicating scent that seemed to have tangled itself around his nerves, pulling tight. His mouth almost watered, his senses burning to life in the space of a heartbeat.

No.

Hastily, he pulled himself up. He couldn't allow thoughts like that to sneak into his mind, even for a moment. It didn't matter a damn if this woman was the sexiest female on earth—and he refused to listen to his senses' insistence that that might just be the case—she was not for him. She was *forbidden* to him, dammit. They were on opposite sides of a huge divide and, frankly, it was better it stayed that way. From what he had heard, she was too much trouble to be worth any transient pleasure. And he already had too much on his conscience as it was.

'My apologies,' he said stiffly, imposing control on his voice in the hope that the rest of his senses would follow. 'I am not going to hurt you.'

'Do you think that if you say it often enough I'll be forced to believe you?' she challenged. 'What's that phrase about protesting too much?'

He wasn't sure if she had deliberately flung the question at him to distract him, but it worked. Puzzled, he reacted without thinking, taking his foot from the door and, sensing the lessening of pressure against her hand, she acted instinctively, pushing the door back against him and whirling away from him, dashing back inside the house.

If she could just reach the phone, she could call the police, Clemmie told herself. Or she could hope to get right through the house and out of the back door. She didn't trust for one minute his declaration that he had no intention of hurting her. He meant trouble, she was sure. Some deeply primitive instinct told her that, gorgeous or not, he was dangerous right through to the bone.

But she hadn't pushed the door quite soon enough. She knew the moment that he stopped it from closing, the silence instead of the bang of wood on wood. He had stepped into the hallway; was right behind her. Every nerve, every muscle tensed in anticipation of his coming to claim her, to grab at her shoulder or her arms. But, unbelievably, as she dashed into the kitchen she heard him come to a halt.

'Clementina.'

Whatever she had expected, it wasn't that. Wasn't the use of her name—her full name. The one that no one here in England used. The one that no one even knew *was* her real name. And the sound of it stopped her dead, freezing her into stillness in the middle of her tiny kitchen.

'Clementina—please.'

Please? Now she had to be hearing things. He couldn't have said that. He wouldn't have said *please*—would he?

'I'm not coming any further,' he said with careful control. 'I'm going to stay here and we should talk. Let me explain—my name is Karim Al Khalifa.'

Through the buzzing in her head, Clemmie heard the words so differently. She had been expecting to hear that name, or one so very like it, that she believed he'd said what she'd anticipated.

'Now I know you're lying.'

She tossed the words over her shoulder, turning her head just far enough to see that he had actually halted as he had said, just outside the kitchen door.

'I don't know how you know that I was waiting for someone to come here from Sheikh Al Khalifa, but it sure as blazes wasn't you. I've seen a picture of the man who was coming and he's at least twice your age, has a beard. The photo's on my computer—it was in the email…'

'Was,' he inserted, cold and sharp. 'The important word there is "was".'

'What *are* you talking about?'

Needing to see him to look into his face, meet his eyes, to try and read just what was going on inside his handsome head, she made herself turn to confront him and immediately wished she hadn't. The dark glaze of his eyes was like black ice, making her stomach lurch. At the same time she felt the clench of her nerves in another, very different sort of response. A very female, very sensual sort of reaction. One that made her throat ache in a way that had nothing to do with fear.

One that was the last thing she wanted, or should even acknowledge she was feeling.

'The man who *was* coming,' he repeated with a dark emphasis. 'But isn't any more.'

'And how do you know…' Clemmie began, only to find that her voice failed her, the rest of the question fading away into an embarrassing squeak. This man knew too much about her situation—but from what sources?

Suddenly, she was nervous in a new way. One that had thoughts of diplomacy, peace treaties, international situations and strong tensions between countries running through her head. Her hands felt damp and she ran them down the sides of her thighs to ease the sensation, her heart clenching painfully as she watched his dark eyes drop to follow the betraying movement.

His eyes lingered in a way that made her shift uncomfortably from one foot to another on the terracotta-tiled floor.

'I know because I organised it,' was the emotionless response. 'My father ordered what was to happen and instructed Adnan to come and fetch you. He also had the photo of the man he'd put in charge of this sent to you so that you knew who was coming. At least those were the original arrangements—but then everything changed.'

'Changed?'

It felt as if her blood was weakening, the strength seeping out of her so that she almost imagined there would be a damp pool collecting on the floor at her feet. Adnan was the name of the man Sheikh Al Khalifa had said he would send. The man who was to see her safe to Rhastaan. And she needed her safety to be guaranteed.

Not everyone was as pleased about this prospective marriage as her father. Sheikh Ankhara, whose lands bordered Rhastaan, and who had always wanted the throne for his own daughter, had made no secret of the fact that he would sabotage it if he could. It was because of a possible threat from him that Sheikh Al Khalifa—*my father,* Karim had said—had taken charge, organising a trusted man to escort her to Nabil.

But now Karim was saying that he had changed those arrangements. Did that mean that something had gone wrong?

'Do you want to sit down?'

Her feelings must have shown in her face. Perhaps the blood had drained from there too.

'Here.'

He had crossed to the sink, snatching up a glass and filling it with water from the tap.

'Take this…'

He pushed it into her hand then closed his own hand around hers as her shockingly nerveless fingers refused to grasp it, coming dangerously close to letting it drop and smash on the tiles.

'Drink it.' It was a command as he lifted the glass to her lips.

She managed a little sip, struggling to swallow even the small amount of water. He was so shockingly close. If she breathed in she could inhale the scent of his skin, the faint tang of some aromatic aftershave. His hands were warm on hers, sending pulses of reaction over her skin, and if she looked up into his dark eyes she could see herself reflected in their depths, a tiny, pale-faced thing with huge eyes that gave away too much. She didn't like how the image made her feel diminished in a way that was as powerful as her awareness of the force and strength of the long body so close to hers, creating a pounding turmoil inside her head.

'Your—did you say your father?'

A sharp, curt nod of that dark head was his only response. He was still holding the glass of water to her lips, not pushing it at her, but making it plain that he believed she needed more. It was a toss-up between easing the painful tightness of her throat or risking making herself sick as she struggled to swallow.

She managed another sip then pushed the glass away. The brief slick of her tongue over her lips did little to ease the way she was feeling. Particularly not when she saw that darkly intent gaze drop to follow the small movement and she actually saw the kick of his pulse at the base of his throat. Was it possible that he was feeling something of the same heated reaction as the one that had seared through her at his touch?

'And who, precisely, is your father?'

'You know his name— you talked of him just now.'

'I talked of Sheikh Al Khalifa, but he can't...' Another nod, as sharp and hard as the first, cut her off in mid-sentence and she had to shake her head violently, sending her dark hair flying as she tried to deny what he was saying. 'No—he can't... Prove it!'

A faint shrug of those broad shoulders dismissed her challenge but all the same he reached into his jacket pocket, pulled out a wallet and flipped it open, holding it up in front of her.

'My name is Karim Al Khalifa,' he said slowly and carefully, as if explaining to a difficult and not very bright child. 'Shamil Al Khalifa is my father—he is also the man whose envoy you were expecting. Isn't he?' he demanded when she could only stare at the driving licence, the bank cards in blank silence.

'But if he—' Clemmie shook her head slowly, unable to take it all in. 'Why would he send you—his *son*…?'

Because if this Karim was the Sheikh's son then that meant he must be a prince in his own right, as rich and powerful—possibly more so—as Nabil, who was the reason for this situation in the first place.

'I was expecting a member of his security team. Someone who would make sure that I travelled safely to Rhastaan and…'

'And met up with your prospective groom,' Karim finished for her, making it clear that he really did know all about the situation; that he was well aware of what was going on.

'Things made it—imperative—that the arrangement we'd put in place could not go ahead as we planned. Plans had to be changed at the last moment.'

'But why?'

'Because it was necessary.'

And that was all the explanation she was going to get, Clemmie was forced to acknowledge as Karim pushed himself upright, straightening his long back and flexing his broad shoulders. He strode to the sink, tossed what was left of the water into it and placed the glass on the draining board. The air around Clemmie suddenly felt uncomfortably cold without the warm strength of his body so close to hers.

'And those plans mean that we don't have any time to waste.' He flung the words over his shoulder, not even troubling to turn and face her as he spoke. 'I hope you've packed as instructed, because we have to leave now.'

'Now?' That brought her to her feet in a rush. *As instructed.* Who did he think he was?

'No way. That's not happening.'

'Oh, but I assure you that it is.'

She'd planned on arguing against this. Or, at the very least, she'd hoped to discuss it with the man who was due to arrive at her cottage. Her birthday was still nine days away. Less than a month, but that made all the difference.

'The contract that was drawn up between my family and the rulers of Rhastaan only comes into effect on December third. The day I turn twenty-three.'

'That day will come soon enough. We'll be in Rhastaan by the time you come of age.'

So he did know everything about her. Was it supposed to reassure, to let her know that he really was in control of the situation? Because reassure was the last thing it did. She had known that one day someone would come for her. It had been decided, signed and sealed thirteen years before, when the son of the Sheikh of Rhastaan was five, and she not quite ten. They had been betrothed, contracted to each other, to be married when Nabil reached adulthood. She had had some years of freedom, time to complete a university course, while their parents waited for her prospective husband to become old enough to wed and to hold the throne of his own kingdom. And now that time was up.

But not yet. Please, not yet.

Clemmie had thought that she would be able to argue with the man who had been sent. That she could at least pull rank just a little, insist on having a day or two's grace before she had to leave. The man she had thought was coming to collect her—an older man, a *family* man, she had hoped—might be someone she could appeal to.

Someone who would give her that breathing space and let her have a chance of fulfilling her promise to Harry.

But this dark, sleek, dangerous panther of a man—would he listen to a word she had to say? Would he give her any sort of chance? She doubted it. Especially when she couldn't tell him—or anyone—the whole truth. She didn't dare. It was vital that she kept Harry's existence a total secret. If anyone ever found out about him then the little boy's future was at risk.

So how could she persuade him?

'I need more time. A few days.'

You have to be joking, the look he turned on her said without words. It made her feel like some small, crawling insect just within crushing reach of his feet in their highly polished handmade shoes. A small, crawling *female* insect. And from the way he looked down his straight slash of a nose, the burn of contempt in the blackness of his eyes, she knew just which of those words he considered to be the greatest possible insult he could toss her way.

She made herself face him, her eyes locking with his, burning with the defiance she felt towards his arrogant decree.

'And who precisely are you to order me around?'

'I told you—I am Karim Al Khalifa, Crown Prince of Markhazad.'

He obviously thought that his cold statement would impress her but he couldn't be more wrong. She'd spent so much time as she grew up with the royal family who were destined to be her family one day. It had been a sterile, regimented existence, with very few moments of freedom. Her father had been determined that she knew how to behave, how to follow court protocol. She had been trained for her role. When she married they would be more than equals, and soon she would be queen.

'Crown Prince, hmm? So why are you here, running errands—'

He hadn't liked that, not one bit. A flame of anger had flared in those polished jet eyes, turning them from ice to fire in the space of a heartbeat. And, contradictorily, that chilled her own blood till she felt it might freeze in her veins.

'I am here representing my father,' he snapped, cutting her off before she could complete the sentence. 'Not running errands. And as my father's representative I insist that you pack your bags and get ready to leave.'

'You can insist all you like. I've no intention of going anywhere with you so I suggest you just turn around and walk out that door.'

'And I have no intention of leaving—at least, not without you.'

How could that gorgeous, sensual mouth make a simple statement sound like the most terrible threat since time began? And the husky appeal of his accent only added to the horror of the contradiction.

'I've come for you. And I'm leaving with you. And that is all there is to it.'

CHAPTER TWO

WAS SHE REALLY going to make this more difficult than he had ever thought? Karim found it hard to believe that this slip of a girl was going to make things so very problematic for him.

And the worst part of it was that he couldn't even tell her the truth. He couldn't reveal to her just what was behind his coming here, the problems and dangers that had meant he had to deal with this himself, rather than leave it to Adnan who, although a member of the security team, was not the right man for the job. Definitely not once Karim had found out that he was secretly in the pay of Ankhara.

His eyes narrowed as he looked into Clementina's face assessingly, wondering just how much he could tell her. How much did she know about Sheikh Ankhara and his ambitions to put his own daughter on the throne of Rhastaan? Karim had no doubt that if Adnan had been the one to collect her, as had originally been planned, then there would have been some unfortunate 'accident' on the journey back. Anything to ensure that she didn't make it to her wedding.

Clementina didn't look like the type of delicate flower who would go into some sort of emotional meltdown if

she realised the risks involved in getting her out of here
and taking her back to Rhastaan, handing her over to her
husband-to-be. On the contrary, she had been hissing and
spitting defiance at him ever since he had arrived, like
some beautiful, hostile, wild cat that had been driven
into a corner and trapped there, her back against the wall.
And just because she was sleek-boned and soft-haired,
he would be all sorts of a fool if he let himself think of
her as any sort of kitten rather than a fully grown cat.
She was far more likely to lash out and scratch him viciously if he tried to touch her, rather than purring and
preening under his caress.

Just for a moment the thought of her arching that elegant back to meet his hands, or rubbing the softness
of her hair against his face made his breath knot in his
throat, his blood heating as his body tightened in the sort
of purely carnal hunger he hadn't known for some time.

Hell, no! This was not the way he had expected to feel
about this woman. It was the last thing he should feel
about the betrothed bride of the young King of Rhastaan. It went against all the laws of honour and trust. It
threatened the reasons why he was here right down to
the very roots that had founded them. It was why he had
had to move away from her earlier, when the purely instinctive move to offer her a drink of water had suddenly
turned into some sort of brutal sensual endurance test.
He hadn't been able to stay there, so close that he could
feel the warmth of her body, see the pulse of her blood
beating blue under the fine skin at the base of her throat.
When she moved, some delicate scent had slipped into
the air and combined with the soft brush of a wandering
strand of her dark silky hair across his face, which caught
on the roughness of the day's growth of dark stubble to

create a burn of response that was almost more than he could endure.

Suddenly he wanted her so much that it hurt. He had never wanted a woman so much and yet she was the last woman he could ever, should ever feel that way about. She was not available; not for him.

She was *forbidden* to him.

So the best damn thing that he could do was get her out of here, on the jet where she would be safe and hidden again, on their way to Rhastaan, and deliver her to her bridegroom just as soon as he possibly could.

'So—are you going to pack?' he demanded, his voice rough with all that he was fighting to hold back.

He wouldn't even meet her eyes though he could tell that was what she wanted. She sought to confront him face to face, challenging everything he said.

Was she really so irresponsible, so careless of the consequences of her actions, that she would defy him out of sheer perversity? That she would put everything so many people had worked towards in jeopardy on a selfish whim? She had been given a touch of, if not freedom, then at least the chance to run on an exceptionally loose rein for a while. But even the most magnificent thoroughbred was the better for a little restraint, a strong grip on the bridle, a light touch of spurs, to keep it under control. Clementina Savanevski, soon to be Queen Clementina of Rhastaan, could not be allowed to run wild any more. And if anyone could be relied on to bring her under control then he was the man to do it. That was one of the reasons why his father had sent him on this mission in the first place.

'Well?'

'I am packed,' she surprised him—stunned him—by

saying. He had been expecting further defiance, further rebellion. In fact, if he was honest he was actually a touch disappointed that she wasn't digging in her neat little heels, bringing up that small chin once more and letting her glorious amber eyes clash with his in pure defiance. He'd expected it, and anticipated the thrill of battle that would come from bringing her back under control.

'You are? Then it's time...'

'But not to leave here,' she disconcerted him by adding. 'I've only packed an overnight bag.'

'That won't be adequate.' She knew that; why was he even having to say it? 'You need to pack everything you want to take with you. You'll not be coming back here again.'

'Oh, but there you're wrong.'

Something had set her soft mouth into a surprisingly hard determined line, and the way she shook her head sent the dark hair flying again, tormenting his nostrils with that subtle floral scent.

'I'm only going away for one night this time—and then I will be back. I'll do my proper packing then. Look...' she broke in hastily when he opened his mouth to reject her outrageous statement and tell her just what he thought of such stupidity '...I can explain.'

'You can try,' Karim growled, fighting the urge to grab her by the arms, bundle her out of the door, into his car and drive away from here just as quickly as he could. That would meet one of the demands of this mission and get her on the road back to Rhastaan as soon as he could.

But it would also defeat the other part of the plan, which was to move her from A to B with as little fuss and publicity as possible. If he virtually kidnapped her—because that would be how she would interpret his actions—

then she would react strongly, possibly go into meltdown and panic completely. She would certainly not go quietly—not this woman. If she started screaming for help or calling for the police, even here in this small village, she would soon draw too much unwanted attention to who they were and where they were going.

'You're not going anywhere. Not for one night—not for any time at all.'

'But… Please…'

Hastily, she seemed to adjust her frame of mind, altering her tone to match so that it was suddenly disturbingly soft and cajoling. Obviously, she had decided to try to entice him round to her way of thinking. And the shocking thing was the way that just hearing that low, almost gentle tone changed his mood. He wanted to hear more of that voice, could imagine it murmuring to him in bed, whispering temptation in the heated darkness of his room. And that was not an image he needed in his mind right now.

'Haven't you ever wanted—needed—to keep a promise? So much so that you would do anything at all to make sure you did just that?'

'What?' His brows drew together in a dark frown. 'Of course I have.' It was why he was here now. 'But…'

'Then you'll know exactly how I'm feeling right now. I made a promise…'

'To whom?'

'To Har—to someone,' she corrected hastily, obviously horrified that she had almost blurted out the truth. 'Someone who really matters to me.'

She had been about to give someone's name. A man's? *Harry? Someone who really matters to me.*

'Nothing matters—' Karim's tone was harsh and

unyielding. His face seemed carved from stone, not a muscle moving to reveal any sympathy or understanding. 'Nothing should matter more than the promises you made—your commitment to Nabil.'

'I know all about my *commitment* to Nabil and, believe me, I mean—' Something caught in her throat, making the words tangle there, tight as a knot, so that she had to struggle to force them out. 'I mean to honour it.'

She had no choice. None at all. Not unless she wanted to risk the ruin of international relations between two powerful kingdoms. The possible outbreak of hostilities. The destruction of her family's reputation. Hadn't her father drummed it into her from the moment he had signed the documents? He had made it sound as if it was her sacred duty. She had been fifteen before she'd realised just how much he was getting out of it himself, that the luxury they lived in had been bought from the sale of his own daughter.

'But not yet.'

'You will be twenty-three in nine days' time.' Could his voice be any more cold, any more inflexible? 'You do not have any more time to delay. You've had your freedom, been let off the leash for a while; now it is time to consider your duty.'

'Consider my duty!'

Clemmie threw up her hands in a gesture that was a blend of exasperation and despair.

'Do you think I've ever done anything else? That I've ever been able to forget it?'

'Then you will know why...' Karim put in, but she ploughed on, unable to hold back any longer.

'And *let off the leash*! You make me sound like a naughty puppy dog that has to be brought to heel.'

If the cap fits… his expression said. That was all she was in his eyes. A naughty, disobedient puppy who had been running wild for far too long. She could almost see him snapping his fingers and declaring 'Heel—now!'

She had not been able to tell anyone why she had wanted to leave Markhazad in the first place. She had had to go, while she still could. Once she was married, once she was queen, her life would be lived within the confines of the palace walls, subject to her husband's control, his to command. And she would have lost her last chance to spend time with the only other member of her family. The little boy who had now stolen her heart completely.

'You are to be a queen,' Karim said now, his tone dark and disapproving. 'You should learn to behave like one.'

'Unlike my mother?' Clemmie challenged.

Everyone who knew of her story must know how her English mother had run away from the court, leaving husband and daughter behind, never to be seen again. Clemmie winced away from the memory of how it had felt to be left alone, abandoned by her one defender from her father's worst excesses. Those had been the worst years of her life. It was only recently, in the letter from her maternal grandmother that had been delivered to her after the old lady had died, that she had learned why her mother had had to run. The unplanned, late in life baby she had been determined to hide from her husband. He was a secret that Clemmie was now just as determined to keep, whatever it cost her.

She knew how little her father had valued her because she was only a daughter. She had no needs or dreams of her own. Her only value to him had been in the marriage market, sold to the highest bidder. What he might have done if he knew he had the son he had dreamed of made her shudder to think.

'I'll behave like one when I am a queen! Until then…'

She watched that frown darken, felt a shiver run over her scalp and slither down her spine. She had a suspicion that she knew what he was thinking but she didn't dare challenge it in case it meant he subjected her to more questioning that might push her to drop something revealing about Harry and his circumstances.

'There is no "until then". From this moment on you are the prospective Queen of Rhastaan, and I have been sent to fetch you home for your wedding and then your coronation.'

'But I promised! And if he…'

'He…' Karim pounced on the word like a cat on a mouse, his eyes gleaming with the thrill of the chase. '*He*. Just who is he?'

Clemmie bit down hard on her lower lip in distress at how close she had come to giving herself away. She should know better. Even after less than half an hour in this man's company, it was obvious that he was not the sort of person who was easily side-tracked or misled.

'N-no one. Just a friend. Someone I met while I was living here in England. It's his birthday soon and I promised him I'd be at his party.'

What was it they said—that if you were going to lie, then lie as close to the truth as you possibly could? He was focused on her so completely that she had little hope of getting away from him…unless…

'And you think that you can delay our journey—the plans for the reception and the wedding that are already underway—for a *party*?'

'But I promised! It'll break his heart…'

'And you expect me to believe that?' Dark eyes turned glacial as he flung the question at her. 'Just because you're about to become a princess doesn't mean that I have to believe in the fairy tales you make up.'

'It's not a fairy tale. I have to see—to see…' The realisation of the danger in giving away just what she had to do dried her mouth and had the words shrivelling up into silence.

'You have to see…?' Karim queried cynically. 'Just what is more important than the upcoming wedding—the future of the peace treaty?'

My family. My baby brother. *Harry.* The words beat inside her head, creating a terrible clenching sensation in her stomach that made her feel both nauseous and dry-mouthed in the same moment. A deadly combination.

But at the back of her mind there was the idea that had come to her like a flash of inspiration just moments before. It might just work. And she was desperate enough to try anything.

'Who is this man—your lover?'

That was just so ridiculous that she was close to laughing out loud. Did he really think that she had come to England to meet up with a man? But perhaps it might almost be worth letting him think that for now. At least it would distract him from the truth. And while he was distracted…

'Oh, okay! You win.' She hoped it sounded yielding enough. 'It seems I have no choice so I'll go and get my bag. Look, why don't you make a coffee or something? If we're going to have to travel, we might as well have a drink before we go.'

He still eyed her with suspicion and he didn't show any sign of moving towards the kettle as she walked past him and made her way up the stairs, her feet thumping on the uncarpeted wood. She walked noisily across the floor of her small bedroom, the one that was to the left off the landing, thankfully not the one directly above the kitchen. She had no doubt that Karim Al Khalifa was still standing, alert as a predatory hunter, listening to any sounds that reached him from above.

Determinedly, she added to the sound effects he would be waiting to hear by banging open the door of the elderly pine wardrobe, rattling the coat hangers inside. There was really no need to do any such thing. The small overnight bag she had prepared earlier was still lying, full and firmly zipped up, on the bed. But Karim would be expecting her to pack more than that. He thought she was leaving with him for ever. For the rest of her life.

The thought made her rattle some more coat hangers even more viciously, wishing she could throw some of them at Karim's handsome head.

Karim Al Khalifa. The name reverberated in her head, making her pause to think. He was the son of the Sheikh—a friend of Nabil's late father—who had arranged all this. So why had someone so important—the Crown Prince, after all—come on a mission like this? He had never explained that.

'Clementina?'

Karim's voice, sharp with impatience, came up the narrow staircase. He had clearly noted her silence. And he just as clearly wanted to be on his way. He wouldn't be prepared to wait much longer.

'Nearly done!' She hoped her unconcerned tone was convincing. 'Be down in a minute.'

She had to be out of here. Grabbing the small overnight bag and slinging its longer strap around her neck, and grabbing her handbag, she crept over to the half-open window. Karim might be big and strong and powerful but she had the advantage over him here. Several childhood holidays in England, visiting her English grandmother, had given her a detailed knowledge of this old house and the secret ways in and out of it that had been fun and exciting for a tomboyish teenager.

There was a trellis up the side of the wall, a heavy rich growth of ivy that was thick and strong enough to support her weight even though she was now no longer thirteen and just growing into her womanly form. With luck she could scramble down it, get to her car before he had even realised she had gone silent in the room above him.

But as she eased the window open fully, a last minute thought struck her. This wasn't just a personal thing; there were so many other implications of all this—political ones, international treaties. If she just disappeared then, she shivered at the thought of the trouble it might cause. The repercussions of her behaviour. On her country. On him.

There was a notepad and pen beside her bed and she snatched these up, scribbling down five hasty words, adding her signature as an afterthought.

'Clementina!'

What little patience Karim had was wearing thin.

'Just a minute—or would you like to come and pack for me?' she challenged.

The thought of him doing just that—coming upstairs, into her room, into her *bedroom*—made her heart lurch up into her throat, snatching her breath from her. But his growled response made her feel more relaxed.

'Get on with it then.'

'Oh, I will!'

Leaving the note lying in the middle of the bed where he couldn't possibly miss it, she edged towards the window, her bare feet silent on the floor, her bag on one arm. She didn't dare risk opening the window any further in case it creaked, the wood scraping against wood.

Sliding out backwards, her feet found the spaces in the trellis work that held the ivy tight against the wall with the ease of long-held memory. She prayed it would still hold her—they were both ten years older, herself and the criss-crossed wood. And she was definitely inches taller, pounds heavier. Her toes found the footholds, her hands knowing just where to grab to support herself on the way down. Holding her breath, she let the ivy take all her weight, inched her way down the wall, down to the ground at the back of the cottage, landing with a small sigh of relief as her feet touched the gravel.

'So far so good...'

Her battered red Mini was parked several metres away, its small size and well-worn paintwork totally overshadowed by the big black beast of a SUV that was drawn up just outside the front door. A car as sleek and powerful as the man himself, Clemmie told herself as she wrenched the driver's door open, tossed the bags on to the back seat, flinging herself after them and pushing her key into the ignition almost before she was settled.

The moment that the Mini's engine roared into life was her last chance. Karim had to hear it and would come running so it was now or never. Not even bothering to fasten her seat belt—that could come later—she let off the brake, pushed her foot down on the accelerator and set the car off down the drive at breakneck speed.

She thought she saw the flash of movement—the opening of the door—the appearance of a tall, dark, powerful figure in the empty space, but she didn't take the time to be sure. She needed to focus on the road ahead.

'I'm coming, Harry!'

Pieces of gravel spurted up from under her car's tyres as she headed for the lane and, after that, the motorway and freedom.

At least for now.

CHAPTER THREE

THE SNOW THAT had been threatening from the moment she'd woken up was falling steadily by the time that Clemmie turned off the motorway and headed back to the village. Huge white flakes whirled in front of her windscreen and the elderly wipers had trouble pushing them aside so that she could see the road.

'Oh, come on!' she muttered out loud, concentrating fiercely on steering as carefully as possible. After just over nine months in England, and most of that spent in much warmer and easier weather conditions, she was unused to driving over icy roads, and the addition of the slippery coating of snow made the situation even more treacherous.

Added to that, her elderly car was not exactly in the best state for difficult weather driving. Because she had basically run away from home when she had found out about Harry, not taking much money with her, and not wanting to use her bank cards in case someone found where she was staying, she had bought the cheapest, oldest car she could afford. A decision that had seemed wise at the time, but which she was really regretting now.

Particularly when the engine started to splutter in a worrying way, and the rather worn tyres spun on the frozen surface. If only she had the sort of powerful, brand new four-wheel drive that had brought Karim to the cottage. That beast would have eaten up the miles between the small market town where Harry lived and the moorland village where she had made her temporary home with no trouble.

'Karim.'

Just the thought of him took her attention so that her concentration on her driving went along with it. For a couple of dangerous seconds, the car drifted towards the centre of the road, only coming back under control as she shook her head sharply, reminding herself of where she was.

But the thought of coming face to face with Karim once again made her stomach nerves tighten and twist into painful knots.

Karim Al Khalifa would be waiting for her when she got home. OK, perhaps he wouldn't actually be in the house, but she knew that as soon as he realised she was back, he would be there on the doorstep once again, demanding that she come with him, travel with him back to Rhastaan.

And to her wedding.

Once again the wheel jerked under her convulsive grip, and the unpleasant groaning sound that came from the engine made her wince in distress.

There was no avoiding it now. No hope of gaining any more time or hoping for a reprieve. Her twenty-third birthday was coming up fast, and Nabil had come of age last month. The promises their parents had made to each other would have to be kept. The marriage that had been arranged all those years before must now take place. Or the consequences were unthinkable.

And Karim had been sent to make sure that she kept her word.

Just for a moment the image of Nabil as she had last seen him floated behind her eyes. A gangling youth—not much more than a boy, with hooded eyes, a whisper of a moustache under his hooked nose and a sullen mouth, and her stomach clenched on a pang of nerves. But perhaps he had changed, grown up in the time since she had been at the court. He would be a year older after all.

And it was really rather unfair to consider him in the same thought as Karim Al Khalifa. Karim, the dark and devastating. Karim, with the tall and muscular frame that dominated a room so effortlessly. With the sexy, deep-toned voice, the powerful yet somehow elegant hands, the polished jet eyes and the stunning, outrageously lush thick lashes that framed them.

'What am I doing?'

Clemmie's hands tightened round the steering wheel until her knuckles showed white.

Up ahead, on the horizon at the top of the hill, almost concealed by the wildly whirling snow, the outline of the cottage appeared etched against the heavy grey-whiteness of the sky. Home. Or it should have felt like home, like coming back to safety, warmth and comfort after the long and difficult journey.

This little cottage had been the only sort of home she had ever known. Holidays with her English grandmother had given her a tiny taste of freedom from the rules and protocol of the court. Used to the burning heat of Balakhar and Rhastaan, she had loved the peace and quiet, the green fields that surrounded it, the sweeping view spread out from where it stood high on the hill. She had lived a much simpler, very different way of life with her grandmother, how different she hadn't fully realised until she had seen the happy, relaxed childhood Harry was now enjoying with his adoptive parents. They might not have anything like the luxuries she had known but they had one great treasure—the love they shared. And the freedom she was determined to preserve for Harry at all costs.

But the cottage no longer felt like home. Instead, it seemed as if she was heading foolishly into a trap, putting her head into the lion's jaws. And the sleek, dark predator who had turned her home into an alien, hostile environment was Karim Al Khalifa.

But the problem was that she wasn't thinking of him as that predator. She wasn't even remembering him as the cold-eyed, tight-jawed, arrogant representative of the Sheikh of Markhazad. The Crown Prince of Markhazad himself. All she could focus on right now was the man himself.

And what a man.

Shivering pulses of excitement sparked along her nerves at just the memory, the recollection of having him so close, the scent of his skin. He was not a man to be alone with in the confined space of her small cottage. He was pure temptation, and tempted was something she couldn't afford to be—not now, not ever.

Just for a second Clemmie considered putting the car into a turn and heading back the way she had come. Back to the house where she had just left Harry, so happy and secure, worn out after the excitement and enjoyment of his birthday party. Surely Arthur and Mary Clendon, Harry's adoptive parents, would give her support, somewhere to stay…

'No!'

She couldn't go back on her word. The word she had

given to her father and the Sheikh. However much she felt her insides twist in apprehension at the thought of the future, she had made her promise and she had to stick by it. If she didn't, then someone else would come looking for her—after all, Karim had found her easily enough. And they would find Harry.

Surely her memory had to be playing her false. Karim couldn't have possibly been that devastating. That sexy. Could he?

Well, it seemed she wasn't due to have her memory jogged any time tonight at least, she told herself as she swung the little car in through the battered gates and pulled to a halt at the side of the small house. Wherever Karim was this evening, it wasn't here at Hawthorn Cottage. There was no sign of the big hulk of his car, and all the lights were off inside the house. Obviously, he had decided to go somewhere else, probably somewhere where he could have much more comfort than her small home could provide.

So was that flutter in her stomach one of relief or disappointment? She didn't dare to pursue the question any further, afraid of what it might reveal, as she pulled on the brake and switched off the engine. Not before time, she acknowledged. The silence that fell as the rattle died away made it only too clear that what she had been hearing was the death throes of the elderly car. It certainly wasn't going to take her very much further after tonight. The snow—heavy and drifting now, piling up against the walls of the cottage and blocking the narrow lane—had been the very last straw.

It was almost the last straw for her too, as she got out of the car and straight into a snowdrift that was nearly up to her thighs. Cold and wet slid into her shoes, making her shudder and she grabbed her bag, dashing towards the door. It wasn't locked, of course, she realised belatedly as she pushed it open. In her haste to be gone yesterday, to get away from Karim, she hadn't thought about locking anything after her, just to get on the road.

Another wild fall of snow whirled around her, so thick and heavy that she couldn't see more than a few feet in front of her as she stumbled into the house, deeply grateful for the warmth that even the old-fashioned central heating had thrown out while she was away. A quick glance out of the window showed that the snow had already piled inches deep on top of her car.

'Going nowhere else tonight,' she muttered, shrugging out of her coat and hanging it on a hook on the wall.

So did that mean that Karim wouldn't be able to make it to the cottage either? Did she actually have an extra night's grace?

She needed a coffee and perhaps some food before she thought about her next move, she told herself, pulling open the door into the living room. But before that she'd get the fire going to keep the house warm all through the night. She didn't know if she could rely on the heating and on several bitter nights she had actually slept downstairs on the settee with a coal fire glowing in the grate. It looked as if this was going to be one of those nights tonight.

'Good evening, Clementina,' a voice came to her from across the room. A dark, rich, male voice that she recognised in the space of a jolting, stunned heartbeat.

'What?'

Whirling in a panic, Clemmie almost flung herself towards the light switch, stabbing a finger at it in her haste to illuminate the room.

She already knew what she would see but her thoughts still reeled in shock as she came face to face with the reality. It was one thing to realise that Karim was there, in the house, silent and still, waiting for her. Quite another to confront the reality and see him sitting there, tall and proud, impossibly big, impossibly dark, ominously dangerous, his polished jet eyes fixed on her face. He was wearing another pair of jeans and a grey cashmere sweater that hugged the honed lines of his powerful chest. Simple, casual clothing but of such high quality that they looked out of place against the shabby surroundings, the worn upholstery of the armchair that seemed barely large enough to contain the lean strong frame of the powerful man who looked every bit the King's son that he was.

Surprisingly, he had a sleek tablet computer in his hands, one that he touched briefly to switch it off before letting it drop down on to his knees.

'Good evening, Clementina,' he said again, turning on a smile that was barely there and then gone again, leaving an impression of threat, of danger, without a word having to be said. 'I'm glad you made it back home.'

Was that doubt in his voice? Deliberate provocation to imply that this was the last place he expected to see her?

'I said that I would!' Clemmie protested sharply. 'And I left a note.'

Karim nodded slowly, reaching out for a piece of paper that lay on the table beside his chair. Clemmie recognised the note she had left lying on the bed and she couldn't suppress the faint shiver that skittered over her skin at the thought of what his mood must have been like when he had found it.

'"I'll be back tomorrow",' Karim read aloud, his accent making the words sound strangely alien. '"Promise".'

'I promised. And I kept my word.'

'So you did.'

And she'd surprised him there, Karim admitted. He'd been quite prepared for her to have taken off for good, turning her back on everything she had promised and leaving the situation in the most dangerous and difficult stage possible. He'd even organised contingency plans to move into action if that happened. After all, he'd had emergency plans in place before he'd even started out on the journey to England and all it would have taken would have been a couple of phone calls, and the backup team could have moved into action. He'd almost made those phone calls in the first moments after he'd lost patience with her so-called 'packing' and headed upstairs to the bedroom to bring her down, ready or not. Then he'd seen the open window, felt the icy blast of wintry air sneaking through the gaping space. He'd heard the sound of her car's engine picking up speed, heading away from the cottage. But then he'd seen the note on the bed.

'You didn't think that I would?'

'To be honest—no.'

Putting aside the tablet, he uncoiled from the uncomfortable chair, stretching cramped muscles as he did so. The tracking device he'd left on her car had worked well. When he had known that she was heading home, he had settled down to wait, listening for the sound of her car coming up to the door. Then he'd stayed silent and still so as not to have her turning and running.

'But then did you give me a reason to trust you?'

'Um...no.'

Her eyes dropped away from him as she spoke and she actually chewed at her lower lip, white teeth biting down hard on the soft pink flesh in a way that made him wince inwardly. He wanted to reach out and put his hand to her mouth, stopping the nervous gesture, but instinct held him back though his fingers twitched in anticipation of the contact. He could already feel the heat of her body, the scent of her skin reaching him and the sizzle of electricity down his nerves was like a brand on his flesh. He felt hungry, wanting in a way that was darkly carnal, just barely under control.

'I did run out on you.'

If he hadn't already met her, if he didn't know her voice, her scent and those stunning amber eyes, he might think that this was not Clementina but her double. An identical twin who had stepped in at the last minute to replace her wilder, less conventional sister. This woman was a cooler prospect altogether. Her long dark hair was caught into a shining tail that fell sleekly down her back. Her porcelain skin and golden eyes were free of any make-up—they didn't need any—and the curling black lashes that framed her gaze were impossibly thick and lush without any cosmetic enhancement.

This woman was a princess—a potential queen through and through. In spite of the fact that her clothing was once more on the far side of casual, worn denim jeans with holes at the knees and frayed hems, and an elderly dark pink jumper that had shrunk in the wash or was deliberately designed to give a disturbing glimpse of peachy skin on a tight stomach and narrow waist when she moved. She was tall and elegant. And hellishly beautiful.

But then her eyes came up fast to meet his and there was the burn of defiance in their depths.

'I did leave a note! And all I asked for was another twenty-four hours!'

The wilder Clementina was back as she tossed back her hair. He'd liked the wild Clementina better—hell, he'd loved the wild one even though he hadn't been able to show it. She'd thrown him off balance when he was already tight on edge with all that had happened. The news about his father. About Nabil. About his security chief.

'Would it have hurt so much to give me that?' she challenged.

'Not if I could have been sure that all you really wanted was those twenty-four hours.'

'I said so, didn't I? And you didn't believe me.'

'It depended on what you wanted to do with that extra day—where you planned to go. You ran away from the palace once before. How was I to know if you were setting off to some other hideaway or if you ever planned to come back.'

'I said that I would!' She turned on him a look from those brilliant eyes that was searingly scornful, even with a touch of pity threaded through it. 'It must be hellish being you—being so suspicious of everyone. Is there anyone you can trust? Anyone you can believe in?'

I believed in Razi. In spite of himself, Karim couldn't stop the thought from sliding into his mind. He had put his trust in his brother and look where that had got him. The worst failure of his life. Two deaths he hadn't been able to prevent. A whole change of life, the old one turned inside out. A new role that he had never wanted. Even a bride he had almost had to marry out of duty, if that hadn't been decided against.

'I had no reason to believe in you.'

Dark memories made his words as cold as black ice,

turning the atmosphere inside the room colder than the wintry scene outside.

'And I had no way of knowing that you were simply heading for a birthday party in Lilac Close...'

That got through to her. If he had thought that her eyes were amazing before, they were stunning now, open wide in shock and questioning bewilderment. The knowledge that he had shaken her out of her defiance gave him some satisfaction in return for the way she had escaped yesterday, leaving him with his mission unaccomplished. She had lost all colour now, her cheeks parchment-white, in contrast to the rich dark fall of her hair, those impossible eyelashes.

'How did you know?' Her voice sounded rough and raw, as if it came from a painfully dry throat.

She really didn't know who she was dealing with and the satisfaction at having wrong-footed her so completely was like a roar in his blood.

'It was easy.'

She was still staring at him as he headed for the hall, wrenching open the door. The wild fury of the snowstorm made him wince. It had been nothing like as bad as this when he had driven back to the cottage this morning. There must have been inches—more—that had fallen while he had been inside, waiting for Clementina to arrive. No wonder the reception for his computer had been spotty to say the least.

Hunching his shoulders and ducking his head, he headed out towards where her tiny elderly car was parked, its tyres already halfway deep in the drifts.

Just what was he doing now? Clemmie asked herself, as something that was not just the cold but something more, something deeper and rawer than the icy blast of the wind from outside crept round her neck and shoulders, making her shiver miserably. It was something about Karim himself. About the way he had looked at her, the ice in his eyes, the blank emotionlessness of his tone. He had been sent to fetch her and that was the one thing he was concentrated on, like a hunting dog with the scent of its prey in its nostrils. He was never going to let her go.

But how had he known where she had been? And what did that mean for Harry's safety? She could only stare in confusion as Karim dropped to his knees in the snow, reaching under the car at the front.

Jeans that were as tight a fit as that ought to be illegal. Especially over taut, muscled buttocks like this man possessed...

What *was* she thinking? Clemmie couldn't believe that the thought had flashed into her mind. She had known from a very early age that she was never going to be able to choose her own partner, her own husband. And she had also known that keeping herself respectable, not letting any scandal seep out about her was essential to her reputation. So she had never had the freedom to enjoy the company of the opposite sex like other girls, and had never even let herself think about such things. Instead, she had focused on her studies, on the books that absorbed her, the lessons with her tutor. She had never been allowed to go out to clubs or the cinema like other girls and so had missed out on chatter about boys, about fashion, even music.

Only a few months of getting to know Mary Clendon, who was just six years older than her, had changed her viewpoint, and her knowledge, on a lot of things. But she hadn't expected it to have changed to such an extent! She had never had thoughts like that about any man before.

And she had to start having them with the man who was the most unsuitable—the most inappropriate— person possible.

But Karim was getting up now, moving lithely from his position in the snow to stand upright, brushing briefly at the damp flakes still clinging to his knees before he headed back towards the cottage. The snow was whirling even more heavily, making it seem as if he was making his way through a thick white curtain, his face barely visible, his whole body just a black blur. This way, he should seem so very different. That strange, primitive, uncomfortable feeling that he seemed to spark off just by existing should be diluted by the curtain of snow.

The truth was that it was just the opposite. The contrast with the wild delicacy of the snow made him seem bigger, stronger, darker than ever, head down against the howling wind, and she felt her heart jump, skittering against her ribs as he loomed closer to the door. He came back in a rush to stride into the hall, shaking the snow from his big frame, his dark hair, like some wild animal reaching shelter from a storm.

'Here.'

He tossed something at her, something so small that it was only instinct that had her hand coming out to stop it falling to the floor.

'What?'

She stared down at the tiny metallic disk in blank confusion, not recognising it in any way.

'What is this?'

She glanced up as she spoke, meeting that darkly searching gaze head-on. But then something in his expression, the set of that sensual mouth hit home to her and she knew—she just knew. And there had been that tablet computer he had been studying when she had walked in on him in the sitting room. She had briefly glimpsed something that had looked like a map as he had put it down; a blinking cursor that marked where someone—where *she* had been.

'A tracking device!'

The words exploded from her in a blaze of indignant fury.

Did he know how this made her feel? She had been hunted as if she was a criminal and he had tracked her down. But why should he give a damn how she felt? It was why he was here; what he had come here to do.

'It's a bloody tracking device!' She tossed the disk at him, not caring that it landed on his cheek.

He didn't flinch; barely blinked and just a small brusque movement of his head sent the disk tumbling to the floor.

'And don't frown at me!' she flung at him as she saw those straight black brows twitch together in disapproval at her tone or the vehemence of her words. 'What's one little swear word in comparison to this? Or don't princesses swear in your country?'

Mistake. She knew it as she saw his expression change, his mouth tighten.

'So you remember that you are a princess,' he declared icily. 'Soon to be a queen.'

Every word was tightly enunciated, particularly the titles. He couldn't have made the atmosphere any colder if he'd tried and at that moment a freezing flurry of snow whirled in through the open door, making Clemmie shiver convulsively. With a single backward kick of one booted foot, Karim slammed the door shut and the sudden silence and stillness was unnerving. There was so little space in the small hallway and he seemed bigger, stronger than ever before. The scent of his skin coiled round her senses like some intoxicating drug, making her mouth dry, her head spin.

'And you claimed that you were a prince—Crown Prince, if I remember rightly.'

A crown prince who knew about such security devices. If he was the prince he claimed to be. A sudden rush of apprehension hit home, the room seeming to swing round her on a wave of near panic. What if he had lied all the time? If he was never who he claimed to be?

Had she done something very stupid?

He was between her and the door this time. Even if she flattened herself against the wall, there was no way he would let her squeeze past. He would grab her in an instant, hold her tight...

Shockingly, the fear that came with that thought was blended with an unholy flash of something that had no place in this situation at all. How could she feel a heated *excitement* at imagining those strong hands coming out, fastening around her arms, pulling her close...?

Suddenly she felt overdressed in the angora jumper. It really was far too warm in here. Or was that heat coming from *inside* her rather than the outside?

'I am exactly who I said I am.' The cold flicker of rich black eyelashes dismissed her question as unimportant.

'Then how do you know about such things?' Clemmie nodded towards the small disk that still lay on the floor, pushing at it with the toe of one leather boot. 'Is that the sort of hobby that crown princes have nowadays?'

'I wasn't always the Crown Prince. I had a brother. Razi.'

Had. That took away the heat in her blood, and the bleakness of his eyes made her heart twist.

'What happened?' She had to force the words out because the answer to them was so obvious.

'He died.' Cold and desolate and blunt as a hammer.

'Oh, no…' Having just begun to get to know Harry, she couldn't imagine how it would feel to lose a brother in such a shocking way. 'I'm sorry.'

It was instinctive to reach out a hand to him, but at the same time a brutal sense of self-preservation had her freezing, not having made the connection, when his iced eyes dropped to watch her and then flicked back up to her face, his expression blank and shuttered off.

'I was a security expert—in charge of defence and particularly my brother's safety.'

'But he died—so you failed him?'

Nerves made her say it. Nerves that tightened to screaming pitch when she saw the dark cloud of a scowl that distorted his stunning features, the white lines etched round his nose and mouth.

'He died in a car crash—it was his own driving that caused the accident.'

And that was all he was going to say on the subject, though she was sure there was more. There had to be more. It was hidden behind the tightly clenched jaw, the skin that was drawn too tight over powerfully carved facial bones. *Don't ask*—every line of his expression screamed it without words.

'I…' Clemmie began but Karim was looking at his watch and frowning in a very different way.

'It's time we were on our way.'

'But I need to pack.'

'And you think I am going to fall for that again?' His scorn scoured off a much needed protective layer of her skin. 'You have your overnight bag already.' A nod of his head indicated where the bag still lay where she had dropped it as she had come through the door. 'Anything else you might need will be provided on the way. Nabil has already sent clothes for his princess. They will be on the plane, waiting for you there.'

And Clemmie could just imagine what sort of clothing that would be. Traditional costumes, formal and controlled, covering almost every inch of her body. The days of the freedom of tee shirts and jeans, her hair flying loose, were over. Already, and well before she was ready, the doors of the palace of Rhastaan were closing around her.

'I see.'

There was no point in arguing. Karim was not likely to yield on this or on any other point. She might as well beat her fists against the rigid stone of the cottage walls as beg him to give her any more time.

'Then let's get out of here.'

'You'll have to move your car first,' Karim told her. 'Mine is parked round the back and you're blocking me in. On second thoughts...' He reached for the car key that she had tossed on to the small table in the hall. 'I'll drive—and don't even think about running off.'

'I wouldn't! I only went...' Her voice died away. Did he know why she had gone or just where she had gone? 'I only asked for twenty-four hours—and I said I'd be back. I am back and I'm not planning on running off. You have to believe me.'

Strangely, he did, Karim admitted—today, at least.

Yesterday he'd had a very different opinion of her. But yesterday he'd been angry, tense, too much to think of and collecting Nabil's errant bride being one more thing he didn't want on his shoulders. His father's heart problems and the suspicion that they had been brought on by the stress of the loss of his eldest son and heir had been the last straw. He couldn't get away from the fact that if he had refused to give in to Razi's demand that he have no security detail, his brother might still be here.

Today he felt differently. And it wasn't just because she had come back when she'd said. This new, calmer, dignified Clementina was a very different prospect from the wild, defiant creature who had opened the door to him yesterday and had sneaked out of the house at the first opportunity.

But some instinct had made him give her the twenty-four hours she had asked for. The tracking device had shown that she was at Lilac Close. A few discreet enquiries had revealed that she was friends with the family who lived there. Who were holding a birthday party for their young son. He'd decided to give her the chance and wait.

He was surprisingly glad that he had. And when the door had opened and she'd walked in something had changed inside him. Something unexpected and unsettling. Something he didn't want to take out and face. Not when he had to get this mission completed and one princess delivered to her prospective bridegroom, putting his father's mind at rest on this at least.

He'd already been delayed twenty-four hours too long. It was time they were on the road and heading out of here.

There was no chance of that, Karim realised only a very short time later. He'd already had doubts when he went outside again. Yet more snow had piled up around

Clementina's car. The wheels were half hidden under the drifting snow, the path to the road had been obliterated, and the garden was a white-out. The vehicle was going to be very little use in these conditions. It was lucky he had his four-wheel drive in the yard at the back of the house. If he could only get it on to the road.

But the little car's engine refused to start. Every time he turned the key in the ignition there was a dreadful grating, rasping noise that sounded as if the elderly car was breathing its last. It choked and spluttered—and died with a shudder. One that made him curse and slam his hands down on the steering wheel in exasperation.

'Is there a problem?' Clementina had come out of the house and was leaning down to the window, frowning in concern.

'You could say that.' Once more he tried turning the key. There wasn't even a groan from the engine. 'This car isn't going anywhere today—tonight,' he amended, glaring up at the darkening sky.

'Perhaps if I steered and you pushed…'

'We could try.'

'OK then.' She made a move to hurry out of the way of the opening car door. 'Let me into the driver's seat and I'll… Oh!'

The sentence broke off on a sharp cry of distress as she stepped on a patch of ice hidden under the snow. With a yelp, she fought to stay upright, one leg going one way, the other heading in the opposite direction. Her foot twisted under her, throwing her completely off balance and she fell headlong, landing heavily in a deep snowdrift.

CHAPTER FOUR

'KARIM!'

Her cry of distress was too high, too shocked, to be anything but genuine, setting his nerves on edge and pushing him out of the car as fast as his reflexes would allow.

'Clementina...'

She was struggling to get up, slipped a little and then collapsed again on a small moan.

'What hurts?' Because it was obvious that something did.

'My ankle...'

She was biting her lip hard and only by diverting his attention to the right ankle she had indicated with a wave did he stop himself from pressing his fingers against her mouth to stop the damaging action.

'I fell over on it—twisted it...'

There was nothing to see. Nothing, that was, except the temptation of soft pale flesh, delicate bones, the base of a long slender leg... He ran his hands over the skin of her ankle, pressed gently. Fought against the burn of response that flashed up his nerves as he did so.

'Can you stand?'

He knew his tone was rough and abrupt; didn't need

the reproachful look she cast at him. Reproach that melted into defiance as her chin came up and her mouth firmed.

'I can try.'

Stubbornly, she ignored the hand he held out to her, relying instead on supporting herself on the car's bumper as she hauled herself up. Then, just as she stood upright, she gave another gasping cry as she tried to put her weight on the injured limb.

'OK…'

He caught her before she fell, swung her off the ground and up into his arms.

'Let's get you inside.'

He sensed her rebellion, the tensing of her body, but then, clearly recognising that she wasn't going to manage this on her own, she made herself relax against him. He was grateful for the need to watch his step on the icy path, the fight against the whirling snow as he hurried inside. It distracted him from the feel of her, warm and soft against him. The perfume of her skin rose up, tantalising his senses, and the softness of her hair was like silk against his cheek.

Karim didn't know if he was relieved or sorry when he made it inside the house, shouldering his way along the narrow hall and into the living room. He laid her down on the settee, not caring if the haste of his movements, the abruptness of his actions made it seem as if he was glad to be relieved of the burden of her weight. He *was* relieved, but not because her weight was too much for him to carry. He'd managed much heavier weights over much longer distances before now. But nothing he'd ever carried before had made his heart beat so fast, his breath tangle in his throat so that he was breathing as hard as if he'd run a marathon.

'I'll take your boot off.'

It was a good thing that there wasn't a visible pulse in her ankle, Clemmie reflected as she watched Karim's dark silky head bend over her foot, unlacing and easing the boot from her foot. If there was then he would be sure to see the effect his closeness was having on her, the way that her heartbeat responded to the touch of his hands, the warmth of his breath on her skin. It made her insides twist, her nerves tangle.

This was the first time that she'd seen all that strength and power used in a very different way. A gentle, caring, helpful way. In the moment that he'd picked her up she had felt as if a shield had come round her, blocking off the cold blast of the snowstorm, protecting her from it. And being held against the warmth and strength of his chest had felt like being enclosed in the strongest, most wonderful hug ever, with the heavy regular beat of his heart just under her cheek.

Then she had felt nothing but warmth, but now she felt alternately burningly hot and then shiveringly cold, as if she was in the grip of some delirious fever. The heat in her blood was raw and primitive, a visceral feeling that clawed at her, fraying away her sense of self, leaving her feeling out of control and wildly adrift. She had never felt this way before and it shocked and disturbed her, making her pull away from Karim's grip as she sat up hastily, wanting to escape from it.

'I'll do that,' she snapped, hiding her real feelings behind a mask of indignation.

She wanted to move as far from Karim as possible, but in the same moment that she twisted away she felt surprisingly lost and bereft, needing the warm protection of his body—needing so much more.

'I can manage…'

Unfastening the boot, pulling it from her foot was no problem at all but she made herself focus on it as if it was a struggle, rather than face the real struggle that was going on inside her. Her heart was thudding unevenly, her breath ragged and uneven.

'Are you all right?'

He'd heard the way she was breathing, put the wrong sort of interpretation on it. But that was the way she wanted him to interpret it, wasn't it?

'I'm fine.'

Even in her own ears it didn't sound convincing, no matter how emphatic she made it, so she put on a hiss of discomfort as she pulled the boot from her foot and tossed it to the floor.

'I might have sprained this —it's swollen.'

No, that had been a mistake, as it brought him back to her, those long, square-tipped fingers touching her ankle lightly, testing, stroking…

More! The word burned inside her head and she almost choked trying to swallow it down. *I want more than this.*

'I think…'

Another mistake. Just speaking had brought his head up, made his gaze lock with hers. She could see the black thickness of his lashes in absurd detail, find a tiny reflected replica of herself in the depths of those amazing eyes. His skin smelt of musk and lemon, making her head spin as she inhaled when she breathed.

'You think?' Something had put that note of huskiness into his voice. The fullness of his mouth had a faint sheen where he had moistened it lightly with his tongue. Had he felt as dry-throated, found it as hard to swallow as she had?

'Perhaps something cold would help ease it—reduce the swelling?'

'Good idea.' He pushed himself upright with a speed and satisfaction that scraped her tight nerves painfully raw. 'Then we might actually be able to get on the road—get out of here.'

Did he have to make it so plain that all that mattered to him was their getting on their way? She must have been totally deluding herself thinking that he might actually respond to her as she was reacting to him. Daft idea. Stupid—crazy idea! Just what would a man like Karim—like Crown Prince Karim Al Khalifa—find of any interest in someone like her? Someone in tatty jeans and a sweater, her hair unstyled and usually just left to fall free. Someone who was happier with books and paintings than the clubs and bars her friends were fascinated by.

Someone who must wear her naiveté and ignorance where the opposite sex was concerned like a brand on her forehead. And show it in every unguarded move, every artless look. A man like Karim would be seen with sophisticated glamorous women. He would be like Nabil who, even though he was so much younger, had already been spotted with beautiful models or actresses. He had the freedom to play the field. To sow his wild oats before tying himself down to the arranged marriage that had been planned for them both.

'Peas,' she said abruptly, her uncomfortable thoughts not giving her room to think of anything extra to make it less stark, less brusque. 'Freezer...'

That was no better but at least she waved her hand in the direction of the kitchen. And at least he followed her vague gesture, moving away so that she had time to catch her breath, fight to bring her heart rate under control.

'Wrapping a bag of frozen peas around it might work.' He didn't need the explanation, was already opening the freezer door and rummaging through the bags and containers in there.

'If I have any peas...'

A sudden thought struck her and she couldn't control her response, unable to hold back the giggle that bubbled up in her chest.

'What is it?'

He didn't sound as irritable as before. In fact there was actually a softening warmth in his tone. Or was she just deceiving herself, wanting to hear it?

'What are you laughing about?'

'I can't believe that we are struggling to find a packet of frozen peas when there is all that ice and snow outside! Can't you just fill a plastic bag with the stuff and wrap that around my ankle?'

'It might work—but—ah!' He pounced on something inside the freezer. 'Not peas——but I'm sure sweetcorn will have exactly the same effect. You have so little food in the freezer,' he said as he came back to crouch down by the settee again. 'Barely enough to feed a bird.'

'I was running it all down, getting ready to move away from here—to Rhastaan— Ouch!'

He had dumped the frozen bag on her ankle with a surprising lack of finesse, nothing like the powerful and contained grace of movement he had showed up to now.

'Did that hurt?'

Frantically, Clemmie shook her head, afraid that he would replace the chill of the frozen vegetables with that disturbing and dangerous warmth of his hands, the unsettling feel of his touch.

'No—just the cold! It was a shock. But I'm sure it will help—'

'It had better. We need to get out of here.'

It was as if the few moments it had taken him to hunt through the freezer had pushed the ice into his soul and turned it hard and glacial all over again. But more likely the truth was that she had been letting her imagination run away with her when she had thought she'd heard that unexpected streak of warmth that had softened his tone.

'You're not still thinking of leaving tonight? You're mad! Have you ever tried driving in conditions like this?'

'I have lived—and driven—in Europe before.'

But not in a snowstorm like the one raging outside, Karim had to admit to himself. Under normal circumstances, he would stay right where he was. But these were not normal circumstances. There was nothing normal about the situation he had been put in, first by his father, then Nabil—and now Clementina.

And there was nothing normal about his reaction to her. The soul-twisting, gut-wrenching, brutally carnal hunger this woman woke in him.

Hell and damnation!

Karim pushed himself to his feet and swung away from watching her as she clamped the bag of frozen sweetcorn around her ankle. He couldn't bear to see the way the colour had left her cheeks and then unexpectedly flooded right back into them again. The way she was still worrying at the softness of her lip and, worst of all, the unexpected vulnerability in her eyes. Each one of those responses would twist at his gut. Taken together, they were lethal to his self-control.

Stupid, stupid, stupid! Karim told himself as he headed for the door. He should know better—he did know better.

But knowing and convincing himself that this was not going to happen was getting harder with each thundering beat that made his pulse thud at his temples.

He hadn't had a woman in a long time. Too long. Another thing that was part of the mess that his life had become in the past six months. The upside down and inside out version of the existence he had once had. And that was nothing like it would ever be again.

Perhaps the time spent outside, trying to get the car going again would give him a much-needed dose of reality. Certainly, the cold of the wind and snow should have the effect of an icy shower to cool the heat of his blood. Permanently, he hoped. When he had looked into Clementina's eyes and seen the bruised pansy darkness there, the heat that had flooded his senses had been a form of madness that had sent his brain into meltdown.

It had been strong enough to make him forget for a moment just who she was, and why he was here. It had made him realise just how much he had pushed aside his own needs to deal with other things.

And those needs had now come rushing back in the form of the one woman who was the last person on earth he should feel those things for.

The snow whirled wildly into his face as he opened the door, making him grimace, bring up his hands against the onslaught. He could barely see through the white curtain but he had no intention of turning back. The exercise and the fight against the cold were the only possible antidote he could think of to the frustration that was burning up inside him.

How much longer was he going to be?

Clemmie could not fight against the restlessness that had assailed her since Karim had disappeared out of the door and let it slam behind him. She needed to know what was happening, when they might get on the road. The evening had started to gather in, filling the room with darkness, but when she had tried to get up to switch on more lights, the pain in her ankle had had her sinking back on to the settee with a cry of distress. But if things got any worse, she was going to have to try again. The cold was beginning to fill the air too and she was starting to feel uncomfortably chilled just sitting here.

She was just about to try to push herself to her feet again when the front door banged open and Karim appeared in the hallway. A Karim who looked more like a moving snowman than anything human, his jacket was so piled up with snow and his hair plastered against the strong bones of his skull by the damp.

'At last!' she said.

She pushed herself up in her seat as he stood on the doormat, stamping his feet to clear them of the clinging snow.

'Are we on our way?'

It was inevitable they must be. That was what he had come for—to collect her and take her back to Rhastaan. She wouldn't—couldn't let the painful clenching of her stomach make her think of how it felt to be starting out on this journey, heading for the life she hadn't chosen but she had known must come to be hers. And leaving behind the only true member of her family she had ever known. Her father didn't count. He had only seen her as a pawn in his political manoeuvrings and her mother had walked out on her without a glance back.

'Shall I get my coat?'

If her voice went up and down unnaturally then surely he would think it was because she was struggling to get to her feet. Even she didn't understand the sudden change in her heartbeat, the skittering of her pulse as she took in the stark contrast between the white of the snow and the dark power of the rest of Karim's body, the heavy silhouette of his frame in the doorway, illuminated by the one hanging light.

'No.'

It was stark and cold, biting as harshly as the wind that sneaked down the hall, taking even more of the minimal warmth from the room so that she shivered in more than physical response. What had happened to the man who had laughed with her over the pack of frozen sweetcorn?

'But I thought…'

'Don't think,' Karim snarled.

He pulled off the snow-laden jacket, tossed it aside, stamping his feet again with a sound that echoed ominously in the silence.

'And don't say another word—not unless you can come up with some clever idea as to how we can get the heap of scrap you call a car to move more than a metre or two.'

'It's not a heap of scrap!' Clemmie flared, coming to the defence of her sweet little car. It might be old, it might be a bit battered, but it was hers and it had spelled freedom and escape when she had needed it most. 'We can't all drive the latest luxury four-wheel…'

'You could if you wanted to—' Karim cut in sharply, bringing her to an abrupt halt '—if you'd stayed with your father or in Rhastaan. As Nabil's queen…'

If Nabil would even let her drive, Clemmie told herself. Young as he was, he was traditionalist enough to insist on his wife staying inside, emerging only with an escort, or with Nabil himself. Women in Rhastaan had not been allowed to drive during his father's reign. So would that be permitted now?

'Now I wonder why—' she began, only to break off as a worrying, disturbing thought hit home like a blow. 'My car won't move?'

'Not an inch, not in these conditions. And as my car is trapped in the yard behind it, then we're stuck. Unless I can get a garage truck out—do you have a number?'

He gestured towards the old-fashioned phone on the hall table. Clemmie's heart sank several degrees lower.

'That's not going to help. I had it cut off as part of my preparations to leave. I've been relying on my mobile, even though the reception's unreliable.'

She pulled her phone out her pocket, checked it, then held it out to him, her face spelling out her disappointment.

'Nothing. Yours? Or your tablet? It was working when I arrived.'

One touch of his thumb to the phone told the same story. Not a single bar to indicate any connection. And it was the same with his computer.

'The Internet's down too—everything. This storm has really damaged everything. So, for the foreseeable future, we're imprisoned here until something changes.'

She wished he hadn't used that word 'imprisoned'. It sounded too stark, too dangerous, too scary to face in a moment like this, isolated in this tiny cottage with a man as dark and ruthlessly determined as Karim Al Khalifa.

'Then what…' she began, wondering just how things could get any worse.

But, even as she spoke, the single light illuminating the hall flickered, crackled loudly and then went out, leaving them in total darkness.

'Karim!'

His name was a cry of shock and near panic, the instinct to turn to him coming from somewhere deep and unexpectedly primitive. The blackness around her was thick and almost impenetrable, the only hint of any light coming from the reflected whiteness of the snow beyond the window. She struggled up from her seat on the sofa, the breath hissing in through her teeth as she put her weight on her bruised ankle.

'I'm here.'

Something flared in the darkness. He was using the phone as a torch, the screen lighting the room for a moment. It shone straight up into his face, showing it dark and shuttered, strangely shadowed in the glow, but Clemmie felt that she had never been so pleased to see anyone in her life. The cottage that had previously been safety and home to her now felt like something else entirely. The real world had invaded her sanctuary. It was Karim who had brought that reality, that world in with him, and yet it was Karim that she felt she could turn to. She was glad that he was here. Only one day earlier he had invaded her life, shocking and disturbing her, and yet without him she would have felt lost and adrift on a sea as wild as the storm raging outside.

Karim seemed almost like part of that storm. Harsh and forceful as the weather, like some untamed creature that had come in from the night, his power and presence filled the small house. It was strange that the golden tones of his skin, his name and his accent all came from a land of heat and sun, but here, in the dark and wildness of the icy snow, he still had a power that seemed at one with the elements. This was her home and he was the intruder, but in the darkness and the cold she was grateful for the strength of his very physical company.

'The power's gone…' Stupid and weak as it sounded, it was all she could manage. 'Are you sure we're stuck here for the night?'

'Certain.'

He'd been flicking switches, checking plugs, to make sure that it was not just the bulb or the wiring in the hall and now he was nodding grimly, mouth clamped tight over the anger he clearly would not allow himself to express.

'Nothing, damn it. Do you have a torch? Candles? I need to conserve the power on my phone.'

'Candles in the cupboard under the sink. My torch is in the car.'

She'd thought she might need it on the journey to visit Harry, not once she was back safe in her own home. It was a struggle to just stand there and watch him as he groped his way to the kitchen, hunted in the cupboard. Rattled by all that had happened, and with her twisted ankle still nagging at her painfully, she was so tempted to move to his side, fling her arms around him…feel his strength close around her as it had done when he had picked her up from the snow outside. What stopped her was an instinctive feeling that that would be overstepping an invisible line, risking…

Risking what? A stunningly physical response or, more likely, an immediate rejection—or, even worse, a careful, condescending putting her away from him so that he could get on with the practical matter that he was focused on. She couldn't bear the humiliation of that and it was more than enough to hold her where she was in spite of the yearning that still twisted in her stomach.

A scratching sound of match on box from the kitchen seemed unnaturally loud in the silence. There was a small flare, and the flickering flame of the candle added a tiny light to the darkness.

'There are no holders...'

'No, but we could stick them on saucers,' Clemmie told him, making her way gingerly into the kitchen.

Luckily the cupboard containing the plates and cups was at the other end of the kitchen so, even feeling her way with her hands, she was in no danger of touching him. But she could still see that stunning face in the flickering candle flame, could scent his skin and his hair, drying slowly after the exposure to the snow. She could even see the tiny flecks of the white flakes that decked his long lashes like miniature diamonds and her mouth itched to kiss them away, licking the moisture from his lids with her tongue.

And where had that thought come from? Shock at the way her mind was working had her banging the saucers down on the kitchen worktop with a distinct crash. She had never felt like this with anyone before. And not just because she had tried to keep her mind off such things. She had just never felt this way ever.

'Careful!' Karim's reproof was low and strangely touched with warmth. It was as if he knew only too well what was going through her mind and that thought made her hand shake as she reached for another of the candles.

'Careful yourself—they're my saucers—my candles...'

To her horror she had mistimed the reach, her fingers grabbing at the candle Karim held rather than the spare unlit ones in his other hand. In the same moment the awkward movement twisted at her sore ankle again, making her overbalance and tumble headlong towards him.

'*Careful!*'

It was so very different this time. Every trace of that warmth, the light amusement had faded from the single word and the edge on his tone sent shivers down her spine. Shivers that combined with the shock of electricity where her fingers had closed over the hand that held the candle. It was impossible not to think of the shape she held, long and hard, and capable of such heat.

She had one moment to try to recover, one moment of looking up straight into his eyes and seeing the darkness there that was more than the shadows surrounding them, the burn of something that was more than the reflection of the flame he held between them. But then, as she almost overbalanced, he reacted swiftly, dropping the candle into the sink so that she didn't fall dangerously close to it but instead stumbled right into his arms.

In the darkness again, it was more than she had anticipated. More than she could ever have expected. Her face was up against his chest, pressed into the softness of the cashmere, crushed against the hardness of collarbone and ribcage, inhaling the scent of his skin, feeling the heat and the muscles in his throat against her brow. She heard him draw in a sharp breath, sensed him swallow hard, wished she could do the same to ease the choking dryness in her own mouth.

She felt his hands come out to hold her, stop her from falling, and her breath caught in her throat as the heat of those hard palms reached her through her clothing, searing the skin on her thighs, her waist. She could have sworn that his hands lingered, curling closer, holding her against him so that she couldn't break free even if she'd wanted to. But breaking free was the last thing on her mind. Her heart had taken off at an alarming rate, blood thundering in her ears. But Karim's pulse rate was as cool and controlled as if he had simply just caught hold of the handle of a broom or mop—rather than a living breathing woman.

And yet...

'Shall we try again?'

There was a definite sardonic edge to the question, an almost brutal stiffness in the way he caught her arms and straightened her up, moving her away from him as if he suddenly felt that her touch would contaminate him. She could sense no reluctance to let her go, catch no sense of regret in that calmly indifferent voice. But just for a second she had been crushed up against him and even as the heat of her own response had flooded through her she had known that he had to be feeling something too. There was no denying the hard and heated evidence of his body crammed against hers; the evidence of a carnal hunger that not even a virgin with as little experience of men as she had could possibly mistake in any way. It could have—should have—frightened her but instead it sent a secret, stinging thrill running through her.

'Karim...'

Protest, encouragement or question? She didn't know, didn't care. Her head was swimming, every cell in her body seemed to be on fire at just the thought that a man like this—this man—could want her in that way. She ached and needed in a way she'd never thought possible, heat and moisture waking deep inside. And she hoped...

But already he was bending, picking up the candle. He turned to pull the saucers towards him, dismissing her from his thoughts, before reaching again for the box of matches. It was business as usual, and he was cold and distant again. So withdrawn that she began to believe she had imagined any other reaction. Was she really so desperate, so like some schoolgirl in the middle of her first heavy crush, that she was allowing herself to dream that the most devastating man she had ever met would want her, of all people?

As the light from the candles flooded into the darkness it seemed as if it was followed by a shiver of reality that reproached her for fooling herself. In the same moment that the flame illuminated some sections of the room, it also darkened and deepened the shadows of others, making them bleak and impenetrable as Karim's shuttered face. And with it came an awareness of the way that the atmosphere in the room had changed, physically as well as mentally.

CHAPTER FIVE

'THE...THE ELECTRICITY going out means that the heating has gone off too,' she managed, needing to say something to break the silence that had tightened round her. 'This house is going to get really cold very fast.'

It was already starting to chill rapidly in a way for which even Karim's glacial stare couldn't take the blame. The eerie sound of the wind howling around outside, rattling the elderly windows in their ill-fitting frames, added to the uncomfortable atmosphere.

'You have a fire.' Karim nodded towards the open grate.

'If it will light!' Clemmie acknowledged, knowing from bitter experience how difficult that could be. 'I've spent I don't know how many hours fighting with the damn thing in the past.'

'It will light.'

Karim's statement was resolute, adamant. The fire would do as it was told. It would light; it had no choice.

And it did light, of course. With an ease that made a mockery of all the times she had battled with the old-fashioned grate, he soon had strong flames catching on the wood he'd laid as kindling, licking around the coal.

The crackling sound it made, the sparks that flew up the chimney promised that warmth would soon follow.

Which, of course, it did. Karim was in charge and nothing dared defy him. And Clemmie had to admit that she was more than thankful to see the golden glow fill the grate, feel the heat reaching out to touch skin that was now chilled through as the darkness closed in around them, the candles providing only a minimum of light. They would need to ration them if the electricity stayed off much longer. The half dozen or so she had in the cupboard would barely last the night. She didn't want to admit to herself that some of the ice that seemed to have filled her veins had come from the realisation of just what a fool she had been. Imagining that Karim of all people could actually find her attractive—could want her!

The way he had immediately turned his attention to the task in hand, clearly forgetting all about her and any connection she might have imagined they'd made, told her in no uncertain terms that that fantasy had been all hers. And a fantasy was what it was.

'Do you have any food for this evening?'

Karim kept his eyes focused on the fire as he spoke. It had been bad enough in the dark with her. The half-light of the candles and the fire was too alluring where it played over the warm curves of Clementina's body, put an extra spark into the depth of her eyes. Being blind accentuated all your other senses and, though he hadn't actually been blind, being lost in the complete darkness had had the same effect.

He had felt the warmth of her skin, inhaled the subtle floral and spice scent of her perfume. A perfume that was threaded through with the intensely personal aroma of the feminine body that had come so close to his. He had felt the warmth of her skin through the denim of her jeans when his hands lingered, longing, tempted, around the curve of her hips, the indentation of her waist. And in the deep silence, all outside muffled by the heavy coating of snow that had fallen, he could hear the soft sound of her breathing, knew the moment when it caught in her throat and then broke again in a faint hiccup of response to his touch.

Fool! Bloody stupid fool!

He rammed the poker in amongst the hot coals, feeling that he knew exactly how they must feel. He had arrived at the cottage—was it less than forty-eight hours before?—thinking that all he had to do was to get the woman he had been sent to collect into his car, drive her to the airport, and deliver her to her prospective bridegroom. But from the moment he had seen Clementina Savanevski he had known he was in trouble.

How badly in trouble he hadn't realised quite then.

Suddenly his life and the plan he had for it had been turned on its head. Clementina had been nothing like he had expected and he had never anticipated the force of his own response to her. She had already delayed their departure by her disappearing act—and now this!

'That's the bad news.'

Her voice came from behind him and he knew he should turn to face her. But for now he wanted to stay turned away, to focus his attention on the fire before him, to tell himself that the heat of the flames was what was burning him up inside. It had nothing to do with anything else.

Nothing.

'What's the bad news?'

No, dammit, the fire was settled and going fine. He

was going to look like all sorts of a fool if he didn't turn.
So much so that she would suspect there was something
up and he didn't want her thinking any such thing. He
had made it seem as if the practicalities—candles, light,
warmth—were all that mattered to him. They were all
that should matter to him. And he didn't want to let any
suspicion of anything else slide into her mind.

'What's the bad news?' he demanded again as he
swung round.

She was standing behind the old shabby settee, holding
on to the back in a way that suddenly made him remember her injured ankle and curse himself for forgetting.
Without that they might still have been on their way out
of here, but she'd fallen and he'd had to bring her inside.
Another delay to add to the ones that had ruined every
last detail of the plans he'd had to fulfil his promise to his
father and then get on with his own life while he could.

Cursing silently, he felt for the phone that he had
pushed into the back pocket of his jeans and checked it
again. The screen told him all he needed to know. There
wasn't a hint of reception. Not a single bar to show even
the hope of any call getting through. They were well
and truly trapped. As he acknowledged the thought the
whirling wind of the storm outside built up in power and
ferocity to emphasise the point.

'The food.'

She'd noticed his abstraction and was frowning faintly.

'There might be some bits and pieces in the fridge—
but I won't be able to do much with them. The cooker
is electric...'

A wave of her hand indicated the elderly and inade-
quately fitted kitchen.

'So that's gone—so has the kettle. I can offer you a sandwich...'

'I'll make it.'

Karim was already moving towards the kitchen. Did he have to make it so obvious he was impatient and anxious to be away from her? Clemmie wondered. If he had checked his phone once, he'd checked it a hundred times and he had only given up on moving her car when the storm had driven him inside.

'I'll do it!' she protested, pushing him aside as she hobbled into the other room. 'Small and tatty as it is, this is my house! You can't come in here and throw your weight around just because you're Crown Prince of somewhere...'

'I was thinking of your ankle.' It was a mocking drawl, one that made her stiffen her back in defiance. 'Can you manage to stand on it?'

'I'm fine.'

She would do it or die in the attempt, Clemmie told herself, grabbing the remains of a loaf from the bread bin and slamming it down on to the worktop. She was already regretting moving much at all, with her ankle aching and protesting fiercely when she put her weight on it. She opened the fridge door awkwardly and peered in, balancing precariously on her sound leg.

'Cheese? Salad?'

The exclamation of annoyance from behind her should have warned her, but she was so determined on not looking at him that she missed it completely. All she knew was that she was suddenly grabbed from behind, snatched up into the air and carried forcibly back into the sitting room. There Karim dumped her unceremoniously on to the settee and pushed her back into the cushions with a firm hand when she struggled to get up again.

'Stay there,' he said in the sort of voice he might use to control a dog. One he expected to be obeyed.

Clemmie decided against fighting him over this. He'd been right about her ankle, though it galled her to have to admit it, and the warmth of the fire was welcome after the sneaking chill of the kitchen. She huddled closer to the grate and hugged a cushion tightly for comfort. It did nothing to wipe away the burn of Karim's touch, ease the uneven lurch of her heart. The scent of his skin still lingered on her sleeve where he had held her and, believing he was occupied with the food, she couldn't resist the primal urge to rub her cheek against it, inhaling deeply.

'Food... Such as it is.'

She jumped like a startled cat as a plate came over the back of the settee, pushed almost into her face. Had he seen anything? Had he caught the betraying reaction she'd just given in to? With the scent of his hands still in her nostrils she felt the nerves in her body spring into painful pins and needles life as Karim came close to the fire. Would he sit beside her on the sofa? She didn't know if she could bear it, cope with it, if he did. But in the same heartbeat she wanted it; longed for it with a burn that scorched her nerves.

So it was impossible to snatch back the sigh that escaped her when Karim took the only other seat in the room, pulling the battered brown armchair up to the fire as he sat down with his own sandwich on a plate. She saw that the sound had caught his attention, watched that warning frown appear between his dark brows, and nerved herself for the inevitable sarcastic comment.

Surprisingly it didn't come.

'Why do you live here? Like this,' Karim demanded instead.

The way he looked round the room, dark eyes assessing, made her grit her teeth. She knew the cottage was shabby. But she liked it that way. It was the way that Nan had left it when she'd died and it brought back such wonderful happy memories of those brief childhood visits.

'I'm sorry if it's not the sort of palace that you are used to.'

'Nor the sort of palace *you* are used to,' Karim parried. 'And very definitely not the sort of place you will be living in from now on.'

Don't remind me! Did he really think that would be the sort of thing that would make her think differently about this cottage? That she would actually prefer the marble palace of Rhastaan where her life had been signed away as a child and from which she could never hope to escape?

'But this place is my own! All mine and no one else's.'

And until Karim's arrival, no one from Markhazad or any of the surrounding desert kingdoms had known anything about it. He had invaded her privacy, stalking into her home like some dark, arrogant wild cat, taking with him her last traces of seclusion and solitude. From now on her life would not be her own. She would live in the public eye if she ever set foot outside the palace. And inside… Her mind skittered away from considering the prospect of life with the husband who had been chosen for her, the emptiness of a political marriage from which she had no escape.

If he had looked like Karim, though…

'Yours?' Karim queried.

She really had his attention now. That probing gaze,

dark with disbelief, was fixed on her face, and a frown had snapped his black brows together.

'My grandmother lived here, and I visited sometimes when I was a child. She left me the cottage in her will—and—well, there didn't seem much point in changing it seeing as I was only here for such a short time and...'

She had foolishly taken a small bite of her sandwich and now her throat closed sharply over the bread so that she almost choked. She grabbed at the glass of water, all they had to drink, and swigged it desperately, hoping that he would miss the tears in her eyes or at least take them for the result of her coughing fit rather than a reaction to the cruel combination of past memories and the prospect of the future that had assailed her. Karim didn't move an inch, didn't even blink, his own sandwich part raised from his plate but frozen in mid-air. She could feel the burn of his searing stare, those dark eyes seeming to strip away a defensive layer of skin and leaving her raw and vulnerable underneath.

'Two day-old bread!' she managed by way of an explanation, waving her own sandwich in front of her face in the hope of distracting him. 'Too dry.'

It was too, she realised with a grimace as she made herself force another mouthful down. She had been expecting to move on from the cottage, so her supplies of food had been deliberately run down.

'So you were planning on going back?' He'd picked up on what she had been about to say without her having to complete the sentence.

That brought her head back, her chin coming up in defiance as she blinked the betraying tears away from her eyes in order to be able to face him. In the firelight, shadows flickered and danced across his rough-carved face, making it impossible to read what thoughts the black ice of his eyes really held deep inside them.

'Don't sound so surprised. Of course I was going back.' The prospect of what might happen if she hadn't made her shudder inwardly. 'In fact there was no need for your father to send you—or anyone else to come and fetch me.'

Oh, but there was. Karim prayed that his reaction didn't show on his face. He had no wish to have her panicking and making things so much worse. If they could get any worse.

His appetite vanishing in the blink of an eye, he tossed his sandwich down on to his plate and slammed it on to the small coffee table. He was supposed to be out of here now, and well on his way back to Rhastaan. In fact they should have been there already, landing at the airport where Nabil's security men would be waiting to take over. He would be free of his duty, of the promises that had been made, free of the burden of responsibility for Clementina, and on his way back to his own life.

Except that the changes in that life meant that he would never again be really free. No longer the 'spare' to Razi's heir, with the extra degrees of independence that had brought, he was now learning what it meant to be the future Sheikh of Markhazad. Belatedly, he felt he had begun to understand just why a sense of rebelliousness, of restlessness had driven his brother. He also had to try to be both sons to his father, who had felt the loss of his heir so terribly.

But to think of Clementina as a burden grated against something deep inside. Her position and the promises his father had made, the peace treaties that were at risk now, were what made this situation so difficult. Without them, being with this beautiful woman, whose face was lit by the flames in the hearth, putting a glow into her eyes, tinting her skin with gold, would be no burden at all.

Hell, no!

Ferociously he slammed a door shut in his mind, cutting out the dangerous thoughts. But it was too late. Already his senses had responded, his blood flooding with a heat that had nothing to do with the burning coals that were only making the smallest impact on the encroaching cold. His gaze fixed on the softness of her lips, gilded by the light, so full, so soft that his own mouth hungered to take them, to plunder their sweetness, feel them give way under his, yield to the invasion of his tongue. He wanted to tangle his hands in the fall of her hair, inhale the intimate scent of her body, feel the softness of her breasts against him as he had when he'd carried her into the house after her fall in the snow.

Damnation, he wanted more than that. He wanted her on her back on this rug right in front of the fire. He wanted her under him, holding him, her body arching up to meet his, pressing herself closer…

No.

Grabbing his glass of water, he downed the entire contents in a series of harsh, powerful gulps that did nothing to douse the fires inside him. His body ached, the hardness between his legs making it impossible to sit comfortably, so that he pushed himself to his feet and paced around the room, finding a new frustration in the impossibly small space that confined him. What he needed was a brutal workout, a punishing run for miles until he was exhausted, or an ice-cold shower to subdue his demanding libido.

All of which were impossible for him, even the cold

shower. Unless he went outside into the snowstorm, of course. And he could just imagine Clementina's reaction if he did any such thing.

And, the way he was feeling, he doubted that even jumping into one of the snowdrifts would do anything to cool the heat that had been building up inside him ever since he had first met Clementina.

She was watching him now, her eyes wide with confusion and bewilderment, and who could blame her? He was acting like a captured wolf, trapped in too small a cage. He had to get a grip and distract himself from the hunger that was eating at him.

Talking. That might do it. Talk about anything—anything but sex. Think about anything but sex. And then when he was out of here he would find the nearest, most willing woman and lose himself in her. It might take more than one but at least he could have fun trying.

Now, what had they been talking about? The cottage and the fact that she had come here—running away from her duty.

'So why didn't you tell anyone where you were—and that you'd be back?'

It was the last thing Clementina had been expecting. She had been sure that he had something else on his mind, something that had brought that black scowl to his face, tightened the muscles in his long body until they made him stand as if he was ready for a fight.

'Leave another note like the one I left you?'

Broad shoulders shrugged off her challenge, her shaky defiance seeming to bounce off those taut muscles.

'I doubt very much that I'd have been believed. And then…'

But no, that was going too far. He already knew where

she had been last night. The address was obviously filed away in some database on his computer, along with the trail that the tracking device had followed to Mary's house. If she let anyone suspect that Harry existed, that he had been adopted after her mother's unexpected death, then it would be the easiest thing to hunt down 3 Lilac Close and…

Following his example, she tossed the bread and cheese down on to her plate and pushed it aside, unable to think of eating any more. What she was doing would protect Harry—and Mary and Arthur. It would give them the future that she couldn't hope for herself. She had signed the cottage away to the Clendons and she could only hope that they, and especially Harry, would love it as much as she had.

'Yet you left me a note—and expected it to be believed.'

And even now she was still asking herself why. Not why she had left it. That had been the only honourable thing she could do. She couldn't just have taken off out of here without leaving some communication that said she was coming back, that the future that was all mapped out for her was one she accepted—she had to accept.

But she didn't quite know why she had thought that it mattered particularly to leave it for *him*—and that he would believe she had meant it.

'But you didn't really believe me—did you?' she challenged. 'You didn't need to, for one thing—you had that tracking device on my car. You could have come and picked me up at any point.'

'I could—but you seemed to be having such fun.'

'Fun that isn't part of my royal duties…'

The words faded away from her tongue, leaving her mouth dry and tight.

'I was having...you saw?'

Karim didn't condescend to give her an answer, but his total stillness told her all she needed to know.

'You followed me!'

He didn't even blink.

'I came here to fetch you back to Rhastaan. It is my duty to make sure that you arrive there safely and in time for the wedding ceremony.'

Something in the word 'safely' caught on a raw edge of Clemmie's nerves, making her frown in uncertainty. But there was something else that had slid into her mind, something that now seemed to explode in a shock reaction.

'You followed me—you saw where I was—you saw I was...h-having fun.' So had he seen Harry too? Had he looked through the window and seen the obvious affection she had for the little boy and he for her? Could he now tell someone...?

'But you didn't fetch me from there. You watched and then you came back here and waited for me to come home. Why?'

'I have been asking myself that too.'

'And how have you answered it?'

Another of those expressive shoulder shrugs but this time it was not just dismissive. Instead she would have said that it had a touch of uncertainty about it except that uncertainty was not something she could possibly associate with Karim in any way.

'I wanted to see what would happen.'

'But if I hadn't come back—if I'd stayed or moved on somewhere else... No, don't answer that!'

She caught the gleam of something disturbing and dangerous in that rough-hewn face. Something that the flickering candlelight made even more worrying as it cast shadows across his stunning features. She knew what would have happened if she'd tried anything else. He would have come after her like the hunting cat she'd imagined him to be earlier, and when he'd caught up with her...

Something cold and nasty slid down her spine at just the thought of what would have happened then. But, in the same moment, her pulse also jumped at the image of him coming after her, hunting her down, making her his.

Oh—that was stupid! Quite the most impossible image! If this man hunted her down, it was only to collect her and take her back to another man—to her prospective bridegroom. And he was only doing that because of this strongly felt sense of *duty* that he kept harping on about. Did she need any further evidence that he had never considered her as a person in all this, but only as the 'target', the errant princess he must return to her arranged marriage, no consideration as to whether she was willing or not coming into it?

'Tell me something...why is it that you are here—? Yes, I know you've told me that you've come to escort me back to Nabil. But why *you*? Surely there must be other security men—other people you could have sent to fetch me.'

Other security men who wouldn't have disturbed her as much as this man did. Who wouldn't have sparked off these wild, sensual fantasies that had been plaguing her ever since Karim had walked into her life.

'Why you?'

She'd touched on some raw nerve there; the change in his face, in his stance, gave it all away. He swung towards the windows, pulling the curtains closed on the night with a rough, jerky movement. With the reflected light of the snow shut out, the small room seemed even darker and more confined, claustrophobically so, and Karim's lean muscular body filled the space with a sense of power that it seemed impossible the tiny cottage could contain. Clemmie didn't know if the tiny hairs at the back of her neck had lifted in apprehension or excitement. She only knew that it suddenly seemed as if the heat from the fire couldn't reach her and she was shivering in shock and reaction.

'My father had promised Nabil's family that he would make sure you reached Rhastaan safely. He owed them that, after Nabil's father had saved his life once in a helicopter accident. It was a matter of honour.'

And that honour meant more than any consideration of the person he was dealing with. The need to get her back to Rhastaan overriding anything else.

'But he has been taken ill—heart problems—that meant he had to hand the task over to someone else.'

And that was all she was. 'The task' who would be handed over like a parcel that needed delivery. If he had stabbed a knife between her ribs he couldn't have wounded her more.

'And only you could keep that honour? You don't have the loyalty of your own security team?'

If she'd picked up her glass of water and flung it in his face, he couldn't have reacted more sharply. It was as if she was watching a metal door slamming closed behind his eyes, shutting her off from everything in his thoughts, blanking out his expression completely.

'You don't!'

The realisation was sharp, shocking like a stab of light

into her mind and closing off her throat, taking her breath with it.

'You can't trust your own men.'

Her voice came and went like a radio with faulty tuning and the strength seemed to be draining from her legs, seeping away from her, leaving her trembling with shock.

'My father's men.' Karim's tone was flat, totally deadpan, his face mirroring his expressionless response. 'Or, rather, one—as far as we know for now. We found that he was working for Ankhara.'

Ankhara. The man whose very name was a threat to her own security, who was determined to prevent the marriage to Nabil from going ahead. Who wouldn't let a mere woman stand in the way of his ruthless ambition.

Surely the room couldn't have got so very much colder in the space of several uneven heartbeats? The fire in the hearth was burning brighter than ever but the heat didn't seem to be reaching out to her. Instead she was chilled right through to the bone.

'And he was the one who was supposed to come and fetch me?'

A brusque, curt nod was his only answer, not a word being spoken.

'So you came instead of him.'

To make sure that the job was done properly. Because of that sense of honour he had referred to. The cold that was creeping through her body was there because of her own fault. Somewhere along the line, weakly, foolishly, she had allowed herself to think, to dream, however briefly, that there was the possibility that Karim had come to protect her specially. That he had cared just a little bit because—because it was her? What sort of foolishness had she let creep into her thoughts, making her feel that she *mattered*? At least to him. But the truth was that she mattered to no one.

It was a matter of honour.

Karim's honour, and that of his father, his country. The country where he now was Crown Prince after the loss of his brother. He took that role very seriously, it seemed.

CHAPTER SIX

THE SMALL ROOM seemed to shrink even more, the darkness closing in around her as she faced up to the truth of what was happening. She was just a pawn in so many political games. She wasn't a person, just a piece on a political chessboard. She shivered convulsively, unable to hold back the instinctive response to her thoughts.

'Are you cold?' Those sharp black eyes had caught her reaction, and he was moving forward hastily. 'Shall I put some more coal on the fire—build it up?'

'No.' Her shake of the head was determined, almost wild, sending her hair flying around her face. 'No, thanks.'

All she wanted was to go away and hide somewhere, go into the darkness with her thoughts. Close her eyes and try to hold on to that last image of Harry as he waved from the window when she had driven off. The last time she would ever see the baby brother she was doing this for. Surely Karim, who said that he had lost a brother too—and in a far more permanent way—would understand.

But then she looked up into those opaque eyes, all emotion wiped away—if there had ever been any there in the first place—and she knew that she was dreaming even more if she allowed herself to think that he even saw her as a person. She was that point of honour that had to be dealt with. He would do his duty, deliver her to wherever she needed to be—where he needed her to be—and then he would go on his way and forget her, never even looking back for a second.

'I'm tired,' she managed, avoiding the real issue that tormented her. 'I want to go to bed—to sleep.'

He didn't even try to hide the way he looked at his watch, checking the time, and just that single sidelong glance told its own story, reminding her of the frequent occasions on which he had done just that already tonight. Checking his phone, his computer, frustrated by the delay that kept them trapped here together. Impatient and anxious to be on his way. To get this matter of duty over and done with, the responsibility that his father had passed on to him, handed over to the people who really wanted her.

And then he could go home, satisfied that he had done his duty. Honour would be served.

'Yes, I know it's early,' she snapped, flinging her own scathing glance at the grandfather clock in the corner, its large white face only barely revealed in the flickering light of the flames. 'But I'm tired. I had a late night last night. I was talking with my friends,' she added with even more of an edge as she saw his dark head come up, black eyes narrowing sharply as he stared at her down the long, straight beak of his nose, nostrils actually flaring as if he had caught some distasteful smell just beneath them.

Harry had been restless, overexcited by the party and then unhappy at the thought that she was going away, that his beloved Clemmie would be leaving in the morning and was unlikely to be coming back. In order to let Mary have a much needed night's sleep, and to indulge herself with one last long night together before those dreadful final farewells, she had sat with the little boy, reading him story after story, and then finally rocking him to sleep in her arms. She had been so afraid of disturbing him that she had sat there for over an hour until she had felt that she could ease herself away and leave him sleeping. As a result she had barely had more than a couple of hours' rest herself.

'We could do something…'

Karim cursed himself for letting the truth about the situation with Ankhara slip. It had had exactly the result he had dreaded, set her off in a panic so that now she was restless and unsettled as a nervous cat. He doubted very much that she would be likely to sleep as she had declared, even though the shadows under her eyes did seem to speak of her need to rest. They had darkened since he had seen her first, making him wonder just what had happened in the days since he had arrived at the cottage. What had happened last night? He had waited, watched, until all the lights in the house had gone out, but all he had seen before that was some kid's party, and, later, a group of mothers arriving to take their little ones home.

'And what, exactly, would you propose?' Her head was flung back, huge eyes widening even more as she faced him. 'Play some music, perhaps. Or watch a film on DVD—oh, no, I forgot—we don't have any electricity, do we. So that's a no then.'

'We could talk.'

Talk! What the hell was he thinking about even suggesting it? Talking meant her moving her lips, drawing attention to the wideness of her mouth, the soft fullness of those rose-tinted lips. Every time she spoke, or when she had opened her mouth to eat or drink, all he had been able to think of had been the way those lips would feel under his, how they would part to the pressure of his tongue. How her mouth would taste deep inside, warm and moist in an intimate caress.

It was all he could do now not to stare fixedly at that mouth, or reach out a hand to trace a finger along the bow shape of her lips.

'Talk? No, thanks. I've had enough lectures on duty and honour from you and everyone else to last me a lifetime.'

He'd missed a beat, watching her lips and tongue frame those words, wanting...

'Something else then.' He sounded as if he'd swallowed broken glass, his throat husky and raw, so that she frowned at him when she heard it.

'Something else?' She rolled her eyes in exasperation. 'Precisely what? Oh—perhaps you'd like to try a board game—I know Nan has some somewhere. A little old-fashioned looking but they don't really change, do they? Can I challenge you to a game of Ludo or perhaps you'd prefer Snakes and Ladders?'

She couldn't make it plainer that she was being sarcastic, but he couldn't resist taking her up on it, teasing her deliberately.

'Why not? If that's what's available. And I've never played either of those—I have to admit to being intrigued to find out just what sort of game goes by the name of— Ludo? And what the devil is Serpents and Ladders?'

'Snakes. It's a board game—they both are. And you're not going to convince me that you actually want...'

'Oh, but I do.'

The look she turned on him as she tested the truth of his assertion was impatience, indignation and total disbelief all in one. The trouble was that it was pure provocation at the same time, the wicked gleam in her eyes, the faint curl at the corner of her mouth. He hoped to hell that these ridiculously named games would have something to hold his attention, distract him from looking at her, keeping his eyes on the board or something so that he wasn't so tempted.

Her little hiss of irritation was so appealing that it was worth having suggested this just to hear it, and to see the spark in her eyes as she told him without words that he was going to regret this. The pert challenge of her rear pushing against the denim of her jeans as she bent over a drawer in the sideboard to pull out the box of games was much more difficult to resist and his palms itched to smooth across the taut buttocks, curving over the swell of her hips.

Hell—no! That was the way to destruction and devastation. Why did the one woman to make him this hot and hard in so long have to be the woman who was barred from him? The woman who would destroy his honour and that of his family—his country—if he tangled with her. It would be one hell of a lot easier if she wasn't giving off signals that a blind man could read at a hundred paces. She was as drawn to him as he was to her, but they could not, they *must* not act on it.

Needing to hide the brutally physical effect she was having on him, he sat down hard on the settee she had just vacated and forced his attention on to the boxes she had lifted from the drawer. It wasn't easy. The swing of her hair as she placed the boxes on the table brushed against his face in a way that was a torment to his heightened senses, and her position as she bent to open the top gave a savagely tempting glimpse of the shadowed val-

ley of her cleavage and the creamy curves of her breasts.
Only by digging his teeth hard into his lower lip, almost
drawing blood, did he manage to hold back his groan of
primitive response.

'So tell me the rules…because there are rules, I pre-
sume?'

Weren't there always rules? Rules that ran your life
on regimented lines. Rules that would cause chaos if
broken. The scar on his chest stung as if in response to
his thoughts and he rubbed at it abstractedly. If he had
needed any reminder of what happened when the rules
got twisted and shattered, it was right there, underneath
his shirt, etched into his skin. His life had been built
on loyalty. Loyalty to his father, to his older brother the
Crown Prince, to his country. Those had been the rules—
until he'd bent them so that his brother could ease up on
the protocol he fretted at. As a result, those rules had
been blown so wide apart that new ones had to be put
in their place.

And Razi was dead, his reputation buried with him

But at least these rules were simple. It was, after all,
just a child's game, with die and counters, cartoon images
of brightly coloured snakes, ladders of various lengths.
It did help to distract him—barely. The truth was that he
could play the game with just one quarter of his concentration, the rest he tried to fix on other matters—keeping
the fire alight, removing the guttering stubs of candles
and replacing them with new ones, checking his phone,
his computer, to see if the connection had been restored.
It never had, only adding an extra mental burn to the rage
of his physical frustration.

At the same time, there was a strangely intense relaxation in what he was doing. If someone had told him at

the start of this mission that he would end up sitting opposite the gorgeous, sexy, beddable woman he had been sent
to collect—playing a child's game and actually *enjoying
it*, Karim told himself half an hour or so later, he would
never have believed them. And if they had told him that
the woman he was sitting opposite was the woman who
made his body harden and hunger in a way no woman in
the rest of the world had ever done—and he hadn't been
able to do a thing about it— he would have declared that
they were crazy. Totally out of their heads. There was
no way he was going to accept any mission that put him
into such a position, and to hell with the repercussions.

But no one had told him, no one had warned him. And
he was here, now, with irresistible temptation in the female form sitting opposite—so close—too close—and
he was having to clamp down hard on every carnal impulse that made him a man.

But at least she had calmed down. She seemed to have
pushed away the realisation that there was a possible
threat to her, a danger from the plotters and manipula-
tors who didn't want her marriage to go ahead. She had
lost that look of the startled rabbit caught in the head-
lights of an oncoming car, and she was focusing on the
game. She was also fiercely competitive, biting her lip
in disappointment when she hit a snake, or crowing in
delight when he did the same, especially when it was the
longest snake on the board.

'Down!' She laughed, the sound tangling round his
insides and pulling hard. 'Go on—right down to thirteen
again! I'm going to win this game.'

'Not if I can help it!'

Glancing up into Karim's face, lit for a moment then
shadowed again as the flames played over his features,

Clemmie saw the way his mouth had softened slightly, his eyes less like deep black ice. He thought he'd settled her down, she knew. He believed he had distracted her from the thought that out there, in the wildness of the storm, someone was hunting them—hunting her. And he had almost succeeded.

He'd be doing a better job of it if he wasn't so intent on looking at his phone, tapping the screen of his tablet, to check on what was happening. The small frequent movement set her teeth on edge, reminding her that not all was as peaceful and warm as the small firelit room.

And yet, in the strangest way, she felt a relaxation such as she had never known before. Not since she had played these games with her grandmother. The simple moves of the game, the heat of the fire, the flickering light of the candles, all created an enclosed space, a sanctuary, where there was just the two of them, and the rest of the world was shut out beyond the thick stone walls of the cottage. The desultory conversation drifted over a range of topics, nothing too deep, nothing too controversial. She had never felt so free in her life. Never believed that she could actually say what she wanted, express herself openly, and not be slapped down verbally as she was at court, or warned with a black frown or worse from her father if she ventured into forbidden territory.

She even felt comfortable with the physical sensations that were racing through her body, stinging at her nerves, as she shared this confined space with the big dark man who had invaded her life. She *wanted* to know the fizz of excitement that made it almost impossible to sit still. She wanted to hear the rough texture of his voice scraping across her skin, allow herself the luxury of leaning forward, apparently to move her counter over the board, but in fact to inhale the scent of his body and let it intoxicate her in the most sensual way.

'Five…'

Karim totted up the number of dots on the bright red die and counted the spaces as he moved his counter along, narrowly missing the same long ladder that had taken her own token almost within reach of the end goal. She was so intent on watching his long-fingered hand, the tanned skin, the clean, cared-for nails…imagining what that strength, that control would feel like on her own skin, how it would be if it lost control, that her breath quickened in her lungs, her mouth drying fast.

'My turn…'

As she reached for the die and the shaker, her hand touched his, the burn of electricity sizzling over every nerve, making her gasp in uncontrolled shock.

'What?'

His dark head came up sharply, black eyes burning into hers so that she almost flinched away from their force on her skin.

'N—nothing…'

Her voice cracked and broke in the middle as she tried to swallow to ease the tension in her throat.

'My turn,' she managed again.

'OK—no!'

It was worse this time because he reached out to still her hand, long fingers closing over hers, warm and hard and… She tensed herself to pull away, then found she couldn't make herself do it.

'Not your turn—not yet. I have to…'

His attention was back on the board, allowing her a moment to snatch in a much needed breath. Was it con-

fusion or the rush of loss as he released her hand that
clouded her thoughts? Karim was counting again.

'Thought so.'

Blankly, she watched as he took his counter back to
his original square on the board and one elegant finger
stabbed at the following numbers. Then he moved his
token, not to the long ladder but to one of the most fear-
some-looking snakes and slid down it, right to the tip of
its tail, six rows below.

It took a couple of unsteady heartbeats for her to realise what she had just seen and to count back again,
checking it out.

'That's five,' she managed at last.

'And I originally made a mistake and counted six.
It's fine now.'

'You didn't have to.' Was the snow falling even more
heavily outside, whipped up by the wind, or was that the
race of her heart pulsing in her ears? 'I hadn't noticed.'

Of course she hadn't noticed. She'd been so busy
watching him, watching his hands, the down-dropped
lids as he focused on the board. The jet-black arc of his
long lashes resting above those knife-sharp cheekbones,
shadowing the olive skin. She'd been watching the movement of his lips as he counted the squares, imagining
how it would feel, how it would taste to have those lips
on hers. *Wanting* his mouth on hers.

'I didn't see…'

Her tongue stumbled over the words, tangling up on
itself so that she wasn't sure that what she said was even
comprehensible.

'But I did—'

His eyes lifted again, seeming to spear her on his intent gaze. Hot colour flashed over her skin, making it

burn so fiercely that she was grateful for the flickering shadows that hid the changing colour of her complexion.

'And if I had not corrected it, it would have been cheating.'

He made it sound like the worst sin possible.

'And you are such a man of honour.'

The look he turned on her made ice drops skitter down her spine. It was both challenge and agreement. *Don't ever doubt it*, he might have said, and she *didn't* doubt it. How could she possibly? But there was a darkness and a tension behind the words that tightened her throat in a sense of apprehension at the thought of something coming closer, growing more dangerous, like a premonition that would affect her life in an ominously threatening way.

Feeling cold through to the bone in a way that no warmth from the fire could banish, she forced her eyes away from his, focusing intently on the board in front of her. Up another ladder, down a snake…straight up to the last few numbers and then…

'I won!'

The triumph was a soaring rush of adrenalin, a dangerous mix with the fast beat of her heart, the hungry need she had never known before. And yet, underneath it all, that worrying chill still lingered disturbingly.

'You won…' Karim conceded and then he took all that triumph and excitement away, leaving only the chill, by yet another glance at his watch, his phone. 'Another game?'

'No, thanks. I'm tired.'

It was true. With the rushing away of all that heated response, pushed from her soul by bitter disappointment at the realisation that her imaginings were just that—

fantasy—she felt drained and lost, bone-weary. She nerved herself for the sarcastic comment—something on the lines of running away—or hiding.

It didn't come. Instead, with another of those infuriating glances at his watch, Karim simply nodded, picking up the counters, the die, and tossing them back into the box.

It was like riding some emotional roller coaster, one moment allowing herself to go up, up into the heady air of believing he was interested—that he might know something of the way she was feeling, and experience it too. Only to be knocked right back down again in the space of a heartbeat as one more casual glance at his watch told its own story.

The relaxed, enjoyable evening—the evening she *had thought* was relaxed and enjoyable but in fact had probably just been him tolerating her, going along with things to pass the time and distract her, was over. She was dismissed, his thoughts turning to something else entirely. He didn't have to say that all he wanted was to get out of here and deliver her to her husband-to-be. It was written into every action he took, hidden under the careful mask of politeness.

Now she really was tired. She felt like a balloon when all the air had escaped from a small leak, limp and flat, but the thought of heading up into the icebox that was her bedroom held no appeal at all. Karim was moving, getting to his feet, picking up cushions from the settee, dropping them on to the floor.

'What are you doing?'

'Your bed.' A wave of his hand indicated the sofa. 'Mine.' This time he gestured towards the cushions at his feet. 'You don't want to freeze upstairs.'

'N—no…' It was disconcerting, almost as if he had read her thoughts.

'A bit of a tight fit, but it will have to do. I'll get some blankets.'

She had been tired, but would she be able to sleep now? Clemmie asked herself when, a few minutes later, she was ensconced on the settee and firmly wrapped in the blankets Karim had brought down from the bedroom. She was cosy enough—physically at least—but a sneaking chill was winding its way around her thoughts.

Was Karim really acting out of consideration for her or was he merely settling there on the floor to keep a watch over her, make sure she didn't attempt another escape during the night? She'd freeze to death if she did; the knee-length pink tee shirt style nightdress she had pulled on was modest enough but no protection against the bitter night, but clearly he didn't trust her. Turning restlessly on the lumpy sofa, she fought to get comfortable. It was impossible to get her thoughts straight on Karim. One moment he seemed to care just a bit. The next she was sure he was only doing that duty he believed was so important. Her eyes went to where Karim still sat in the one chair, a black, bulky figure in the darkness. Now that the candles had been extinguished for safety, the only light came from the glow of the fire, banked down ready to last through the night. His arms rested along his thighs, shoulders hunched forward as he stared into the grate. Was she destined only ever to have ambiguous feelings about him?

That thought made her stomach clench at the realisation that her time with him was ebbing away fast. Once the dawn came he would find some way of getting the car moved, getting them on their way. And if the future had seemed grim enough before, the thought of the loveless political marriage she had to make hovering like a black cloud on the horizon, now the prospect of getting there and watching Karim walk away out of her life seemed impossible, unbearable. How had he come to mean so much to her in such a short space of time? And how could she let him go when they reached Rhastaan?

Let him go! Burying her face in the blanket, she forced back the bite of acid in her mouth. She wouldn't *let* him go. *She* would have no part of it. He would just turn and walk away from her. Job done. Duty fulfilled. Not a single look back.

Somehow she fell asleep but in her dreams there were dark shapes and shadows haunting her mind, chasing after her. She was running, calling out for Karim, but he was ahead of her. Always ahead of her, walking away, and no matter how fast she tried to run, he was always so far ahead of her even though he was just walking. But her father and Ankhara were behind her, catching her up, coming closer with every step they took.

'No…' She wished she could shake them off but they were coming closer. 'No—*no*!'

'Clementina…'

Someone had caught up with her, caught her. They were holding her arm, shaking her…

'Clementina.'

She knew that voice—recognised it… A rush of memory jolted her awake, bringing her upright in shock, eyes wide, staring into the dark face that had haunted all her dreams but only because it had always been turned away from her. Now he was here, so close, perched on the edge of the settee, his hands closed about her arms, the heat of his palms burning into her skin. He had discarded his

sweater and the trousers he had been wearing, his only
covering a white tee shirt and dark boxers. She could
barely see his features in the shadows but the dark pools
of his eyes drew her in.

He was too close. She was drowning. She could hardly
breathe, the little air she could snatch in tangling in her
throat as she stared up at him. And that air was touched
with the scent of his skin, still warm from the blankets
he'd been sleeping in.

'What happened?'

'I—was scared. Ankhara…'

Hell, he'd really messed up, Karim reproached himself, telling her about Ankhara. Nightmares were bad
enough; the thrashing of her body and the way she'd
moaned in her sleep had brought him awake fast. She'd
been dreaming about the man who'd sent men after them.
Who would try to put a stop to this marriage if he possibly could.

'It's all right.'

Did she know what it did to him to see the way her
eyes had widened, deep as lakes in the whiteness of
her face? How could he ever have thought her the wild,
careless party girl she'd been described to him as? The
woman who had carelessly tossed her duty to her family, to her country, aside when she had set out to seek her
own pleasure, heedless of anyone else. There was more
to it than that. Another reason why she had come here.
He didn't know what it was but he was sure there was
something underneath her apparent recklessness. Perhaps it was something to do with this Harry—whoever
he was. A friend? A lover?

'Clementina, it's all right—you're safe.'

And she would be safe if he had anything to do with

it, he vowed inwardly. He would make sure she reached Rhastaan safely if it was the last thing he did. He didn't allow himself to acknowledge that that vow was made for Clementina herself, not just for the debt he owed to Nabil's family.

'C-Clemmie…' Her voice was low and husky, that trace of breathlessness still lingering in a way that tugged at his nerves.

'What?'

'Clemmic,' she said again, more strongly this time. 'My—friends—call me Clemmie.'

'Is that what we are? Friends?'

The battle he was having with the sexual hunger that had flared as soon as he had taken her in his arms to waken her made his question rough and raw, catching on her mood, changing it in a second. She frowned, bit down on the softness of her lower lip as she considered, then shrugged in a way he couldn't interpret. Not with his head full of forbidden thoughts of how he wanted to reach out and ease her lips apart, stop her from injuring the soft flesh. He wanted to soothe the injury she was inflicting on herself with the sweep of his tongue. She was so close, the scent of her body so warm that he could almost taste her on each breath he drew in, and the cotton boxers provided little or no concealment of the aching hardness that those thoughts, the enticement of her body had built between his legs.

'If that's how you want it,' she muttered. 'After all, what else could we be?'

'What else indeed,' he agreed, nodding slowly. Then, seeing her shiver in the night air, he frowned sharply. 'You should get back under the blankets—go to sleep.'

Her eyes met his, shadowed and defiant.

'I don't want to sleep. I'm afraid that if I close my eyes it will all come back again.'

'But you need to rest...' And he needed to get the hell away from her before he gave in to the carnal thoughts that were frying his brain.

'Couldn't you hold me?'

It was the last thing he had expected, the last thing he needed, and it knocked him off balance for a moment, almost reeling back where he sat.

'Clemmie...' His voice was thick, rough, and it was only when he heard himself say it that he realised he had conceded and used the name she wanted him to call her.

Her pink tongue slicked over her lips, leaving behind a gleam of moisture that had a kick of cruel temptation out of all proportion to its size. Hunger clawed at him, forcing him to clamp his mouth shut on a groan of response.

'Please hold me. Just till I get back to sleep.'

She moved the blanket aside, opening a space under it for him to join her, and the movement revealed the slender pale length of her legs, the sight draining all the moisture from his mouth in a second. He tried to speak, to tell her how crazy this would be—how *wrong*—but his voice failed him and she was already talking again, taking his silence for some sort of concession of agreement.

'I don't think I could possibly sleep if you don't. And you must be cold out there in what you're wearing.'

He was cold. In spite of the fire, there was no real warmth in the air and he was thinking longingly of being under the blankets and huddling into them.

But the truth was that he was also thinking more longingly of being under the blankets *with her* and holding her close. In spite of the cold, his body burned at the thought.

'*Please*,' she said again in a voice that took all his strength from him.

He was lost.

CHAPTER SEVEN

'IF YOU PROMISE to go to sleep...'

'I promise.'

Surely this was hell, Karim told himself as she scooted over and he eased himself into the small space that she had left for him. Hell was not eternal fire or demons torturing you. Hell was a cosy nest in a too-small bed with a woman he ached to possess but was forbidden to touch. He could only pray that she would go to sleep fast.

'How am I supposed to sleep with you sitting there like you have a broom handle for a spine?' Clemmie protested, the warmth of her breath shivering over his skin.

'There's not much room...'

'Then curl up closer...'

She suited actions to the words, her movement building the heat in their little cocoon to boiling point. Damn it, was she really that naïve or—his heart skipped a beat with a heavy thud—was she doing this deliberately?

'Sleep!' he growled roughly, his lips brushing the silky hair on the top of her head, fine strands catching on his skin, on the roughness of his day-old stubble as they did so.

Sleep!

Clemmie barely caught back the word of protest as she

lct her face rest against his chest. How was she expected
to sleep like this? Her whole body was wildly awake, her
heart pounding, her breathing suddenly raw and heavy
in her lungs. The strength of the arms holding her were
at once a source of comfort and dangerous excitement
and the hard bones of his ribcage seemed to be made
specially to support her head. The heat of his skin had
turned the comfort she had been looking for into an in-
ferno of need that pulsed between her legs in a way she
had never known before.

This then was *desire*. This was what it felt like to want
a man—this particular man—in the way that a woman
was meant to feel.

She wanted—*needed*—to feel more of him. One hand
stroking across the white cotton of his tee shirt, she could
feel the thud of his heart under her fingertips, the smoothness of skin, the...

The movement stilled, her head lifting slightly, at the
unexpected thickening and roughness where everywhere
else there had been smooth skin.

'What's this?'

'Clemmie—'

She caught the note of warning but ignored it. Her fingers brushed against the swollen hardness of his lower
body as she pushed at the hem of his tee shirt at his
waist. It almost made her pause, the realisation of what
it meant sending shockwaves of reaction through every
inch of her. But the new and very different tension in the
powerful body beside her told her that she was touching on something that mattered, something that came
close to the innermost part of this man, and she was not
to be put off.

'What's wrong?'

She pushed the white cotton aside, bunching it up around his shoulders and then caught her breath in shock at what she had exposed.

'Damn it, Clemmie...'

With a muttered curse, Karim twisted sharply, catching hold of her wrists and imprisoning them in the strength of his hands. But not before she had registered what was there. Even in the dim light from the fire, the disfiguring ridges and lines were plain to see. The scars that marked one side of his chest, marring the sleek beauty of the bronzed skin, untouched by the haze of crisp black hair that covered so much of his torso.

'But what happened? When?'

He was only relatively newly healed. The scars were still pink and new, not yet easing into the silvery lines that followed the softening effects of time.

'How?'

He wasn't going to answer; she could see it in the set of his face, the way that his beautiful mouth was clamped tight shut, the red burn of the fire throwing shadows on and off the hard planes of his cheeks.

She'd seen that sort of tension once before. When he had spoken of his brother and the fact that he had died. The scars were connected with that incident; she had no doubt of that. Karim didn't need to say a word; the emotional truth was etched on to his face, no matter how much he might want to dodge away from her seeking eyes.

He didn't try, though. Instead he met her questioning gaze head-on, the light of challenge flaring in the darkness of his eyes. His grip on her wrists had softened now, letting her ease herself away, and Clemmie let her fingertips drift over the damaged skin, her breath catching as she saw the change in his face, the way his eyelids dropped briefly to shut himself off from her.

'What happened to your brother? I mean—I know he died in a car crash, but—you were there, weren't you?'

'I was in the car behind.'

He sounded as if the words had been dragged out of him. If it hadn't been for the darkness, the silence of the night, she wouldn't have caught the words, they were so low, so soft.

'He wanted to see a woman—not the woman he was betrothed to marry. So he'd dismissed the security detail, but I couldn't let him go out without any protection. I followed him.'

A long pause, another obvious effort to make himself go on.

'I made the mistake of letting him see me in the mirror so he drove too fast to get away from me. He took a bend carelessly... By the time I reached them his car was on fire.'

'And you tried to get him out.'

It wasn't a question; it was a statement. She knew without any sort of doubt that that was how he had been injured, scarred.

'I...'

Whatever he had been about to say was choked off as she bent her head to press her lips to his wounded skin, acknowledging silently the way he must have tried—the horror of having failed as the fire had driven him back. Softly she kissed her way over the long scar, acknowledging the courage it must have taken to earn it.

'Clementina...'

Her name hissed in between his teeth but she barely heard it. She was lost, drugged on the taste of him, the scent of his skin. Her tongue slid over the ridges of the scar, tasting the slightly salty tang of his skin, and she heard the beat of his heart quicken and deepen, sounding like thunder in her ears. Her own heart was racing, primitive feelings, sensations she had never known before stirring deep inside her, pulsing between her legs. She wanted to crawl on top of Karim, hold him, lose herself in him.

This was what sexual hunger was all about; why it was spoken of in those tones that had made her feel it could never be as powerful or as intense as it was implied. But the way she was feeling now told her that she had underestimated its force, its potential for wild abandonment. The room had faded into blackness, the faint crackle of the fire barely audible in her ears. There was only her and this man…this man who made her feel what it was really like to be a woman.

'Clemmie…'

It was raw and rough, a sound of protest or surrender and she couldn't tell which. But then his hands tangled in her hair, yanking her face up to his.

The mood in the room changed totally in the space of an uneven heartbeat. This wasn't warm or gentle or even considerate. It was dark and harsh and dangerous. Everything about Karim was hard. His facial features seemed to have been carved from stone. His mouth was clamped into a tight forceful line, his chest and arms were like rocks against her cheeks. And the erection that she was crushed up against was like burning steel, threatening to brand her as his.

'Damn you, woman!' he muttered again and the last word came out harshly against her lips as his head swooped and his mouth took hers, crushing her lips back against her teeth as he plundered the softness between them.

His hands were tighter in her hair now, holding her head, twisting it till it was in the perfect position where he wanted it. The perfect position for his kiss. A kiss that was like nothing she had ever known before.

Their mouths fused and everything Clemmie had thought she had known about male and female interaction, about sexual interest or excitement was obliterated from her mind in one explosive moment. This was nothing like the tentative clumsy, or even the pushy secret kisses of the few boys she had met at college. There was nothing boyish about this at all. It was all male, the hunger of a fully grown man, and it roused all that was woman in her. It had such force and power, such heat, that it was like being kissed by a volcano. It was the kiss of a man who knew what he wanted and was determined to take it.

And what he wanted was her.

Clemmie's mind was spinning, whirling, her ability to think spiralling off into the darkness somewhere so that she could no longer keep track of it. Somewhere under the molten lava in her mind, created by Karim's kiss, firing her blood, was a warning thought that she should not let this happen; that she should say no and push him away. Push herself away. But that weak protesting thought was drowned out by the stronger, fiercer need that thundered along every nerve, pounding at her temples, driving away any other sort of awareness.

It was wild and carnal, primitive in the extreme, but it was what she wanted now. It was all that she wanted. Karim was all that she wanted. Karim and his kiss, hot and heavy on her mouth. His touch on her skin, searing a path over her legs, her hips, her waist, heading inexorably upwards, towards her aching breasts, the hardened nipples hungry for his caress.

His possession…

Something blew a fuse in Clemmie's thoughts, forcing her to realise that the modest tee shirt nightie was no longer anything like so modest. It was no barrier at all to those urgently seeking fingers. Her nightdress was rucked up well past her waist, her naked legs were tangled with his, smooth skin against the muscular power of long, hair-covered masculine limbs. The feel of his hot skin under her hands was like bathing in liquid fire. She wanted to touch all of him, kiss all of him, feel all of him, all at one time.

'Karim…'

She mouthed his name against his skin, taking in the taste of him as she muttered the word. The hair on his chest pricked at her tongue, soft electrical impulses that made her shiver in response. She needed to writhe nearer, pressing herself against the length of his body.

Karim muttered something in a language she didn't understand, his teeth grazing her neck softly, and with a sudden movement he took possession of the breasts he had exposed to his caresses, making Clemmie gasp aloud and rear up slightly, flinging back her head in a rush of response. But a moment later she regretted the slight break of contact, needing more, so that she dropped her face down to his again, her hair forming a soft curtain around them as she took the kiss she wanted—needed.

The heat of his erection pressed against the moist curls between her legs, but her body hungered for more. She yearned to feel the full heat and power of him without even the barrier of his underwear, fine though it was.

With a hungry murmur deep in her throat, she slipped her hands between them, finding the elasticated waistband and tugging at it, wanting to draw it down. She felt the tension in his body in a new and disturbing way; one she wanted to ignore because she was afraid of what it meant.

'Clemmie! No!'

Karim bucked underneath her, his reaction as violent as if he had been stung. And what she feared was there in his tone, in the warning she didn't want to hear.

'Hellfire, lady... I— No! *I said no!*'

He twisted away, caught her hands again and held them prisoner at the wrist. She could feel his heart thudding against his ribcage and knew that he was every bit as aroused as she was, every bit as hungry. But he was determined to deny it.

'Karim!' she protested, her voice thick with need. 'Don't do this. I want you—why are you doing this?'

The breath he snatched in was raw and ragged, grating its way into his lungs.

'We can't do this. We must not. You know why.'

She knew he was trying to appeal to her sense of reason but it wasn't going to work. She didn't want it to work. She didn't feel at all reasonable. She *wanted* this. Wanted it with every beat of her heart.

'Do I?'

Deliberately she wriggled against him, smiling under the cover of her hair as she heard his groan, felt the tension in the long body beside her.

'I don't see why. This is almost the last night of my single life—my last night of freedom—surely I can spend it as I want—with who I want.'

'If you were anyone else, then yes.'

His voice scraped over her nerves, waking restraints

and scruples that had never been there before. It was as if someone had lifted away the blankets, doused the fire, and the cold, creeping sense of misery that oozed over her skin was almost overwhelming.

Almost. But underneath the sense of hesitation that chilled the heat of her hunger there was another, more rebellious feeling that flared and burned away her qualms. It throbbed to the beat of the pulse between her legs, impossible to deny.

She had spent her life living according to her father's calculated rules. Settlements that had been decided for her and about her but without any consent or even knowledge on her part. She hadn't even *lived* her life. It had all been dictated for her by her parent's ambition. But here, tonight, she had one chance—her only chance—to live as other women her age had the freedom to live. The freedom to…

No—her thoughts danced away from the dangerous four-letter word she had almost allowed into her mind. There was no love in this.

She couldn't fall in love in less than forty-eight hours with a man who had been a stranger until she had opened the door to him—was it really only yesterday? It wasn't love; it was lust—but lust was a new and exciting feeling. One she had never experienced before. One she was sure she was never likely to feel when she was forced into a diplomatic marriage with a man she didn't know. No, not a man—a boy—nearly five years younger than her.

She would never experience the joy and excitement of falling in love. But she could experience *this*. It might be all she would ever have to sustain her in the arid, desolate years that lay ahead.

'But we are who we are and this can never be. It is forbidden. You are forbidden.'

'Not tonight.'

Increasing anxiety, the nagging ache of withdrawal as the stinging excitement ebbed painfully, leaving every inch of her burning and hungry, made her voice desperate.

'Tonight we are just two people, alone in the dark. This cottage is miles from anywhere, and the snow has isolated us even more. There's no one to see us, no one to know.'

'We would know.' His voice sounded as if it was fraying at the edges. 'I would know.'

'But we need never...'

Something about his terrible stillness, the way his head was turned away from her, his eyes refusing to meet hers, staring into the fire instead, sent a shaft of ice slicing through her. It froze her into an immobility to match his, her heart quailing deep inside.

'Is it—'

She couldn't manage to say it, didn't want to say it. But it had to be faced. In her naiveté, had she made the most terrible mistake, imagining something that wasn't there? Had she put her own longings on to the moment, creating a scenario she wanted, but one that had never been there at all?

'Don't you want me?'

Karim's answer was a deep, soul-felt groan.

'Not want you?' He was almost laughing when he said it. But it was a laugh that broke in the middle.

'Not want you? Dear God, lady, but does this...' he turned so that the heat and hardness of his erection was pressed against her naked stomach '...feel like I don't want you?'

It felt like the exact opposite so that her heart leapt a little then sank back down again as she saw the hard set lines of his face.

'I want you so much that it's tearing me apart.'

'Then why? Why not? Karim—you want me—I want you. So why can't we…?'

'No!'

It was a wild explosion of sound, underlined by the violent movement of his long frame, pulling away from her and jack-knifing off the settee in a savage rush.

'No. Damn you to hell, woman, you are not going to tempt me this way. This ends now. Once and for all. It's over. Done. It's never going to happen.'

'But…'

In spite of herself, she rose up on to her knees on the cushions, letting the blanket slip away from her to pool around her legs as she held a hand out to him, trying to reach him. She saw those dark eyes sear over her exposed naked body and it felt as if he had actually flayed the skin from her flesh, leaving her raw and bleeding.

'Don't touch me!' he commanded. 'Don't ever touch me again! I want nothing to do with you—nothing but the job I was sent here to do. I will deliver you to Nabil—to your promised husband.' Could he have injected the words with any more venom? 'And then I will never see you again.'

And he would only be happy when that had happened. He didn't have to say the words. They were there in the darkly savage way he spoke, the burn of violent rejection in his eyes.

Already he was turning away from her, grabbing at the jeans and sweater discarded on a nearby chair, pushing himself into them with rough, angry movements. But when he stamped his feet into his boots and headed for the door, Clemmie couldn't just keep silent and watch him go.

'Where are you going?'

'Outside. In case you haven't noticed—it's raining.'

A brusque jerk of his head indicated the windows, where Clemmie now noticed that water rather than snow was lashing against the glass. A slow dawn was starting too, bringing a faint tinge of light to the sky.

'I will get your car moving— or find a connection for the phone.'

He would do it if it killed him. The declaration was stamped into every line of his face, turning every muscle to stone.

'And while I'm out you should get dressed and be ready to leave. I want to be out of here as soon as it's physically possible.'

Out of here and away from her. Or at least on his way to delivering her to Nabil to pay off a debt of honour. He made her sound like a parcel for which someone had paid express delivery. He was not the passionate lover she had dreamed of, nothing but a cold, hard man intent on using her for his own ends, just as her father had done.

Clemmie shivered in the rush of icy air that had flooded into the small room as Karim yanked open the door and she grabbed at the blankets, pulling them up around her, even over her head, huddling into them for protection.

But it wasn't the cold that he had let into the cottage that made her shudder. Instead the feeling came from deep inside, a terrible sensation of rejection and embarrassment at the way she had behaved. Tossed violently on an unknown sea of physical feelings, she had lost all thought of sanity and self-preservation and had thrown herself at him like some wild creature, driven only by her baser instincts.

The blankets were doing no good. She pulled them closer round her, but they felt rough and uncomfortable against her sensitised skin. Every nerve, every sense that Karim had awoken now stung with an arousal that refused to die down. Even the cotton of her nightdress was uncomfortable against her still peaking nipples and so much of her body was an ache of frustrated hunger that it felt like a bruise over every inch of her. She longed to call Karim back, to beg him to reawaken the excitement that had driven all thought from her mind, left her at the mercy of primal needs that were too strong to be contained.

It was no wonder that she had never needed to fight to resist the sort of temptation that she might have been assailed by. She had never known it. Never experienced anything like real temptation before. But one touch, one kiss from this man and all her defences had been blown apart, leaving her gasping and vulnerable, unable to even form the word *No* in her mind, let alone speak it.

But she hadn't needed to say no. Karim had said it for her. Whatever she had felt for him, he had felt nothing of the same. He might have wanted her physically; she was not so naïve as to be unaware of just what the powerful response of his body meant. But he hadn't wanted *her*.

She had thought—had hoped—that she had found a way to ensure that her first time with a man was, if not out of love and truly something special, then at least with someone who made *her* feel special. Someone who excited her like no man had ever done in her life before. And Karim had made her feel that way. His touch had

sent delight through every inch of her body, at least until
he had pushed her from him, rejecting her so violently
that she still felt the bruises on her soul. And instead of a
wonderful, exciting initiation into womanhood, she just
felt grubby and limp, like a discarded rag.

Slowly, awkwardly, Clemmie got to her feet. Her ankle
still ached, though she realised she had forgotten all about
it when she was in Karim's arms. Her legs didn't quite
feel us if they belonged to her and she swayed where she
stood as she tried to gather her strength. She just wanted
to go and hide, but she knew that Karim was not going
to allow that to happen.

If she needed any reminder then the sound from outside brought her head up sharply, knowing she was already on borrowed time. The hiccup and cough of her old
car's engine finally breaking into life, the rattling roar
that told its own tale. Karim had somehow got it started
and very soon he would have moved it out of the way,
freeing his own vehicle to take to the road and drive them
both away from here.

He would expect her to be ready and waiting to go
with him when he came back into the house.

Just for a minute Clemmie considered rebelling. She
would just sit here and…but as the hooded blanket slid
from her head to her shoulders, reminding her that underneath the brown wool she was just about naked, the
tee shirt nightdress still rucked up above her waist, all
the fight went out of her in a rush. She didn't want Karim
coming back and finding her still as he had left her, discarded and unwanted, in a miserable bundle on the sofa.
She would be dressed and on her feet, ready to face him.

Ready to go.

Slowly she looked round at the small shabby room in

the cottage that had been her home for the past months. The place that been her haven, her sanctuary from the negotiations that had taken her life away, the promises that her father had made on her behalf. But it was no longer her sanctuary. In a couple of days it had changed completely and all because of Karim.

Karim had invaded her space, he had taken away her privacy, her security—her self-respect—and nothing would ever be the same again.

So she might as well go now and face the future that lay ahead of her. Her brief, foolish dreams of finding anything else to put in their place had shattered, falling at her feet in piles of dust. There was nothing more for her, nothing to look forward to, to hope for. She'd had her short taste of freedom and it was over. She had no possibility of avoiding her future any longer. So she would dress, and collect her last few belongings and when Karim returned he would find her waiting, if not ready, for the marriage that had been planned out for her when she was a child.

It was time to forget about dreams and to accept the future that fate and her father had decided for her.

CHAPTER EIGHT

ENGLAND WAS A lifetime away.

Three days. Thousands of miles. The other side of the world. And she felt as if she'd lived a whole lifetime since then.

Clemmie stood by the high window and stared out at Rhastaan city spread out below her at the foot of the hill on which the palace was built. If anything brought home to her how much her life had changed, then it was this city set on the outskirts of the desert, a heavy heat haze hovering on the horizon and a total lack of any wind to stir the flags on the royal buildings.

If she opened the window, then the ferocious heat of the day would rush into the room, fighting against the almost brutal air-conditioning that kept the place cool. Kept it liveable in. It was amazing just how quickly she had got used to a very different atmosphere, very different temperatures so that in spite of the fact that it was the sort of environment she'd grown up in, the raw heat of this desert kingdom was almost unbearable. She was actually longing for the cold of the little cottage that had been her home, her haven for such a short time. Here, she was surrounded by every comfort, every luxury, and yet she would trade it all in an instant for another few days of feeling free, of really being herself as she had been in Yorkshire.

But that was never going to happen.

With a deep, dragging sigh, Clemmie turned away from the window and moved back into her room, her bare feet making no sound on the pink veined marble tiles, the turquoise silk of her long robe sliding sensuously over their polished surface. Another thing that she would gladly go without if she could. The robe might be made from the finest silk, be decorated with beautiful embroidery and have been made exactly to her measurements but she longed for the battered jeans and tee shirts she had lived in before.

Clemmie plonked herself down on a padded stool and stared at her reflection in the dressing table mirror. She barely recognised herself, with her make-up done in a way she would never have chosen, heavy kohl outlining her eyes, rich red lipstick emphasising her mouth. And her hair…!

The wild dark locks had been pushed and pinned into an ornate arrangement of smooth, elaborate curls that pulled at her scalp and made her head itch. She was the woman her father had wanted her to be, trained her to be, but she couldn't help wondering what Karim, who had wanted her to look and behave like a future queen, would think of it.

Karim.

Just his name sounded alien inside her head. He had come into her life in a storm and had turned it upside down. For a few crazy, dangerous hours she had thought that he might be more than just the man who had been sent to collect her. That he could be something special. She couldn't have been more wrong.

If she had needed anything to drive that home to her, then the journey here would have been all that it would have taken. She might as well have been a piece of luggage that he had collected and had to deliver to Nabil, he had spared her so little attention. With her car out of the way, he had grabbed her small case, taking it out to dump it in his vehicle, then, opening the front passenger door, he had stood there waiting for her, not a word being spoken. When she had come past him to slide into her seat he had held himself stiff as a statue hewn from granite, keeping well back from touching her. Only his eyes had moved but when she had met his gaze it had been hard as polished jet and every bit as impenetrable.

Had he spoken more than one sentence to her?

'Seat belt...'

The command had been tossed at her as he'd climbed into the car beside her and put the key in the ignition. And then that had been it. Silence. When she'd tried to speak, he had just flicked a sidelong glance at her and then made a gesture to where the rain that had replaced the snow was lashing against the windscreen, reducing visibility to a minimum and making driving conditions very difficult.

'I need to concentrate.' It was clipped, blunt, totally dismissive. And then he had added, 'We need to get to the airport and on a plane to Rhastaan before Ankhara finds out where we are.'

If there was anything guaranteed to clamp her mouth shut, then it was that. How could she have forgotten about the man who was set against her marriage to Nabil? He was the head of a group who would do almost anything to make sure that the alliance that marriage represented never took place. Huddling into the raincoat she had pulled on over jeans and a jumper, she pulled her jacket tightly round her, chilled to the bone in a way that had little to do with the weather and was more the result of her thoughts.

Whatever else had happened between them, she needed Karim to get her to Rhastaan safely. He had been sent to protect her, and that was clearly what he was intent on doing—that and nothing more. She could do nothing but go along with him and do as she was told, for now.

It had been the same at the airport. Clemmie had been ushered from the car, through a bewildering series of gates and up into the private jet before she had fully registered just where they were. All formalities were dealt with by Karim, her luggage was loaded on board—and once she was settled in the plane, safely belted into her comfortable seat, it was Karim who disappeared into the cockpit to pilot them to Rhastaan himself. She hadn't seen him from the moment they had taken off until just before landing. Or, if he had come back into the cabin at any point, she hadn't been aware of it. Once in the air, and with her body finally feeling warm and something close to relaxed after the small meal and a hot drink prepared by an attentive stewardess, the stress of the past couple of days and the broken night had caught up with her and she'd fallen fast asleep. She'd only woken when the same stewardess had touched her shoulder to warn her to fasten herself in for landing.

'Madam…'

A careful cough, a quiet voice, drew her attention now to where Aliya, the maid who had been assigned to her on arrival at the palace, stood in the doorway.

'You have a visitor, madam—downstairs.'

Nabil. Who else could it be? She had been waiting for this summons ever since they had arrived at the palace.

In fact she had been surprised to find that her husband-to-be hadn't been at the airport to greet them, or at least arranged a meeting as soon as the sleek black car with the darkly tinted windows had swept up to the palace. She had nerved herself for it, determined not to show any weakness in front of Karim. He believed she had tried to run away from her responsibilities, that she was not fit to be a queen. So she would not let him see that she was afraid, or that she was concerned in any way. Head high, back straight, she had stalked into the palace, expecting to see Nabil.

And had only been met by his High Chamberlain.

Since then she had been alone in the palace apartment assigned to her. No one to talk to. No one to keep her company. Once from her window she had seen Nabil, walking in the courtyard.

He had been talking to a young woman, small, dark, very pretty, his head bent towards her, and he hadn't noticed Clemmie at her window, watching them. For a moment she had considered going out to speak to him but in the end had changed her mind. This relationship, this marriage had been forced on both of them when they were too young to do anything about it. It was best to leave things until Nabil was ready to come to her. But after that she had heard that he had left the capital, flying out to his summer palace. Obviously he was no keener than her to get this marriage underway.

So now, it seemed, the summons she had been expecting had finally arrived. Squaring her shoulders, she drew in a deep breath as she nodded to Aliya.

'I'm coming.'

The man who was waiting in the reception room on the ground floor was bigger than she had expected. Taller, broader in every way than she might have anticipated of a boy who had just had his eighteenth birthday. He was standing as she had been minutes before, staring out of the window, head slightly bent, one strong hand braced against the wall. And it was that hand that gave him away as she came nearer, recognising a gold signet ring on the fourth finger.

'I… Karim?'

Had her heart really leapt up into her throat, pounding so hard that it seemed to have cut off her breathing, making her pulse thunder in her ears?

He took his time about turning round, making her feel that perhaps he had known she was there in spite of the soundless steps that had taken her into the room, closer to him.

'Clementina…'

The slight inclination of his dark head was the only acknowledgement of her position here at this court. He was a High Prince too, his attitude said, and as such he wasn't going to bow to her. Which was fine with Clemmie. The truth was that she was already sick of all the bowing and scraping she had received. It would have been bad enough anyway, but after the months of freedom, of living like an ordinary woman in her grandmother's cottage, it seemed even more over the top.

'Or should I say, Princess Clementina?'

'Oh, please don't!'

She was too busy taking in the sight of him standing there, big and strong and even more gorgeous than before, to think about holding her tongue and just let the words escape. She had never seen Karim in traditional robes before, the flowing white garment contrasting startlingly with the bronze tones of his skin, the polished jet of his eyes. He had discarded the headdress and the black silk of his hair gleamed in the shafts of sunlight that came in through the leaded windows.

She knew she had missed him, but she hadn't known how much until now he was here again, standing before her, tall and powerful and devastating. She felt like someone who had been starving and who had suddenly had an incredible feast placed before her so that she didn't know where to look first, what to enjoy most. How could two days' absence have felt so long? How could this man have become so central to her life in the space of less than a week? And how had she survived the past days with the huge hole in her life that he had left behind?

'I did ask you to call me Clemmie.'

'But that was in another time, another place.'

Another lifetime, his tone said, forcing her to remember how he had reacted to her naïve attempts at seduction, the way he had assiduously kept so distant from her. He had delivered his parcel, completed his mission and he was done...

So why was he here now?

'I have come to say goodbye.'

It was as if Karim had read her thoughts as he offered the flat-voiced explanation of his appearance here. If the truth was told, she had never imagined that she would see him again and just to have the chance to see his face, hear his voice was more than she had dreamed of. But...

'Goodbye?'

He should never have come, Karim acknowledged as he saw her huge eyes widen in shock and surprise. He had told himself that he wouldn't ever see her again. That it was so much better that way—the only way. He had made a vow to fulfil his father's debt of honour and deliver Clementina to Nabil, and he had done just that. His duty done, honour satisfied, he was free to leave and go back home. Back to take responsibilities from the shoulders of his ailing father, to take the reins of government of the country he had never thought he would come to rule.

'What else is there to say between us?'

His conscience gave a nasty twist when she saw the flinch she gave at his tone. She tried to hide it, of course, bringing her head up and meeting his eyes so defiantly that it was all he could do to bite back a smile. So the other Clementina, the wild, mutinous creature who had answered the door to him that first day at the cottage, was still there underneath this new version. The tall, elegant woman in turquoise silk, that wild hair tamed and sleeked into an ornate arrangement, who had stunned him into silence when he had turned to see her standing there.

It was the wild-haired, barefoot creature he'd first seen he remembered when awake. But it was that other Clementina, skin warm from the nest of blankets, silken hair spread out over his chest, the sound of her voice whispering his name in his ear who'd haunted his dreams. That memory made him toss and turn in restless hunger so that he had woken, bathed in sweat and with his heart racing, his body hard even from imagining her. Her choking cry of *'I want you...'* was always there inside his head, driving him to a feeling of near-madness as he tried to rid himself of it.

He had told himself that the only sane way to deal with this was to go, never looking back. To put her behind him and head home, to the life that was now his and that she could never be a part of. That was best—for both of them.

So why the hell had he found it impossible to leave without seeing her one last time? Why had he come here now, like this, like some fool of a naïve adolescent unable to tear himself away from the current object of his adoration? Because that was all she was, all she could ever be. Today's sexual fantasy. One he could easily replace with another willing, warm—and much less dangerous—woman in his bed.

No, that thought had been a mistake. The idea of any woman in his bed only reminded him of how it had felt to hold Clementina so close. To know she was warm and willing—and totally forbidden to him. It had almost torn him apart to say no to her then. It would destroy him to remember it over again.

'You are here, where you belong, with your future ahead of you. Your birthday will be very soon.'

'Four days.' It was only a whisper so that he had to lean forward to catch it then immediately cursed himself for doing so as a waft of some heady floral perfume, mixed dangerously with the clean ultra-feminine scent of her skin tantalised his senses and made his lower body ache in hungry response.

To conceal his reaction he nodded sharply, taking a much-needed step back and leaning against a high carved pillar.

'Your wedding will be arranged soon and your coronation immediately after that.'

'My destiny.'

It was stronger this time, infused with the defiance he had expected. But there was something else, something that stiffened her slender neck, brought that pretty chin up just a touch too high. There was a new sheen behind those thick, lustrous eyelashes, something that betrayed an emotion she was determined to hold back and not quite succeeding.

'I will be Queen of Rhastaan.'

'You will.'

It was strangely difficult to nod in response. His own neck seemed to have seized up, his head refusing to move. He had been forced up against the thing he didn't want to think of. The image of Clemmie—*Clementina*—as Nabil's wife. In Nabil's bed. That long sexy body entwined with the younger man's plumper frame, her mouth kissing him, her legs opening…

Hell and damnation—no! With a ruthless effort he forced his hands to uncurl from the fists into which they had clenched, knowing without looking that the crescent shapes of his nails would be etched into his palms from the pressure he'd exerted on them.

The memories of the Clemmie he had known were the ones he had to push aside—for good. If anything brought home to him why that was vital then this woman, the tall, regal creature whose ornate make-up had nothing like the impact of her fresh-faced beauty, was a statement without words of all that came between them.

Clemmie was the woman he wanted most in all the world. But she was not just any woman. And he was not just any man. What he wanted had no place at all in what must happen, no matter how it clawed at his soul to acknowledge it. The Clemmie of the cottage no longer existed. There was only the future queen of Rhastaan. *This* was the Princess Clementina he must turn his back on or bring his country and his family's reputation down lower than Razi had already taken it.

'And my part in all this is done. I heard this morning that Ankhara's man has been found and captured. He will not be able to interfere in anything ever again. And you will be in no further danger from him.'

'So you are free to go. To get back to your own life. I should thank you for bringing me here safely...'

Could her voice have any less life in it? Clemmie wondered. She couldn't find the strength to say anything more, or ease up on the rigid control she was imposing on herself. If she did then she feared she would break down, reveal the turmoil that was churning viciously inside her, maybe even risk saying the one thing she knew she should never say.

'Don't go...'

The words reverberated inside her skull, making her head go back in horror as she heard her own voice and realised that she had done exactly what she had told herself she must *not* do. She should have clamped her lips tight over the words but they had escaped and now that they were said she couldn't call them back.

'Don't...'

Could his eyes get any blacker, his face stiffen more into marble stillness? He was looking at her in such shock that she wished the ground would open at her feet and swallow her whole.

'Do not say such a thing.'

His hand had come up, flattening against his chest, just below the base of his strong throat. Underneath his fingers, hidden now by the fine white material of his robe, were the scars she had felt on his body, the marks that had marred the beautiful tanned skin. Skin she had once been able to touch, to kiss. But only once.

'You don't know what you're saying.'

'Oh, but I do.'

In for a penny, in for a pound. She'd told herself she must never say anything—but, now that she had, there was little point in holding back any more. They had no future. No hope of any time together. But they did at least have this. And she was going to snatch at her one chance of letting him know how she felt.

'I've missed you. So much.'

'I've been busy.'

What had she expected him to say? That he had missed her too? Stupid, stupid, stupid! A naïve fantasy— a child's dream.

'Busy with more of those duties that are so important to you?'

The dark frown that snapped his black brows together almost unnerved her. But she didn't care. She refused to let that icy stare freeze her into silence. If this was the last time she could spend with him—the last time she would see him—then she wasn't going to waste it in pretending to feel anything other than what was really in her heart.

'I hope they were fascinating—and fulfilling. Unlike our night together.'

That made the heavy eyelids drop down over the glittering eyes, narrowing them to just slits, the burn of his scrutiny gleaming behind the thick black lashes.

'We did not have a night together.'

His voice was thick with a rejection that burned like acid deep inside. But her memories—memories she had relived over and over since she had arrived in Rhastaan— gave her the strength to go on.

'We could have had.'

Violently he shook his head, swinging away from her, turning towards the door.

'You were unhappy—afraid. You had nightmares… and I comforted you.'

'And that was all you did?' Clemmie challenged.

'All…' It sounded as if it came from a strangled throat,

rough and raw, and that determined her that she was not going to let him get away with it.

'Liar,' she said softly, then, encouraged by the way he had frozen, absolutely still, she made herself go on. 'You are a liar,' she said more forcefully, 'and a coward not to admit it. I'm not afraid to say I wanted more.'

Had she overstepped the mark, pushed him to a point where he wouldn't take any more? She saw his long body stiffen, recognised with a clench of the nerves in her stomach, a twist to her heart, the small movement towards the door, away from her. A movement that he stilled then reversed only a moment later.

'I wanted more…' he conceded and it was only as she tasted the faint tang of blood on her tongue that Clemmie realised just how hard her teeth had been digging into her lower lip, breaking the skin under their sharpness.

'I wanted you,' she croaked. 'And you…'

The words died in her throat as he swung back to face her, the livid burn of his eyes stark and harsh against the tautness of his skin, the white marks that were drawn tight at his nose and mouth.

You wanted me…

She tried to say it. She opened her mouth, once, twice. Her lips moved but no sound came out. No words were needed. But then she looked into his eyes and what she saw there meant that the words didn't need to be said.

Not those at least. But there was something she had to say before she could let him go. He had to hear it and then she would see if he could still walk out of the door.

CHAPTER NINE

'You wanted me but it was more than that.'

'How could it be more? We were just a man and a woman...'

'We weren't *just* anything. Don't you believe that there must be one person who is truly special—one person who's meant for us, for however short a time? Someone we meet who changes our life, puts our existence on a new path once and for ever.'

She thought he wasn't going to respond. That his mouth and his whole being had frozen so that he had lost all ability, all need to say a word. Then suddenly he blinked hard, just once, shutting his thoughts off from her.

'No,' he said, cold and stark, totally ruthless. 'No, I don't believe such fanciful nonsense.'

'But your brother—he was going to be married. He must have loved... No?' She broke off as the violent shake of his head, the tight line of his mouth rejected everything she said.

'What has love got to do with it?' he said.

'It's usual...' Clemmie began then caught the way he was looking at her and backed down hastily. Karim nodded grimly.

'My brother's marriage was carefully arranged, planned for the best, for the future, to bring together our country and hers for their mutual benefit—like yours.'

It was stabbing, pointed, deliberately so.

'He knew it and so did she. They both knew their duty.'

There was something behind those words, something she couldn't interpret. There had been an unusual emphasis on that, *'They both knew their duty'*, even with Karim's personal emphasis on duty and honour, that scraped over nerves that seemed too close to the surface. The memory of the look he had turned on her when she had questioned his miscounting on the game of Snakes and Ladders came back to haunt her so that she shifted uneasily from one foot to the other and then back again.

'And his fiancée—what happened to her when your brother died? What would have been her *duty* then?'

'And mine.' It was flat, toneless, as opaque as his eyes.

'And yours?'

She had a nasty creeping sensation that she knew what he meant but she didn't want to accept it. But his reply took away that faint hope.

'With my brother gone, I was the Crown Prince. I inherited everything—his title, his lands—his fiancée.'

'His...You would have married the woman who had been engaged to your brother? She would have become your wife?'

Why ever not? What else would I do? He didn't have to say the words; they were there in the cold-eyed look he turned on her.

'The marriage was arranged between the Princess of Salahara and the Crown Prince of Markhazad. It didn't matter who held the title.'

'So you…' Was this behind the way he had behaved in the cottage? Why he had held back, pushed her aside as if she was contaminating him. 'You're married?'

If his expression had been cold before, it was positively glacial now. She'd trampled in unawares, and the glare he turned on her sent a damp shiver crawling down her spine.

'I am not married. She would not have me.'

Was the woman mad? Clemmie had no idea what his brother had been like, but given the chance of having Karim as her husband—arranged marriage or not—what woman would be crazy enough to turn down the idea?

'I don't believe you. There had to be more to it than that.'

'There was.'

Well, she'd pushed for that answer, but did she really want to hear the rest of what he had to say? Her throat felt so tight and horribly dry that she couldn't have asked him to stop if she'd tried.

Karim stalked away from her, the beautiful white robe swirling around his taut frame, his dark gaze fixed on a point some distance beyond the window. A point that she was convinced he was not actually seeing.

'Meleya was promised to my brother almost from birth. Then, when she was eighteen, she came to live in the palace, to get to know him. Their marriage was arranged—a date fixed, but my brother was out of the palace a lot. He was restless, unsettled. One day I followed him. I saw him with another woman.'

Cold, stiff, deeply disapproving of the way his brother had behaved. Did this man have no gentler streak in him, no understanding of what the softer feelings might mean? Was there only *duty* and *honour* in his make-up?

'That was the day that Razi crashed his car,' he said.

Did Karim know how his hand had moved to his chest, to rub at the spot where the scars, barely healed by time, ridged his skin under the fine material of his robe? Clemmie didn't need reminding just how he had got the damage to his body.

'You tried to save him.' And, of course, to save the honour of his family.

'I tried to get them both out. I failed.'

Did he even realise who he was speaking to? His eyes still had that unfocused stare into the distance.

'She was a married woman—married to someone else.'

Clemmie's throat closed up, shutting off her breath so that she thought she was going to choke. No wonder he felt so strongly about these things. It was no surprise after seeing his brother die in such circumstances. The pain of loss must be like the scars on his body. Healed over but still there, still needing to be lived around.

'Meleya's father refused to let her marry anyone from my brother's family.'

And that would have been the final insult, the final realisation that his brother had damaged the honour of his family, so that even his arranged bride would turn away. Clemmie felt that she could see why Karim had felt obliged to come and fetch her, to fulfil the debt his father owed, to restore his family's honour in the eyes of his world.

Impulsively she moved forward, laid a hand on his arm.

'I'm sorry.'

Polished jet eyes dropped to where her hand rested against his, her fingers manicured now, nails polished and groomed in a way they had never been before. Then he lifted his gaze again, clashed with hers, and held.

She should move away, Clemmie told herself. Should take her hand from his arm and step back as far away as possible. If she was wise—if she was sensible...

But she didn't feel sensible. She didn't want to move away. Even when she saw his head move, angling slightly so that she knew what was coming. His eyes were fixed on her lips, so intent that she could almost taste him already, know the pressure of his mouth on hers. And she wanted it. Needed it like breathing.

It was her last chance. The last time. He had said that he had come here to say goodbye and she knew that nothing could possibly change that. How could the man who valued honour so much—and now she knew why—ever do anything else? This was the last time she would see him. The last time she would touch him. The last time she would...

She didn't know if she moved first or if it was Karim. She only knew that at some place, halfway between them, their lips met and clung, breath mingling, eyes closing the better to experience the sensations that were flaring through every nerve, every cell.

Her hands twisted in his, turning, clutching, clinging. Time evaporated, their surroundings disappearing into a buzzing haze. There was only her and this man who just by existing had taught her what it meant to be a woman. How it meant to feel as a woman. To know the wild and carnal force that was sexual need, sexual hunger. She didn't care what might come between them, what Karim might put between them, she only knew that what she wanted was right here and now, in this place and—her breath escaped in a choking cry as his arms closed round her, hauling her tight up against him.

Swinging her round, he almost slammed her up against the wall, the marble hard and cold against her spine, the turquoise silk little to no protection against its cold smoothness. She welcomed it. She needed it to keep her in reality, her feet on this planet. Everywhere else in her was fire and heat, a conflagration that pulsed with every beat of her heart.

She was crushed between him and the wall, feeling the hardness of his need pressed against her and, with an instinct as old as time, she moved, adjusted her position so that his erection was held in the cradle of her pelvis, as close as she could get to the hungry pulse low down in her own body.

'Clemen...' Karim began but because she feared what he might say in spite of the evidence of his body against hers, she reached up, laced her fingers in the dark, crisp hair and pulled his head down to meet hers, her mouth opening to his.

He tasted wonderful. He felt wonderful. The jet-black hair slid under her fingers, the strong bones of his skull hard against their tips. He smelt wonderful, the scent of his body enclosing her like incense, making her senses spin. She couldn't believe that it had only been a couple of days since she had been close to him like this. It felt like a lifetime since he had been in the cocoon of blankets and had held her close.

But she had wanted more then and she wanted more now. In fact, she'd had more then. She'd had the real closeness of skin on skin, the touch of his hands on her flesh.

And it still hadn't been enough.

It could never be enough. The hunger that had started then had only grown in the time in between. The yearning that had built with the thought that Karim had left, that he had gone out of her life was overwhelming, taking her over. He'd come to say goodbye and she couldn't let him go, couldn't end it now without knowing, without experiencing more. It was obvious that Nabil wasn't interested in her. He might be bound to her by law, by diplomacy, but he had yet to show any interest in her as a person.

Her future might be mapped out for her by others, dictated by treaties and politics, but there were still a few days before those treaties came into being, before she was actually twenty-three. And for the first time in her life she was in the arms of a man who made her heart pound, who heated her blood, and drove all rational thought from her mind. She wanted this. She wanted Karim. No one else could ever create this feeling inside her. This need. This hunger. She wasn't going to waste this excitement, this magic on anyone else.

His mouth was at the base of her throat, his teeth grazing the fine skin over her racing pulse, his lips hot on her skin as he muttered her name, thick and raw. But it was when his hand skimmed up over her body, making her breasts burn, her nipples sting, that she moaned her hunger aloud, wild and unrestrained. The fire between her legs was making her writhe against Karim's hard powerful form, heat and moisture flooding her with every touch, every kiss. He was tugging at the turquoise silk, wrenching it aside, ripping the fine fabric as he did so, the tearing sound telling her that his own control was lost as much as hers. He was oblivious to where he was, to the fact that there was only the door between them and the rest of the palace.

Between them and total exposure.

'We can't do this here...'

She pulled his head up again, muttered the words roughly against his lips, terrified not so much that anyone might hear but that he might try to speak, to deny what was between them. They only had today. Just a few short hours. Surely he would not deny her... He couldn't...

She wasn't going to give him the chance as she clamped her mouth against his, met the invasion of his tongue with the welcome of her own. Somehow, awkwardly, sideways, she edged him towards the secret inner stairway she had discovered only the previous day. The small staircase that was used by the royal family only, hidden from public view. With Karim's back against the wall this time, she urged him onwards, upwards, holding his head prisoner against hers with one hand while she let her other hand stroke over his straining body, touching, caressing, teasing, deliberately tormenting him so that he wouldn't be able to think, to have any hesitation. She caught his moans of response in her own mouth, tasting his breath and the hunger on it as she urged him up towards the door to her room, each step a near stumble of need and yearning as they climbed blind, somehow making it to the landing without mishap.

'Inside...'

Clemmie knew she sounded breathless but it wasn't the climb that had made her that way. She was burning with frustration as the long robes that Karim wore came between her demanding hands and the need to touch his skin, to feel the heat of his flesh.

'Clemmie...'

The door slammed back against the wall, the sound reverberating round the silent palace. Clemmie tensed, hearing Karim's shaken voice, fearful that it was now when he would say that this had to stop. She had barely survived his rejection once before. She didn't know if she could endure it over again.

But Karim's hands were on her arms as he whirled her into the room and kicked the door to behind them. The spinning motion carried them part way across the floor, heading almost to the huge silk-covered bed that stood on a small dais in the centre of the room.

Almost but not quite. Somehow Karim took hold of the crazy dance that had caught them up. He stopped the careering path across the marble floor, almost stumbled, almost lost his footing. Almost.

But then he had a hold of himself, and of Clemmie. With a hasty adjustment, he brought them both to a halt, holding her upright while her head still spun with disorientation and desperate need, the room swinging round her so that she would have fallen if it was not for that powerful grip on her arms, hard fingers digging into her flesh so that she could almost feel the bruises forming under the pressure.

'Stop!'

The single word was both a command and a threat, bringing her to a halt even more strongly than his hold on her. She blinked hard, trying to clear her eyes, to meet the powerful glare of his, and shivered as she saw herself reflected once more in the polished jet depths as she had been on the night in the cottage. A night that seemed like a lifetime away.

'Karim…'

He couldn't be doing this again, could he? He couldn't

be so cruel—so dishonest! Because to insist on her stopping now could only be a lie. It had to be, with the burn of arousal scoring the knife-edges of his cheeks, the furious beat of his heart under the powerful ribcage. He was still hard and hot against her so why the hell was he...?

'Karim...'

She wriggled frantically in his hold, managed to raise her hands to his face, wincing as she felt the granite hardness of the muscles that tightened against her caress, the furious jerk of his chin as he repelled her touch. Surely this couldn't be happening, not when he had been the one who had been kissing her, caressing her in the room below.

'Karim—please...'

If he wouldn't let her touch him, then perhaps she could reach him some other way. Her slippers had been lost somewhere along the crazy journey up the stairs so that she had to stand on tiptoe to reach, but somehow she managed to reach up and press a soft and, she hoped, enticing kiss in the hard plane of his cheek. Her mouth lingered just for a moment as the tang of his skin burned against her tongue, the intensely personal flavour of his skin scalding her senses. The moment was a singing delight and a terrible torment all in one as she felt the hardness of him against her, her breasts crushed to the rigidity of his chest, the thunder of his heart a physical sensation against them. The scent of his body surrounded her, enclosing her in a cloud of warm sensation, and that taste on her lips...

'No!' Karim's voice was a rough animal growl in her ear, the snarl of a savage cat that faced an intruder into its territory. An alien, unwelcome intruder.

'But...'

'I said no!'

Suddenly the room was spinning round her again, more sickeningly this time. She wasn't aware of just what had happened, wasn't aware of anything at all until she hit the side of the bed, landing with a gasp of shock on the silken covers where he had flung her with force, away from him.

For a moment as she looked up into his eyes Karim looked as stunned as she felt, some wild force glazing his eyes, making them look like polished black glass. But then he blinked and the movement wiped away every trace of emotion.

'I do not want you,' he stated flatly.

But that was too much. She had felt the tension, the heat in his long body. She had known the taste and pressure of his kisses. Her body still burned and stung where his hands had moved over her skin, the pressure urgent with need.

'Liar,' she said softly, then repeated more strongly, conviction giving her voice added force. 'You are a liar and that is the most impossible untruth. You could at least be honest.'

Karim's proud head went back as if he had been slapped in the face, dark eyes narrowing violently. For a moment Clemmie thought that he was going to fling something at her, verbally if not physically, or at least that he was going to spin on his heel and stalk out of the room. But then he drew in a deep breath, his nostrils flaring as he did so, and nodded, slow and controlled. And it was the control that worried her.

'And what, precisely, would that achieve?'

It would mean so much to her. It would give her something to hold on to in the dark, arid future that lay ahead of her. It would leave her with one happy memory to know that one man—*this* man—had actually wanted her for her and not because of the money, the power, the treaties that came with her. He had wanted her solely because she excited him. Because she was a woman and he was a man.

But she couldn't say that. It would be like ripping her soul from her body and laying it out in front of him for him to scorn, or, even worse, to ignore completely.

'It would be the *honourable* thing,' she flung at him and knew a bittersweet sense of triumph as she saw the tiny, almost imperceptible twist to his beautiful mouth that told her dart had hit home.

'Oh, would it, Princess?' he questioned and her heart seemed to turn to ashes inside her.

Princess, he had said. And that single word put her right in her place, telling her exactly what he thought about her. He might be attracted to her physically, he might even hunger for her as much as she did him, but she was still just the 'mission' he had been sent on. The runaway bride he had been sent to collect. The would-be queen he had to ensure would reach the throne.

So that his honour could be satisfied.

'It would be honourable to take this situation and make it even worse than it is?'

Karim prowled closer to where she lay in the middle of the bed, the fine material of his robe whispering across the marble floor. Clemmie shifted restlessly, pushed herself up on to her knees to face him.

'I—don't understand.'

'You wanted honesty—well, here's honesty…'

Suddenly she didn't want him to say anything. That frankness she had wanted now seemed so dangerous, so threatening. Yet she had pushed him to say it and she couldn't find the words to stop him. But it was too late.

'I do want you.' Karim's black eyes burned down into her wide amber ones, searing right into her thoughts. 'I want you like hell. Never doubt it.'

His hand flashed out, caught hold of hers, held it for a moment against his body, his fingers flattening hers against the swollen heat of his erection under the fine material. Just for the space of a couple of jerky heart-beats but then he released her and took several steps back, away from her.

'I want you so much that it's tearing me to pieces not to have you. But what does that do for us?'

There was a hard band around her skull, across her forehead and digging into her temples and it was tighten-ing with every heartbeat, twisting cruelly. What was that saying about being careful what you asked for? Karim had given her what she wanted—what she had thought she wanted. She had forced it from him. He had said the words she had claimed, to herself, she wanted to hear.

And all that it had done was to put an even greater distance between them.

'It… You know it was an arranged marriage. One I had no part in, no agreement given. I was just a child. My father sold me!'

'The agreement is still binding. You are here to be-come Nabil's Queen.'

But I don't want to be Nabil's anything! The words burned on the edge of her tongue but she knew the danger they would bring if she spoke them. It was bad enough to know that they were inside her head but if she heard them spoken aloud, between her and Karim, then there was never any going back. How had she managed to live her life, get this far, without ever really facing up to the nightmare that her future was going to be? She knew now why she had made herself keep so much to herself. She had known instinctively that if she had come out from the glass dome she had built around herself she would never be able to go through with this.

But Karim had walked into her life, shattered that glass dome beyond repair. He had forced her out of her seclusion and let the real world in, and, like the story of Pandora opening that box, there was no chance of ever getting anything back inside again. There wasn't even that one tiny little thing called Hope left to offer her anything.

'But not yet...' she said.

Clemmie uncoiled herself from the bed and pushed herself to her feet, needing to be able to look him in the eye, not stare up at him from where she was. His height already gave him too much of an advantage.

'The agreement between our countries—my official marriage to Nabil—is only legal when I am twenty-three.'

The flashing glare he turned on her warned her not to go on but she couldn't give in. She was fighting for her life.

'And Nabil doesn't care! He wasn't even here to welcome me and I saw him—with another girl.'

It wasn't really any evidence of anything, but Karim's reaction was. A faint flicker of something across his set features, in the darkness of his eyes, told her that he knew more about this than he was letting on. And that gave her the strength to carry on.

'He has to take me as his Queen—to accept me formally. Before then, I'm free—I can be with anyone else—with you. Like I was that night in the cottage.'

The memories were there at the back of his mind; she could read them in the way he veiled his eyes behind those long lashes, the tight set to his mouth. But he was not going to let them into his rational thoughts.

'You were never mine.' It was a cold, blank statement.

'I could have been!'

'No, you could not. You were not mine. You are Nabil's.'

'Nabil didn't own me. I was not his possession. He still doesn't.'

'You were forbidden. I was sent to bring you here because everyone—Nabil—my father—my country—trusted me. I will not betray their trust.'

'Because you are a man of honour.'

'You make it sound as if it's an insult.'

'Oh, no—'

'Then we are back where we started, I think.'

Karim pushed both his hands through the black silk of his hair and rubbed his palms over his face, closing his eyes off from her for a moment.

'Princess...' There was that word again, driving home what he wanted without anything else needing to be said. 'I came to say goodbye—that is the only thing that needs to be spoken between us.'

No... Please, no...

She tried to say it; opened her mouth, once, twice, but no sound would come out. Karim would not have listened either. That much was evident from the opaque look in his eyes, expressionless as a carved statue.

'So—goodbye.'

His bow was just a faint sketch of a movement, no feeling behind it. An inclination of the head, a swift turn and he was heading for the door, taking everything he had brought into her life with him. Surely he would not be able to walk away from her, turn his back on her. But it seemed that Karim was perfectly capable of doing just that.

How did she argue against that? What could she possibly put before him to make him stop, listen…change his mind?

'But I love you!'

CHAPTER TEN

SILENCE.

Total, shocking, frightening silence. Nothing more. All that had changed was that Karim now stood stock-still, the long line of his back turned against her, his head held high, his eyes fixed straight ahead. Other than that total stillness, he gave no indication of having heard her, so would she have to say those words again?

She would if she needed to. Because as soon as she had spoken them she had known how true they were. How far she had come from their first meeting that had brought her awakening, then knowledge of how it felt to be a woman, to now—to this, when she knew how to *love* as a woman, with all that a woman's heart was capable of. And she knew that that woman's love was strong enough to endure whatever the future held for her if she could just have this one day, one night—one time of loving Karim and creating memories to hold in her heart when the arranged marriage closed round her and imprisoned her for life.

'I...'

She'd opened her mouth to say it again but at last Karim had moved. Slowly he turned to face her.

'You love me?'

Did he expect her to deny it? Did he *want* her to deny it? Was that what was behind that stony expression, the tightly drawn muscles? Whatever he thought, it was impossible to turn back now.

'Yes, I love you.'

It felt better, more right, every time she said it. This feeling had been growing silently and secretly like a seedling uncurling under the earth, ready to push the little green spike out into the sunshine. That spike was there now, out in the light, and she recognised it for what it was. And she was glad to see it. So grateful to know that at least she had experienced this feeling once in her life. She loved this man and she would never have to live out her days not knowing what this felt like.

'I love you.' She said it again because she wanted to and because it made her smile.

A smile that was not mirrored on Karim's set face.

'Why do you love me?'

What sort of a question was that? He had knocked her off her feet in the moment he had appeared on her doorstep and nothing had been the same ever since.

'Isn't it obvious? I love you for who you are. For your courage in trying to rescue your brother. Your loyalty to your father and your country.' That had sent him out on this mission when he could have delegated it to someone else. 'And your sense of honour. You couldn't even cheat in a game of Snakes and Ladders, for heaven's sake.'

Her laugh, already brittle, shattered into tiny pieces as she saw the look he gave her.

'Then you will understand why I do this.'

'Yes—no—'

Now she saw where he was going and a cruel hand

reached out to grip her heart, twist it brutally so that she gasped in pain.

'But you don't have to. I don't want you to!'

Dark brows snapped together in a dangerous frown.

'It is not what you *want*—or what I want. It is what must be. You are legally promised to Nabil.'

'But…' Clemmie's protest faded on her tongue as Karim held his hand up to silence her. But it was the look in his eyes that took the sound from her mouth.

'You say that you love me—so you must love me as I am. All of me.'

He paused, waited a nicely calculated moment to drive the words home.

'The man I am. My sense of honour.'

Her wounded heart had actually stopped beating. She could no longer breathe, and knew that every trace of blood must have faded from her cheeks, leaving them whiter than the pillows on her bed.

'No…' she moaned, so low that he must have had to strain to hear it. But she knew that, hear it or not, he understood what she was trying to say—and would refute it. 'Please, no…just once.'

Even as she said it, she knew that there was no 'just once'. *Just once* would break the moral code he lived by. It would bring them together and destroy them in the very same moment. But the alternative would break her heart.

There was no alternative.

'When…' It was all she could manage, knowing with a dreadful sense of inevitability just what the answer would be.

'Now.'

It would destroy him if he stayed, Karim admitted. He couldn't remain in her company any longer and not pull her down on to that bed and make love to her. Not do as she asked, as she so obviously wanted. Hell, she had offered herself on a plate. He wanted it too; so much that the hunger was tearing his guts apart, and he didn't know how he could walk to the door without looking back.

She was so damn gorgeous—temptation personified. But—*love*?

If anything had convinced him that he was right to do this the way he had to, then that word was right up there. He had no right to stay unless he could offer her love in return. Hellfire, he had no right to stay at all. She had been forbidden to him from the start, and she was forbidden to him now. The repercussions of acting on the carnal hunger he felt would have the equivalent effect of a nuclear explosion. He couldn't offer her any hope of anything else, so he had no right to stay when doing so would only destroy her future as well.

'If I don't do this then I can never be the man you love. I will be someone else entirely.'

She understood that all right. He watched her take it in, absorb it, and realise the deepest truth of what he was saying. She nodded silently, eyes huge in the pallor of her face. Something—pride, defiance, anger?—held the muscles in her jaw and chin tight, but those amber eyes were shadowed with something that it twisted his conscience brutally to see.

He didn't have the time, or the right to try to make this any gentler. Hard and sharp—and fast—was the only way to do this now.

'Goodbye, Princess.'

And then, to his horror, he saw that she was doing that thing with her mouth, digging her sharp white teeth into the soft flesh of her lower lip. It was impossible to stand by and watch it this last time. Without fully being aware of having acted, he moved across the room, his hand going under her chin—a chin he only just realised was quivering with the force of control she was imposing on it—as he lifted her face to his.

'Don't...'

With his thumb he pressed her mouth open slightly, easing her lip away from the worrying force of her teeth. But he had made two mistakes. The first was the worst. He had touched her and now he knew that he would live for ever with this feel of her flesh against his, the warm scent of her breath on his skin. And, this close up, he could see the betraying shimmer of her eyes. His own reflection blurred in that sheen. She couldn't make this any harder for him—but at least he could make it as easy as possible for her. He could get out of here now, fast, and leave her to get on with her life.

But he couldn't go without one last kiss.

His first kiss was meant to be firm and fast. Just dropped on to her forehead. An unemotional, uninvolved farewell. But the minute his lips touched her skin he knew that would not be enough. Every male sense he possessed demanded more.

With gentle fingers under her chin, he lifted her face again and bent his head. The last kiss was softer, lingered longer, put all the hunger he felt into its pressure on her mouth. So much so that he felt he was getting dragged into a storm of sensuality that threatened to close over his head and drown him.

With an effort that tore at his being, he wrenched himself away.

'Goodbye, Clemmie.'

It physically hurt to walk towards the door. His body

screamed in angry protest but he forced himself to ignore it. This time he was going. He was not looking back. He was *not*…

It was only when he was out of the room and in the corridor beyond that he realised he had been holding his breath all the time so that he had to let it go in one great wrenching, gasping, brutal rush. The door closed behind him so that at last he was unobserved, and, taking a moment or two to find a way of breathing again, he forced himself forward. He got himself out of the palace the only way he could. By putting one foot in front of the other and never looking back.

Clemmie watched the door close behind Karim with eyes that burned cruelly, aching and dry. The tears that had been so close had vanished now. She couldn't let herself cry. She wouldn't let herself. She had told Karim that she loved him and he had still walked out on her. He had turned and walked out of the door, never once looking back.

And the real problem was that she understood perfectly why he had done that.

She had just let the man she loved walk out of her life. She couldn't do anything else. He was so right about that. If he had stayed, if he had taken what she offered, then he would not have been the man she had fallen in love with. She had lost her heart to a man of honour, never thinking of having that code of honour turned against her in a way that had ripped the soul from her body.

She loved him but she hated him for being so right about that. She couldn't fault his reasons for behaving as he had, however much she wished he had never done so. She could argue with anyone, with herself—but she couldn't argue with him.

She couldn't argue with Karim.

Her hand crept up to her mouth, her fingers pressing on her lips to hold the memory of his kiss for as long as she could possibly manage. Already the moisture from his mouth was drying, but she could still taste the essence of him on her lips. If she could have found a way to call him back, to see a way out of this, then she would have done.

But the truth was that there was no way out. She could not call him back without destroying the man he was. The man she loved for his integrity. He would not be the man of honour—if he had stayed—and how could she hate him for being such a man, even if it had destroyed her one chance at happiness?

She had thought once before that she had had to face the fate that lay ahead of her with a heavy heart and a sense of dread. But now that future seemed so much darker, so much bleaker because she had had just a taste, just a glimpse of how wonderful the alternative might have been.

An alternative that was now closed to her for ever.

CHAPTER ELEVEN

'HE HAS DONE *what*?'

Karim could not believe what he had just heard. He recognised the words but they just did not make any sense. Or, rather, they did make sense but not one he dared to put his trust in.

'Nabil has renounced her—revoked the marriage agreement,' his father stated again, holding out the sheet of paper he had been reading from. Karim snatched it, stared at it, but the words danced before his eyes.

'It is his right,' his father said calmly. 'It was always part of the treaty agreement.'

His right, maybe…but why? The words stilled, settled, and at last he could read…

'He has renounced her…' he echoed his father's words in a very different tone, his voice thick with the implications of this for Clementina, for Rhastaan—for him. 'But why?'

The rest of the message made things clearer in one way—but so much more confusing in another. His father might not recognise it, but there could be no doubt in Karim's mind just who was behind this.

It seemed that under interrogation Adnan—the ex-security man who had been in Ankhara's pay—had told

Nabil of the night that Karim and Clemmie had spent together alone in the cottage. A night that her prospective
fiancée and everyone at his court had put a very different—a damning—interpretation on instead of the real
one. No names were mentioned in the report his father
had received, but Karim knew only too well who was
the man involved. His conscience twisted at the thought.

But still things didn't make sense. No matter what accusations had been thrown at her, all Clemmie had had
to do was to tell the truth. That nothing had happened.
Why had she not said anything, flung Nabil's accusations in his face?

'It was Nabil's right—Nabil's decision,' his father was
saying now. The older man's face had so much more colour now and his strength was improving daily. 'Our part
in this is over. You fulfilled my vow to the boy's father.
Honour is satisfied.'

Honour is satisfied.

The words that should have meant so much now rang
hollow in Karim's thoughts. Honour might be satisfied,
but he was not. How could he be when every day since
he had come back from Rhastaan seemed shadowed,
hollow—empty?

But I love you! Clemmie's impassioned cry echoed
in his thoughts, taking him back to the terrible day in
Nabil's palace when he had felt as if he was being torn
in half as he had had to walk away from her.

Because she was Nabil's promised bride: the prospective Queen of Rhastaan. Which she was no longer.

The sound inside his head was so loud that he was
stunned his father hadn't actually heard it. It was deaf-
ening enough to make his head reel, his thoughts spin.

It was the sound of chains dropping away, falling to

the floor. The chains that had bound both him and Clemmie. Tying them into a situation where they could have no hope of ever being true to themselves.

Of ever being just a man and a woman.

Once again he was back in Nabil's palace, recalling how he had looked at Clemmie, decked out in the silken robe, the ornate hairstyle, the elaborate make-up that marked her out as the promised Queen of Rhastaan. The woman who was forbidden to him.

No longer.

All that had been stripped away. She was no longer Princess Clementina, but just Clemmie Savancvski. Then he had wished that she was no princess, but just a woman—as she was now.

And in these circumstances, he was just a man. The man that Clemmie had enchanted from the moment he had first met her, and whose absence had darkened and frustrated his existence ever since.

And as just a man and a woman, was it possible that they could begin again?

'Happy Birthday to you! Happy Birthday to you!'

The chirpy refrain ran through Clemmie's head over and over, its bright, cheerful sound totally at odds with her mood.

Today was her twenty-third birthday, but there were no festivities, nothing in the world she felt at all like celebrating. Her life was so totally different from the way she had thought it would be. The path she had thought she was to take was now closed to her and she had no real idea of where she would go. She felt lost and unsure, and so cold!

With a shiver she wrapped her arms around herself,

pacing around the room in an attempt to warm herself when even the fire she'd lit didn't seem to have enough heat to take the bite out of the air. Was it just because she had become accustomed to living in the heat of the desert—for a short while at least—so that she felt the cold more than before? Or was it the truth that the chill came more from inside, from her heart, rather than the wintry weather?

It was all so very different from the day just forty-eight hours before, when she had been summoned to the throne room to meet with Nabil at last.

Clemmie sighed and moved aside the curtains at the window, staring out at the icy rain that lashed against the glass. The sun had been high and fierce in Rhastaan then and it was probably still shining down on Nabil and his new princess. The girl he had wanted all the time to take as his bride. The girl he had cast her aside for.

The morning had been like any other since arriving at the palace. Her breakfast tray had been brought to her, clothes laid out for her—a long silken dress in fuchsia pink. Her maid had been as attentive as ever, her eyes down bent, her attitude totally respectful. If there had been anything in the air, something to warn her of what was coming, she hadn't noticed it. But then she had been so down, her spirits so very low after the way that Karim had walked out on her two nights before, that she had gone through her dressing, the styling of her hair, the application of the ornate make-up, like an automaton. There had to be some way out of this but for the life of her she couldn't think of one.

In the end it was Nabil himself who had come up with the escape clause. And not in the way she had anticipated.

The sound of footsteps coming down the stairs had her

swinging round from the window, plastering the necessary smile on to her face as a small, dark-haired bundle of energy came thundering into the room, followed more sedately by his mother.

'Clemmie!' Harry flung himself into her welcoming arms, enveloping her in a huge hug. ''appy birfday!'

'Do you think he'll ever get tired of saying it?' she asked Mary as their eyes met over the top of the dark, shining head.

'I doubt it,' her friend laughed. 'After all, this is the first year he's had a big sister to wish a happy birthday to.'

'Well, I hope there will be dozens and dozens more.' With an effort she managed to smooth out the shake in her voice, that smile a little less fixed and forced now. 'After all, it looks like this will be my home from now on.'

'Such a tiny place after what you could have had.' Mary's gaze went round the small shabby room. 'When I think of what you've had taken from you.'

'Oh, no,' Clemmie hastened to reassure her. 'What was taken from me? A marriage I didn't want. To a man I didn't love and who didn't want me. A kingdom I could never have belonged in.'

On the positive side, she'd gained her freedom from her father's tyrannical rule and now had the chance to develop a real relationship with her adored little brother.

'True enough.' Mary nodded, picking up Harry's coat in preparation for the journey home. 'Looked at that way, you didn't really lose so very much after all.'

Mary had to say that, Clemmie admitted to herself. Because she hadn't been told the whole story. So she knew nothing about the real loss she'd endured in all this. The emptiness that tore at her heart. The loss of the man she had fallen headlong in love with. Fallen so deeply and so completely that now her life felt as if it had a gaping, raw hole right at the centre of it.

'And even the peace treaty managed to work out in the end—after some heavy-duty diplomacy.'

'But only because you let Nabil get away with everything he wanted. You could have put up more of a fight; told him how wrong he'd got everything.'

Clemmie felt a chill slide down her spine as her friend's words made her remember her last day in the palace at Rhastaan, the accusations that Nabil had flung at her.

'I didn't want to fight—and what good would it have done?'

The only fight she'd had in her had been to declare the truth. And that would have made matters so much worse.

'But he threw you out. Now even your own father won't have you back. You told me what he said.' Mary shook her head, her eyes darkened with concern for her friend.

'"You are tainted—what man will want you now?"' Clemmie echoed her father's dismissive response.

'I will.' The voice came from behind her. From where the battered wooden door had opened silently, allowing a man to come into the room.

A man. *The man.* The man she had thought that she would never ever see again.

A man who seemed taller, darker, more dangerous than he had ever been before. She had met this man here when he had come for her. He had taken her back to Rhastaan because he had been given the task by his father and because his honour demanded that he carried out that debt which his family owed to Nabil. He had handed her over…

And then he had walked away from her because, in spite of the fact that he admitted he wanted her, hungered for her more than he could bear, his damned *honour* demanded that he did so.

She had told him that she loved him; that she wanted him as much as he wanted her and he had still walked away.

Now Karim was back in her life and she had no idea why he was here or what his plans might be.

'Karim…' It was just a breath, a whisper of reaction.

'Clementina.'

There was much more strength in his response but his voice was rough and uneven as if it was fraying at the edges. He barely looked around the room, taking no notice of Mary and the little boy who was gaping at this new arrival in frank curiosity.

He was hardly dressed for the cruel weather outside. A supple leather jacket, a tee shirt that was so wet from the rain that the dark curls on his chest showed through the white material. The black silky hair was plastered to the fine bones of his skull, his bronzed skin slick with the rain so that his high cheekbones looked sharp as knives. But it was the burn of the dark eyes above them that caught and held her, stopping the breath in her lungs.

Those black eyes were fixed on her face, his stare so intent it burned away the topmost protective layers of skin, leaving her raw and exposed underneath. Her own gaze was caught and held, mesmerised, unable to look away, trapped into immobility no matter how wildly her mind screamed at her to break away. To run.

But to run from him or to him? She had no idea and her brain couldn't compute any possible answer.

'Clemmie...' Mary tried for her attention, her tone making it plain that she knew there was little chance of her being noticed. 'I think I should go. Harry—come here—get your coat on.'

Something in the thickening atmosphere in the room had communicated itself to the little boy and he made no protest, didn't even resist when his mother bundled him into his coat, then grabbed for her own jacket. And still the connection between Clemmie and Karim was locked, absorbed, almost a physical thing, a spider's web of connection, so fine and yet impossible to break.

'Call me...'

Mary was bustling Harry out of the room, but she turned for a moment in the doorway to glare both at Karim and then at Clemmie, but in such very different ways.

'If you need me...'

'She will.'

Karim might have been speaking to the air; not the slightest turn of his head acknowledged Mary's presence behind him. And Clemmie could only bring herself to dip her head in agreement, unable to drag her eyes away from the man before her.

The slam of the door behind her friend and Harry made her blink once, hard. But when she looked again *he* was still there.

'What are you doing here?' She forced the words out, hearing them crack in the middle.

Not even the flicker of a smile warmed his face.

'You know why I'm here,' he said harshly. 'I've come for you.'

The words he had used the first time he had come here. On the day that he had appeared at the door of the cottage. Then he had taken her life, her heart, into those powerful hands of his and turned them inside out.

So *was* she crazy to feel so glad to see him? She didn't know, didn't care, only knew that her heart had leapt at the sight of him and that she was glad for the chance to spend a few more hours in his company. A few more hours when her eyes could linger on the dark strength of his face. When she could hear his voice. When the hunger that had haunted her nights, made her toss and turn, waking in sweat-soaked sheets, now had physical form. And he was only metres away from her.

'How do we do this?'

Was he feeling anything like the way she was? Had the same yearning she was feeling put that rough laughter into his voice? Was there really just a shabby rug on the floor between them or had an enormous chasm opened up at their feet that she didn't know how to cross to reach him?

Suddenly Karim flung his arms open wide, stretching the white tee shirt tight across his chest, his eyes burning into hers.

'Hell and damnation, Clementina, we can do this now. Come here. Come to me before I go crazy with wanting you.'

She wanted it too. She wanted his arms around her so much but in the same breath her mind was warning her, telling her that she knew nothing of his reasons for being here. Nothing except that he had come for her. She took one hesitant step forward and then it was as if just the movement had broken the spell that held her frozen.

One more step—and then another. And then she was

running—flying it felt like—over the floor to where he stood waiting for her, those powerful arms still outstretched.

He was moving too, rushing towards her so that they met—collided—with such force that Clemmie lost her footing, stumbled, fell, taking Karim with her. She landed on the settee, the breath driven from her lungs as the weight of Karim's body crushed her, her gasp of surprise snatched from her lips as his mouth took hers. The taste of him went straight to her head like the most potent fiery spirit, intoxicating her in a second. It was all she wanted but it was not enough. How could it ever be enough when this was what she needed, what she'd longed for? She'd only been apart from him for a few days but those days had left her starved, desperate for this. In the moment that he lifted his body slightly she thought he might move away from her and grabbed at his shoulders, at his head, clenching desperate fingers in the crisp darkness of his hair to hold him still, close to her.

'No… Don't leave me…' It was a yearning cry and she felt rather than heard the laughter that shook his long body.

'No,' he muttered, rough against her lips. 'Definitely no. I have travelled halfway across the world for this. I have no intention of giving up now.'

He had only moved to pull her underneath him so that the heat and weight of his body pressed her into the scattered cushions of the sofa. He was almost crushing the breath out of her but she welcomed the heated imprisonment, knowing that this was what she had been dreaming of at nights, what she had been longing for through the days.

His mouth was on hers, his tongue seeking hers, tasting her, inviting her, provoking her. She followed his lead so gladly, her head spinning with the joy of it, the sensual force of his kisses making her mind blow apart. The wet tee shirt was damp against her face but she didn't care. It brought home to her that this was no fantasy, no figment of her imagination. It was real—it was true. He was here, with her and this was actually happening.

He tasted wonderful. He smelled wonderful. He felt wonderful. He was all male and everything about her that was female was responding to his touch on her skin, his fingers tangling in her hair. His hands were everywhere, touching, caressing, enticing, demanding. When he curved them over her breasts, cupping her through the soft wool of her sweater, she arched her back up to meet the caress, pressing herself against his touch. Needing more.

Her own hands were scrabbling at his clothes, tugging the leather jacket off and discarding it somewhere on the floor. The tee shirt followed it, tangling crazily, wildly with her own sweater as he pulled it off to allow him freer access to the curves of her breasts pushing against the pink silk of her bra. A moment later that too had joined the growing bundle of their clothes on the floor and Clemmie's breath hissed in between her teeth as skin burned against skin and she felt she would pass out from the pleasure the intimate friction brought her.

His mouth was at her breast now, suckling her, delicately at first, then harder, deeper, stronger. Drawing her distended nipple deep into his mouth and scraping his teeth gently over it so that she moaned aloud in uncontrolled response.

'More…more…'

She panted it from between dry lips, her body writhing under his, knowing what she wanted and yet not daring to believe that it might actually be within her grasp. That she might actually know the truth of this man's possession.

'There will be more—I promise,' Karim assured her, thick-voiced. 'I've waited—and wanted—and now I've come to take my reward—and to give you all that you need. Like this…'

Another set of heated kisses were pressed against her other breast, licking it, nibbling at it until it was burning in sensation like the first.

'And this…'

That wicked mouth moved lower, sliding down over her skin, kissing its way to where the waistband of her jeans was an unwanted barrier. Clemmie's breath caught in her throat as she waited, frozen, yearning, needing…

He paused for just a moment, tracing the line of her belt with the warmth of his tongue, and then he flicked open the buckle, slid down the zip, following the line of pale skin that he had exposed with yet more kisses as he tugged the soft denim from her hips.

'Yes—oh, yes.'

Her hands tangled in the dark hair, holding him tight against her while her most intimate core pulsed in hungry anticipation, needing more, needing it now—and yet not wanting to lose a minute of every wonderful sensation he was creating in her. Bolder than she had ever anticipated being, she found the fastening of his jeans, tugging them open, fighting to push them off. Karim helped her, lifting his hips so that the material slipped down his legs, kicking them off the edge of the sofa before he came to settle, warm and strong, and so very powerful, between her opening thighs.

She was naked to him now. Naked and open and so very willing. The fear she might have thought would intervene, making her pause and hesitate, didn't strike at all. Instead it was Karim who paused, drawing in a deep ragged breath, and he looked down into her eyes, searching for what he needed in her face.

'This is your first time...' The rough growl of his voice told him how hard he was finding it to keep his control for long enough to ask the question. 'Are you...?'

'Yes.' Her kiss, hot, hungry, passionate, closed off the question he had been about to ask. He didn't need to ask but she still had to reassure him, couldn't let him wonder, doubt for a minute that this was what she wanted. 'I couldn't be any surer—I've waited so long—too long!'

The last word was a cry of shock and delight as, not needing any further encouragement, Karim yielded to the hungry force that was pulsing through him and eased himself inside her, sliding deep surprisingly easily where she was slick and moist with wanting him.

'All right?' he breathed, raw and uneven, and she couldn't find a word to answer him. She could only nod again and again, pushing herself against him, opening up to him, drawing him in.

'Yes...' she managed as he shifted his weight, pressed harder, further.

Just for a moment there was a burning pain, a stinging discomfort that had her gasping, fingers digging into the hard naked shoulders above her, eyes open wide. For a couple of heartbeats she froze, waiting until the burn had subsided, but then she relaxed back against him, moving her hips to encourage him, slowly, tentatively at first then more confidently, faster, meeting every powerful thrust of his strong body into hers.

You're mine.

The words sang inside her head as she gave herself up to the sensations that took over her body, loving the way they were building up, reaching for something just out of reach, something so wonderful she didn't dare to begin to imagine it.

You're mine and I'm yours—yours—*yours...*

And then there was no possibility of words, or thoughts, only feelings and wonder. Whatever had been out of reach was now rushing towards her, wild and glorious and out of this world. She opened herself up to it and let it take her, let him push her right over the edge into a brilliant and explosive world where there was nothing but herself and Karim and the sensations that they had created between them.

CHAPTER TWELVE

THE NIGHT HAD slipped away from them, burned up in heat and hunger and wonderful, glorious fulfilment. At some point exhaustion had claimed them and they had dropped into sleep that had swamped them totally, keeping them unconscious until outside, beyond the window, the late winter sun finally began to rise.

Fingers of light crept under Clemmie's closed lids, bringing her awake, and slowly, gingerly she stirred, easing herself up from the nest of blankets they had built around them at some point in the darkness of the night. With a smile that recalled the delights of their lovemaking she looked down at where Karim's dark head rested against the crumpled pillows, one arm flung up beside it.

Karim. Her lover and her love. The man who had made her his so completely through the night.

In the new light the scars on his chest looked raw and angry, making her heart clench at the thought of him being hurt so badly. And at remembering that he had got them trying—but failing—to rescue his brother. With gentle fingertips she traced the brutal lines, smoothing a soft caress over them. She heard his breath hiss in between his teeth and lifted her head to look into those black, watchful eyes.

'Did I hurt you? I'm sorry...'

'No.'

He caught her chin in firm but gentle fingers, holding her still when she would have turned away, bringing his head down so very close to hers that she could feel the warmth of his breath on her skin.

'No,' he said again, deeper, rougher as his gaze seared her. 'You caused me no pain. But I was surprised. Soraya hated the scars.'

She knew there had been other women before her but still it gave her heart a twist to hear her name.

'But why? They were won in honour.'

The word fell into a pool of silence, making her world tilt sharply just once, then back again but to a point where she felt she no longer had a sense of balance. She had been so happy to see him reappear in her life that she hadn't been able to think before she had flung herself into his arms. His touch had been like putting a flame to the blue touchpaper on an explosive, instantly devastating, destroying any hope of thinking rationally. She had given herself to him again and again without a care for her own safety or the protection of her heart. But now she could think and those unwanted thoughts reminded her that she had no idea at all what, other than the lust that had so clearly driven him, had brought him here.

I have travelled halfway across the world for this, he had said. But could he have travelled so very far *only* for that? No matter how powerfully he had wanted her, was that enough?

Because he *had* wanted her. How could she ever doubt that when her body still sang with the after-effects of the fulfilment she had known, parts of her aching, the delicate inner tissues bruised in a way she welcomed as the proof of her initiation into womanhood. The evidence of a man's—*this* man's—need of her, the hunger that his body had felt for hers. And hers for him.

But he had felt that before and because she had been promised to someone else his honour had kept him from acting on it. Now she was no longer forbidden, they were both free...

Free to do what?

Free to do what they wanted. She knew that *this*—the heated passion they had just shared—was what Karim had wanted all along. He had never offered her anything else. But she had longed for more. If he had nothing more to give her then she would have to find the strength to be content with what he offered.

Uncomfortable and restless, she eased her chin free of Karim's grasp and wriggled upright, pulling one of the blankets with her and clutching it to her breasts as she stared into the glowing embers of the fire. The heat scorched her eyes but the burn was nothing compared with the sting of unshed tears that pushed at the back of them.

'Clemmie...?'

She felt Karim move behind her, the sudden rush of cooler air as he eased away from her, propping himself up against the arm of the settee.

'What is it?'

'Nothing.'

It was just a mutter, low and gruff, and she wouldn't have believed herself either, so she wasn't surprised when she heard Karim's response.

'Liar!'

There was a touch of laughter in the half-amused reproach. But it was the other half of his tone that stabbed and twisted deep in her soul. A blunt fingertip touched at the back of her neck then slid gently down her spine. The gentle caress made her shiver as it stirred once again the hungry physical responses she might have thought were at least dormant for a while. But it seemed they were still there, just below the surface, waking at just a touch, and threatening to swamp her mind.

And she needed to think.

'Don't!'

She flinched away from his touch rather more violently than she had intended. The gentle touch was like the scrape of thorns with her nerves so very near the surface. She knew the mistake she had made when she sensed the tension in the powerful body behind her, the freezing of the movement of his hand.

'What is it?' Karim asked, his tone putting an edge on the question. 'Did I hurt you? Is that it?'

'No. Of course you didn't hurt me.'

At least, not in the way he meant. He had been a wonderful lover, careful, considerate, gentle when she had needed him to be so, and responsive enough to recognise when gentleness was the last thing she wanted.

'I mean—well, of course it was bound to be a little—difficult at first—but that was all. I wanted you. I wanted this.'

There was silence behind her as he absorbed that. He would not be satisfied, she knew, and the nerves in her stomach twisted into painful knots as she waited for what would come next.

'Then what is it? What is it you are not telling me…? Look at me!'

It was a command she didn't dare to disobey. If she turned she feared that he would see the truth that must be written on her face. But if she didn't then he would know something was up—and he wouldn't give her any peace until he found out what it was. Five days ago, in despair, she had told him that she loved him and had had to watch as he turned his back and walked away from her. She didn't think she could cope with risking that happening again.

'I'm sorry...' Dragging up the strength from somewhere deep inside, she turned to face him, flashing a smile that she hoped was convincing. 'I was just—trying to absorb all that has happened.'

If she looked into his eyes she would be unable to go on so she forced herself to focus on the dark hairs on his chest, watching them rise and fall with each breath he took. His breathing was deep and regular, quite unlike her own tight, shallow gasps.

'After all, it's not even a fortnight since I was here, packing, knowing that my birthday—and my wedding— was just days away. And then you appeared at my door.'

Had there been a tiny jolt in the regular, even beat of his heart? She could have sworn that just for a second something had made him react.

'And then you disappeared out of the window—to see that little boy?'

When he had first arrived, Karim recalled, the small boy had been hugging her tight. As soon as he had appeared, her friend had bundled the child into his coat and left with him hastily. But not before he had caught sight of the small sturdy body, the dark hair, the face that had been an almost mirror image of the one that was now in front of him. The shock that was clear on Clemmie's face told him he was right.

'She called him Harry,' he said quietly. 'And the first

day you tried to get extra time—to go and see someone—you began to say his name then cut it off.'

He didn't need her to give any response. It was there in her eyes, in the film of tears that caught the firelight and multiplied it.

'He is your brother?'

Clemmie's head moved slowly in a nod of acknowledgement.

'My mother ran from my father when she realised she was pregnant.' Her voice was low and hesitant, but it grew in confidence as she told her story. 'She was terrified that this child would be taken and—sold—into marriage as I had been, and she was determined that nothing like that would happen to this new baby. She knew she was already ill, so she gave him up for adoption and sadly she died very soon after he was born.'

'So this is why you came here, to look for him?'

She'd come to trace her one other family member not, as her reputation had declared, just to have some time of freedom, some fun, before she married.

'Yes. I found out about him when I learned that Mother had come here, to Nan's cottage, before she died. She left me a note that told me who had adopted Harry and I just had to see him, if only once. But I couldn't tell anyone about him.'

Karim felt the shudder that shook her slender body as a reproach without words. Intent on fulfilling his duty, locked into that code of honour, he hadn't spared enough thought for the effect it had had on her, the prospect of her life being taken away from her. Arranged marriages were so common in his world. It was only when he had come up against this one that he had been made to reconsider.

'If my father had known, he wouldn't have hesitated to take him back—to use him for his own ends.'

'He will never learn of him from me.' Karim reached out and covered her shaking hands with his own, looking deep into her eyes. 'You are under my protection now. Your father will never touch you again.'

Her laughter was shaken, right to the core. There wasn't even a trace of humour left in it.

'He wouldn't want me. He'll be happy if he never sees me again. Nabil has discarded me and now, as far as my father is concerned, my reputation is ruined. I bring the shadow of that scandal with me.'

Black cold fury sliced through Karim like a blade of ice and he reached out to pull her close, her head resting against his chest where his heart thudded in anger. As soon as skin touched skin he felt the bite of sexual need as it flooded his body, but he had to clamp down hard on it, fighting a brutal battle with the desire that threatened to destroy his ability to think.

For now he had to think. He had to know.

'If I had realised that Ankhara's man had known about our night together...'

The dark head that rested over his heart stirred slightly, and he felt the new tension in her body.

'We weren't *together.*'

Not for her want of trying. And now, with the scent of her skin around him, the softness of her flesh against his hands, he didn't know how he had managed to hold back, how he had ever been able to deny himself this pleasure, this satisfaction. But could it ever be more than that?

'Why didn't you tell Nabil that you were still innocent? That nothing had happened?'

'And he'd have believed that?'

She hadn't been mistaken then, Clemmie realised. The steady pulse under her cheek had definitely missed a beat. Held this close, this tight, she couldn't be unaware that he was as hot and hard and ready for her as if they had never made love at all that night. Her own senses were responding to that knowledge, her body softening, moisture dewing the folds between her legs as an answering beat set up in her blood in response to the pound of Karim's heart.

All she would have to do was to turn closer in to him. To lift her face and press her mouth against his, smooth her hands down over the powerful ribcage, towards the thrust of his erection under the blankets. She could entice him into lovemaking and this awkward, difficult conversation would never have to be. She would never have to risk hearing him say that she had done it all for nothing. That she had played hazard with her future, her reputation, to get out of the contract that bound her to Nabil for only a few nights of heated passion. A blazing sexual affair that was going nowhere.

'How could I tell him that when it would have been a lie? When he had only to look into my face—into my eyes—to know.'

Because something *had* happened. Something that had changed her life, changed her entirely. After that one night with Karim she could never be the same woman ever again. And it hadn't been sex that had changed it, though it might just as well have been. If he had made love to her then he couldn't have changed her any more than he had just by being himself.

By being the man she had fallen in love with.

She had been deluding herself to think that she could ever go through with the arranged marriage that had been

set up for her. She had been sleepwalking towards a fate
that she had no idea how it really was, how it would really feel. She had never really known what feelings were
possible in a female heart, just what was possible between
a man and a woman. What being in love truly meant and
how shockingly powerful the feelings could be.

'Something had happened. And I couldn't pretend that
it hadn't.'

Something as earth-shattering, as elementally powerful as a volcano exploding and spewing red-hot lava
into the atmosphere. It had changed her for ever and she
had known that there was no hiding it, no pretending
from here on in.

'I told him that I was no longer the woman he thought
I was   that I could never be the wife he wanted.'

She tried for a raw, jerky laugh of irony, only to find
that it cracked and broke in the middle.

'It turned out that I wasn't the wife he wanted at all,
anyway. He was only too grateful to me because he had
been looking for an excuse not to go ahead with our marriage—but to marry Shamila instead. Apparently she's
already pregnant with his child.'

The deep sigh that Karim drew in lifted her head but
then she let it drop again. She knew that the only way
she could know what he was thinking was to look into
his eyes and try to read what was going on there. But she
still didn't have the courage to do that.

'You could have been a queen.' His voice was rough
and ragged. 'You turned down a kingdom—for what?'

For love.

But she didn't dare to say it.

'I didn't want it. I don't think I'm cut out to be a queen.'

'I would be proud to have you as my queen.'

Clemmie felt as if her head was about to explode. Had he really said...?

But Karim was moving, lifting her from her position against his chest, turning her so that from not daring to look into his eyes, she now couldn't look anywhere else at all.

'Why didn't you come to me?'

Oh, she'd thought about it. But she hadn't been able to bring herself to do it. If she and Karim were to have any future then he had to come to her of his own free will. Because he wanted to. Her heart wedged up high in her throat at the thought that he had done just that. But was there more than *wanting* behind his appearance here?

'Because you would have felt honour-bound to marry me, knowing that my reputation was ruined.'

She was right about that, Karim's slow nod acknowledged silently.

'Is that how you wanted it?' she asked sharply. 'That I would come running to you?'

'You told me that you loved me. Was that not true?'

Clemmie pulled away from him, wrapping the blanket tighter around herself, needing it like a suit of armour to hold her together when she feared she might start to crumble from the inside. Defiantly she lifted her chin, held her jaw as tight as she could.

'I told you that I loved you but you said nothing in return. Except to hold on tight to your honour. Was I supposed to take what little you had to offer—take this—?'

A wild wave of her hand indicated the tumbled blankets, the crumpled cushions where the scent of their mingled bodies still lingered. The gesture threatened her grip on the concealing blanket but she suddenly found she didn't care.

'And not ask for more because I loved you.'

'Loved?' Karim questioned and Clemmie didn't know how to answer him. She didn't even know how the question was being asked. Was it possible that he believed her love had not been as strong as she had declared it to be?

'Less than one week, Clemmie—is that all the time your love lasted?'

He almost sounded as if he was teasing her. And yet there was a rawness to his voice, a searching look in those deep dark eyes, that caught her up sharp and left her wondering...

'It was more than you gave me. More than you have for me...'

He closed his eyes for a moment as he shook his head and when he opened them again she felt the look he gave her go straight as an arrow to her heart.

'No, Clemmie. It wasn't like that. I didn't know what was happening to me. That night—that first night we spent here—you got under my skin and I've never been able to free myself from you. That night was the closest thing to crazy I have ever been, and I haven't felt in control of anything since. I had made a vow to my country—to my father—and I had to keep it. I had to walk away. By doing that, I kept my honour, but I lost you.'

Lost. It was such a small word but such a strong, emotive one, a world wrapped up in just four letters.

'And then I heard that you had defied Nabil—that you'd told him there was someone else. I could only pray it could be me. I had to come—to see if you still felt the way you had then.'

I have travelled halfway across the world for this. I have no intention of giving up now.

But he still hadn't said what *this* was.

'You came for someone who has lost her reputation?' Her voice wobbled dangerously on the words. 'What will that do for your so important honour?'

Karim's shake of his head was a violent rejection of her bitter question, the flash of rejection that accompanied it.

'I don't care about honour any more when I'm with you.'

'And you expect me to believe you?'

Once more those black eyes dropped to the tangled bed, then came back over her half-covered body, up to her face, warm as a caress.

'So what was that just now? And all the night long…?'

'That—that was just sex.'

'Just sex?'

Karim's voice had dropped an octave, deep and disturbingly sincere as he took her hand.

'For me, that will never be *just* anything. Not with you. And isn't there a line in the wedding service—*with my body I thee worship*. What is worship if not honour? I want to honour you—to worship you with my body for the rest of my life if you will let me.'

He lifted the hand he held to his mouth, turned it so that he could press a kiss against her palm. The gentleness of the caress tore at her heart and she knew that this was what she wanted for the rest of her life too.

'Clemmie…' Over her hand, Karim looked deep into her eyes. 'Will you let me? Will you marry me?'

She didn't want to ask the question but it had to be said. If he didn't answer it with the words she needed then how could she marry him, no matter how much she loved him? She had only just escaped from the prospect of one loveless marriage, so how could she ever tie herself down in another one?

'As…as a matter of honour?'

She'd thought—hoped—prayed that he would say no but instead he inclined his head in a slow, thoughtful nod.

'Yes, as a matter of honour…but not in the way you mean it.'

'What other way is there? Your honour demands that we should marry and so…'

And so she could never agree. Because she wanted more—needed so much more. But deep inside there was a weakness, a shadow on her heart that urged her to say yes.

'Not *my* honour.' Karim's tone was deep and dark, huskily intent. 'My honour no longer matters in this. What matters is the honour that you would do me if you agreed to be my bride. I can think of no other woman I could ever want as much. No other woman I could ever love as much.'

Love. That small, softly spoken word caught on her nerves and hung there, making her head reel. Could she really believe—had he actually said…?

'Love?'

'Yes, love,' he assured her. 'I love you and I have done almost from the moment that we met. I knew it when you climbed out of that window and went to Harry—and, in spite of everything my training had taught me, I waited. I waited for you to come back as you'd promised you would. I knew you would—I wanted you to come back. I wanted you.'

It was a low caressing whisper, sincerity in every word he spoke.

'I wanted you more than any woman I had ever met—

but it was more than that. I wanted you to be free to be the woman you really were. We were trapped in a situation that we couldn't control. Your father's scheming, those political treaties, my family's debt of honour had us trapped. I couldn't set us free—you were the only one who could do that when you told Nabil the truth.'

Reaching out, he touched her face, cupping her cheek softly in the palm of his hand, so that she could feel the faint tremor in his fingers that told her just how much he meant this.

'Clementina, you are my love, my honour. You are all I want out of life. All I need. But without you I am nothing. I love you and I want to do so till the end of my days. So please, tell me that your love is still there. Please say that you will marry me and make the rest of my life complete.'

And there was only one possible way she could answer that. Leaning her head to one side, she pressed her cheek against his hand and smiled deep into his eyes.

'I will, my love,' she told him, strong and sure. 'It will be an honour to be your wife.'

* * * * *

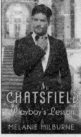

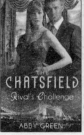

Join the Mills & Boon Book Club

Want to read more **Modern**™ books?
We're offering you **2 more** absolutely **FREE!**

We'll also treat you to these fabulous extras:

- 🌹 **Exclusive offers and much more!**
- 🌹 **FREE home delivery**
- 🌹 **FREE books and gifts with our special rewards scheme**

Get your free books now!

visit www.millsandboon.co.uk/bookclub
or call Customer Relations on 020 8288 2888